REVENANCE

REVENANCE

TERENCE BLACKER

BLOOMSBURY

First published 1996

This paperback edition first published 1997

Copyright © 1996 by Terence Blacker

The moral right of the author has been asserted

Bloomsbury Publishing Plc, 38 Soho Square, London W1V 5DF

A CIP catalogue record for this book is available
from the British Library

ISBN 0 7475 2794 6

10 9 8 7 6 5 4 3 2 1

Typeset by Hewer Text Composition Services, Edinburgh
Printed in Great Britain by Cox & Wyman Limited, Reading

For my parents

OVER THE CENTURIES, the people of Burthorpe have become accustomed to the idea that the outside world has no more than a brief and passing interest in their little village, that for most people it is no more than a step along the way to somewhere altogether more exceptional.

The grand events of history have somehow passed Burthorpe by. The arrival of the Romans in Diss, the visit of Elizabeth to Redgrave in 1578 and the resulting plague of the following year, the great fire that swept through town in 1640, the fourteen-hour football match between Suffolk and Norfolk that took place on the fields of Palgrave in 1738, the Roydon Riots of 1823: at these great local dramas, Burthorpe was no more than a spectator, in one of the cheaper seats, with an impeded view.

Glance through the pages of the *Diss Press* today, and you will find that little has changed. Three miles down the railway track, in Mellis, a lovelorn milkman parked his float on the level-crossing and was hurled into oblivion, silver-tops and all, by the Norwich to London express. In Occold, the middle-aged vicar ran off with an eighteen-year-old girl groom. Beyond Stuston, a border dispute between farmers ended in murder. And Burthorpe? The nearest Burthorpe has come to making the front page of the *DP* was in 1989 when an RAF Harrier Jet swooped low over the village roofs, narrowly missing the tower of St Botolph's, before crashing into a field some four hundred yards away. 'VILLAGE IN MIRACLE ESCAPE', ran the *DP* headline.

There is a logical reason for Burthorpe's anonymity. On the local ordnance survey map you will see, cutting like welts through the village, a crisscross of lines (roads, the railway, a river, the border between Norfolk and Suffolk), giving it a scarred and fractured look. This place has always been a means to an end – nine hundred years ago, for pilgrims on the way to the shrine of St Edmund in Hoxne, today for holidaymakers heading for Great Yarmouth – and the ever deepening paths between its houses have served to divide the community from itself.

There have been those who, trying to explain the inexplicable, have argued that it was Burthorpe's very lack of individuality that caused the events described in these pages, that its invisibility as a village had in some strange way infected its inhabitants, making them unusually vulnerable and restless. Just as some people attract accidents, it was said, so the people of Burthorpe created out of the murk of their own psyches the revenance that was to take place in their village.

Personally, I doubt it.

There was an undertaker's wife called Alison, a thanatologist called Dr Larwood, a landowner called Simon Pygott. There were the inhabitants of a small East Anglian village. Then, for a while, there was Margaret Cowper.

It could have happened anywhere, but it happened in Burthorpe.

1

THAT'S BOOTIFUL!
This week's Bootiful Baby is Darren Pearson of Farthing
Lane, Burthorpe. According to Mum Cathy Pearson, Darren
has been a bouncing little handful since the day he was born
on February 15th this year. Altogether now, Aaaaaah!
*Another contestant in our Bootiful Baby competition will be
in next week's* DP.

A LOUD, PLANGENT NOTE, F# rising slowly to a
G, then down again to the F#, echoed around the redbrick
houses of Scrope Rise, blending with other country
sounds of that November afternoon: the wistful cry of
a police siren from the direction of Bressingham, the impatient buzz of
an electric saw, the distant roar of two American Phantoms, appearing
briefly between the grey clouds, the sound of their jets drowning Gary
Preston's new guitar. A tractor made its way through the small
housing estate, spreading mud liberally on the tarmac and verges
as it transported sugar beet from one of the fields beyond Long
Meadow to an outside yard at Hall Farm.

As it passed, the trailer brushed against the brambles of a blackberry
bush, disturbing what, to a passing stranger, might have appeared to
be a shank of sheep's wool, or maybe a wisp of smoke from the fire of
some travellers whose camp could be seen beyond the railway track.
Only a smudge of red amidst the grey, like the spot of blood in a

fertilised egg, suggested an entity outside the normally accepted laws of nature.

The object moved from the bush and hesitated briefly, resisting the wind, on the muddy verge of the road. It gathered, almost reluctantly, at the entrance to Scrope Rise, then made its way slowly along the hedgerow of Railway Drive, up the incline towards the main road, where it crossed, buffeted high in the air by the slipstream of passing cars. It rested briefly amidst the spokes and crossbars outside Burthorpe Bikes, then moved down the hill, past the village shop, where H.T. Pearson could be seen standing amidst his half-empty shelves, as if daring anyone to enter, across Long Green, through the graveyard of St Botolph's Church, by Burthorpe Primary School from where piping voices could be heard singing to the accompaniment of an out-of-tune piano, and so to the entrance of Turville Funeral Home, where it stayed for a full ten minutes.

Slowly at first, then gathering speed, it skimmed the village pond, startling a moorhen, and crossed the muddy field littered with small corrugated-iron arcs in which Charlie Watson kept his pigs, over the stream – until recently a river but now redirected beyond village bounds. There, overlooking the valley, hidden away from the road and from the other houses in the village, was Garston Hall, outside which were parked two cars, a mud-spattered Range Rover and a dark-blue Saab.

It must have been a Tuesday afternoon, because at that moment Simon Pygott was in bed with Rose Hope, whose duties as editor of the *Diss Press* allowed her this weekly window in her diary for a light, low-grade affair with the master of Garston Hall.

The cloud entered the house through a gap where the paving stone under the front door had been worn away. Crossing the hall, it ascended perpendicularly on to the upstairs landing. From a bedroom nearby, the sound of a bedboard banging rhythmically against a wall confirmed that Pygott and his guest were fully occupied. Hesitating briefly at the door to the bedroom, the grey shape passed over Simon's broad, hairless back and entered an adjoining bedroom.

It was in that dressing-room less than a minute, during which time the amorous scuffle reached its conclusion, Simon's crescendo of

4

grunts (not unlike the sound he made when calling Jess, his Golden Labrador) accompanied by an angry gasp of relief from his lover. Had either of them opened their eyes as they lay there in that moment of post-coital calm, they would have been startled to see a pile of Susan Pygott's clothes – jeans, shirt, underclothes, shoes even – being transported across the bedroom to the corridor as if by an invisible hand. They floated over the banisters to the hall, where a small practical problem impeded their progress. Gently, the clothes were laid on the large mahogany table below a portrait of Sir Marcus Pygott. The grey shape explored the ground floor of the Hall, finding at last a kitchen window ajar. Pausing briefly to hear the low voices from upstairs, the cloud embraced Susan Pygott's clothes and made good its escape.

By now, an early afternoon gloom was settling on Burthorpe. Soon mothers would be collecting their children from the school, the volume of traffic through the village would increase. Avoiding roads, houses, even the sewage farm that adjoined Watson's piggeries, the cloud bore its burden to a glade, protected from view by a tangle of willow and hazel, beside a stream skirting Mileham Fen.

Minutes later, the grey cloud was following Errol Pryce as he trudged down Farthing Lane, hands deep in the pockets of his mud-spattered combat jacket, towards the cottage of the late Ned Simpkin, a local carpenter.

Subterfuge came naturally to Errol. His plump and tanned features, the homely paunch spilling over his dirty jeans, his tall, gangling frame may have seemed to be those of a simple man of the soil, a Burthorpian born and bred, but the small, dark eyes, amused and canny, suggested another reality.

Glancing over his shoulder but unaware that he was being followed, Errol opened the garden gate and walked quickly across Ned's lawn, treading heavily on the plants of a surprisingly trim border on which the old man had imposed an order lacking from the rest of his life.

The front curtains of the cottage were drawn. Errol took the small path around the back of the house. Moving a rusty oil barrel to the back wall, he pulled himself on to the roof of the porch, cracking tiles as he went. Shading his eyes against the glass, he peered into the front lounge where Ned had been found yesterday, stretched out on his back in front of the television, the cigarette in his right hand burnt down to his gnarled, cold fingers, leaving a thin tower of ash pointing to the ceiling.

Nothing in the house seemed to Errol worth the effort of breaking and entering. Lowering himself on to the side of the roof, he stepped on to the barrel, and jumped down.

Darkness was closing in. He reached into his pocket for a small torch. Hearing a car approach he stood still for a moment. Then as the car accelerated away towards Redgrave, he returned the barrel to its place, lit the torch, and made his way down a garden path to Ned's workshop. Casually, Errol looked at the heavy padlock on the latch across the door, then walked behind the barn where, under a corrugated-iron lean-to, some timber was neatly stacked.

He ran a calloused hand over a heavy ten-foot oak beam, unmarked but for a few rusting timber nails. There were three more pitch-pine beams, slightly smaller. It was as he considered how best to relieve Ned's estate of a few lengths of timber that Errol became aware of a sound behind him, like the dripping of a tap.

He turned, shining his torch at the ground. Something was splashing on to a strip of plastic sacking, making soft dark explosions on the bright-yellow surface. He directed the beam upwards. The liquid appeared to be dripping through a crack in the roof, black and viscid. Puzzled, Errol squatted beside the plastic, tentatively running his third finger across the small, dark pool gathering upon it. The torchlight showed a red stain on his fingertip, too light in colour to be creosote and too thin to be paint. Tentatively, he licked a finger, then stood up slowly.

An unimaginative man, Errol was not easily alarmed. He stood for a moment, considering the situation. It was blood. Dripping through the roof. At the house of a man recently dead. Under the circumstances, Errol seemed to conclude, it would perhaps be sensible to return later for the timber. He turned to go.

It was then that, unmistakably, he heard the sound of a slow scraping, a heaving, across the corrugated iron above his head. A drip of something fell on his shoulder, causing him to start and let his torch fall into the stacked wood. Swearing softly, he swooped down to grab the torch, tearing the back of his hand on a timber nail. An icy breeze seemed to burst from the wood, making him gasp and lose his balance, the toe of his boot catching one of the beams. With a crash, the beam fell sideways on to a stack of heavy poplar posts which, coming down on him like a slow, rolling avalanche, knocked Errol to the floor.

For a few seconds he lay still, concerned that the thunderous noise might have alerted a passer-by. Then, in the silence and darkness, he shifted his left leg, trapped under the wood. A stabbing pain from his knee caused him to curse anew. He lifted the stakes one by one from him. Within a minute and a half, he was free. No limbs were broken. Slowly, painfully, he hobbled away, past the cottage, down the path, along the road and into his van.

It was only as he sat in the driver's seat that Errol became aware that something was wrong, an inexpressible discomfort. Then he realised what it was. The reassuring bulge of banknotes that he kept in his back pocket was no longer there. For the briefest of moments he considered returning to Ned's shed. Then, with a curse, he started the engine and drove away down Farthing Lane in the direction of the village.

The grey cloud moved quickly to the Turville Funeral Home where its manager Matthew Turville, a dark, slim man in his late thirties, had left his secretary Mrs Kirby working on invoices in the office, had put on a heavy rubber apron, and was now in the bright, white-tiled Preparation Room, looking down at Ned Simpkin who lay naked on the lipped, metal embalming table.

Ned's slight, reedy form seemed to glow palely, the scars of a lifetime's manual work showing up darkly beneath the fluorescent lighting, as he stared upwards, his chin bound in place by tape. Matthew ran a hand down one of the old man's bony shanks as thoughtfully as a cabinet-maker inspecting a fine board of oak. He turned the head slightly, noting that the whiskery ears had been faintly discoloured by cardiac blue. Ned was, on the face of it, unpromising material. Concave-chested, his back curved by decades of work, with a rattish, orange-toothed countenance, he had been an unlovely man when alive, and the two days spent undiscovered at his cottage had done little to improve his appearance. Already patches of putrescent green, purple and brown were faintly visible through the grey hairs of his chest.

'Right, Ned.' Matthew washed his hands in a basin near by, dried them, and pulled on a pair of rubber gloves. 'Let's be having you.'

As Matthew leant forward, a lock of his heavy dark hair fell across his right eye, temporarily giving him the look of a moody adolescent. He turned the body slightly, revealing the dark skin around its dorsal area where, after seventy-one years, Ned's blood had finally come to rest, lying as still as a stagnant pool of rainwater in a blocked drain.

Leaving Ned on his side, Matthew crouched down and pinched some loose skin at the back of the leg. He reached for a hooked stainless-steel needle and, as gently as if Ned were still alive, eased it deep into the back of the knee, raising the artery, then inserted into it the drainage tube leading to an embalming machine nearby. He repeated the process in six other places around the torso, buttocks and limbs. Two other, larger tubes were attached to the jugular vein in Ned's neck and under his rib-cage. Matthew switched on the machine and, as the fluid worked its way around the body, he massaged the flesh with long, easy strokes, forcing out Ned's tired old blood which darkened the larger pipes as, sluggishly, reluctantly, it left the body.

If hurried, embalming could be a messy business but, despite his arteriosclerosis, Ned's circulatory system was in good order. Matthew worked slowly and with care. Noticing a thin, yellow trace of serum oozing across the skin below one of the tubes, he wiped it carefully with a cloth soaked in surgical spirit, before turning his attention to Ned's face.

It was a full thirty minutes before the work was completed. Standing back, he surveyed a new Ned Simpkin, his back straighter, his skin clean and glowing, his expression no longer furtive and evasive but direct, honest and strong. Under the undertaker's hands, Ned had been transformed. Matthew took off the rubber gloves, threw them in a bin, then turned to the bench in the corner on which he had left the cerecloth.

There was a knock at the door. Matthew closed his eyes, letting his head fall back in a brief moment of exasperation. 'Who is it?' he asked.

'It's me.' The voice was soft, faintly apologetic. 'Are you busy?'

Sighing, Matthew rinsed his hands. He opened the door slightly without taking off the security chain. 'I'm up to my elbows in Ned Simpkin.'

'I was visiting a property.'

'It's really not a good moment.'

'Two minutes. Please.'

Matthew hesitated. 'Hang on,' he said, closing the door. He picked up the shroud, shook it out and laid it over Simpkin's body. Then he unbolted the door.

'Chains, bolts, honestly.' Sarah Dunn ambled into the room, a woman in her early thirties, her hair slightly too blonde, her dark suit marginally too clinging, to be entirely correct in an estate agent. She kissed Matthew lightly on the lips. 'What's the problem? Bodysnatchers?'

'Families. There are some things it's better for them not to see.'

She looked up at Matthew, ran her right hand through his dark hair in a confident, proprietorial way. 'What a thoughtful man,' she said.

She wandered over to the embalming table and lifted up the shroud. 'Yuk.'

Matthew stood by the door. 'I'm working,' he said.

'Honestly. You're always in such a hurry these days.' Sarah pulled the shroud back over Ned's face like someone making a bed. 'It was just that I was going to see a house on Magpie Green. It's empty. I thought you might like to see it, too.'

'What about poor old Ned? If I leave him much longer, he'll be as brown and hard as baked clay.'

'Let him bake for a bit.' Sarah was toying with the edge of his rubber apron.

'Sarah, please.'

'Ned's body can wait.' Sarah reached for Matthew under his apron. 'Mine can't.'

As if in response, there was a long, low gurgle from the direction of the corpse.

'Fucking hell, Matthew, he's still alive.' Sarah backed towards the door.

'Chemical reaction,' said Matthew, glancing uncertainly in the direction of the body. The cerecloth covering Ned's face seemed to be rising, as if it were part of a bizarre conjuring trick.

'Matthew, look!'

He walked over to the table and, with only a moment's hesitation, lifted the shroud. Like a giant, fungoid growth, Ned's tongue extruded from his mouth, blue and erect. The effect of the open mouth had been to tug at the facial tissue, widening his eyes into an expression of grotesque disapproval.

'Ugh, that's disgusting, Matthew.' Sarah was quickly putting on her shoes. 'It looks like a – '

'Happens sometimes,' said Matthew unconvincingly. 'I'll need to work on this.'

'You do that.' Sarah stood at the door, her face turned away from the laying-out table. 'Will you be there on Saturday?'

'Hope so.'

'We need to talk.'

With a final shudder, she left, closing the door behind her.

Frowning, Matthew gazed at Ned Simpkin's contorted features. He was about to remove the sheet when he noticed, across the front of it, a smear, a reddish stain, too light in colour to have been caused by coagulated blood.

He picked up the sheet; the waxed material seemed oddly cold, even allowing for the low temperature at which the Preparation Room was kept.

A soiled cerecloth. Matthew shook his head. Then, tossing it on to the bench, he turned back to the table to complete the work on Ned's face.

The cloud rose high over the rooftops of Burthorpe, then descended rapidly over the village pond to the garden of a small cottage where Matthew lived with his wife Alison and their children, Stephen and Kate. It settled in the large yew tree in the front garden startling a blackbird that was roosting in its thick branches.

Lights shone from every window of Yew Tree Cottage, seeming to warm the chill winter air. They illuminated the lawn where, two yards away, a mole was creating a small hillock of dark moist earth. Tomorrow morning, Matthew would rake over this and other fresh molehills, tossing the occasional stone excavated by the mole over the wall. During their ten years of marriage, the Turvilles had waged a hopeless, weaponless war against moles; they had left mothballs down the burrows, borrowed a vibrating machine from Charlie Watson. One evening Alison, a keen student of local folklore, had knelt beside a yew tree and had prayed to the god of moles to vacate their lawn. More violent methods, gas or traps, had been forbidden by the children. In the end, humans and moles had reached a kind of accommodation.

There was movement inside the house, too. In the small, low-ceilinged sitting-room adjoining the kitchen, Stephen sat at the piano practising scales, glancing occasionally at a television nearby. The compromise between duty and pleasure, which some take a lifetime to understand, already seemed second nature to him. Now and then, his mother corrected a false note from the kitchen. Stephen, without protest, completed the scales, then started again, incorporating the correction.

Kate sat at the kitchen table, an exercise book in front of her, while her mother stood beside her, cutting beans for dinner. Seen from the garden, they presented a picture of generational female unity: the daughter's light curls tangled like half-consumed candy floss, her metal-framed glasses held in place by a strip of pink tape, the mother's fine blonde hair falling forward on each side of the pale, light-boned features of her face.

Suddenly Alison looked up and, for several seconds, stared out of the kitchen window, as if she had seen something in the gloom outside or had heard someone approaching. Then Kate tugged at her mother's arm and, with a little frown of irritation, Alison Turville returned her attention to domestic life.

The cloud hovered by the yew tree for a moment then, rising high into the air, turned back to the fen.

2

CAMELOT COMES TO BURTHORPE!
Visitors to the historical Greyhound Inn, Burthorpe, are in for
a surprise as from this week. Proprietors Norman and Carol
Lownes have refurbished their establishment along the lines
of King Arthur and his famous Round Table!

With the help of well-known theming consultant Larry
Feathers of Norwich, the sixteenth-century Greyhound has
been transformed into an Olde England extravaganza. From
the Lancelot Lounge to the Camelot Carvery, not to mention
the splendid Excalibur Conference Centre, it's a veritable
wallow in the glorious days of old when knights were bold.

'We did want to change the name,' says Norman. 'I came
up with "That's Shallott", which I thought was quite
chucklesome but the Mid-Suffolk Heritage Committee told
us that it was historically inappropriate, so we stuck with the
Greyhound.'

Never mind, for local knights and their ladies, the new,
improved Greyhound Inn seems certain to be the Holy Grail!
Diss Press *readers have the opportunity to sample the delights
of the Greyhound Inn for themselves – and at reduced rates!
Produce this* DP *article over the next fifteen days and you can
have 25 per cent off room prices. For bookings, ring 01379
72189.*

A SPINDLY MAN WITH the beginnings of a paunch, Norman Lownes stood behind the bar in the Lancelot Lounge. His square shoulders and trim, sarcastic moustache gave him the air of an ex-army officer who had retained his modest military rank for civilian life, who harboured darkly right-wing fantasies deep in his soul, and who would die before his time, his body a mess of stress-induced pathogens. It was possible that Norman had once been good-looking – in photographs, he could look quite reasonable even now – but there was something about the resentful wince, the ever-present note of droning complaint in his voice, that was as depressing as warm winter drizzle.

Being something of a student of human nature, Norman prided himself on being able to judge people by the way they carried themselves: the square-shouldered, head-of-the-family strut of a dad, the grey glide of the representative, the young couple who seem to enter the lobby crotch first (no, we do *not* rent rooms by the hour).

So it was with the small woman with curly dark hair who walked into the lounge bar that Tuesday evening. As she made her way past a table where a group of workers from Dick's Ducks were drinking, glancing on her way at Errol Pryce who sat with his wife June in ill-tempered silence, his left leg stretched out on a stool, Norman saw not the midnight curls, the slim body, the slight, almost childish features, but the long-paced, easy walk, the cowboy roll of those sharp little shoulders. It was a student walk, he thought, but one with the confidence of the new breed of female area manager. An unappealing combination. Trouble.

She stood in front of the bar, as Norman pulled a pint, ignoring her. 'I'd like a room, please,' she said.

'Single? Double? Family?'

'Just for me. For a month.'

Norman looked up and was, for a moment, caught in the unblinking stare of those wide grey eyes. Then he pursed his lips, his moustache bristling like the fur on the back of a startled ginger cat. 'Month? We'll need a deposit.'

'Of course.' The troublemaker, whose figure was now being considered by several of the men in the bar, reached into the pocket of her jeans and pulled out a thick wad of dirty £20 notes. 'How much will you need?'

'£80.'

With a smile that seemed to contain more warmth than was justified by the occasion, she gave him four notes.

Norman took down the registration book from a shelf behind him. 'Help you with your luggage in a moment,' he muttered.

'I have none.'

'Ah.' He looked up sharply, then gazed across the room as if something more interesting had attracted his attention. If at this point he had been able to find an excuse to turn away this woman, this student area manager, he would have – particularly since his wife Carol, who had grown tired of the way he discouraged customers because he didn't like the look of them, was nowhere to be seen.

Yet, in the end, he didn't quite have the nerve to lose a month's half-board just because the prospective guest had an over-confident walk and no suitcases. 'Name?' he asked.

'Margaret Cowper. That's with a "W".'

'Mrs, Miss or' – Norman winced stagily – 'Ms?'

'Miss.'

'Hmm.' Norman wrote down the name and looked at it carefully as if still considering whether she should be admitted. Almost certainly, she was the type of customer who would smuggle men upstairs and try to get away with paying for a single room, or tear pages out of the courtesy copies of *Country Living* or, worst of all, sit alone in the Carvery eating a meal while reading a bloody book.

'This way, please, miss.' He nodded in the direction of the door. 'I'll show you to the Guinevere Suite.'

She walked through the lounge, ignoring the stares of local drinkers. Norman followed her, raising his eyebrows as he passed the lads from Dick's Ducks. He gave a knowing wink. Personally he had no time at all for that sort of thing, but he had to keep up appearances.

My light was but a taper, my warmth the fire built from mammocks and log-ends carried back from the fen. My children lay sleeping when he arrived as if somehow it were the will of the

Lord that His servant should not be disturbed. He would be there once or twice a week, under cover of darkness, leaving that bayard that would be recognised throughout the parish tethered to the cart behind the cottage, out of sight from the lane.

He would embrace me, then would take his chair on the other side of the fire, talking all the time of his work, of the gossip of the parish, laughing at the ways of country people. As he spoke to me, those small eyes, set in the beautiful, ravaged landscape of his face, would watch as I listened, smiling, now and then asking a question, to which he would reply, as if addressing a much-loved, but simple village dawcock.

Meg, he would sometimes say. Where would I be without my Meg? And he would talk sweetly, mocking me gently, his make, his miting, his Meg.

Soon he would stand up, extend a hand to me. We would lean together in front of the fire. Then we would go to my bed in the corner.

If one of the children stirred in the night, he would put his arm around me, hold me back.

In the morning, he would be awake at the first cock's crow from the village. He would sit up in bed, his mind already far from the cottage, full of the words and the duties of the day. He scarcely looked at me as he dressed and pulled on his boots and reached for the grey pilch lying across the bed.

The Lord be with you, I said once, as I lay, naked and cold, looking up at him.

He laughed, as if at some parish jangle.

Soon I would be listening to the squeak of leather, the click of hoof upon flint, as he left me with the children in the early morning darkness. Two coins, a crowch for his make, his miting, had been left on the bench by the door.

Through the coat of grime on its double-glazed windowpanes, bright winter sunlight illuminated the Guinevere Suite, where Margaret lay in the narrow bed, its slightly damp blankets pulled to her chin. She smiled as heavy vehicles changing gear around the corner outside sent a shudder through the room, shaking her to the marrow of her bones.

Last night she had been so tired that not even the clamour of voices from the drinking room below had kept her awake. She had drifted off to sleep, the sound of human voices and laughter from the bar downstairs rumbling like waves beneath her.

She opened and closed her eyes, several times. Then, turning on to her side, she gazed at the patterned wallpaper. A blue knight, courting a pink maid beneath a bright-green oak: the tableau was repeated from floor to ceiling. Margaret followed the procession of knights and ladies and oaks around the room, as if searching for a development, some small variation in the scene. She bit the fleshy tissue on the inside of her mouth, winced, then smiled. She snapped her teeth together. Pinching each side of her face, she pulled the skin downwards, simultaneously pushing her small pink tongue through her lips, like Ned's yesterday at the Home.

It was past nine o'clock before Margaret sat up on the side of the bed. She looked down at the sight of her pale, delicate feet, which, puppet-like, she lifted one after the other. She stood, swaying briefly as her legs took the weight of her body, then pirouetted, arms outstretched, her hands white in the rays of the winter sun. In front of the window, there was a chest of drawers on which Margaret saw a mirror. She stood in front of it; the reflection caught only the top of her dark hair. She pushed the base of the mirror but, as soon as she stood back, it returned to its original position. She looked around her, then pulled a red metal chair to the middle of the room. When she stood on the chair, her entire figure appeared in the stained, shadowy glass.

She considered herself, head on one side, humming quietly. After a few moments, she stepped down from the chair.

'Colour,' she whispered. She fell to her knees, speading her fingers over the nylon carpet's swirl of pinks, yellows and purples, manmade, invented shades so confident that they owed nothing to nature or to the past or to God. Tracing the pattern with her fingers, she crouched forward, nose to the ground, inhaling the smell of last night's cigarette smoke which rose from the bar below through the floorboards and the dazzling nylon.

There was a sound behind her. Without any sense of embarrassment or hurry, Margaret turned. A middle-aged woman with orange hair of a similar sheen and texture to that of the carpet stood in the doorway.

'Cleaner,' she said. 'Come to clean the room.'

'Thank you.' Margaret stood up, making no attempt to cover her nakedness. For a moment, the two women stood in silence.

'Sign.' The cleaner raised her voice as if Margaret were foreign or simple-minded. She pointed to a plastic sign reading, 'PRITHEE SILENCE! GENTLE FOLKE AT RESTE!' hanging on the door handle. 'You should put up the sign if you don't want to be disturbed.'

Muttering grumpily, she left, clattering her plastic bucket against the door.

Norman Lownes was wiping the tables in the Camelot Carvery when Margaret made her way quietly into the room and sat at one of the tables. He allowed several seconds to elapse before acknowledging her presence.

'Breakfast seven-thirty to nine-thirty,' he said. He glanced at the clock on the wall. 'You've missed the bus by almost ten minutes.'

'The bus? I wanted to eat.'

'Kitchen's working on lunch now.'

'I'll have some lunch then.'

Norman wiped another table, pursing his lips. 'Twelve o'clock, lunch,' he said. 'Twelve till three.' Seeing that Margaret had failed to vacate her table, he added, with a hint of apology, 'That's the way we run things here. I think you'll find it's all explained in the guest pack in your room.'

Reaching into the pocket of her jeans, Margaret produced the fat wad of notes. 'I'm hungry,' she said.

Throwing his sponge on to the table, Norman walked behind the bar. 'Snack?' he said irritably. 'Nuts? Nibbles? Pork pie?'

'The pie, please.' Margaret held out a £20 note.

Norman slapped a plastic-wrapped pork pie on the bar. 'I'll put it on the bill,' he said.

Briefly Margaret seemed confused by the idea that she would have to walk to the bar to collect her pie. Then she stood up and made her way across the room.

'Can't eat it in here,' said Norman. 'We're preparing for lunch.'

'I'll go for a walk.'

Mollified that he had won a small victory over a customer, Norman nodded in the direction of the window. 'Cold out. You'll catch your death in that T-shirt.'

'I don't think so,' said Margaret.

In the days before Burthorpe had been dispersed and bisected by road and rail, the Greyhound Inn had been both the focus of village life and a hostelry of distinction. James I and his entourage were said to have stayed there during the King's frequent hunting trips to the area. Later, it had become a popular coaching inn, famous for the huge circular bed which had occupied the room now known as the Excalibur Conference Centre, sleeping up to forty travellers every night. Today, gentrified yet enduringly shabby, its windows fortified against the heavy traffic which thundered past within inches of its walls, the inn still occupied a vantage point overlooking the old and the new Burthorpe, the village and its many divisions.

Across the main road where Margaret stood that morning, a smaller road called Railway Drive led down the hill, past Dr Miles Larwood's cottage on the left. On the right was Scrope Rise, Burthorpe's most recent settlement, a housing estate built in the early eighties. At the time, the Rise's fragile redbrick houses had seemed to represent a small but significant contribution to the new concept of a property-owning democracy, but greed and compromise had soon betrayed these hopes. In exchange for an agreement not to oppose planning permission, the local farmer Charlie Watson had insisted on access to a parcel of land beyond the estate so that now tractors passed through Scrope Rise, spraying mud over the residents' tiny lawns, patios and cars. Megson's, the local firm that had won the contract to build the houses, found themselves over-committed during the building glut and failed to drain the land sufficiently. Today, with every downpour, the south-side residences slipped inexorably towards the railway track fifty yards away. During the great gale of 1987, garages in Scrope Rise had taken wing, one of them coming to rest beyond the Norwich to Ipswich road.

Even the estate's name had been something of a compromise. In exchange for their agreeement to a project that transgressed most of the planning guidelines for the region, opposition councillors on the Planning Committeee had insisted that it should be named after an iconic socialist figure from North Suffolk, or even South Norfolk. There were few to choose from, it had transpired. Thomas Paine, who had worked briefly as a corstet-maker in Diss, had recently given his name to a crafts centre in Garboldisham. John Skelton, the sixteenth-century poet laureate and Rector of Diss, had been commemorated in a new street in the town. In the end, the committee settled on Jane Scrope, a young convent girl for whom Skelton had written a poem of such startling flirtatiousness that, according to some historians, Jane had been obliged to flee to Ipswich. It was agreed by the committee that all evidence pointed to an early case of gender politics, sexual harassment, possibly even child abuse. 'Scrope Rise' was passed without opposition.

Beyond the housing estate, as Railway Drive turned to the left and crossed the railway tracks, a thin plume of smoke and an array of gaudily painted vehicles marked a more recent arrival. This was the community known simply as 'the travellers', a raggle-taggle band of men and women, with their wary, hard-eyed children. In 1986, they had arrived in a procession of rusting caravans, pick-up trucks and converted ice-cream vans, and settled on a piece of scrubland beyond the tracks which had once been Burthorpe Station.

Why did the travellers come to rest when they arrived in Burthorpe? What was it about this little village that decided them to no more a-roving go? Such questions were frequently asked in the Greyhound, or in the market-place in Diss, particularly on Thursday afternoons when they would invade the town to collect their girocheques, with their dirty multicoloured hair and army boots, trailing underfed dogs, toting beer cans, playing guitars on Mere Street and generally upsetting law-abiding townsfolk who had hoped to take advantage of the late-night shopping at Safeway's.

For entrepreneurs like Errol Pryce, the travellers' settlement in Burthorpe had been particularly irksome. In 1985, the railway station, crumbling and mildly vandalised, had been dismantled in the confident expectation that some beady property speculator would buy the site for 'in-filling' with consequent benefit to local builders and sub-contractors. It never happened. Apart from 'this terrible recession' (a catchphrase used to this day to explain all the economic ills that Burthorpe is heir to), the proximity of the Scrope Rise houses – moving closer to the former station with every fall of rain, like children playing Grandmother's Footsteps – discouraged development. To the travellers, economic recession and land slippage were relatively minor problems, and they stayed on.

Despite their wide and general unpopularity, these people had made their own contribution to village life. They helped with the harvest, took casual work when new supermarkets were built. Their presence discouraged Londoners who found themselves in Burthorpe while sniffing about for a weekend cottage. Araminta Winterburn had rather dashingly taken to using a couple of their teenage daughters as babysitters. In a blue caravan with faded red blinds, a woman locally known as the Squealer provided an informal, round-the-clock service of sexual release for the less discriminating of the village men.

Above all, the travellers provided Burthorpe with one particular focus for its many and varied dissatisfactions – a skipping hobgoblin who carried, on his skeletal shoulders, the secret fears, the sins, the nightmares of the entire village. If he had ever had a conventional name, no one in the village was aware of it.

To them, he was simply known as Naughty Boy Dance.

Margaret stood watching the cars. A black van, dented and mud-spattered, ascended Bridge Lane at speed, splashing her as it passed. She caught a glimpse of Errol Pryce behind the wheel, his eyes fixed angrily on the road in front of him. The van slowed at the top of the hill, one brake light glowing, then crossed the main road towards Scrope Rise. As the van disappeared, Margaret turned, taking another bite of her pie, and walked slowly past the green towards the pond. After a few yards, she extracted from her back pocket the thick wad of banknotes and held them under her nose. The money had been sweetened by the aroma of Errol's pipe tobacco, which smelt not unlike the smoke that drifted upwards from the Home late at night.

She returned the money to her pocket, then ran her right hand up her forearm where the delicate dark hair stood out in the cold from her pale flesh. She hesitated outside the H.T. Pearson Convenience Store, considering the dusty jars and tins which, for H.T. Pearson, passed as a window display.

They say that Pearson's father, also called Henry, was a jovial, good-natured man; for some reason, these gifts had not been passed on to his only child. A man of indeterminate late middle years, H.T. Pearson had the clammy, prematurely aged appearance of someone with bowel problems and an unhealthy secret life. For most of the day, he would sit, straight-backed, on a small wooden stool behind the counter. His only moment of genuine pleasure occurred when schoolgirls, returning home from Diss Comprehensive, called in at the shop. As they entered, Pearson's tall, bald figure would rear up from behind the counter like an erection. He would watch them in a sweet agony of confusion, simultaneously anxious that they might be disordering or stealing from his shelves, yet longing for them to stay, filling his shop with the smell of the classroom, with their dirty little laughter.

Recently even this innocent pleasure had been seriously diminished. Last term, Pearson had been appalled, *scandalised*, to discover that the uniform at Diss Comprehensive had been 'rationalised'. Girls were to wear trousers. He had felt quite sick with rage when the first two sets of entirely covered legs had entered his shop. He had prayed that there might be an element of choice for his girls – this was a democracy, for Christ's sake – but no. The only time he saw young legs these days was during the holidays and frankly they were never quite the same without the uniform. Such was his distress that H.T. Pearson had been obliged to send a letter to the *Diss Press*.

Dear Sir
DOWN WITH THESE TROUSERS!
Am I alone in being appalled by the recent change in uniform imposed on pupils of the fair sex at Diss Comprehensive? The traditional garb was smart, practical and attractive to look at. I'm no stick-in-the-mud when it comes to change but surely this

craze for the 'unisex look' has now gone too far. After all, variety is the spice of life!
Yours,
Mrs F. Peters,
Wortham

It had never been printed. Briefly, H.T. Pearson had worried that an investigative reporter from the *DP*, discovering that there was no Mrs Peters in Wortham, would follow the trail to his door. In the end, he concluded it had been the humorous headline that had counted against him – there was little room for innocent levity in the *DP*. So, gloomily, he was coming to terms with the new uniform. It was not the first time that reality had let him down and that his imagination had been required to take up the slack.

Pearson's store was convenient only in name. The minimal and unappetising selection of goods ranged sparingly along the shop's dusty shelves gave the place a fifties ration-book feel. Even when an item was sold, the shopkeeper would part with it like a man losing a small but precious family heirloom. Only his duties as sub-postmaster, handing out stamps or child benefit allowances, gave Pearson any sense of satisfaction, authority. When Margaret entered his shop, the door producing a misleadingly cheerful 'ping', he was seated in his Post Office cubicle, blinking at her mournfully like some doomed, ill-kept animal at a small rural zoo.

Eyeing his customer with suspicion, he left his cubicle, and stood behind the counter, leaning forward on his big, soft, shiny fists.

'Yes?'

'Hello. The woman looked up from a small display of soup cans with an expression of dazed delight.

'Can I help you?'

The woman approached the counter. 'Smoke, please.'

'Smoke.'

'Please.'

'Ah. Matches? Firelighters? Two-bob rockets? I don't sell smoke as such. Sorry.'

She pointed to the small selection of cigarettes displayed behind the counter. 'One of those, please.'

'Cigarettes, we call them. Which brand?'

'I don't mind.'

Pearson reached for a packet of twenty Benson & Hedges and laid them briskly on the counter like a man playing a trump card. '£2.70.'

She handed over a £20 note which the shopkeeper held up to the light before reluctantly placing in his till. By the time he had handed her the change, the woman had opened the packet and had put a cigarette between her lips. Pocketing it with another smile, she turned towards the door.

H.T. Pearson watched her leave the shop. Small hands: for an instant, he saw those thin wrists held by one of his big hands, those whippy little bones flexing under his great male strength. Closing the door behind her, the woman stood hands in pockets, looking down Bridge Lane, the unlit cigarette drooping from her mouth in what seemed to him a self-consciously melodramatic way. Then, as if reaching some kind of decision, she gave a curt nod of her head. Smoke billowed from her mouth. Pearson frowned, intrigued in spite of himself. As she wandered down the hill, he walked to the front of the shop and peered after her. 'Nice buttocks,' he said quietly; he had always considered himself to be something of a buttocks man.

By Burthorpe's standards, it was a poor crowd that had gathered at the gates to the Funeral Home to mark Ned Simpkin's last journey. Charlie Watson, a tall, forbidding man who exuded the natural melancholy of a farmer, looked uncomfortable in his dark suit. By contrast, the Williamson sisters from Palgrave seemed entirely at home in matching grey coats and skirts; although they had hardly known Ned, they would frequently travel from Palgrave for funerals, their only regular social occasions. Thurston Farr, the plumber, was there and so, more surprisingly, was Jenny Dine, wife of one of his neighbours, who, so far as anyone knew, had been no particular friend of Ned's. Her appearance at the funeral was later to prompt rumours that the old man had been richer than expected and that his will would contain pleasant surprises for those who had extended to him kindnesses of one sort or another in his solitary later years. This speculation (as a result of which a Simpkin brother living in Ipswich appeared in Burthorpe ten days after Ned's ashes were scattered in the Garden of Remembrance) proved to be ill-founded.

It was Matthew Turville's habit to stand at the entrance to the Funeral Home, greeting the mourners, circulating amongst them with discreet words of condolence until the hearse, driven by his part-time employee Jim Garnham, arrived. Then he would close the neat, white-painted gate.

Arms crossed, Margaret watched him as he spoke, brows furrowed on his smooth dark features, to Charlie Watson. Unfortunately, Matthew was wearing his father's three-piece mourning suit which, even though it had been taken in and modified by Taylor's the Tailor's in Diss, somehow bestowed on him an air of slightly bogus middle-aged *gravitas*.

Glancing up the hill in the direction from which Jim and the hearse were due at any moment to appear, Matthew noticed for the first time the slight, pale presence of a woman in dark jeans and a T-shirt standing beyond the gate. For the briefest of moments, their eyes met, before Matthew looked away to resume his conversation with Charlie Watson.

Margaret lit another cigarette, then turned to walk back up the hill.

The sound of a small engine cut the air as Naughty Boy Dance gunned his Honda scooter up Railway Drive. With the quickest of glances, he joined the main road, then took a quick right turn behind St Botolph's Church, past Burthorpe Primary. As he passed Margaret, his dirty blond hair streamed behind him. He was laughing.

The black van appeared at the top of the hill some two hundred yards behind. Margaret caught a glimpse of Errol Pryce's features, pale and tense like a bomber pilot's, as it flashed by in pursuit.

Unwisely, Dance took the road across the fen, allowing Errol to gain on him as they drove down the long straight road. By the time the scooter reappeared in the village, having looped around Wortham, there was no more than seventy yards between them.

Naughty Boy Dance was approaching the Greyhound when he heard a loud crack to his left. Glancing across, he sensed movement within the mature trees surrounding the pond. Only when he heard, above the wind rushing past his ears, a loud crash behind him did he brake and look back down the road. A tall lime tree lay across the road between him and Pryce's van, which had turned and skidded sideways into its bare branches. For a moment, Dance considered whether he should return to help the builder, but then the front door of the van slid back and Errol stepped out, and stood, hands on hips, a figure of comical exasperation, beyond the fallen tree.

The unmistakable sound of distressed metal caused Dr Miles Larwood to look up from his computer screen. It was not unusual for minor accidents to occur on the main road up the hill from his cottage: there were blind turnings, cars emerging sleepily from side roads into the path of the rushing traffic.

Miles stood up in his paper-strewn, low-ceilinged room. Out of the window he saw Mr Lewis, a pensioner who lived across the road in Scrope Rise, hurrying up the hill, a jemmy in his hand. Vaguely, Miles wondered whether he should follow Lewis, gather around the accident with the other villagers, comfort weeping passengers, wave traffic past, call the services, help prise the stricken vehicles apart with the crowbar, but in the end he stayed where he was. Not good when it came to emergencies, Miles sensed that he would merely get in the way of other, more practical men.

He sighed, sat down and rolled himself a cigarette. Then, catching the reflection of his face in the window, he looked away quickly.

These days there was something scuffed and used about Miles Larwood. Beneath the sandy locks of hair that descended stringily on to the collar of his shirt, he had the stooped shoulders and papery complexion of a man who had spent too much of his life in libraries, whose attention to academic detail had been achieved at considerable cost in terms of general physical comeliness. There had been those, some ten or twenty years ago, who had found in his gaunt, distracted features a sort of ascetic charm, but as his nature (solitary and ruminative) found expression in his face, as the muscle tone slackened around his cheeks and chin, as his own concern for matters of personal appearance, particularly in the nasal area, grew ever more haphazard, it had seemed that Miles's reputation and conversation – neither of which were exceptional – now counted as his strongest personal attributes. Recently he had begun to feel rather more than his forty-five years.

He thought of the crash. It was little comfort that no one actually expected him to become involved in the small dramas of village life. Miles picked a damp fleck of Old Holborn from his upper lip and examined it.

As an academic, a teacher, a writer, he feared that he was seen as something of an odd fish by the locals. At last summer's Burthorpe fête, for example, he had found himself in the tea tent, talking to Nina Hebden, an edgy, thin-faced, pretty woman whose darting eyes and outrageous comments suggested an intelligence turned sour by boredom and inaction. He had actually told Nina that he was writing a book.

'A book?' she had said. 'But how riveting. What's it about?'

'It's called *Regional Death Studies: A Resource Handbook*.'

'Ah.' She had frowned. 'Does one dare ask what Regional Death Studies might be?'

'Yes, I'm researching into thanatological aspects of local history – the sociology, folklore, economy, eschatology, ritual, philology, even' – he had laughed nervously – 'the erotology of death and mourning.'

'Golly.' Nina had glanced around restlessly. 'Well I'll be jiggered.'

Too late, he shifted the conversation to his part-time teaching job at the Anglia Institute in Ipswich. A chill had descended on the exchange and, soon afterwards, Nina had drifted away, doubtless to more congenial company.

Perhaps it would change. Maybe, once the resource handbook was completed and published, Miles's status within the village would be established. Just as Stuston currently boasted a TV cook and Palgrave housed the writer of Suffolk crime stories (*Death in Mellis* and *Eye Spy* being her best-known titles), so Dr Miles Larwood, the eminent thanatologist, would become that rare phenomenon, a Burthorpe man known outside Burthorpe. It was possible.

Miles laid the damp remains of his roll-up on a stained scallop-shell ashtray and faced the computer screen again. Before he had been interrupted, he had been grappling with 'Death and affectivity: towards a theory of thanatophilia', a keynote entry in the handbook in which he hoped to relate the medieval notion of the Good Death, via eighteenth-century gothic necrophiliac obsession, to contemporary eroto-morbidity as specifically expressed in the fictions of J.G. Ballard, but now he felt distracted, depressed even.

What was the point? What good did it do, this isolation from the real world of collisions and emotion and contact? First the work, then the life: that had been the standard under which he had marched down the years. But what if the work was no good? What if it was good but unrecognised? What if the work turned out to be no more than an escape from that messy, uncontrollable project called life? What if the work never ended, but stretched into infinity like death itself? These questions haunted Miles. Every day, he felt older, less secure in himself, a castaway drifting slowly from the shore of normal, everyday existence on the rickety raft of intellectual exploration.

He glanced through his notes, then tapped out on the computer keyboard:

'OLD JOHNNY'
See MARSH FEVER IN C17 ESSEX.

PLAGUE IN DISS, 1579
See THE CONTAGIOUS COURT: QUEEN ELIZABETH'S
TOURS, EFFECTS OF.

TRANSI
See THE CORPSE IN C14 THANATOLOGICAL ART.

HAEMORRHOIDS, MENSTRUAL PAINS AND TUMOURS
Cured by perspirations of the dead, see THE CURATIVE
CORPSE.

ANATOMISTS, HEALING HANDS OF
See THE CURATIVE CORPSE.

SHROUDS, CORPSES' APPARENT CONSUMPTION OF
See REVENANCE, THEORY OF.

WARMTH, POST-MORTEM
See DECOMPOSITION AND THE FOLKLORE OF
AFTERLIFE and CREMATION, ENVIRONMENTAL IM-
PLICATIONS OF.

MOURNING CLOTHES
See APOTROPAICS AND DISGUISE: PERCEIVED DE-
FENCES AGAINST THE RETURN OF THE DEAD.

Miles sat back and rubbed his eyes. So much to research, so little time. Scholarship was a demanding mistress.

3

SIMON PYGOTT STOOD with his back to the inglenook fire in the library of Garston Hall, one foot resting lightly on the plump fawn body of his Golden Labrador Jess. Tall, broad-shouldered, with sleek, well-groomed hair, Simon seemed to fill the fireplace with his outsize good looks. The mobile telephone into which he was speaking appeared toy-like against his large, handsome head, as if it had been designed for a smaller, less certain race of human beings than the one into which Simon had been born.

'Unspeakable in pursuit of the what?'

At the other end of the telephone, Rose Hope was explaining one of those clever-arse references in which she specialised and which had always made Simon feel uneasy. He hated not getting jokes – sometimes, at a dinner party, he'd give a great, honest, appreciative guffaw of laughter when things seemed to be moving into what he called humorous mode – but, with Rose, he was never quite sure what was expected. Her wit was sneaky and indirect. He had never known a girl who was quite so competitive in her conversation.

'Ah yes. Pryce is unspeakable and Naughty Boy, I see, well – ' Simon picked up a copy of the *Diss Press* which lay on a fireside table nearby. 'Now the real reason for my calling the esteemed editor of the *DP* is to ask what the bloody hell she's doing giving a bunch of raggedy-arsed protesters free publicity at her lover's expense.'

There was a volley of protests from the other end of the telephone.

'"Around the villages, Burthorpe".' He read from the paper, his voice heavy with disapproval. '"A group of environmental protesters temporarily held up clearance work on Beggar's Hill, an ancient woodland on the Garston Hall estate, last Thursday. Police said the activists came from outside the area. This Saturday's car-boot sale will take place at blah-blah . . ." Yes, I know you tucked it away among the coffee mornings and bring-and-buy sales – but it was still there, wasn't it? Honestly, darling, this does sweet bugger all for what I call my local credibility.'

Simon sat down slowly as Rose explained one of her schemes. 'I hate interviews,' he said eventually. 'Always ends in tears.' Extending his right leg, he pushed an oak log towards the centre of the fire, half-listening as Rose explained how we lived in an age of publicity, of presentation.

'Publicity,' he muttered. 'Every move I've made over the past few years ends up with publicity. Sell a bit of farmland to make the Scrope Rise estate. Flog off a couple of Gainsboroughs. Chop down a few trees. I get the publicity all right. But it's never Mr Pygott, the sensible landowner pursuing prudent housekeeping measures – *oh* no – it's Pygott at it again, betraying the community.'

The editor pursued her argument.

'The Heritage Committee?' Simon smiled patiently. 'Darling, they're the worst of the lot. Every time they open their mouths about

Garston, it seems to cost me another couple of grand. Last time I heard from them, it was to tell me I wasn't allowed to sell the family papers to some university in America. Not allowed! Surely that couldn't be right. But it was. And why?' Simon put on a nasal, bureaucratic whine. 'Because we represent the interests of the community, Mr Pygott.'

Rose tried to interrupt but this was something about which Simon felt really rather strongly. 'Was it the community that was given monastery land by Henry VIII? Did the community design and build this place?' he asked. 'Where was the community to be found over all those centuries when my bloody family developed the park and the estate, took on tenant farmers, gave employment to virtually every snot-nosed, drooling ne'er-do-well in the district? Living off the Pygott family, that's where the community was. And now these people have the gall to pronounce upon what I can or can't sell. Haemorrhage Committee, I call it.'

Simon sighed wearily and listened to the editor's argument for a moment. 'All right, bring the tape tomorrow. I'll say a few words and you cobble it together . . . Debrief, how d'you mean –?' He laughed unconvincingly. 'Oh yes, right – you debrief me and I'll debrief you, very good.' Hanging up, he stabbed at the telephone and laid it on the table beside him.

'Bloody woman,' he muttered.

He stared ahead of him, picturing Rose in his mind: the aggressive little hairstyle, the tape-recorder in her bag, the jeans, the long striding legs which didn't quite meet at the top as if – Simon shuddered at the thought – they had been worn away by the efforts of her countless lovers. He wondered vaguely whether it was time to move on, what he called romantically.

At his feet, Jess shifted slightly to allow the heat of the fire to warm another part of his anatomy.

'Old dog, you're a lazy bastard.'

Jess raised his grey-whiskered face and thumped the mat with his tail.

'What are you?' Simon leant forward and slapped the pink exposed stomach with the copy of the *Diss Press*. There was a moment of mute adoration between the dog and its master.

'Bloody duty. Bloody teeown ceeouncil,' Simon said loudly. Jess looked up, pricking his ears as if some important code-word relating to exercise or food had been pronounced. 'Sodding heritage.'

There was no doubt, Simon reflected, that he was in seriously bad form these days. Quite often he found himself pondering, never previously having been the pondering type. All around him he saw the scrofulous ranks of the concerned, the community; behind him, more oppressive still, was the weight of history, represented by those distinguished Pygotts of the past, several of whom were looking down at him in wordless expectation, from the west wall of the library. Sir Thomas Pygott, the merchant of Norwich who had become a court favourite (and, some said, lover) of Queen Elizabeth. Next to Sir Thomas was Sir Malory Pygott, a pasty-faced cove with a pointed beard, who had played host to James I. His son Sir Henry had remained loyal to the Crown during the Civil War and was rewarded at the Restoration with yet more land and patronage. So it had continued down the centuries, generation after generation of Pygotts deploying the family's influence and money to support king and country and, in the process, acquiring yet more influence and money. *Mediocra firma* was the Pygott family motto and that was the way it had always been. Moderate things were the most lasting. Moderate land, moderate power, a moderate but lasting contribution to national life and one's own family.

It had been simple then and, bloody hell, it should be simple now. History was like the stock market: there were times to buy and times to sell. After centuries of adding to its portfolio, the Pygott family was temporarily obliged to go liquid, divesting itself of some household stock, the odd bit of woodland. His ancestors, he was convinced, would have appreciated this. After all, the Pygotts had never been afraid of change when the time was right.

Simon stood up and wandered over to an ancient radiogram which stood in the corner of the library, crouched down and put on a record. The mournful voice of Connie Francis singing 'Where the Boys Are' filled the room.

There *was* something about all this that seemed a little tiresome, slightly bothering. Simon Pygott walked back to the inglenook and stared at a portrait of the latest generation, which was hanging over the fire. Despite the glowing yellows and blues with which the artist had worked, giving the picture a strange backlit quality, it radiated an undeniable melancholy. These days his wife Susan spent her time in London, the boys were at prep school, his father had died in Italy last year. It occurred to Simon that, like the books in the library and the oaks in the park, the Pygott family itself was being dispersed.

He nudged Jess with his right foot, then winked at the animal. The dog had always been a quick learner – Charlie had taught him how to die for the queen in one afternoon – but, in spite of hours of training, he had never got the hang of the old winking trick. Suddenly, a brighter look of expectation entered Jess's eyes.

'That's right, you clever old thing.' Simon smiled. 'It's time for dins for you, then party for me.' He stood up and stretched. 'It's going to be a hell of a thrash.'

Hands sunk deep into the pockets of his cavalry twills, Simon whistled tunelessly through his teeth as he followed his dog towards the door, the steel tips of his shoe-heels echoing around the empty shelves of the library.

'It says ten on the box but it comes up generous.'

'So it does. Very generous.'

Margaret smiled at the manager of the Catwalk Fashion Boutique of Mere Street, Diss.

'Very popular with our younger clients.' The manager touched the garish bomber jacket whose splashes of greens and purples reflected last year's ersatz druggy look. 'Teenagers and suchlike.'

'Younger?' Margaret turned in front of a full-length mirror, touching at the lime-green trousers, glancing at the blue boots with thick soles.

'Not necessarily,' said the manager carefully. 'They look good on all sorts of people. You've got the figure for it.'

'I'll take them all,' said Margaret.

The manager made to remove the jacket, but Margaret stepped back. 'No, I'll keep it on,' she said.

'Of course, madam.'

'I'll need more money soon,' she said, as she paid.

'Don't we all,' said the manager.

Moments later, Margaret stepped out of the Catwalk Fashion Boutique, freshly clad and carrying Susan Pygott's clothes in a plastic bag.

Mere Street was busy in the late afternoon gloom and, for a moment, Margaret stood back to watch the shoppers. This little street, a matter of two hundred yards linking the space in front of the mere to the market-place, had appeared, over the years, to take on a new character every few months. Once it had been a thoroughfare. Then, as the vehicles grew larger and faster, humans and machines had seemed to do battle in the narrow confines between the two rows of shops. The humans had won, first reducing the flow of traffic, then staunching it altogether to make the street into a great pavement, marked by benches and litter bins. Trade had reflected this uncertainty. Today the shop adjoining the Catwalk Boutique sold videos and greetings cards. Two years ago, it had been a vegetarian foodstore; before that, briefly, an estate agent, after Wrens Tea Shop had closed down. It was as if the street were looking for a new identity to wear but that so far nothing had fitted.

And yet reminders of the street it had once been still survived: sides of pork hanging in the butcher, a solitary cockerel that strutted among the shoppers and made its way every Friday to the stalls in the market-place where it pecked among the debris.

'Like the jacket.'

A group of teenage schoolgirls had gathered outside Woolworth's. They had been laughing at Margaret, leaning against one another, hiding their faces, when one of them, a plump, unlovely creature with cropped hair, called out, 'Yeah, really great jacket, that.'

'I like it, too.' Unsteady in her new shoes, Margaret made her way slowly towards them.

'Really, like, colourful.'

One of the other girls asked her, with an adolescent attempt at a sneer, how much she had paid for it.

'£49.99.'

'Yeah?' The big girl stood in front of Margaret, chewing open-mouthed. 'Give you a tenner for it. I could use it on the guy for Bonfire Night.'

Margaret stared at her for a moment, her eyes wide and unblinking.

33

'You like green?' she asked.

'Yeah, but not puke-green like that jacket.' The other girls cackled with pleasure.

'Good.'

'What d'you mean goo – ?' The girl doubled over. 'Shit,' she gasped. 'My stomach.'

'You shall have green menses.'

'That evil bitch has given me a stomach ache.'

'What's menses?' asked one of the others.

Margaret turned and walked towards the mere.

The musket.

For a moment sounds and smells fill the head. Horses' hooves, the creak of timber as ox-carts and waterlags make their way through the mud, the clamour of travellers and tinkers by St Mary's, the call of a lamb separated from its mother on the meadow beyond the water, and the bells, always the church bells.

The musket. His Reverend's mutton. A hackney for our master's holy rod. Make way for the mare.

I can hear the laughter still.

It was early evening at Yew Tree Cottage, a time of business and tension as the pressures of school and work spilt untidily into the home, before the rhythm of domestic life had established itself. Kate Turville had been collected from her ballet lesson in Eye and was with her brother Stephen watching television in the sitting-room, from where the niggle and whine of an Australian soap opera could be heard. Matthew was in the small study at the back of the house, working on plans for the new Garden of Remembrance. Soon Alison would prepare supper, after which the children's bedtime would have to be negotiated, then some school papers needed marking, but now she moved through the house, clearing up, wiping down, straightening and ordering with casual, brisk economy.

It was odd what having a family and home could do to a person. Before she had married Matthew, Alison had been as slobbish and easygoing as any other student teacher, yet now the domestic impulse was part of her character, as if tidying away the errant toys, scattered cushions and discarded mugs of Yew Tree Cottage were not so much housekeeping as marriage-keeping, life-keeping.

They had been here for twelve years. Once, this building had been a dull and anonymous labourer's cottage: unpainted, fragile, its beams buckled and rotting, it had looked as if a brisk gust of winter wind or extravagant fall of snow would bring it down.

They had worked on the house. While Matthew replaced the beams and fitted new windows, Alison cut back the brambles in the garden. As she painted the kitchen, the bedrooms, the little hall, he retiled the roof, then dressed the house in a lime wash of Suffolk pink. Every weekend they had worked, calling out to one another over the sound of a radio during the good times, or, when things were difficult between them tapping and scrubbing in studious silence. Eight months pregnant with Stephen, Alison was still tiling the kitchen. When the children were four and one, she was working on the garden, weeding, planting, pruning.

It was as if the house had been saved by love. Once the poor abandoned village beggar, it had been warmed and fed and reclothed. With its brightly coloured walls, white windows and dark peg tiles, Yew Tree Cottage had reclaimed its rightful place in Burthorpe, settling into the hollow behind the village pond, glowing with such a sense of ease and accord and the general rightness of things that, in the summer, strangers driving by would slow down to gaze at the house and the garden, soothing their fretful lives with its tranquillity and confidence. And there would be Alison, watering-can in hand, Matthew attending a faulty lock on the front door, Stephen reading a book on the lawn, Kate kicking at a tennis ball.

The marriage had ripened and matured as, through pain and experience, the Turvilles had come to understand each other's points of frailty, areas of conversation that represented risk, jokes and references to be avoided. The landscape of their own love had also been tamed and brought to a satisfactory state of order. Within Alison, there had been a barely perceptible shift of interest from her husband to the family as a whole, from the children she taught as a part-time supply teacher to her more private ambitions as a landscape gardener.

Sometimes she would gaze at Matthew as he worked on the house and would imagine the day when, the children gone, the two of them would be alone again at Yew Tree Cottage, the successful business-man and the fulfilled artist.

He had changed, too. The presence of children, of a tolerant wife, had mellowed him. The impatience he had shown when bemused by the ways of marriage in the early days had given way to affectionate resignation. These days he rarely raised his voice, he gave his time happily to the children, defused moments of marital tension in the traditional way, with charm and flowers. Over the past two years they had taken to locking the bedroom door on Sunday mornings when they would make love with languid, economical affection. It had become their secret, part of a marital code, a good-humoured threat or a promise. 'I'll discuss this with you on Sunday morning,' she would say with a smile over the dinner table; sometimes a raised eyebrow, a quizzical 'Sunday?' would be enough.

Each of the children had played a part in this process of gentle maturity. Stephen's nine-year progress had sometimes seemed like a miracle of good fortune. He had slept well as a baby. His graduation from nappies had been trouble-free. At Burthorpe Primary, he had shown enough talent in his lessons, sport and music as to earn the gratitude of teachers without sacrificing the popularity of his peers. What for others might have been problematical parents – mother a teacher at his school, father the local undertaker – showed not the slightest sign of weighing him down or holding him back.

Kate's young life had unified her parents in a different way. Hers had been a difficult birth. An unlovely baby, she had been afflicted by colic during the early months and, even when this abated, she habitually slept badly. Her eyes were weak and, by the age of four, she had been obliged to wear glasses all the time. Her broad features, angry, frizzy hair, and angular character had strained her teachers' talent for euphemism. Towards her brother, she showed feelings of jealousy and love, rage and hero-worship. In school reports, there were references to 'communication problems', but then there had been times when she had communicated all too effectively, wetting her bed, daubing the carpets with paint and, last Christmas, cutting up cigars belonging to Alison's father and leaving them floating in the bowl of the downstairs lavatory. On Sunday mornings, she would often kick at the locked door of her parents' bedroom until one of them, irritated and flustered, opened it to her. She tried their patience, and sometimes they talked about her in low, worried tones, late into the night.

Alison stood in the kitchen and glanced at her watch. Then she opened the kitchen fridge, took out a bottle of white wine and poured two glasses. She turned down a saucepan that was boiling on the cooker and took a glass to the study.

She opened the door softly. 'Winning?' she asked.

Matthew started. Across the desk in front of him lay a series of computer spreadsheets, the top left-hand corner of which contained the words, 'Turville Funeral Home: Proposal for Expansion and Development'. He stared at a map that laid out the Garden of Remembrance he had designed after extensive research into market leaders in the funerary business in Europe and America.

'You'd think it would be simple,' he said. 'Burthorpe needs business development. Our Garden of Remembrance is the perfect spot. We buy Chapel Meadow from Simon Pygott and move there. But, at every stage, there's a problem.'

'You haven't actually approached Simon yet.' Alison placed the glass of wine on the desk.

'Colin Dunn says he's skint. Simon never says no to money. It's planning permission that's going to be the problem.'

'I thought everyone was in favour of business parks these days.'

'It's something about moving the Garden. Been here for over a hundred years. People are strange about these things. Superstitious.

'Remember you've got a father-in-law who's a solicitor. If you need him.'

Matthew winced. 'I'd prefer not to get your father involved. He always manages to alienate people.'

Laughing gently, Alison placed a hand on Matthew's shoulder. 'You've to do it your own way, haven't you?'

'Colin's brought Miles Larwood in. Reckons a bit of academic credibility could swing the planning committee.'

'And how will you get Larwood's credibility?'

'Colin has a plan.'

'Ah.' Alison kissed the top of her husband's head. 'Kate's going on about a pony again,' she said.

Matthew groaned. 'Great timing.'

'I told her that her life was full enough already. She said it was full of things she hated.'

'A pony. I don't believe it.'

'Friendly, it's going to be called.'

'Jees.' Matthew looked up with that new anxiety that Alison had recently noticed within him. 'What did you say to her?'

'I said we'd see.'

'We'd see means yes.'

'Not necessarily. She's surprisingly mature about these things.'

'She'll lose interest, just like she always does. You'll be left with some hairy bloody nag to look after.'

'Stephen has so much.'

'Thanks to his own efforts.'

Alison gave a derisive little laugh. 'Your psychology,' she said, walking to the door. 'You haven't a clue.'

'It's really not the moment,' said Matthew glancing back at the papers on his desk. 'I have to give this to Colin at the dinner tonight.'

'Poor hardworking Daddy,' said Alison. 'Another of his busy evenings.'

The words hung dangerously in the air for a moment.

'You could have come if you'd wanted,' Matthew said quietly.

'Don't wake me up when you come in.' Alison closed the door behind her.

Matthew sat at his desk, staring bleakly at the plan in front of him. Then, slowly, he ran his hands across the paper. He saw Sarah Dunn, her full body, the freckles around her shoulders, the way she looked up at him. He traced a wide 'V' on the plan as if following the curve of her collar-bones downwards to her breasts. He thought of the party at Garston Hall tonight where the two of them would meet and, almost certainly, make love. He shook his head and resumed his work.

Already the lie was there, a minor seepage of harm leaking into the turbulent healthy flow of life at Yew Tree Cottage. Because she understood her husband, Alison had recognised the lie almost as soon as it had entered the house. It might have been a shady business arrangement, some bizarre addiction; her discovery that it was no more than a weekly tryst with Sarah Dunn came almost as a relief. It had not been sexual yearning, Alison was sure, that had led Matthew to Sarah's bed, but merely the innocent desire for social and professional betterment, a side of his character which, by a certain irony, she had always liked. When they had been first married, it had been she who had urged him to assert himself more, to express his ambition by getting out, becoming one of Burthorpe's movers and shakers. He was certainly getting out now, not to mention moving and shaking. So perhaps, in some strange way, the tiny but critical chemical reaction that had brought the lie into existence had originated with her.

Nor was Matthew the tortured adulterer. Sometimes he would reflect on his affair, checking himself for signs of guilt. There were few. What harm could seeing Sarah do to his marriage? A release from the daily round of domestic and professional duties, it probably made him a better father and husband. To be pampered, praised, to be adored once a week in circumstances that would never get out of control, must surely make him a mellower, more positive person. He looked at his marriage from every possible perspective, concluding that the effects of the affair on himself and his family were, for the most part, beneficial. It added a splash of colour, the merest hint of invigorating danger, which fully justified the small amount of deception involved.

So the lie, a small spot of corruption, settled at Yew Tree Cottage, remained in the air that they all breathed, touching each member of the family, even the children. Instinctively, Stephen had learnt when to defuse tension between his parents, diverting attention from them on to himself. Kate was less observant but seemed to absorb the unexpressed feelings around her through her skin. She looked at her family and saw herself as a separate being, less intelligent, less good-looking, less normal, less happy. The lie worked on her every waking moment of her day; even when she was asleep, dreaming of Friendly, her life was being quietly contaminated.

All this had been watched, noted and understood.

Margaret lay in her bath in the Guinevere Suite. Her legs ached, a blister had formed on one of her heels, a cigarette lay smouldering in a saucer beside the bath. She smiled as she considered her body, soft-skinned under the water.

After a few moments, she stepped from the bath, dried herself, then put on her coloured bomber jacket. Returning to the bedroom, she removed the 'PRITHEE SILENCE! GENTLE FOLKE AT REST!' sign from the handle, and hung it outside the door, which she locked. She opened the window, slightly, then drew the curtains. Having removed her jacket, she lay on the bed and switched off the bedside lamp.

Lying in the darkness for a full minute, Margaret sighed, as if suddenly reluctant to leave the Guinevere Suite in order to witness a dinner at Garston Hall. Then she closed her eyes, drawing her elbows into her back, the heels of her tiny feet upwards so that in the darkness they gathered just below where her neck had been and the joints and curves of her body became a confusion of white and red which in a matter of seconds lost definition and faded to grey.

The sounds of the public bar downstairs grew fainter.

4

SMOKE, EXPENSIVE AND blue, floated up towards the high ceiling of the dining-room, above the murmur of conversation, the chink of glass and silver, the discreet snip of a cigar-cutter, the occasional flurry of laughter – chamber music of the soul to Simon Pygott who sat, eyes half-closed at the head of the table, a Romeo y Julieta cigar dangling from his hand. When it reached the ceiling, the smoke flattened like thin summer cloud, then coalesced with another greyness, already there, rather as the members of the Garston Hall set were said to coalesce as the end of evenings such as these drew to a close.

Simon smiled lazily. Being at the centre of a social set that had become a local byword for scandal and moral turpitude rather amused him. For centuries, Garston had been known for its parties. Now, thanks to him, that tradition had been maintained, albeit in a more modern version.

Much of the rumour was nonsense, of course. Nothing as callow as an orgy, as suburban as a swapping party, took place at Garston Hall. There were occasions, it was true, when husbands neglected to leave with the wife with whom they had arrived, when the traditionally shambolic pastime of adultery was put on a more formalised, ordered footing than usual, but then so what? At least, at Garston, one knew where one stood. Everyone was playing by the same rules.

How had it all happened? Simon gazed benevolently around the dining-room table. Apart from the Frenchwoman, whose morals were pretty much as one would expect, there was no one here who was particularly what he called fast. Within the set, certain unspoken standards applied – new guests who proved to be too keen (eager, swivel-eyed gropers, clammy-palmed group enthusiasts, benders, watchers, pain merchants) were as unwelcome as those who, like Miles Larwood or Matthew Turville's little wife Alison, were thought unlikely to be keen enough.

The Hall of course played its part. Something about its comfortable, ill-lit rooms, its air of unforced decadence, liberated guests of their normal inhibitions, taking them away from the dreary world of domestic responsibility by providing an agreeable, stimulating theatre for their games. This dining-room seen by day, for example, would seem dusty and anonymous. By candlelight at night, the cracks in the oak panelling, the faded velvet of the curtains in the dining-room somehow contributed to the comforting sophistication of the occasion.

Although there were no particular rules to these dinners, a certain rhythm had become established. Conversation during the first part of the evening would cover the usual topics – staff, property, the misbehaviour of nannies, tales from prep schools, rumours of a new by-pass. Only when the food and wine had been consumed, followed invariably by brandy, port or what Rose Hope called 'puff' would a certain mellow air of expectation descend upon the group. Then things might start to happen.

Not every guest was entirely happy with the things that happened. There were those who, for reasons of character, class or self-esteem, found themselves at the lower end of the hierarchy and were therefore obliged to accept roles in its sexual playlets that were not always welcome. With a shudder, Simon recalled the occasion when, no doubt for the best of motives, Peter Hebden had left the hall without his wife Nina. Dutifully, but with sinking heart, Simon had taken her to bed but it had all proved to be a ghastly mistake. Elbows, knees, a nervy, bruising over-eagerness and, worst of all, conversation. At some ungodly hour, Nina had asked him about Susan. Why she spent so much time in London, did he miss her, was he happy?

Good God. Playing what he called the wife card was bad enough form at the best of times and frankly, four in the morning, starkers in the marital bed, after a night of notable dissatisfaction all round, was some way from being the best of times.

Simon closed his eyes as Colin Dunn, Nina's brother-in-law and current lover, recounted one of his interminable anecdotes. Where would Susan be now? Doubtless at some dark, expensive nightspot inflicting yet more GBH on the old credit card in the company of some youth with floppy hair and an eye to the main chance. Since she had moved down to London, announcing that she had produced two heirs for the Pygott line, seen them both off to prep school and that it was time for her to get in touch with herself, Susan had very much gone her own way. These days she only returned to Garston during the school holidays and even then did little to disguise her boredom with life in the country, treating his chums as if they were provincials unworthy of her attention.

It had been after her departure that Simon had started entertaining what he called seriously. It was a cloud which turned out to have had a silver lining.

He leant back in his chair and stared upwards. As if reflecting his thoughts, a cloud of smoke still adhered to the ceiling above the table. He waved an arm, disturbing the air. The cloud swirled, parted, then, rather oddly, seemed to resume its former shape.

To his right, Sarah Dunn turned and smiled as if she had forgotten he was there. There was a sparkle in her eyes which, Simon assumed, had something to do with the presence of Matthew Turville beside her.

'Penny for them,' she said.

'I know you wouldn't in your day, but it's different now.'

Alison Turville sat up on her side of the double bed, the cream cotton nightdress and woollen shawl around her narrow shoulders giving her an eccentric, grandmotherly look as she spoke into the telephone. 'Matthew likes dinner parties. They bore me. He needs these people for business. I prefer to get some sleep.'

She laughed, glancing at the clock beside the bed. One of the few things she had in common with her mother was an inability to sleep. Often the problems befogged by events during the day could be seen with feverish clarity when the world slumbered.

'Oh, he gets back at one o'clock, two, sometimes later,' she was saying. 'You know how these things go on. No. He's not like that. All men *aren't*. Honestly, Mum, when did you become so cynical?' She imagined her mother sitting up in the single bed that seemed neat and uncreased even when she was in it. Across the room, his back turned, his face to the wall, would be her father, snoring gently in a rare moment of repose.

'Can't sleep.' The door to Alison's bedroom opened. Kate stood in the doorway, rubbing her eyes at the light.

'I'd better go, Mum. Kate's woken up.' She laughed again. 'Yes, another insomniac in the family.'

After she had put the telephone down, she patted the bed beside her. 'In you get,' she said. 'Daddy will put you back later.'

Kate climbed on to the bed, under the bedclothes, moving close to her mother. 'Who was that?'

'Grandma. She sent her love.'

'Why can't I sleep?'

Alison sighed, took off her shawl, and switching off the bedside lamp, pulled the covers over both of them. 'It means your head's full of ideas. It means you're a clever girl.'

Kate gave an audible smile.

Was it true? Alison held her daughter closer to her. Sometimes, when she looked into the children's bedroom at night, Stephen would be asleep but Kate seemed to be in a sort of trance, staring impassively into the darkness, asleep yet awake, as if she were seeing things that no one else could see.

'What are we going to do tomorrow?'

'Well, the first thing I'm going to do is put out the sacks for the dustmen. Then the papers will be delivered – perhaps we'll have some letters from the postman. I've got to book a visit from the piano-tuner.' As she spoke, she found something distantly disturbing about this murmured litany of chores, domestic duties and events which punctuated their days. The man from Anglia Water to test the water for nitrates, someone from Eastern Electricity to check the meters, maybe Pardew the Vicar on one of his occasional rounds. And she too would be fulfilling a similar function for the people she visited: the recorder teacher, the tennis coach, the schools, the charity shop in Diss where she occasionally helped out. All of their lives were suspended on a carefully arranged net of humdrum yet important calls and visits and duties.

Kate shifted beside her. 'What's that noise?' she asked.

Alison listened for a moment. 'Must be the washing-machine,' she said. 'It's rumbling away, like we're a big ship sailing through the night and that's our engine.'

'Perhaps we'll sink.'

'Don't be silly. What a thought.'

'Charlie's gone green.' Simon sat back in his chair and puffed at his cigar disconsolately.

'Green? What *are* you talking about?' asked Sarah Dunn.

'Got a letter from him this morning. "Dear Daddy, I have just given up meat because I disapprove of the means of production. Please can you write to Mr Thompson to tell him it is OK for me to have vegetarian meals."'

'Disapprove. Sweet,' said Sarah. 'I do like the way the young have opinions these days. We wouldn't have dreamt of going green when we were nine.'

'Hmm.' Simon mumbled something to himself.

'Benji asked me why we don't electrocute people like they do in America.' Sarah turned to Matthew, including him in the conversation. 'Rather stumped me, to tell the truth.'

'Don't like it,' said Simon.

'Oh come on, Simon. It's much better to get that sort of thing out of your system when you're young.'

'Oldest son. I blame the school. Sent him there to sort him out, not give him bloody opinions.'

'I say, d'you remember when one of Susan's whippets caught a leveret in the park?' said Sarah. 'Charlie burst into tears and refused to come out of his bedroom.'

'That's all very well when you're five,' said Simon, discomfited both by the mention of his wife's name and the memory of his son's behaviour. 'Should be growing out of it by now. If he turns out to be some sort of bolshie, bloody-minded, nutcrunching anti, I don't know what I'll do.' He glanced moodily at Matthew. 'Kids, eh?' he said, raising his voice and letting his accent slip as he did when talking to his Spanish housekeeper Jaime or to one of the farmworkers. 'Nothing but bovver.'

Matthew smiled politely. 'There's quite a fashion for vegetarianism at the village school,' he said. 'More than half the girls won't touch meat.'

'Charlie isn't a girl,' muttered Simon. 'At least, not yet.'

Half-listening to the conversation, Rose Hope drew slowly upon the fat joint she held in her hand, then, exhaling, surveyed the scene through narrowed eyes. When she had first met Simon, she had been amused and attracted by the heavy, guileless, smooth-faced good looks, the astonishing air of impregnable calm; she had even been touched by the bemused Churchillian grumble with which he responded to events beyond his comprehension (Susan's departure, the farm's downward spiral into insolvency, life). Yet recently she had begun to find that natural confidence irksome. Could *anything* touch Simon, instil in him just the faintest suspicion that the Pygott way of doing things might not be the right way? She was, she supposed, becoming bored by all this. For some time, she had told herself that the events in the village would be perfect material for the moment when she would return to London to write a book or work on one of the national papers as she deserved. Soon, she thought. It would have to be soon.

To her left, Colin Dunn, Burthorpe's richest man, was staring woozily across the table at his wife and the local undertaker.

'Bit of an odd man out, that Matthew,' said Rose.

'Too bloody right,' said Colin. 'What d'you think of him?'

'Decorative. But no Einstein.'

'I'm buying his crematorium garden off him.' Colin spoke without enthusiasm. 'Sarah's idea. Setting up a business park in Burthorpe.'

'And where will Matthew put his stiffs?'

'Oh, you know. There's a little scheme. He's on the move, as these people tend to be.' Colin gazed at the joint that Rose now held in front of him. 'Oh cheers, love,' he said, taking it.

As it happened, Colin had been thinking about Sarah and himself and relationships and sex, wondering vaguely whether their marriage would ever become anything more than a convenient, well-organised partnership. She asked much of him – not just tolerance of her own affairs but the expectation that he would play the game, too. On his left thigh, Colin felt the hand of Sarah's sister Nina, its fingers digging into his flesh like the claws of a purring cat. Although the relationship with dotty, enthusiastic Nina was an amusing enough sideshow, he had recently been surprised to find himself fantasising about his wife while making love to his mistress. He couldn't believe that was either healthy or normal.

Hoping that Nina would desist for a moment from gouging his thigh, he passed the joint to her.

Quite suddenly, Nina wanted Colin more than anything in the world. Taking the joint with her left hand, she continued to squeeze his thigh as he turned back to Rose, the haggard journalist who had gained access to their group via Simon's bed. Nina knew it was unhealthy, this affair with Sarah's husband, but she had decided that, games apart, Colin was the man to make sense of her senseless life. One day, quite soon, she hoped, she would stop drinking, and speaking out of turn, and behaving badly at parties, and tell her husband and the world that what had once been a spot of fun was rather more serious. Colin and Nina – it even sounded right. Arranging her face in a suitably disagreeable expression, she faced her husband who sat across the table. 'Want this?' she asked, holding the joint out to him.

Peter Hebden had been listening closely to his neighbour at dinner, the enchanting Agnès Babineau, but he had of course been aware of the way his wife was inclining towards Colin, like a sapling in the wind. What a relief that was. In the early days of their marriage, Peter had enjoyed Nina's shyness – her insecurity made him feel so much more secure himself – but soon her wilfully eccentric behaviour had become tiresome, all that swearing and drinking at lunchtime and taking off her clothes in company. So now she was seeing her sister's husband. Good. Let Colin take the heat for a while. Peter had other, more urgent concerns.

'*Mais dis donc, mon cher –*' Agnès Babineau, olive-skinned and animated, was relating how she had managed to negotiate the acquisition of an eighteenth-century grandfather clock after a recent auction. Listening, Peter smiled and nodded, bewitched by the curiously provocative turn to the lips, those dark, humorous eyes, the dark heavy hair, the plump yet pliable body.

'We,' he said, imagining them together in London, at the theatre, turning heads, Hebden with his French mistress. He held out the joint to her. 'Voilar.'

'*Tu es gentil.*' Agnès bestowed a teasing smile upon this big-boned, freckled, overgrown Englishman whose eyes watched her lips as she spoke. She inspected the sodden object in her hand and, with ill-concealed distaste, stubbed it out in an ashtray. These Englishmen were so predictable – give them what they least understood and they'd adore you for it. Her ex-husband Jay, a novelist of *gauchiste* inclination, had found endlessly seductive her ability to make money. This awkward puppy, Anglo-Saxon from his bouncy, curly head down to the heavy, expensive soles of his shoes, craved the forbidden, the soft, the fragrant, the foreign. *Eh bien. Ça peut se faire.* Agnès sensed an acquisition.

'What's this I hear about Naughty Boy Dance?' Simon Pygott was asking Matthew in a loud voice.

'Dance? I haven't heard any – '

'Didn't your missus teach him at the village school?'

'He left,' said Matthew. 'Dance must be fifteen now.'

'Whoever taught him did a good job.' Colin Dunn spoke languidly, gazing down at his hands. 'Thieving. Drugs. Vandalism. And never getting caught.'

'That's what's so wonderful about modern education, darling.' Nina spoke brightly, leaning lightly against Colin. 'In the playground, you learn how to sniff glue and break into cars. In the classroom, you discover *why* you sniff glue and break into cars. It's what they call a rounded education.'

'Little bastard.' Peter Hebden forgot Agnès for a moment. 'Stands for everything I dislike about the new Burthorpe. Dishonest, no respect for his betters, scruffy, probably pumping himself with every kind of controlled substance. Scrounges on the dole. Doesn't pay a bloody penny of tax. I mean, have you *seen* those travellers down by the railway?'

'It's their dogs I feel sorry for,' said Sarah vaguely.

'Even if he was caught, he'd wriggle out of it.' For the first time, Colin Dunn addressed Matthew directly as if somehow he bore responsibility for events among Burthorpe's lower classes. 'Some bloody social worker would explain that it's not really his fault but society's. We are all guilty.'

'God, I'm glad I sent the boys away,' muttered Simon. 'Everything's changing in the village, complicated. In the old days, one would have given Dance a job on the farm and he'd have been happy with it.'

'A job? Christ, Simon, you're as bad as the bloody social workers,' said Colin.

'Yes, probably not a good idea.' Simon stared mournfully ahead of him, then smiled at his guests. 'Shall we adjourn to the library?'

Sarah touched Matthew lightly on the arm. 'The chapel,' she said softly. 'Not long now.'

In the early hours of the morning, while the rest of the world was sleeping or engaged in leisure pursuits traditionally associated with the weekend, Miles Larwood was at his word-processor. Normally the contrast between his nocturnal activity, pushing back the perameters of scholarship, and theirs, splashing around in the shallows of mindless self-indulgence, would have afforded him a sharp sense of worth and purpose, but tonight, inescapably, he felt stale and restless.

An hour ago, he had returned from a visit to the flat in Norwich of Dr Katherine Porter. Nothing had precisely gone wrong during the evening: the Chablis had been cold, the pre-prepared dinner modest but acceptable, the conversation professional and no duller than usual. Then after coffee, they had – no, Miles didn't want to think about that. There had been times over recent months when he had managed to convince himself that a partnership of modest pleasures, economically shared, suited his needs as an intellectual, but tonight that partnership had merely seemed sad and evasive. He had hurried back to his work but the futility of the evening had somehow infected his researches.

He skipped from entry to entry, trying to find a connection, a pattern. The advantage of writing a resource handbook, he had once thought, lay in its loose structure: one could circle about, completing minor entries, approaching by stealth the book's central argument. But what was this central argument? Obviously it had to have one – a governing thematic which would one day be debated in *The Thanatologist* or even in academic journals – but how long would Miles have to wait before it emerged?

DOUBLE BURIAL, PROCEDURE OF
Until the seventeenth century, it was quite normal for those of noble blood to be 'divided' *post mortem*, a process involving two or sometimes three (see CHARLES V OF FRANCE, THE THREE TOMBS OF) distinct burial situations.

The death of Henry VIII in 1547 is a well-documented case study of death-related behaviours. His body was first 'spurged', that is, washed with aromatic water. The bowels were then emptied ('cleansing') and the royal rectum plugged. Intestines were removed between the bottom of the rib-cage and the pelvic region ('bowelling') and blood vessels cauterised ('searing'). After the inner cavities were embalmed, the outer surface of the body was 'dressed' with application of balms and a mixture of resins and volatile oils. 'Furnishing' involved the placing of the '*sudarium*', a square of linen that covered the face, and covering the corpse with cerecloth.[1]

The viscera was placed in a lead box and buried separately at St George's Chapel, Windsor following extensive thanatoptic devotions.

'SPURGING'
See DOUBLE BURIAL, PROCEDURE OF.

---

[1] A more detailed account of the death of Henry VIII can be found in J. Litten's *The English Way of Death* (Hale, 1991).

'CLEANSING'
See DOUBLE BURIAL, PROCEDURE OF.

'BOWELLING'
See DOUBLE BURIAL, PROCEDURE OF.

'SEARING'
See DOUBLE BURIAL, PROCEDURE OF.

'FURNISHING'
See DOUBLE BURIAL, PROCEDURE OF.

LAYING OUT, THE WORKING-CLASS MODEL

According to Elizabeth Roberts[1], some of the most significant protagonists in death-related situations of early twentieth-century Lancashire were the local women known as 'layers-out'. These were highly respected, unpaid individuals who, until the 1902 Midwives Act, had often been midwives. The layer-out would place pennies on the corpse's eyes, plug the nostrils and anus and put a prayer book beneath the chin to keep it in place. The corpse would be then visited by people in the neighbourhood, including children. 'When there was a funeral, it was like going to the cinema,' one Lancastrian told Roberts[2].

IMPRESSION MANAGEMENT AND 'MR POST'

The art of placing the relations of the dead at their ease forms an essential part of funerary services in America.

The corpse is described as a 'guest' and invariably referred to by his/her first name. To avoid unnecessary distress, calls over the intercom for morgue attendants to attend a post-mortem are disguised with a euphemistic 'Mr Post, Mr Post, please report to your office'. Funeral directors are fully trained in grief therapy and what the American undertaker Vanderlyne R. Pyne has described as 'dramaturgical discipline in the management of one's face and voice' in order to to present 'an actual affective response'[1] is regarded as an essential skill.

---

[1] 'The Lancashire Way of Death' in *Death, Ritual and Bereavement*, edited by R. Halbrooke (Routledge & Kegan Paul, 1989).
[2] Obviously an element of chronological displacement is involved in this reminiscence since popular cinema had, at that point of time, yet to reach Lancashire, or anywhere else.
[1] Vanderlyne R. Pyne, *Caretaker of the Dead: The American Funeral Director* (Irvington, 1975)

The age-old thematic connection between death and sex is
powerfully expressed in the nineteenth-century belief – mor-
alistic mythmaking under the guise of science – that the act of
onanistic

Miles groaned and sat back in his chair. Gloomily he poured himself
another whisky and looked at the clock on the wall. It was almost two
in the morning. Mention of the *petit mort* had reminded him of
Dr Katherine Porter. He stood up and switched off his word-processor. The entry could wait until tomorrow.

For several years, the tiny chapel set by the stream running through
Chapel Meadow had been used as an extra bedroom for the use of
guests at Garston Hall. Simon Pygott had come to this arrangement
not in any spirit of anti-religious rebellion but for practical reasons.
The sixteenth-century building was too small to be of any use for
anything apart from the occasional family funeral and had fallen into
disuse even in this area. The last Pygott to die, Simon's father
Humphrey, had insisted in his will that he should be buried at his
local church in Tuscany.

Shortly afterwards, Susan Pygott had suggested that the chapel
could be used as a bedroom by guests at the large weekend parties that
were regularly held at the Hall. A double mattress, a modest pine
cupboard containing sheets and blankets, a paraffin stove and a small
gas lamp were placed in the vestry. Occasionally visitors were
reluctant to sleep in the family burial chamber but, for couples
who relished the exotic, it turned out to be a rather amusing and
original attraction.

There were no more grand parties now, and the bed was rarely
made up with clean sheets. Yet Simon still allowed the chapel to be
used by couples who, for practical reasons, were unable to entertain
one another at home.

Sarah Dunn lay on the mattress, covered by a sheet, watching the
shadowy figure of Matthew Turville as he undressed, carefully folding
over a pew his touchingly vulgar dinner jacket, which looked as if it

had been borrowed from a junior waiter working at a hotel in Ipswich. It occurred to her that she was in danger of becoming rather over-involved with this man. He had retained the innocent ambition, that sense of the possible, that Colin had once had before his drive had deteriorated into sullen, middle-aged greed. Matthew, Sarah thought, didn't just desire money (which was rather unattractive in a man), but he wanted success, a place in society.

With some difficulty, Matthew was untying his bow-tie. One of the first times he had visited the hall, he had been rather cruelly mocked for wearing a clip-on. A quick learner, he had never made that mistake again.

'I don't think frills on the dress shirt are quite the thing, darling,' she said.

He glanced down at the shirt, which Alison had recently bought him. 'It was a present.'

'Plain dress shirt. Believe me on this.' She smiled as he unbuttoned the buttons between the frills and, with a hint of impatience, threw the shirt on the stone floor. His muscular torso never ceased to fill her with wonder. Whereas the texture of men like Colin had a sort of pale doughiness, Matthew actually had muscles. Why was that? she wondered. Something to do with background, perhaps.

'I gave Colin my projection,' said Matthew.

'Good.'

'He didn't seem that interested, to tell the truth.'

'Of course he was interested. I'll make him interested.'

Matthew started suddenly, looking into darkness behind him.

'What's the matter?' Sarah sat up on the mattress, holding the sheet to her chest, like a fifties film star in a coy bedroom scene. 'Matthew?'

'My back went cold.'

'Draught. Come here. I'll warm you up.'

'No, it wasn't a draught. It was like something slimy being laid on my shoulders.'

'Don't you dare give me the creeps, Matthew Turville.'

'Sorry.' Matthew laughed. 'Must have been my imagination.' He crossed his arms and rubbed his shoulders, a strangely girlish gesture.

'Either that or you were goosed by the ghost of Garston.' Sarah let the sheet slip. 'Let's put on a show for him.'

Matthew scurried in front of the altar and on to the mattress. Only when he was between the sheets did he remove his boxer shorts.

'God, what a shy boy we are.' Sarah leant on one elbow, laying her left hand on Matthew's chest. Her fingertips softly strummed his rib-cage, then descended into the hollow of his stomach, over the bone of his hip, to scratch the dark stubble of his upper thigh.

Matthew stared at the ceiling. 'It's awkward at these things. Colin and I both know I'm about to make an offer for Chapel Meadow. Simon has a good idea that something's up. Yet all we talk about is our kids or Naughty Boy Dance.'

'I've been thinking about you all day,' she said quietly in the darkness. She knelt, facing him, then touched his forehead, ran her right hand through his hair. He closed his eyes.

One of the many things she liked about Matthew Turville was that he really wasn't very highly sexed. In her experience, men tended to take on an entirely different character when they got her into bed – there was a change within them, a sudden shift of interest to their own need, urgent and rather off-puttingly crotch-centric. It was as if life and sex belonged to entirely different universes of feeling and behaviour. Colin, for example, became a grinning, monosyllabic fool, his eyes glazed, his lips wet with desire. In the early days of their marriage, this change might occur in the middle of a meal, or while they were watching television. She knew at that moment there would be no sense out of him until he had found his own ghastly little personal release. There was something faintly insulting about the process – it made her feel like a business deal that needed urgently to be negotiated on behalf of impatient shareholders. Afterwards, in the time-honoured husbandly fashion, he would quickly fall asleep. Once or twice, out of curiosity or spite, she had tried to strike up a conversation after sex, but his speech would be slurred and spastic, as if it were a distillation of his brains that had been spent and which now trickled, cold and sticky, between her legs. She shivered.

'Did you feel it?' Matthew opened his eyes.

'Hmm?'

'The cold. The draught.'

'Yes, I think I must have.' She lay across his chest and whispered, 'This is the best moment.'

It was a feeling she had never been able to explain to Matthew, the idea that the greatest, most intense intimacy occurred at this instant of unresolved need. Once they started, they would become just another mating couple; now they were lovers. The cut and thrust of sex could never quite live up to the pure potential of anticipation.

'I think I can improve on it,' he said, increasing his pressure on her arm.

'Don't move,' she said.

She loved to see the gentle, unfocused look that descended on his eyes when they made love, as if she were an erotic fairy godmother and had cast a magic spell on him.

Suddenly, he shifted beneath her. 'There,' he whispered, turning his head to the right. 'On my shoulder. Now.'

Sarah stopped moving. 'Not the bloody draught again.'

'I swear I'm not inventing this.' Matthew's eyes were wide, his face paler than it had been.

She laid a hand on his shoulder. 'There's nothing there, Matthew. Honestly, you've been smoking too much. You'll be seeing dinosaurs coming out of the ceiling next.'

'It felt damp, almost alive. It . . . moved across me.'

'Silly.' She arched her back, stretched both hands behind her, then pulled the sheet over her shoulder, like a cloak. Leaning forward, she made a tent for their bodies. Her face an inch from his, her nipples caressing his chest, she watched the glaze of pleasure settle back on to his features.

As the sheet began to move again, a silver sheen descended upon the whiteness, first on to her shoulders, then into the undulating valley in the small of her back. Unheard, behind the quickening breaths of the lovers, a low, soft exhalation of longing filled the chapel.

When they left, an hour later, neither Matthew nor Sarah saw the gash of red, still shining damply, on the small stained-glass window above the altar.

5

AROUND THE VILLAGES

Burthorpe A spate of thefts has been reported in and around
Burthorpe this week. On Tuesday, the sum of £160 went
missing from the till at the H.T. Pearson Convenience Store.
An undisclosed amount of cash, but no credit cards, was
taken from a safe at Manor Farm the following day. After the
mid-week football clash between Burthorpe FC and Palgrave
FC, several players returned to the pavilion to find money
missing from their wallets. At St Botolph's Church, the spire
fund 'kitty' has been mysteriously emptied without the lock
being broken. 'We are dealing with a sneak thief, possibly
more than one, possibly a gang of youngsters,' said DC
Penman of Eye Police. 'We have not ruled out the possibility
of incomers, maybe from the London area, being involved.'
Police are advising locals to be vigilant as far their personal
possessions and cash are concerned.

Report on the Burthope v. Palgrave match on page 32.

FOR A VILLAGE without any noticeable charm,
Burthorpe has been remarkably successful in attracting
new inhabitants. People, usually on their way to somewhere else, have been snagged into staying here, like rust
along a pipe, or the calcification of an ageing artery.

Although locals have tended to complain about these so-called
'incomers', their arrival has, on the whole, had an invigorating effect
on the village. A comparison of the civic and personal contributions of

H.T. Pearson and Errol Pryce would reveal, for example, that it was the long-term resident whose character, conversation and merchandise were daily confirmations of the greyness of Burthorpe life while the incomer (as Errol, almost thirty years after his arrival here, was still regarded) at least added a certain colour.

Pearson should by rights have been a village stalwart; his family had been here so long that almost certainly, among the crowd watching Elizabeth I's progress through Palgrave in 1578, there would have been a Pearson forebear, complaining lugubriously about the disruption. The personal life of today's H.T. Pearson was, like his shop, a cold, unwelcoming place. His father had died of a heart attack in 1973, his mother resided in a nursing home near Dickleburgh but, since 1993, had been unable (mercifully, some said) to recognise that the awkward, bald man who visited her once a week was her son. As for pastimes, Pearson indulged an angry and perverse fantasy life fuelled by thoughts of his younger clientele and by monthly parcels received from the Adult Video Club of Ipswich. His entrepreneurial contribution to Burthorpe has been less adventurous: in 1976, he changed the name of his shop from Pearson's to the H.T. Pearson Convenience Store. In 1983, he installed some new lino. An experiment with a cheese counter in 1987 was abandoned after a couple of months.

By contrast, the presence of Errol Pryce had had an undeniably catalytic effect on village life; when Errol was around (and somehow Errol always was around), Burthorpians would be wary and awake, on their guard. While today he was vociferous in his opposition to incomers unless they represented an opportunity for profit, Pryce himself arrived from London in 1968, a time when East Anglia had become a popular destination for those wishing to embrace a quasi-alternative lifestyle. He bought a barn, converted it, presiding with a deceptively gentle authority over a motley band of wastrels, hedonists and part-time revolutionaries. During the seventies, as the great hippy flood subsided, members of Errol's commune drifted disconsolately back to London or their parents, leaving, like a faint tide-mark, the few semi-bohemians who lived in the village to this day: Araminta Winterburn, the occasional illustrator of children's books, a furniture-maker called Balfe, Grant Wilson who, oddly, had become a great expert on computer software. Errol himself sold the barn to a

57

restaurateur from Saxmundham, and moved easily into the world of building and property development. Since his two children had grown up and left home, his personal life had centred around his wife June, a large, angry woman with a complexion the colour of honey-roast ham.

There had been other ingredients in the mix of old and new that is Burthorpe. The mid-eighties saw an influx of commercially minded folk attracted by the false dawn of rural economic recovery. After the subsequent riot of bankruptcy, suicide, nervous breakdown and broken marriage, a few stayed on and now worked in modest employment in Norwich or Ipswich or Bury.

More recently, commuters to London had taken advantage of an improved railway service. They could be seen, whey-faced and distracted, driving to or from Diss Station, or, at weekends, pottering about in cardigans and slacks, washing the car, visiting the golf club, dreaming perhaps of a return to suburbia.

If there was any topic that unified the disparate elements of old and new in Burthorpe, it was the presence of the one group of incomers whom everyone felt justified in disliking.

The fall in property values, the refusal of the local authorities to build a by-pass, the decline in churchgoing, the increase in crime, the lack of jobs or investment in local industry, the generalised moral shiftlessness of the village youth: they could all be traced back to the arrival of the diddicoys and hippies, the scroungers and gyppos of Railway Drive.

Apart from the occasional contribution to the letters column, complaining queasily of the blight of broken-down vans and litter that defaced the once beautiful village of Burthorpe, there was little or no reference to the travellers in the *DP* or other local papers, but when reports of theft referred to 'incomers', readers understood. H.T. Pearson banned them from his shop. Errol Pryce plotted and planned, awaiting an opportunity to reclaim the wasteground beyond the tracks for the God-fearing, tax-paying folks of Burthorpe.

Gavin 'Naughty Boy' Dance moved about his ice-cream van, listening to the machine-gun beat and lonely wordless wail of a D.J. Rufus ambient mix emanating through earphones which led to a small personal stereo in the front pocket of his jeans. It was almost eleven o'clock on a Saturday morning. He checked a small cupboard for food, took a bottle of milk out of a fridge and sniffed it. Glancing briefly in the direction of the bed, he stepped out of the door, securing it from the outside with a heavy chain and padlock. He looked across at a caravan nearby – its red blinds were drawn down, no sound was to be heard. One of its tyres, he noticed, was soft and would need attention. Pulling a small bike from the darkness under his van, he jumped on. Soon he had crossed the track and was making his way down the lane behind Scrope Rise and had disappeared.

The older Dance had grown, the less visible he had become to the people of Burthorpe. At the age of five, when he had first been locked out of the caravan to spend the day wandering around the site by the railway, a sandwich and a packet of Smarties in the pocket of his grimy dungarees, he had acquired a reputation as a noisy little bastard, a bottle-kicking, foul-mouthed troublemaker with defiant eyes and a formidable, if often incomprehensible, armoury of abuse. By the age of seven, he was a familiar sight in Burthorpe, often when other children were at school. There had been some question of his being taken into care at the age of ten, his thieving exploits (bikes, mostly, but also a handbag taken from an unlocked car) having brought him to the attention of the Diss police; surprisingly, a woman claiming to be his mother had made a favourable impression on local social workers and was allowed to keep him at home. Neither her nickname, the Squealer, nor its precise origin was known to the authorities.

Since then, Dance had become a Burthorpe legend, an emblem of the present-day corruption and evil of youth. He had attended his comprehensive school just long enough to avoid the attentions of local authorities but he was a solitary boy whose wiry frame and unblinking, expressionless eyes discouraged contact with other children. Rarely seen, except when racing his scooter down lanes, across stubble fields, or riding a mountain bike on the roads, he was generally assumed to be responsible for whatever outrages against local property happened to be reported in the *Diss Press*. Frequently, the police would visit his yellow-and-green ice-cream van. No stolen goods had ever been found.

Dance left his bike under a hawthorn hedge to the north of Mileham

Fen. Nearby an elderly man and his wife were walking their dog, unaware of his presence as he made his way with the arrogant stealth of a fox across the road, and north up a narrow path flanked by blackberry bushes. He hesitated on the brow of a hill, leaning against a young oak tree as he looked into the valley below. He rolled a thin cigarette and lit up, scanning the outbuildings of Charlie Watson's farm. He switched off the angry whisper of sound in his ear.

He loped forward, puffing occasionally at the cigarette pinched in the thin fingers of his right hand. Pausing briefly before he broke cover, he threw the cigarette into a ditch before walking, hands in pockets, eyes ahead of him, past the haystack, the silo, two tractors, an old trailer with two flat tyres. Glancing briefly towards the Watsons' house, he crossed the yard, then stood before a shed door, its bolt held in place by a heavy padlock. He pulled an old screwdriver from his back pocket and, in less than thirty seconds, the latch holding the padlock hung uselessly from the door. He pocketed the screws, then walked in.

He strode quickly to a cupboard at the back of the shed. With deft fingers, he opened it, removed a plastic container and poured most of the contents into a shopping bag he took from the back pocket of his jeans, before replacing it and closing the door to the cupboard. When he emerged from the shed, he reached for the screws, returning the latch to its former state.

In a glade by the stream on the fen, he cleared some damp brown leaves to reveal a small wooden panel that covered a disused fox's earth. He placed the powder deep into the dark soil, withdrawing a brown envelope from which he took a £20 note before returning it to the hole.

Five minutes later, he was cycling through the village. He stopped at Burthorpe Garage and bought two cans of baked beans, a Mars Bar and some bread. When he returned to the ice-cream van, he looked around him as he unlocked the padlock, as if, even now, some representative of law and order might appear. He entered the van, talking, cooing and laughing as he went.

When he arrived, he was unlike any person I had seen. So big, so haut, like a great colourful bird sent down to us from Heaven.

After a year at the house, I was used to a certain order of things but, beside him, Master Greves had been as a sheep is to a lion.

For a man of God, he was a restless soul, forever eating or drinking or talking or scheming with various jolivets of the parish. That first night, I stood in the back parlour, listening to his laughter, that harsh voice, like the scolding of a rook, echoing through the house. I knew then that he would change all our lives, although, of course, I had no idea by how much.

That energy. We had never seen anything like it. He seemed to live off gnaring disputation, whether it was with a neighbour, an envoy from the court, or with one of the many townfolk to whom he had taken a dislike. It was as if a lust for contention stoked the fires of his whole being.

I knew nothing of books but, from the respect accorded to him by his guests, I could see that he was a learned man. He would quote from Pliny or the ars moriendi, which he claimed to have translated, and they would nod as if this conceit had been passed down to him by the good Lord Himself. How did he know so much? That was the true mystery. Even when I knew him well, I never saw him read for any period of time. He would weigh an open Bible in his hand on a Saturday night, now and then opening one of his Latin books, as if to confirm an item of knowledge that he already knew. He remembered well and, at some earlier point in his busy life, had acquired the art of conversation, that is, the ability to conceal meaning behind a wall of words.

I'm not saying he deceived. There were those who, behind their hands, accused him of being no more than a royl of court whose only religion was his own advancement, but I was never among them. He had beliefs and he would fight for them. Once he told me that he had seen the inside of a prison, having spoken out of turn in the wrong company and, although he later told me the true story (he had stood for a debt which had failed and had been punished with a seven-day sojourn in the house of Lady Margaret), I have little doubt that, somewhere within his large, self-serving soul, there was proper virtue of some sort.

In his heavy cloak, enhached in lime and silver, he would swoop about the house, appearing when one least expected it. One day he startled me while I was gathering nept and parsley in the garden. I turned and there he was, watching me from the shadow of the doorway, a smile across those big, uneven, beautifully ugly features. He said something in Latin, a favourite trick when discountenanced, and disappeared back into the house.

After a month, he demanded that it should be I who waited upon him at table. I would stand, hands in front of me, as he ate. Often he would have his working book beside him into which, between mouthfuls, he would write, sometimes reading out lines to me. I would respond nervously with a nod or a muttered compliment although being, I imagine, little more than fourteen years old and entirely unschooled, I understood nothing of what he said.

Then, one evening, he asked me to sit at the table. I lowered myself on to a chair, perched there nervously like a sparrow about to take wing. Several meals were taken like this before, with particular gruffness, he requested that I sit, not at the end of the table but on the seat beside him. He would eat and write, occasionally looking up at me with that peculiar mocking look in his small brown eyes which I had once taken to be threatening but now saw differently.

One evening, having finished his meal, he laid down his pen and placed a broad, rough hand on my two hands, clasped in front of me. Blessed are the meek, my child, he said, raising one of my hands to his lips. For they shall inherit the earth.

Uncertain as to how to respond to this beneficence, I bowed my head and replied, as I thought fit, Amen. With a laugh as loud as a crash of thunder, he dropped my hand and stood up, his green cowl brushing my face as he quit the room.

For a moment, I stood there, staring at the five flames of the candle before me. His recule lay open on the table beside his place. The words spilt down the centre of the page, narrow and curling, like the Devil's tail.

It was Saturday afternoon and Mrs Enid Kirby was earning some money for the Christmas she would never see by working overtime at the Turville Funeral Home.

For Enid, this was simply 'the Home'. Visitors to Matthew's office may, more often than not, have worn black and been more down in the dumps than usual, yet she had somehow managed to isolate herself from the gloomy side of the business, rather as workers in a munitions factory rarely think of flying limbs and eviscerated corpses as they turn the ratchet on a shiny piece of steel.

Enid disliked unpleasantness and, so long as she avoided Matthew's work-station, the small building, called the Preparation Room, to where clients were delivered, there was no greater risk of anything untoward occurring to her in working hours than in any other office. Technical terms – 'call', 'visit', 'laying out', 'aftercare service' – flickered across her screen as she worked on the accounts. To her considerable relief, the precise state of the client was never mentioned.

Strangely, Enid felt ill at ease, sitting in the office, all alone, the telephone never ringing, the mortal remains of one Frieda Wilcox, account number 1034, awaiting burial next Tuesday in the laying-out room twenty yards from where she sat. She worked quickly, mumbling to herself as her fingers tapped the keyboard.

Something beyond the silence was bothering her. The computer screen in front of her, normally a greyish colour, had acquired an odd glow in its top left-hand corner which she had never seen before. It reminded her of the occasion her television had gone on the blink last year, when everything on the screen had turned blue, except this screen wasn't blue (it really seemed to be getting worse, moving downwards), it was red. She switched to another programme but the fault continued to spread, like a watery stain of red ink on blotting paper. When almost the entire screen had changed colour, Enid decided that she would finish the invoice on which she was working and go home.

She tapped a key. The small outline of a mouse appeared on the right of the screen. She had always thought that computer designers' obsessions with the rodent kingdom were somewhat unfortunate and, even now, would hesitate to place her hand on the plastic item in her right hand they insisted on calling a mouse. It came as no particular surprise that the darned things were appearing as symbols of something or other on the screen.

She pressed two more keys. A pair of computer mice appeared. Enid was about to reach for the manual when the screen, now a vivid red, began to fill with mice, and not just computer mice, harmless little symbols, but moving, animate, really rather large creatures, some bigger than others, tumbling and falling over one another. Perhaps it was one of those computer bugs she had been told about – the machine had become infected by some horrid kids' game. She was surprised to find that she was having difficulty in breathing, that her skin was clammy and damp. She shivered, the dull pulsing sound in her head seeming to obscure some other sound, which was sharper, more familiar and specific.

Slowly, she extended her right hand to the screen. Her fingers felt a surface that was sticky, porous. When she turned her fingertips towards her, they seemed by some trick of the light to be as red as the screen. It was then that she identified the second sound behind the rhythm of her blood beating in her ears. It was like the scribbling of a fountain pen on paper, or the whisper of voices in a church, but was somehow more urgent, more feral, as if an army of rodents was approaching.

The screen changed. A vast rat, dark and sheened, with angry pink eyes, was gazing at her through the screen. It bared long yellow teeth at Enid and began to gnaw at the inside of the monitor as if wanting to escape, to reach her.

She tried to scream, but now the breath wasn't there. Instead there was a terrible, unbearable ache in her chest that suddenly made any cry for help, any word, beyond her ebbing strength. With a genteel little moan, Enid crumpled to the floor, her eyes fixed on the glistening red computer screen. Around her, the room grew murky and indistinct, until all she could see was a long tunnel at the end of which a spot of light was receding, growing ever smaller, fainter, more distant. Then, with a small, damp click, it disappeared and darkness was everywhere.

Pale, blinking behind his tortoiseshell glasses, Freddie Pierpoint stood with Simon Pygott surveying what had once been the woodland of Beggar's Hill. The heavy Barbour jacket which Pierpoint had borrowed from Simon hung slackly from his shoulders, adding a scrawny vulnerability to the air of bleak disapproval which had been part of

Freddie's character for as long as Simon had known him. From bespectacled, bottom-scratching unfortunate at Eton to senior, distinguished City accountant, it had been a long, straight road, and his essential personality had changed little over the years.

Simon had found Freddie's general attitude, the wan superciliousness of a town-dweller, particularly irksome over this weekend. It had been Freddie, after all, who had insisted that they needed to discuss money. Simon, attempting to make this tedious event a touch jollier by turning it into something of a social occasion, had suggested that, since Mrs Pygott had elected to make an appearance, Freddie should come down to Garston for the weekend, bring along a lady friend if he wished. Yet, for all the pleasure old Freddie had expressed so far, he might have been back at Eton on a muddy touchline, watching a match against Marlborough on a wet Tuesday afternoon.

'Without my new Woodmaster 2300, this would have been a *hell* of a mess.' Simon ran the rubber tip of his walking-stick across the broad, freshly cut stump of a beech tree which had been felled the previous day. Around his feet lay the greens, yellows and golds of its leaves. 'Over two acres down in a week. Cut up in beams and planks within the month. Best investment I ever made.'

'Hired?' asked Freddie.

'Bloody hell, no,' said Pygott. 'Mug's game hiring. I worked it out that, if I hired a Woodmaster for two years, I could have bought it.'

'But would you need a Woodmaster for two years?'

Simon smiled triumphantly. 'That's the beauty of it. This new machine's so bloody efficient, it'll have done its job in three months.'

Freddie said nothing for a while. Then, in a monotone as irritating as the drowsy buzz of a trapped bluebottle, he murmured, 'But, Simon, if the job only takes three months, you wouldn't *need* to hire it for two years.'

'Hmm?' Simon looked across the park. It was odd how an apparently intelligent man like Freddie simply didn't understand the ways of the countryside and tried to apply a dull, City logic to matters of farming instinct. 'I just don't like hiring.' He spoke more sharply than he had intended. 'Machinery's always hopeless. You're dependent on other people. This way, at the end of the job, we've got the best saw on the market available for future use. There, sitting in the big barn.'

'How long do trees take to grow?' Freddie was wearing a pained smile. 'I mean, when will you actually be using your precious Woodmaster again?'

Simon frowned as he thought this through. 'All right, Freddie, we've talked quite enough about this.' He picked up a wedge of newly cut wood and threw it as hard as he could. Ears pricked, his dog Jess waddled off in the direction he had thrown it, before losing interest after a few strides. 'I'm a farmer, you're a money man. You look after the cashflow and I'll concern myself with the running of the estate.' He turned back to the Hall. 'Let's rejoin the girls,' he said briskly. 'It's time for tea.'

Freddie followed half a pace behind Simon, head down, warily avoiding cowpats. 'Simon, there's no point in avoiding this. We really have to talk. To buy machinery, you need to be liquid. And you're not liquid at the moment. Rather far from it, in fact.'

'Timber's been bringing in a bob or two. Wise move, that.'

'It's a drop in the ocean. I've been talking to a partner of mine. We think you're really quite seriously overstretched at the moment. It's time to go pro-active.'

Simon walked more quickly. Everyone seemed to be following him about with bad news these days. 'Sounds like a dog food.' He looked down at Jess. 'Want some Pro-active, old boy?'

'For Christ's sake, Simon. You've got the school fees. Susan's not exactly scrimping herself down in London. Something has to be sold.'

'Bloody Carstairs,' muttered Simon. 'Calls himself my farm manager. Loses me money year after year.'

'He told Susan it was because you keep investing in new plant that you don't really need.'

'Hmm. Plant's my area. Carstairs may be young but he's hopelessly out of date when it comes to the new agricultural technology.'

'Yes?'

'Oh, all right.' Simon shrugged huffily. 'We'll just have to flog some shares if you really insist.'

Freddie exhaled with a quiet moan. 'You don't *have* any shares, Simon. You sold them last year. Surely you remember. There's a trust in the boys' name but, even if we manage to break that, there's not enough to turn you round.'

Simon thought of the Woodmaster 2300 in the big barn. The Topliner combine, the Armer-Salmon Two-Row Beet Harvester, the couple of Case International tractors he had bought only last year. He was proud of his plant. Hearing the sound of good modern machinery at work on his land made him feel alive, useful. He was a real farmer. 'I'm not selling my plant, if that's what you're thinking.'

'Colin Dunn mentioned to me that he could arrange a property deal for you. Some field, was it?'

Simon laughed. 'Chapel Meadow. Best grazing in the park. And it happens to have the family chapel in it. Bloody local undertaker Matthew Turville wants to move his Garden of Remembrance there. Most ridiculous thing I've ever heard.'

'I'm not sure you understand the gravity of your situation. You need a serious injection of cash to survive at Garston. It's either a question of selling land. Or moving house.'

Simon gazed silently across the parkland for a moment. 'Don't like selling land,' he said. 'Against my religion as a farmer.'

'You might have to.'

'I suppose Susan put you up to this,' Simon muttered, a hint of defeat in his voice.

'No one's put me up to anything.'

Simon walked on briskly. 'Let's talk about it after tea, eh?'

As the two men approached the hall, they saw Charlie and Jeremy Pygott staring into the moat. Susan Pygott had insisted that, because there were guests for lunch, they should wear tweed jackets, ties and creased dark trousers – uniforms which, from this distance, made them look like miniature adults. They stood, hands in pockets, with the natural awkwardness of the well-bred Englishman.

'Exeat weekend,' said Simon cheerily. 'Back to school tomorrow.'

'Poor little buggers.' Freddie spoke distantly, as if he were talking to himself. 'I'll always remember that emptiness in the pit of the stomach before you went back to school. Trunks packed, tuckbox full of tins and biscuits. If you can take being sent away at the age of eight, you're ready for anything.'

'That's what boarding-school's all about.' Simon glanced at Freddie, surprised at this sudden and uncharacteristic expression of feeling. 'I mean, it hasn't done you any harm, has it?'

'Who's to know?'

'Anyway, school's completely changed since our day. Labs, copies of the *Independent* in the Common Room, debating societies, all that sort of kit. Unrecognisable.'

'I've always found that institutions don't really change.' Freddie Pierpoint spoke quietly. 'The image alters, the personnel's replaced, but, underneath it all, the ethic of the place, the famous school spirit, is exactly the same – like some nasty little mould contained in the bricks and mortar.'

Simon frowned. 'Come on, Pierpoint. You're not saying there's something wrong with the old school spirit, are you?'

'D'you miss them?' Freddie asked, walking on. 'The boys.'

'Oh, like crazy. Place is a morgue without them.'

Jess was ahead of the men, greeting Charlie and Jeremy in an embarrassed, ingratiating way.

'Jess, come here, you fool,' Simon called out.

'What you got, boys?'

'We saw a pike,' said Jeremy. 'Can I get my airgun?'

'What do you think, Charlie?' Simon put his arm around his older son's shoulders. 'You're the family conscience. Should we let him save the carp by blowing away the pike?'

'Don't mind.' Charlie looked away. The pinched, pale look he adopted during term-time had settled on his face.

'Don't mind?' Simon turned to Freddie Pierpoint. 'Charlie's become a bit of an anti these days – gone what I call green.' He raised his voice with dangerous jocularity. 'We don't believe in killing things, do we, Charlie?'

The boy stared at the ground miserably.

'Actually I don't really mind about the pike, Dad,' said Jeremy.

'Why the hell not? Vicious creatures, pikes. Roach, ducklings – I've even heard stories of them taking puppies that have gone for a swim. Because unfortunately, Mr Pikey's not an anti like Charlie here.'

'It's in his nature,' muttered Charlie.

'And it's in my nature to eat beef,' said Simon. He looked up the hill to where some Friesians were grazing. 'I can't look at a cow without thinking of Sunday lunch – a nice, pink, juicy joint.'

Tears welled up in Charlie's eyes. He seemed about to say something but then turned to walk towards the house, with short urgent steps, hands in pockets.

'It was a *joke*, Charlie,' Simon called after him. As the boy walked on, he sighed. 'Silly old Dad, put his foot in it again.'

'I think you should let him be a vegetarian,' said Jeremy. 'He's not eating very much at school. He always leaves his meat, then he gets in trouble with the pre's and Mr Thompson.'

Simon placed a large, affectionate hand on Jeremy's head. 'Of course he can be a vegetarian, the silly old chump. He'll grow out of it soon enough.'

The three of them walked towards the front door. Through the window, they saw Susan Pygott, a fine-boned woman dressed rather too well for a Saturday afternoon in the country, listening to Val Polson, the garrulous stockbroker who had recently effected a temporary merger with Freddie. The two women raised their hands in unison.

'You two go ahead,' Simon said to Freddie and Jeremy as they entered the hall, 'I'll tell Jaime we need tea.'

He walked upstairs and stood outside the closed door of the boys' bedroom, where he could hear Charlie sniffing miserably. For a moment, he wanted to walk in, talk to the boy, try to explain. Then, reflecting that, at the age of twelve, it was perhaps better if Charlie worked these things out for himself, he walked on slowly to his dressing-room.

Simon closed the door behind him, then sat, with a long sigh, at a dressing-table. He pushed one ivory-backed hairbrush against the other, listening to the satisfying 'click' they made, like a well-struck croquet ball. Like Charlie, he was unsettled by these exeat weekends. One moment they were all there, a family, the next he was alone with Jess once more. Sometimes he thought he heard the boys' laughter from their rooms upstairs, but it was nothing, or Jaime's radio playing in the kitchen. For a few days now and then, Susan would be in residence, a vague, distracted presence around the house. Only when she received calls from London would the martyred expression lift from her face. Simon would hear her laughing into the telephone through the closed door of her bedroom. She sounded like a stranger, someone he had never met.

He stood up, checked his hair, then went downstairs to tell Jaime that tea was required in the sitting-room.

'Freddie seems to think we may have to sell Chapel Meadow,' Simon said casually as, five minutes later, the four adults and Jeremy took tea before an oak fire. 'Matthew Turville wants to turn it into a sort of mortuary.'

'No, Dad.' Jeremy, who was lying beside Jess in front of the fire, protested. 'We can't do that – not Chapel Meadow.'

'We may have to, darling,' said Susan. 'We need the money and there are no shares left to sell.'

Simon looked at his wife with some surprise. Not for the first time that weekend, it occurred to him that Susan may already have discussed their finances with Freddie, that a small conspiracy had been hatched between them. 'Of course, we could always sell the flat in London,' he added.

Susan glanced at him. 'I don't think so, darling. That's not really an option, and well you know it.'

'Sell the flat. Pull in our horns. Consolidate at Garston. Sounds sensible to me.'

'I've never heard anything so ridiculous in all my born days.' Susan sipped at her tea. She smiled down at Jeremy. 'Now where *is* that brother of yours?'

'In the bedroom.'

'Blubbing,' muttered Simon. 'Think I might have been a bit what I call insensitive.'

'I hope he doesn't go round blubbing when he's at school,' said Susan, adding, almost automatically, 'So lucky to be there. The boys have an absolute ball.'

'Jess is getting fatter, Dad.' Jeremy poked at the dog's stomach. The Labrador yelped, moved away sharply, then looked embarrassed at the noise he had made.

'Oh, old thing.' Simon knelt down beside Jess. As he touched Jess's stomach, there was a sharp whimper of pain. He looked up, appalled. 'There's a lump,' he said.

'Oh dear,' said Freddie.

'Mortuaries, lumps.' Susan smiled at her guests. 'What odd tea-time conversations we do have in this house.'

Another social gathering, at the house of the village doctor, Duncan Gillette and his wife Caroline, was taking place that Saturday night. Because she liked the Gillettes and was anyway anxious to quash any rumours that she was becoming hermitic or strange, Alison Turville had accompanied Matthew to the dinner party. To her relief, she found that the Dunns had not been invited (chatting to the mistress of one's husband over a glass of wine being something of a strain, she found) although Sarah's sister Nina was there with her husband, as was Agnès Babineau and, in an unlikely social pairing with the Frenchwoman, Dr Miles Larwood.

It was to Nina Hebden that Alison was talking as the guests gathered in the sitting-room before dinner. Although (or perhaps because) Nina drank rather too much, and, after a couple of drinks, her conversation was liable to nose-dive from the banal to the outrageous, Alison had always felt relaxed with her. The two women were not exactly intimates but they enjoyed a mutual ease which made social or sexual competitiveness unnecessary.

As they discussed their respective children, Alison's eyes must have strayed across the room to Matthew, who was chatting to Agnès Babineau.

'Agnès is on song tonight,' Nina said, following the direction of her eyes.

'On song?' Alison glanced at the Frenchwoman. She was wearing a deceptively demure evening dress which, while revealing little flesh, nonetheless emphasised the gentle valleys and promontories of the promised land.

'Must be getting bored with my husband. She seems to be after yours.'

Alison smiled uneasily. 'She's probably just one of those people who can't talk to a man without flirting.'

'She plays every trick in the book, that woman,' said Nina. 'Look at her. There's the head-forward-peek-a-boo-through-the-curtain-of-hair trick. The hunch-your-shoulders-to-make-your-tits-look-bigger trick. The half-open-mouthed-I'd-like-to-get-my-lips-round-you trick. The casual-fingertip-jerking-off-of-the-wineglass trick, the eager-I-want-it-now-crossing-and-uncrossing-of-the-legs trick. It's not exactly subtle, is it?'

Alison laughed. 'I hadn't studied her that carefully,' she said.

But of course Nina was right. It was probably at that moment that Alison saw with dazzling clarity how, once Matthew became less preoccupied with the Garden of Remembrance, when he became bored with Sarah, or when Sarah became bored with him, he would grow restless, look around, and there would be Agnès Babineau. Or maybe someone else. Infidelity till death us do part. Stretching before her down the years, she saw a great queue of accommodating women, waiting to comfort her husband, to hear his secrets, to share with him the burden of the terrible things he suffered in the name of family life. They would be always be there, like ghosts in the family home, knowing everything about her, somehow remaining young as she grew older and lonelier.

'To tell the truth, I don't give a fuck,' she said quietly.

'Perhaps it's time you did.'

More upset than she realised, Alison shook her head.

'Giving a fuck really does help,' said Nina, raising her voice. 'When Peter started his affair with Agnès, I hated it – the way he was so bloody chirpy all the time, and was always checking himself in the mirror and buying new socks, and muttering in French, and changing his underwear every five minutes. But then I thought, What d'you do? Start a row? Chuck the cheating bastard out? Start looking for someone else who'll turn out to be a cheating bastard, too? Lose the whole bloody set-up just because Peter likes to screw some French tart now and then?'

Frowning, Alison placed a finger to her lips. 'And what do you do?' she asked quietly.

'You give a fuck. You join the party.'

Alison looked back at Matthew and wondered vaguely how her husband would respond if she did indeed join the party. Beyond him and Agnès, Dr Gillette was talking to Miles Larwood. Mistaking the direction of her stare, the doctor glanced at her over Larwood's shoulder. Then, quite unmistakably, he gave her the eye, holding contact with her for that split-second that divides the casually friendly from the intimately enquiring. Dr *Gillette*, a man in his late fifties, the fucking village doctor! Alison looked away quickly. It was all too much.

'Do they all cheat?' she asked Nina. 'Are all of our men at it?'

'Good Lord, I should think so. At least the ones with anything to them do.'

'Sad.'

'Oh? Why?' Nina seemed genuinely surprised. 'I'd rather be married to a cheat than to a drunk or a bore. It's only bodies, after all.'

'Yes.' Alison looked back at the doctor who was once more in earnest conversation with Larwood. 'Isn't it strange how things have changed?' she said. 'It seems only the other day that one disapproved of the bolters and the bounders, all those awful types who walked out on their families.'

'Did we?' Nina seemed to have lost interest and was looking round her. From the hall outside a telephone rang and Dr Gillette left to answer it.

'Now it turns out that the really corrupt ones were the people who stayed, cheating away happily amidst the security of family life.' She laughed bitterly. 'The pillars of the community.'

Nina drained her glass. 'Don't you think you're being a wee bit priggish about all this?' she said.

The telephone had stopped ringing. Gillette returned to Matthew, who stood in earnest conversation with the doctor for a moment, before walking over to where Alison sat with Nina.

'The police have just rung from the office,' he said. 'Apparently something's happened to Enid.'

6

IN MEMORIAM
It's not the words, these are but few
But the memories we have of you
Wife, nana, friend and mother
You were the one for us and no other
Thinking of you this special day
We miss you more than words can say
To the lovely person who looks from above
Her loving family send dearest love.
    FRIEDA KATHLEEN WILCOX
Died 23 November 1994: 'Always in our thoughts'.

MILES LARWOOD HAD dressed down for the meeting at the Turville Funeral Home. Because this was, after all, a business occasion and he was an academic, he wore clothes he usually kept for faculty meetings – a brown T-shirt spilling into faded jeans over pale sockless ankles terminating in scuffed grey trainers. It was a uniform which, he hoped, conveyed the impression of a man who had managed to keep alive the spirit and independence of his youth into proud, if battered, middle age. In the office of Matthew Turville, Miles had seated himself a few feet away from Matthew and Colin Dunn, who sat at a boardroom table near by, discussing costs and projections in low, fiscal murmurs.

Miles gazed through the glass partition that divided the office from that of Matthew's new secretary, Margaret Cowper, who sat before a word-processor, typing slowly and carefully.

He felt awkward here. It was not so much the fact that he was out of place that worried him (Miles prided himself on being out of place almost anywhere except in his study), as an awareness that this meeting, in spite of all appearances, represented a fundamental and painful compromise of principle. His hard-earned intellectual integrity was now part of a marketing package. He had been bought.

The deal had been simple to the point of vulgarity. Miles would add the weight of his academic authority to Matthew and Colin's plan to establish a new Garden of Remembrance in Chapel Meadow; Colin's firm would then finance a new fellowship in thanatology at the Anglia Institute, a post for which there could only be one serious candidate. Habituated as he was to the fashionable new intimacy between learning and business, Miles nonetheless felt sullied by the arrangement.

Beyond the glass, Margaret Cowper sat back in her chair, then turned her head towards Miles. For a few seconds, he found himself gazing into her clear grey eyes before, with a solemn but surprisingly warm smile, she returned to her work. For someone working in an undertaker's office, she seemed peculiarly happy.

'Quite a little popsy, eh?' Colin Dunn spoke loudly, causing Miles to start and turn back to the table.

'Sorry,' he said. 'Attention wandered a bit there.'

'Can't blame you.' Colin smiled in Margaret's direction. 'Magical little thing, isn't she? Clever of Matthew to find her.'

Matthew Turville looked up casually from the balance-sheet. 'She found me,' he said. 'The day after poor old Enid died, she turned up on the doorstep, looking for work. Good timing.'

'Nice having her in the next-door office,' said Colin with a hint of a leer. 'Attending to your every need.'

Matthew gave a defensive little wince. 'She takes a great interest in the running of the business. That's the only need she has to worry about.'

'Of course, I forgot,' said Colin. 'You have your hands rather full, what with one thing' – he paused significantly – 'and another.'

Detecting a faint air of hostility between the two men, Miles drew his chair closer to the table. 'Is it time for my input yet?' he asked.

'Yes, let's do that now,' said Matthew.

Colin stretched. 'Any chance of a cup of tea?'

With a frown of irritation, Matthew rang through to Margaret. Turning back to Colin, he asked, 'Perhaps you could bring Miles up to date on developments.'

'I've been in touch with Susan Pygott who, with the help of their accountant, has been softening up old Simon. Then I had a word or two with a chum on the council's Planning Committee, fed him the usual line about local jobs, premises for new business, benefit to the community, blah blah.'

'You've been busy,' said Miles.

'One chats. One eases things on their way. To tell the truth, I'm a bit more worried about local opposition. Somehow the *DP* seems to have got hold of the story.'

Matthew groaned softly. 'Apparently, even old Pearson in the village shop is getting involved,' he said. 'I heard he was planning to organise some sort of petition.'

'I expect it'll die down,' said Colin. 'The English never protest about anything for long. So –' He darted an insincere smile at Miles. 'What we need to do now is convince the wimp tendency on the committee that taking over Simon's field and filling it with stiffs is something a caring, sharing local council could accept. Which is where you and your local history come in, Miles.'

'Right, fine.' Miles hesitated, like a man ordering his thoughts into a form that would be comprehensible to the layman. 'I've recently been looking into the actual sociology of death. If I could just give you a background resumé.'

'The short version, if possible,' said Colin.

'The model I'm working towards is a contemporary, socially valid response to questions of mortality that have engaged historians and thanatologists over recent years,' said Miles. 'Put simply, each epoch has developed its own form of death. For example, the Middle Ages favoured what's known as the Good Death: a resigned, open attitude towards mortality – death as friend. Then, in the early modern age, there was the Tame Death, an abandonment of worldly goods, of *avaritia*, in favour of a simple funeral – merchants would actually give away their possessions to enter a monastery in order to end their days.'

'Bloody fools,' Colin muttered.

'Then there was the Fearful Death, congruent with the flowering of what we call the gothic sensibility, followed by the strange and romantic Beautiful Death of the Victorians which – '

'Could we just cut to the chase?' said Colin.

'Right.' Miles gave a circular wave with his left hand, as if rolling on the years. 'So, to the twentieth century and what Philippe Ariès describes as the Dirty Death – a new morbidity, the fruit of modern man's paranoia, the effects of the First World War. And finally, from the mid-century to the present day, we've been living at a time of the Silent Death. Medical advances have meant that we've been able to shut death away, to conceal it in hospital wards or hospices as if it's something almost to be ashamed of. In a real sense, we've turned the Good Death on its head. Now we actually don't want to be prepared. Doctors tell us, "He knew nothing about it," "She never felt a thing." We cremate our dead, more and more. Grief has become something about which we're embarrassed. We just want to get it over with.'

'I know the feeling,' said Colin.

'Now this, according to writers like Geoffrey Gorer, is profoundly unhealthy.' Miles paused dramatically, looking from Matthew to Colin. 'So, I was thinking that, if we can convince the committee that the quality of mourning is important for the social fabric of Burthorpe, they're likely to see the need for a new Garden of Remembrance.'

For a moment there was silence in the office.

'A new death.' It was Matthew who spoke. 'We give them a modern version of Miles's Good Death. I like it.'

'Mmm?' Colin had placed both hands behind his head and was watching Margaret as she prepared the tea next door.

'We say we're applying the contemporary, stand-on-your-own-two-feet philosophy – but to those who are no longer standing on their own two feet. Deregulation comes to the graveyard.'

Miles shifted uncomfortably at this misinterpretation but said nothing. As a thanatologist, he had come to see undertakers as stalwarts of the community, caring professionals who, with understanding and a subtle sense of theatre, bestowed on the dead and the grieving a sense of dignity, social cohesion and continuity, but, listening to Matthew, he realised what a sentimental view this was.

'We could develop the argument in our favour,' Matthew was saying. 'The Good Death, The Fearful Death, The Silent Death and now' – he spread his hands eloquently – 'The Consumer Death.'

Colin raised an eyebrow. 'You think they'll buy that?'

'With The Consumer Death, the deceased and the family are given a wider choice of ceremony, of commemoration.'

'Consumer choice,' said Colin. 'That always plays well.'

Anxious to return the discussion to the subject of his research, Miles took two ring-bound documents from his briefcase, one of which he handed to Colin and Matthew. 'This is the summary of my work-in-progress which I'd like to submit to the committee.'

Colin flicked through the pages. '"Witchcraft and gynocentricity in seventeenth-century Bury St Edmunds". Good God. "Medieval love and death: Skelton's remedy". "Contemporary societal influences on concepts of meta-death".' He looked up and smiled. 'This looks absolutely excellent, Miles. Just what was needed.'

Miles shrugged bashfully. 'It's at an early stage as yet. I hope to flesh out the bones of my argument over time. But I'm glad you like it.'

'Like it?' Colin gave a bark of laughter. 'Can't understand a bloody word of it – but it's exactly the sort of pseudo-intellectual, balls-achingly boring, pretentious crap that members of the committee will be impressed by.'

'Actually' – two spots of colour had appeared on Miles's unshaven cheeks – 'this is highly original research data.'

'Yeah yeah.' Colin winked. 'And I'm sure it'll go down very well when you apply for that new fellowship of yours.'

'The fellowship.' Miles's shoulders seemed to sag in defeat. 'Yes, mustn't forget that.'

The door opened and Margaret appeared, carrying a tray.

'Ah.' Colin cleared a space on the table. 'Tea and totty.'

Margaret looked at him coldly. 'Totty?' she said. 'I was just asked for tea.'

He held up both hands in mock surrender. 'Just a joke, love.'

Still frowning, Margaret laid the tray on the table.

'Our main problem is turnover.' Matthew stared gloomily at the papers in front of him. 'We need more deaths.'

Margaret paused on her way out of the door. 'More deaths,' she said quietly.

'What?' Matthew looked up, as if noticing for the first time that his secretary had entered the room. 'Sorry, Margaret, I was just thinking out loud.'

'I see.' With another icy look in Colin's direction, she left the office.

'Yikes,' said Colin. 'That is one dangerous lady.'

'We need to find her somewhere to live,' said Matthew. 'The poor girl's staying at the Greyhound.'

'Ah.' Miles frowned, as if remembering something he had forgotten to mention. 'As it happens, my lodger left yesterday. No warning. Out of the blue. Left me high and dry. There's – well, there's a sort of room available right now.' He petered out and was annoyed to find himself blushing.

'You lucky devil,' muttered Colin.

Christmas was approaching, but it was a Burthorpian Christmas and was celebrated in a quiet, low-key manner without the showy *bonhomie* that marked the day elsewhere. There appeared to be fewer carol-singers than in previous years, and more television. The Christmas tree provided by Charlie Watson for the green was a poor specimen and several of its lights failed to work. H.T. Pearson decorated his store with the same faded streamers and battered tinsel with which he had expressed yuletide spirit over the past five or six years. There was talk, as there always is talk, of a white Christmas, but, as it always does, the day dawned warm, wet and greyly anonymous.

At Garston Hall, the Pygott family celebrated with their usual forced goodwill. The butler Jaime had been allowed to invite a friend called Eric to stay and was working, Simon had thought, as if his mind was on other things. A low point in the day had been the discovery of Simon's last bottle of vintage Dom Pérignon brandy, empty in the kitchen, having been splashed copiously over the Christmas pudding.

The Turville family, less practised in the art of emotional disguise, had a more difficult time. On the afternoon of Christmas Eve, Matthew, who had been taking the day off, left Yew Tree Cottage in something of a hurry, claiming that a minor problem needed to be resolved at the Home. Alison rang the office an hour later and was told by Margaret that Mr Turville had not been in all day. For some minutes after making the call, she sat by the telephone, imagining a furtive exchange of presents between Matthew and Sarah at some secret rendezvous, followed by enough sex to carry them over this traditionally difficult period for adulterers. When Christmas Day came, Stephen and Kate fought over their stockings. Later, as presents were exchanged, Kate occasionally looked out into the garden as if expecting to see a pony tethered to the gate. Calls were made to parents, gratitude and good wishes expressed. A sense of anti-climax hung over the house like a guilty conscience.

Miles Larwood returned to the village on Boxing Day, having spent a comforting two days being treated by his mother in Leicester as if he were still nine years old. His new lodger Margaret Cowper was, he had been concerned to discover, staying alone at Christmas, having, she said, no living relations to whom she was that close. Miles was surprised to find that the prospect of seeing Margaret again had induced in him an unfamiliar tightness in the solar plexus. Perhaps it was because, he reflected, Margaret had turned out to be the perfect lodger: unobtrusive, tidy, quiet. In spite of himself, he found he was intrigued by her discreet and watchful persona, the way in which she almost seemed to be studying the everyday life of the village like a foreigner trying to come to terms with a new country. It had certainly been a fortuitous chance that David Morgan, his previous lodger, had moved out (claiming, rather against character, to have seen and heard 'things' during the night in his bedroom), just when Matthew Turville's secretary had been looking for lodgings. For some reason, he very much hoped that Margaret would be staying with him for a while.

He was never happy here. I see that now. Something in his nature demanded conspiracy and backchat, change and contention. I would stand in my dark corner on those evenings when he entertained, marvelling at the tales he told from a previous life. He despised the vanity of court, but with the rage of one who had himself been seduced by its charms.

And where were the charms of the life he now led? His tutelage was no longer of a prince but of the geese, hens, the squealing tithe-pigs with which parish folk paid what was due to him. His kingdom was no longer London or Windsor but the dark house by the Mere. He marched through the kitchen garden as if he would sweep aside its beehives and its plants simply to make something happen.

He manufactured dissent, simply to keep himself from the mire of dullness. The epitaphs he wrote for parishioners became hymns of loathing. The late John Clarke was mocked as Johnny Jay-Beard. When that simple dogswane, the Reverend Smith of East Wretham, was reputed to have made sport in church with a hawk, my lord railed at him as if he were a philistine in the temple.

Then there were those he once called Venus's lusty female children dear. Many was the time when, in his cups, surrounded by those who passed for friends, that my lord, small eyes steep with the memory of desire, would tell tales of Long Sally or Mannerly Margery. I understood little of what was said but I began to sense that these tales of ribaldry were told not for my lord's tame disciples to endew, but for me, standing in the shadows, hands clasped in front of me, staring at the floor, waiting for the meal to end.

That night, after the men had left, he returned to the room where I was clearing the table. He asked me if such talk troubled me. I told him, truthfully, that it did not. He sat at the head of the table, as if considering a matter of the greatest importance. Both hands about his goblet, staring into his red wine, he spoke of the needs of men, of his loneliness, of God's will that His servants should not be denied the greatest of His gifts, His foison. Yet what foison was this? I understood little or nothing of what he was saying until he stood, quite suddenly, and commanded me to leave off my chores. There was more important work to be done. He took me by the hand and asked me if I understood. I did not, but I said I did.

So it was that, by the flickering tallow of my master's bedroom, I myself became one of Venus's children. He was a very different man that night from the one I had come to know. He said little,

*but seemed rapt, as if bewitched by some mystery beyond his
understanding. There was a tenderness, a sorrow, to him that, over
the hours we were alone in his room, eased my terror of that great
white body, my fear that, whatever was expected of me, I would
be unable to provide, like a pupil being examined on a text that I
had never seen. For most of the night, he held me, turning me this
way and that, examining every gall and scar, breathing in my
scent, worshipping my most secret shames, running his hands over
me as if he were a pilgrim before some holy relic. I grew tired,
reclaimed by his murmured words, pliable to the soft authority of
his touch. As light dawned grey through the small window, he lay
beside me, arranged me as he wanted. Then stroking my face with
one hand, while holding my quaking body with the other, he made
me his own.*

*Afterwards, I cried, both for the pain of the moment and for
fear of what the future held, perhaps also for wonder at what I
had felt. He soothed me, then drew back from the blanket to look
upon me. I covered my shame with my hands. He parted them.
Take this, my blood, he said, lowering his great head to me,
tasting the blood that was drying upon my thighs.*

I held him to me, and we slept.

Although the nights were cold now, Margaret had taken to walking in
the darkness, hands sunk deep in the pockets of her bomber jacket, her
face almost obscured by the floppy khaki hat she had purchased at the
Quartermaster's Daughter Stores in Diss. One evening late in De-
cember, she stood by the village pond, looking up the hill towards the
Greyhound, and breathed deep of the Burthorpe air.

A blue-grey light shone from H.T. Pearson's loft where the shopkeeper would be enjoying a new video, crouched before the thirty-
four-inch screen in an angry fever of anticipation. Across the pond,
there was a light in every window of Yew Tree Cottage as if to protect
the Turville family from some force of darkness outside. The children
were in bed now, and Matthew and Alison were sitting silently in front
of the television news, allowing the clamour of the world's miseries to
drown out, for a few moments, their own unhappiness.

Margaret walked down a narrow path between skeletal hawthorn trees and unkempt blackberry bushes. A single security light shone over the sewage plant, where the lane bifurcated, the main route leading to Diss, the other towards Gaston Hall.

She climbed over a gate that led on to Simon Pygott's land, and stood for a moment in Chapel Meadow. It was the perfect setting for a Garden of Remembrance – out of sight from the road, in a small valley through which ran a stream which one day would be a comfort to grieving folk in black. Above it all, separated only by a stretch of parkland, was Garston Hall. Rural peace, a purling symbol of continuity, overlooked by a great house, reminding us all of man's earthly achievements. No client could wish for a better resting place.

As she walked past the chapel, some night creature – a deer, perhaps – dived through the bushes leading to an adjoining field. She stood, gazing towards Garston Hall, which crouched, like a giant, on the brow of the hill.

Apart from an ancient coach lamp above the large oak front door, the only light shining from the house was visible through the two leaded windows of the library. Avoiding the gravel in front of the Hall, Margaret crept to one of the windows and, for a few moments, gazed upon the master of Garston Hall, who was sitting, a copy of *Farmers' Weekly* on his lap, Jess curled up at his feet. From somewhere in the library, 'Roy Orbison's Greatest Hits' was playing and, on the arm of his chair, Simon now and then tapped his hand as if acknowledging the presence of the music.

Leaving the Hall, Margaret walked north, with more determined steps. She crossed two fields and then, with the lights of Scole before her, she slowed as if held back by some great invisible barrier. A strange sound, like the crackle of burning bushfire, filled the darkness for a moment. She swayed, pushing forward again and again. Only when she stepped back did the sound fade. She stood swaying, eyes closed, a febrile, troubled presence in the night. Breathing deeply, she turned back to Burthorpe.

In the entrance to a beet field, she happened upon a car parked beneath a massive dead elm tree. She hesitated, watching the young couple engaged in a desperate, half-clothed tussle on the back seat. The boy's head was thrown back as the girl rummaged about below, her tangled hair occasionally becoming visible through the misted car window. In the darkness could be heard groans, murmurs, gasps, a muffled symphony of teenage lust.

'We need more deaths.'

Margaret spoke softly, a hint of regret in her voice.

She turned, ignoring the deep plaintive creek of wood behind her, the loud crack, then seconds later, the brief human cry, not of passion now but of terror, that was quickly lost in the confused explosion of sound as the elm crushed the car and its lovers.

'We need more deaths.' Head down, deep in thought, Margaret walked towards the lights of the village.

Rose Hope stood in the arched doorway of Garston Hall, arms crossed, as she watched Simon Pygott walk his dog around the frost-covered lawn.

It was a slow progress. His lowered head moving from side to side, Jess waddled painfully after his master, now and then pausing to consider and sniff at something interesting. Simon walked one step ahead and urged on his dog with a gruff gentleness unrecognisable from the voice with which he addressed Rose, or his wife, or even his children.

Simon had been one of her more intriguing lovers, she thought. Before she had met him, she had never been to bed with a genuine, unreconstructed nob. Countless reformed nobs (public-school socialists, old Harrovian journalists), a few would-be, aspiring nobs, but never a perfect, dyed-in-the-wool specimen, uncorrupted by brains or the real world.

And he was utterly genuine, without a hint of side to him. A glance at Simon Pygott revealed a fresh-faced, loud-voiced, well-bred Englishman of the old school. Dig deeper, get to know him better – let him clamber all over you in bed, for heaven's sake – and you discovered this was no veneer. The same solid grain of traditional wood was to be found all the way through him. No secrets. No fears. Not the slightest twinge of self-doubt.

She had been seeing him, as they say, for almost a year now. Simon had been the right man at the right time. In spite of her feminist beliefs,

Rose had been finding the new tentativeness of men – their much-touted sensitivity, their need to talk, to empathise, the distressing ease with which they allowed their eyes to fill with tears – all rather wearisome. Simon's cheery, clod-hopping confidence was refreshing, seductive even. It was as if by sharing his bed she could huddle under the carapace of certainty which kept the frets and concerns of the outside world at bay.

'Now what?' she had asked Simon after the other guests had left at the end of the first dinner party to which he had invited her.

He had risen to his feet, put a guard in front of the fire, and had stood over her in a way that, had he been any other man, she would have taken to be some sort of sexual presentation. 'I was rather assuming we'd pop upstairs to do bodies,' he had said, extending a beefy hand and helping her to her feet. Any kind of response from her seemed somehow redundant. So they did bodies. She remembered that at some point during that first night, as Simon had huffed and puffed over her, another body had suddenly leapt on to the bed, scratching her leg.

She had yelped, 'Jesus Christ, what the fuck –?'

Simon had glanced over his shoulder and, without breaking his stride, had laughed, 'No, you *cannot* join in, you silly old dog.'

Jess. It was, she supposed, a mark of her growing acceptance of country ways that she now regarded it as entirely natural to find herself, during an act of sexual congress, staring into the dark, mildly curious eyes of a Golden Labrador.

'This dog's getting better, you know.' Simon now stood before her at the front door, looking down at Jess who, exhausted, was entering the house, heading for the library. 'He only managed twice around the lawn yesterday. He's done it three times today.'

Rose sank her hands into the pockets of her jeans and shivered. 'It's cancer, Simon,' she said. 'Not a cold.'

'That's what you say.' Simon extended his right arm in an awkward gentlemanly gesture and followed Rose into the house. 'But he's definitely improving with exercise. The Melchetts' whippet had a tumour in its neck last year. Vet cut it out, now she's catching hares again like billy-oh.' They walked into the library and stood over Jess, who had slumped into his basket in front of the fire. 'Exercise. Then the knife. They're surprisingly tough, Labradors. And he's no age to speak of, is he?'

'No.' Rose sighed, as she sat in an armchair near by. Simon was running his hand over the dog's stomach, where a pronounced fawn hillock betrayed the presence of the tumour. 'Would you get another dog?' she asked.

'Good Lord, no.' He pursed his lips. 'You're going to be around for quite a while, aren't you, my old dog.'

'I wonder – ' Rose paused, considering whether it was a suitable moment to delve into the murk of Simon's subconscious. 'I mean, you don't think that the reason why you're so upset about Jess is that perhaps you're worried about everything else.'

'Hmm?'

'The family. Susan. Having to sell off that field. The fuss in the village. Jess's tumour has come to represent it all – a sort of metaphor.'

There was silence in the library. Then Simon looked up, his face more flushed than it had been. 'You really do speak some unutterable balls sometimes, Rose,' he said. 'Metaphor! You'll never understand how we feel about animals.'

As she watched him gently stroking his dog, Rose wondered whether Simon was suffering from what, in any other person in any other family, might be regarded as a nervous breakdown. The problem was that, in his universe, you didn't break down. You were a bit under the weather, in really rather bad form. Sometimes a chap, it was true, became so seriously under the weather, in such appallingly bad form, that he wandered off into the woods and blew his head off with a twelve-bore shotgun, but members of his family would console themselves with the thought that at least he hadn't gone bonkers, at least he was basically sound when the shooting accident occurred.

'How are you sleeping these days?' she asked.

'Not much. I've had what I call a lot on my mind.'

'I'm worried about you.'

'Nothing to worry about.' Simon continued to stroke the dog's stomach. 'Once we get this old thing back on his feet, I'll be fine. Pygotts don't crack, you know.'

'No.' Rose hesitated. 'No, they run away.'

'What exactly d'you mean by that?'

'Oh, Simon.' She leant forward, her elbows resting on her narrow thighs. 'It's just another family – can't you see that? You walk around with this great weight of tradition on your shoulders. It's difficult enough for each of us to get by without having to belong to a vast team of perfect antecedents.'

'They weren't perfect. But they've done a hell of a lot for Burthorpe, the Pygotts. I just want to do my bit, set up Charlie to do the same after me.'

'Families. I've never understood the attraction. As far as I'm concerned, we're on our own.'

'Easy for you to say that. Just yourself to think of. If everyone behaved like you, a fine set-up it would be. Anarchy.'

'But they do behave like that in the end. Look at your father.'

'He didn't run away. It may have looked that way but he didn't. You'd understand if you had met him.'

'I feel as if I have, the amount you've talked about him.' Rose smiled almost kindly. 'Think about it, Simon. He worked in the City. He got caught with his fingers in the till. He did a runner to Italy, leaving his only son, whose mother had died when he was ten, to face the music on his behalf. Where's the family honour and loyalty in that?'

Simon stared down at Jess, his eyes evading Rose's as if he were a guilty schoolboy.

'You never knew him. Fine man. Smart. Dignified. When he spoke, it was as if he had never been contradicted in his life and never would be – almost like God having a word with you. Piercing blue eyes. Gave you the full glare sometimes. Your hands went clammy, mouth dry. If he asked you to do something, you just didn't ask questions, not necessary. Yours not to what I call reason why.'

'It's this that's bugging you, isn't it?'

'I keep wondering what he would do if he were alive. Decisive, you see. Knew the Pygott way of doing things. When it all got a bit tricky on the business side, he called me back from Cirencester, gave me a slap-up meal, sat me down in front of this fire, brandy, cigar the size of a torpedo. Knew something was up because he had never done that before. Told me there had been one or two problems at the office. Chaps were looking for one of the partners in the firm to do the decent thing, fall on his sword and all that. He'd have to go abroad for a while. Said, your show now, old boy.' Simon paused, as if hearing the voice in his head. 'Just like a Pygott, I thought. Someone has to take the fall, be a man. A Pygott steps forward. I was proud.'

'What an old bastard.'

'So off he went. Next morning. Hurried goodbyes, then toodled off to the airport and on to Italy. Said he'd forward me the address when he got there. Lunchtime, the phone starts ringing. Colleagues. Then investigators, journalists, police. All saying the most unspeakable things about Dad. Where was he? Taking a holiday in Italy, I said. Not sure quite when he'll be back. Got an address? Not as such, expecting word soon. They all got frightfully shirty – thought I was covering up. Held the line, though. Didn't let the family down.'

'And the address?'

'Took a few months to come through.' Simon sat in silence for a moment. 'I sold off some land, couple of farmhouses, paid whatever they asked me to pay. Thought the old man would be quite proud of me when he came back.'

'But he never did.'

'No. He'd set up a shell company in Switzerland, old Dad – rather clever really. Fellow director was Rosemary, his secretary. She followed him out to Italy. They bought a house. Must have been planned for months.'

'Did you visit them?'

'Couple of times. Not a great success, to tell the truth. The secretary wandered about without a top, used bad language in front of the boys, that sort of thing.' Simon looked up, his bland features stricken and confused. 'People seem to leave,' he said suddenly. 'They just go. Sooner or later, they . . . sugar off. Ever since I can remember. First term at Hawtreys, in front of the big house, boys lugging tuckboxes up the steps, bit of blubbing going on here and there. Bye, darling, bye, Mum, bye, old boy, bye, Dad. Off they went. Daimler kicking up the gravel, pale hand waving from the darkness of the car. Somehow it always seems to have been like that.'

There was silence in the library.

'About time you left, too, isn't it?' Simon spoke gruffly.

'Yes.' Rose glanced at her watch. 'I've a call to make in the village.'

'I didn't mean that.'

'Ah. Well, maybe that, too.'

'Not as stupid as I look, you know. A chap can tell.'

'I like you very much, Simon. And I've enjoyed all this. But I think it's time for us to redefine our relationship.'

'What does that mean in English? No more indoor sports?'

'I think not.' Rose stood up and gazed at her former lover. Early in her life, she had discovered that, once she started feeling sorry for a man, it was time to move on. 'I still value our friendship very much.'

'Yes, of course. You would.'

She laid a hand on his shoulder. 'Simon, you're a much better man than your father ever was,' she said.

'Hear that, old dog?' Simon lifted up one of Jess's ears. 'I'm such a good chap that she's walking out on me.' Jess lifted his tail and gave a single weary thump of response. 'No, don't worry, Jess, I'm not going to redefine our relationship.'

As she left the library and made her way to the front door, Rose could hear the master of Garston Hall murmuring gently to his dying dog.

She drove down the pitted drive, past Chapel Meadow. The car shuddered as it crossed a cattle grid before it reached the tall farm buildings that had been built two years previously for Simon's growing armoury of modern machinery. In their early days together, he had shown her around these vast iron sheds, pointing out the drillers and strimmers and cutters and combines that would magically transform the Pygott fortunes. They had gleamed, these monsters, still smelling of the showroom. When she had pointed out that they were ranged almost as if they were in a museum, Simon had lectured her patiently on the need for organisation on a modern farm.

Later, a journalist on the *DP* had commented that it had been a glad day for local heavy-plant salesmen when Simon had taken over the Garston Hall estate. Men who had congratulated themselves on the sale of one agricultural behemoth to the new master of Garston Hall had been astonished to find him returning, months later, for another, as if he were a small boy buying a quarter-pound of sweets. They made him special deals, kept him abreast of the newest and most exciting mechanical advances from Japan or America. Simon became a one-man boom market, adored yet mocked by the reps who sold to him. Rose had tried to broach the subject on one occasion but her questions had been brushed aside. Never a good listener, Simon was effectively deaf when it came to farming techniques.

Beyond the building, some smart new post-and-rails had been erected, beyond which grazed a herd of cattle. To her right were fields which he had let to Charlie Watson at a rent significantly lower than the sum he would have received had he let the fields lie fallow as set-aside. When Colin Dunn had, rather unkindly, pointed this out at a dinner party, a look of stunned surprise had crossed Simon's broad features. Well, he believed in working the land, he had managed to say in the end, adding, almost to himself as an afterthought, 'Bloody European bastards.'

Rose turned left up the hill on to Bridge Lane and drove towards the village.

The problem caused by Harold Pearson's surprisingly successful campaign against the Chapel Meadow development was that more and more frequently the position taken by the *DP* was being questioned. It was known all around Diss that Rose was friendly with Simon Pygott. If anyone were to suspect that, on Tuesday afternoons and occasionally at weekends, she was likely to have been found in his bedroom, the effect on her career could have been unfortunate. For Rose, the *DP* was a stepping-stone to greater things. At this point, she could hardly afford to risk local scandal. She had her reputation to consider.

Now that she had put her relationship with Simon on a more appropriate footing, it would be easier to report dispassionately on the controversy surrounding the new Garden of Remembrance. She parked the car in front of the H.T. Pearson Convenience Store, noticing that the shop window which had once been militantly dull now had a window display at the centre of which was a large poster created by Class 3 of Burthorpe Primary. Underneath was the slogan, 'CHAPEL MEADOW? OVER OUR DEAD BODIES!'.

On every previous occasion when Rose had driven past, the H.T. Pearson Convenience Store had been closed – half-days seemed mysteriously to occur several times during the week – but today there were people inside.

Rose entered the shop and stood for a moment, watching as a mother and her two young children signed a petition that lay on the counter behind which Pearson stood, the very picture of a benign village shopkeeper. 'We're hopeful,' he was saying. 'Not much stirs the average bloke to say "This far and no further" but our little campaign seems to have struck something of a chord.'

'We're all very grateful to you,' said the woman.

The children cowered by their mother as the shopkeeper beamed down at them, blinking behind his spectacles. 'It's what it's all about,' he said smoothly. 'Kids. The next generation. If we don't stick up for them who will?'

After the family had left, Rose stepped forward, extending a hand. 'Rose Hope,' she said. 'I edit the *Diss Press*.'

Pearson shook her hand peremptorily. 'Our friends in the media,' he muttered.

'I'm fascinated by your campaign.' Rose looked down at the petition. 'You really seem to have attracted the children.'

A fleeting shadow of alarm crossed Pearson's face. 'Yes, we have,' he said. He reached under the counter and took out several previous sheets of the petition. He pointed to a name on the third sheet.

'That's a story for the *DP*,' he said. 'Charles Pygott, son of the Hall, supports our protest against his father.'

Rose smiled diplomatically. 'We try to stay out of family disputes,' she said.

'Came down here last Saturday. Looked at the plans, then signed his name. You should talk to him next time he's home from school. You'll know the Pygotts, I expect.'

'Slightly. Maybe we could feature a photograph of your good self, surrounded by young protestors. Do a little interview with you, maybe.'

The shopkeeper seemed to be blushing. 'I'm not very photogenic,' he said. 'But, if it would help the cause.'

'I'll get my people to call you later today. We'll do a good spread in next week's issue.'

She left the shop, and walked quickly towards her car. There was something phony about H.T. Pearson, she thought, something almost sinister. She smiled, starting the car. Even after five years away from the corrupt city, she was still unable to rid herself of the conviction that no one was quite what they appeared to be. Not even a poor, old, big-bottomed village shopkeeper, it seemed, was safe from her cynicism. Sometimes she felt quite ashamed of herself.

7

CHAPEL MEADOW?
OVER OUR DEAD BODIES!

Dear Sirs,

Like many ordinary folk in Burthorpe, I was surprised and
appalled by your editorial (January 3) expressing support for
the proposed new business park in the village and the Garden
of Remembrance development on Chapel Meadow. The *DP*
appears to believe that any kind of development is a 'good
thing' just because it generates jobs and, as you put it, 'keeps
alive our threatened rural communities'.

Alive??? The only people that Chapel Meadow will bring to
Burthorpe will be in pine coffins – in no time our picturesque
little village will become the corpse capital of North Suffolk.
The motives of Simon Pygott are clear, as are those of the
Turville Funeral Home. But why-oh-why is the *DP* support-
ing this scheme?

Please inform your readers that my shop, the H.T. Pearson
Convenience Store, is headquarters for the KEEP
BURTHORPE ALIVE campaign. Protestors from the younger generation are especially welcome – this is their future
we're fighting for!

Yours,

H.T. Pearson,
Burthorpe

THE FAMILY OF Carol Power – mother, father, grandmother, younger sister – made its way across the courtyard towards the Laying-in Room like a small dark cloud of misery. Matthew walked with them, taking his normal position on family visits, a few feet away, available yet unobtrusive. His head was slightly bowed, his hands clasped in front of him. He opened the door to the small brick building and, as the family filed past him, he made eye contact with each of them in turn, conveying in his smile both sympathy and a reassuring competence. He closed the door behind them.

On rare occasions, a family might return briefly to the waiting-room while Matthew made changes to the client's hair or cosmeticisation. The mothers of deceased children or teenagers, in his experience, were particularly fussy in this regard – it was as if their loved one was going to that last party and needed to look just right – but no modifications were required today. Despite the nature of Carol's passing (when the elm had been lifted off by a crane and the crashed roof of the car removed, her head was found to be embedded in Darren Bugg's crotch), she now lay at rest, looking as palely innocent as a novitiate taken by some tragic, but decorous disease. After eight minutes, the party emerged, less composed now, Mrs Power crouched over, round-shouldered, leaning against her husband, followed by their daughter whose arm rested on the shoulders of the weeping grandmother. Matthew, even more sombre than he had been before, gently closed the door, and walked behind them at a discreet distance.

As the family gathered at the main gate, he spoke to Carol's father, offering tea in the Family Room before they returned to the real world. Clearly the invitation was declined, because now Matthew was shaking the hand of each member of the family, murmuring precisely the right words of condolence as they turned to make their way towards their car.

Gazing after the car as it disappeared around the bend in Farthing Lane, Matthew noticed for the first time that Rose Hope's green Saab was parked a few yards down the road from the Home. Now she stepped out and walked unhurriedly to where he stood.

'Sad,' she said.

'Yes. I hate it when they're young.'

'There were just a couple of questions I wanted to ask. More out of curiosity than anything.'

Matthew sighed. 'There was nothing dodgy about the way they died,' he said. 'They were unlucky, that's all.'

'Yes, I know. Accidental death. I was at the inquest.'

'Tree must have been rotten.'

'Like the tree that nearly killed Errol Pryce during the autumn.'

'Yes.' For the first time, Matthew expressed mild interest. 'You think there's a connection?'

'I spoke to the journalist who covered Pryce's crash. He said something about a red mark on the tree that fell. He had assumed that the council had marked it for demolition.' Rose paused. 'There was one on the tree that killed these two as well. And the council use black creosote.'

'A red mark.' Matthew frowned. 'Was it sticky?'

'Not so far as I know.'

'When they found Enid Kirby dead' – he nodded in the direction of the office where Margaret could be seen working – 'there was some sort of red stuff on her computer screen. At the time we assumed it was Enid's blood – she hit her head as she fell to the ground – but I never found that entirely convincing.'

'Sounds unlikely.'

'She died instantly, according to the pathologist. That means that blood would hardly flow at all. I didn't tell the police about the mark because I assumed it was some sort of spoor or insecticide. The window was open.'

For a moment, they stood in silence. Then Matthew glanced at his watch. 'I expect there's some explanation,' he said. 'Sorry I couldn't help.'

'You did,' said Rose.

He walked back to the office.

Margaret looked up as he passed her desk. 'Would you like a coffee, Mr Turville?' she asked.

'Please.' He left the office door ajar and sat heavily in his chair. When Margaret brought him the coffee, he was staring out of the window, deep in thought.

'You look worried,' she said.

'Hmm? Not really.'

'Is it the village shop? The campaign against Chapel Meadow?'

'Yes, that's probably it. Bloody Harold Pearson.'

'He will be no more.'

'Sorry?'

Margaret smiled at her employer. 'I'm sure his protest will soon be no more,' she said. 'You were very good with the Power family. I watched you.'

'It was quite a job.' Matthew stared ahead of him as if contemplating the grotesque corpse that had arrived at the Home, its clothes torn, its limbs in disarray, its face a bloodied parody of teenage desire, and then the tranquil, serene figure that now graced the Laying-in Room. 'I suppose I gave the girl a bit of dignity,' he said.

'Were you thanked?'

'No. They don't thank the undertaker.'

'You are as important as a doctor – more important, perhaps. You prepare people for their last journey.'

Matthew looked up sharply, sensing mockery in Margaret's voice.

She smiled. 'You've just made the Power family whole again,' she said. 'Out of death comes life.'

'I suppose so. Some people don't see it that way, even in the business,' said Matthew distantly. 'My father didn't. Undertaking was just a way of supplementing his income as a builder. There was a slump in trade, his carpenter used to make coffins. And here was something where there was no dip in demand – Dad joined forces with the joiner and set up Turville Funeral Services with Turville Builders. Ended up making more money from undertaking than building, but his heart was never in it.'

'He must be proud of you.' Margaret edged her chair closer to Matthew's desk.

'Hardly. When I was sixteen, I used to ask if I could help with the funerals. Dad was appalled. He wanted me to be a businessman, get away from Burthorpe. In the end, he agreed that I could be a reserve coffin bearer. I loved dressing up in black – the top hat, frock coat. The first time I actually carried a coffin, it was one of the proudest days of my life.'

'Most fathers would be pleased that their son was interested in the business.'

'We're not close.'

'And your wife?'

'I think it slightly embarrasses her. It's not quite respectable.'

'She should be proud. You bring order. I watch your hands as they touch people. They heal.' Margaret shifted in her chair, exposing rather more of her pale thigh. 'They bring change.'

Matthew frowned. 'I hadn't been aware you had seen me at work.'

'I can imagine.'

'In the end, it's just a job.' Matthew held out the empty coffee cup. There were times when he found his new secretary's enthusiasm for the job quite unsettling. 'Now. Are there any letters for me to sign? I must leave early this afternoon.'

'Yes, of course. It's Thursday.'

'Sorry?'

'I'll fetch your letters.' Margaret left the office.

'We can't do it today, Matthew. I'm not well.'

'You could have rung me at the office.'

'It's not something I wanted to explain over the telephone. Just tea and conversation this afternoon, all right?'

'Sounds good to me.'

'God, you're so bloody understanding. Aren't you even going to ask me why?'

'Why?'

'Well. Perhaps I could ask you something first. Have you been entirely faithful to me recently?'

'As faithful as a husband can be.'

'I'm not talking about you and Alison, Matthew – you know that sleeping with your wife doesn't count.'

'Of course I've been faithful.'

'Not even Agnès Babineau?'

'Oh please.'

'Why not? Everyone fucks Agnes at some stage. She's a rite of passage every man has to go through in Burthorpe.'

'Not me.'

'What about Alison? Is she seeing someone?'

97

'Don't be ridiculous, Sarah. What is this?'

'Matthew, something odd's going on . . . down there. Something really rather creepy, I'm afraid.'

'Creepy?'

'You won't believe this, love, but my last period. It was sort of . . . green.'

Sometimes, in those early days, it seemed that nothing, not his parish work, nor his versifying, nor his dreams of court, could rid his mind of thoughts of me and what we might do together. Every day he would visit me in my room at the time in the afternoon when I would take my rest.

Behind that bolted door, the sun shining through the high, narrow window, we would enjoy such wild and innocent pleasures as, it seemed, no man and woman had ever known, deinte beyond custom and shame, beyond love.

One afternoon, our bodies still aglow with delight, he lay beside me, silent, rapt, as if words at last had deserted him.

Look. He teased up two fronds of my secret hair. She has the horns, like the Devil.

I laughed. I pushed him back and studied him likewise, but his hair was flat and damp with flecks of grey around his lower man which lay at rest, quiescent yet dangerous.

He's a hawk, I said. As ramage and untamed as a hawk. I touched it with a gentle kiss. Ware the hawk, I murmured.

Good. Very good.

And at that moment I believed that he was talking of my kisses.

H.T. Pearson turned the ancient Lucozade sign on his door from 'Come In! We're OPEN' to 'Sorry! We're CLOSED'. The time was almost five-thirty-five, firm proof that it had been an unusually busy and profitable day at the Convenience Store. Under normal circumstances, Pearson would express impatience with any shopper bothering him after 5 p.m.; from five-twenty-three onwards, he would stand at the door reminding anyone unwise enough to visit the shop that he was about to close. At five-twenty-nine, the Lucozade sign would be turned around and an array of sliding bolts and mortice locks secured. Nothing gave H.T. Pearson more satisfaction than closing up, whether at the end of the day or (an even more enjoyable moment) at 1 p.m. on Wednesdays and Saturdays. When a late shopper appeared, pushing against the door a minute after closing, Pearson would not even acknowledge their existence with a glance. Denying access to those inefficient enough to ignore the clearly marked sign showing his opening hours afforded the shopkeeper a small shudder of satisfaction. Now and then, an irate individual might stand outside the door, gesticulating, tapping her watch, striding up and down in front of the shop window in an attempt to catch his attention. Pearson would pointedly retire to his storeroom.

Yet today had been different. H.T. Pearson tidied the confectionery, hearing childish voices, seeing eager ink-stained hands scrabbling for lovehearts and jelly beans, carefully signing the petition on his counter. A children's crusade! It made him proud to be a Burthorpian. He ran his great shiny fingers down the list of names, each one of them representing the youth, the hope, the future of his village. They looked up to him, these children, they respected and felt close to him. And, by God, he felt close to them with all their innocence and idealism. There was nothing like a good cause to capture young minds, and this was more important than any protest against fur or animal experimentation, more relevant than any attempt to Save the Whale. Over our dead bodies!

How would he present himself for the *Diss Press* interview? A Pied Piper, perhaps. A man of principle. At the end of the day, this was all about something good and old-fashioned, he would tell Rose Hope, something that the children of Burthorpe understood. He saw himself posing for photographs with some of his young campaigners. He closed his eyes, imagining his hands resting lightly on one each side of him, fingertips in the small valley between their shoulders and collarbones. Trusting, slender bodies leaning against him, their warmth penetrating the thin cotton of their school uniforms. (None of these new school trousers, he would casually insist. This is a protest for traditional values.)

H.T. Pearson felt his breath coming rapidly now, the familiar tingle of need emanating from within the heavy white combinations he wore beneath his shiny dark grey flannel trousers. It was time for relaxation. Humming to himself, he drew down the blind on the shop window. He emptied the till of notes (the change could wait), and made his way upstairs. Briskly, he opened the safe in his bedroom, placed the day's takings on the top shelf where he would count them later. Then he unlocked a small door beside the bathroom which led, by a narrow twisting staircase, to what Pearson described to himself as his 'snug'. Visitors to his flat (that is, Joyce Hubbard, the cleaner) had never been invited to this small room at the top of the house; it was where the most private H.T. Pearson, the true H.T. Pearson, resided.

There was a perceptible change of gait as Pearson crossed the small room to the dormer window and glanced briefly on to the road below. Downstairs he moved with elephantine self-importance, a careworn droop to his shoulders; now there was a tiptoed skittishness to his walk. He opened a small cupboard and removed the uniform, which he laid carefully on the bed. As he changed, he imagined his great crusade setting off for 10, Downing Street in a van from the village green, twenty hand-picked children between twelve and fifteen under the care and guidance of their leader, H.T. Pearson. He reached into a drawer beneath the large TV set in one corner of his snug and took out a cassette which, moving with a whirl and a rustle of nylon, he inserted into the video system. He sat on the bed, eyes fixed on the blank screen.

Traditional values. In a London hotel, he would go to the girls' bedroom and chat to them about the temptations of modern life. He could see them now, their neat white sheets tucked up to their chins. He would explain to them about morality, about standing up for what you believed in, your basic principles. Then he would start discussing the sorts of things boys might ask them to do. One of them – that naughty little red-haired Teresa, perhaps – would laugh.

'What's so amusing, Teresa?'

H.T. Pearson stared at the blank screen, hands trembling, globes of cold sweat starting from his crimson brow and neck, a tepee of desire – no, a marquee – arising before him, almost obscuring the television set.

'You know what I do to naughty girls?'

He pressed the remote control.

This was how H.T. Pearson – on occasions such as this, an inspired director of desire – achieved a level of ecstasy rarely experienced in Burthorpe. Having pushed the wheezing engine of private fantasy into life, he would help it gather speed by running one of his videos (today it was an old favourite, *Naughty Nymphets Through the Looking Glass*) on screen. The combined effect, an irresistible melding of thought and picture, little Teresa doubling with a hulking blonde porno model, involved a complex feat of the imagination unmatched by even our greatest filmic choreographers.

ANNA, *a slatternly eighteen year old dressed implausibly in gymslip and T-shirt, has been playing squash with* ULRIKA, *a lardy brunette. They are returning to the changing-rooms. After their exertions, their shirts adhere damply to their absurdly large breasts. They are watched by the school plumber, a spotty youth with a wispy beard and a seventies haircut.*

(Teresa lies in her hotel bed, looking up in adorable trepidation at the leader of the children's crusade, H.T. Pearson.)

ANNA: Boy, am I puffed! Well played, Ulrika! (*They both take off their T-shirts. The plumber ducks behind a pillar and watches.*)

(H.T. Pearson, smiling with mock anger, walks to the door. He beckons to Teresa. Nervously she gets out of bed.)

ULRIKA (*now naked*): I feel like a shower after all that running about, don't you?

ANNA (*taking off her gymslip*): Yeah, me too.

They both get in the same shower,

(H.T. Pearson explains to Teresa that naughty girls have to come to his bedroom. He takes her small hand. She pulls against him – such a rebellious little thing. Then she follows him out of the dormitory down the corridor. He squeezes her hand. She looks up and smiles. He had been right: she *is* a naughty girl.)

ANNA: Can you reach my back, Ulrika? Yes, that's right . . . Oh . . . Ulrika . . . Ah. (*Both girls gasp and laugh at the feel of one another's bodies. They rapidly become aroused. Unseen by the girls as they romp erotically together in the shower, the plumber takes his clothes off.)*

(Teresa is in H.T. Pearson's bedroom. He is talking to her about traditional values and explaining what happens to naughty girls. She is gazing up at him, afraid yet impressed by his authority.)

ULRIKA (*screams*): A man. I saw a man, Anna! (*The girls huddle together, pressing up against one another in the shower. The naked plumber steps forward, his back to the camera. ANNA and ULRIKA look at his face, then down. They are impressed.*)

PLUMBER: Can I help you with your soaping, ladies?

(H.T. Pearson, like a man in a trance, toys with the lower hem of Teresa's nightdress.)

'Ah,' Pearson gasped to himself as Anna, the Plumber, Ulrika and Teresa became a single object of inexpressible lust in his mind. His eyes ascended epileptically. The moment was approaching, now –

There was a knock on the door.

He lay on the bed, monstrously tumescent. Could that really have been a knock? Who could enter his house, let alone reach his snug?

Another knock. He stood and waddled uncomfortably to the door, in order to ensure that it was locked.

It opened. (*On the threshold stand Anna and Ulrika, back in their gymslips and T-shirts. They both look at his face, then down. They are not impressed.*)

ANNA: You are a foul, depraved old man.

H.T. PEARSON *backs into the room, holding his skimpy schooldress to him like a maiden aunt who has just seen a spider.*

H.T. PEARSON: Wh – who are you?

ULRIKA: We are the naughty nymphets. You know why we're here.

H.T. PEARSON (*backing away in terror*): F – free country. Traditional values.

ULRIKA (*shaking her head*): No way.

H.T. PEARSON: What do you want of me?

ANNA: Open the window, Harold.

H.T. PEARSON *opens the window.*

* * *

102

Tracy had lost her baby. It had been clear for some time that she would be unlikely to go full term – the doctor's face as he examined her last week, the way events, and scandals and rumours around her seemed to have been suspended over the past few days as if the world was holding its breath for the news that we all dreaded. When Dave went to Mothercare and spent his entire wage packet on baby clothes, all hope was lost. It was handled sensitively – anxiety, then pain, then a desolate realisation flickering across Tracy's pale but eloquent features. 'Dave,' she had said. 'I think something's going wrong.' That was a minute ago. They were in the hospital now. A doctor had just said, 'I'm very, very sorry.' It was over. Tracy and Dave clung to one another as if they were both drowning in life's pitiless swell. Oh Dave. Oh Tracy.

Alison Turville reclined on the sofa, a handkerchief in one hand a glass of gin and tonic in the other, her face, her eyes, her nose streaming with grief. Matthew was working late. Stephen was with friends. Kate was listening to her new record upstairs. The credits were rolling now, accompanied by a muted version of the series's theme tune, played in a minor key to mark the solemnity of the occasion. Alison stood up, switched off the television, then slumped back on to the sofa, once again wracked with sobs.

It wasn't like her at all. Over the past month Alison had found herself ambushed by sudden emotion at the most unlikely moments. Not only soap operas, but TV documentaries about pensioners, or the homeless, or refugees, a few bars of 'Close to You' sung by Karen Carpenter, the sound of a songthrush warbling bravely in the orchard. Last week she had suddenly found herself awash with tears while watching Mr Motivator, a muscle-bound black man who appeared on mid-morning TV, filmed leading a group of office workers and schoolchildren in a rhythmic devotional dance to the god of aerobics. It wasn't Mr Motivator that had moved Alison so profoundly. It was the plump, grinning, wobbling, uncoordinated members of the public who swayed behind him in time to the music, mesmerised with pleasure and self-consciousness. Those poor, hopeless fucking losers whose idea of achievement was to appear on television as a backcloth to Mr Motivator. Her heart ached with pity for them. What had the rest of life to offer if this was a high point? She wept for them, for the world, for herself.

Alison walked into the kitchen. She took the lemon out of her drink, sucked the juice of it, then threw it into a bin. As she poured the rest of her drink away, she caught her reflection in the dark window above the sink. There were those who envied her blonde hair, the fact that, after two children, she still had a waist. Her marriage was intact, her house a perfect balance between comfort and aesthetic appeal, her children were healthy and loved her. From Kate's room, she heard the sound of Craze, an all-boy group whose cleverly marketed good looks and bland music had captivated an entire generation of girls at primary school. With her right hand, Alison tucked her hair behind her ear. She touched the wisp of blonde moustache at the corners of her mouth. Life, surely, was good. Even if she did have a husband with a secret life, it was a small, unthreatening secret; he was a caring father. His career was developing. Briefly she saw the family as others might see it. House, job, marriage, children, future: what could be wrong with that?

Yet something was wrong. At this very point when so many of her problems seemed to be receding, she felt trapped, as if some essential, momentous event were approaching and, frightened, elated, she could do nothing to avoid it. Over the past few weeks, she had found herself, almost unconsciously, ordering her life so that the demands and routines of daily existence coincided as rarely as possible with those of her husband. He, absorbed in his work, did the same, so that now they were like two creatures forced to occupy one habitation who avoided skirmishes and stand-offs by following paths and channels that never met. These days, the Turvilles' discussions were of practical matters, family or financial problems which creaked under the burden of a larger, unspoken misery. For a while, Matthew had tried to keep alive their Sunday morning trysts, but Alison shrank from him, as if he were infected by some highly contagious disease.

Even when he was away from the house, his presence remained, oppressive and irritating. Odd shoes left lying around under beds and behind doors, the casual territorial markers of a man used to having a woman in his wake, clearing up. The dark suit, white shirt and tie that hung behind the door, like an empty, imitation Matthew, ready for the the next 'call', the next 'visit'. The bowl of mints on the hall table, there to disguise the smell of whisky on his breath if he was called out during the evening. Alison had tried so hard in the past to see Matthew's work as a profession much like any other, but it had worn her down, this pervasive death-consciousness, the knowledge that every neighbourhood mortality was a small business opportunity. So much of their daily life had been contaminated – hymns on the radio, villagers on their way to church at St Botolph's, flowers, the obituary pages in the newspapers, disaster reports on the television news. And always the telephone, ringing day and night with more grief, more tears, more work. Without apparent effort, Matthew would move into character, his gestures becoming slower and more caring, his voice taking on the low timbre of heartfelt, professional sympathy, as he prepared to leave Yew Tree Cottage and go about his dull, deathly business, a fucking Extra Strong mint in his mouth.

Perhaps, Alison thought, she would go to London for a day – wander among the crowds, enjoy the anonymity, the occasional glances of casual enquiry from passing men. Or join a local group, go to a night class. She had tried that twice already – once when, with vague creative thoughts, she had joined a writers' circle, a group of cheerful pensioners who wrote stories about the war years. Then, a year after abandoning literature, she had been invited by Araminta Winterburn to a local women's group. She had found, somewhat to her surprise, that lesbianism was a popular option among several of her more intellectual friends in the area. It was explained to her how the experience of same-sex relationships was largely a political act, an expression of personal liberty. Feeling freakish and old-fashioned, she had left early.

Through the ceiling above her head, she heard the banal, seductive computer rhythms of Craze's latest hit as it faded, then paused briefly, then recommenced as if Kate was trying to learn every thud and squeak of it off by heart. Alison went upstairs and opened the door to her room.

Kate sat on her bed, surrounded by gaily coloured fragments of material. In her hand was a pair of scissors.

'Kate? What are you doing, love?'

The small, solemn figure continued cutting, blinking now and then behind her thick glasses. 'Don't like ponies,' she said.

'Oh shit.' Alison stared at Kate's new blind, which hung in rags as if a storm of razors had passed through it. 'What on earth have you done?'

'Taken the ponies away.'

Alison saw that the scene portrayed on the blind, that of a busy county show, had had all equestrian activity excised.

Kate held up a piece of fabric on which a small bay animal had somehow remained intact. 'This is Friendly,' she said. She cut the material in half.

For a few seconds Alison stood at the door, caught between parental rage and pity. Then she sat down beside her daughter and put her arm around the small shoulders, hunched angrily against the world. The mocking jauntiness of Craze continued until Alison leant across and switched off the cassette machine. She ran her hand over the fragments of blind, eventually finding a pony that was still intact.

'There you are,' she said. 'Surely this one's Friendly, isn't it?'

The child took the piece of cloth and stared at it, as if considering the question. Then, with dry-eyed seriousness, she put it under her pillow.

'Bath and then bed, I think.' Alison stood up, and took Kate by the hand. 'Let me tell you about something that happened when I was a little girl.'

They walked slowly along the corridor, Alison talking quietly all the time, conjuring up pictures of a lost, golden age of childhood when another child had felt bewildered and alone. The stories continued hypnotically as, in the bathroom, Kate allowed herself to be washed like a baby. 'And yet here I am,' Alison said at one point. 'Look at me now.'

Kate stared at the figure kneeling beside the bath, as if, even without her glasses, she saw far more than any six year old should see. In that moment's silence, Alison almost expected her to say, 'Yes, look at you. Can you wonder that I cut up curtains?' But the little girl remained silent, pushing a yellow plastic duck under the water and holding it there.

From downstairs, they heard sounds of movement. 'Daddy's home,' said Alison, standing up and drying her arms on a towel. 'I'll be back in a moment.'

Matthew was pouring himself a drink. 'Sorry I'm late,' he said without looking up. 'The police seem to have cordoned off the village. Had to drive round the back route.' Then, sensing suddenly the air of dislocation and crisis that hung about the house, he asked, 'What's happened?'

'Kate's cut up her pony blind,' said Alison in a low voice.

'Cut up?'

'Scissors.'

'Oh, for fuck's sake. I only just bought that thing.'

Alison took the glass of whisky from his hand. 'Go and clear up the room,' she said. 'Take down the blind and hang up the curtains from the spare room.'

'This is all I need,' muttered Matthew, his mind still full of Sarah's bizarre gynaecological problems.

'Just do it, Matthew. I'll tell you when you can say goodnight. Don't say a word about this to her.'

She returned to the bathroom.

As if stunned by the enormity of her actions, Kate fell asleep more easily that evening, her hand clasping the cloth pony under her pillow. Matthew and Alison Turville sat up late in the sitting-room, weighed down, as never before, by the burden of parenthood.

They talked of Kate's school, of the pressures on her to perform in exams, of her jealousy of Stephen's easy way through life, of ponies, of encouragement on the one hand and discipline on the other. They considered 'talking to someone', but quickly dismissed this idea. It was a family problem, to be resolved by the family, not by doctors or shrinks.

'Have you noticed how the idea of blame has gone out of the window these days?' Matthew said moodily at one point. 'Whether they're eighteen months or eighteen years, kids are never quite responsible for their own problems. It's always parents, or teachers, or social workers, or society, or life.'

'What?' Alison shook her head and sighed. 'You're not saying a six year old should be a responsible citizen prepared to stand on her own two feet, are you? God, I worry about you sometimes.'

'No, I know we're each the product of our background or' – Matthew waved his left hand wearily – 'whatever. But, when we were small, we had to sort things out for ourselves, didn't we? I mean, can you imagine cutting up curtains when you were six?'

'No.'

'And what would have happened if you had?'

'Some scene of traditional child abuse, I suppose.'

'Exactly. But maybe that was right. Perhaps all this parental anxiety, this assumption of our own guilt, actually does more harm than good. If you're not responsible when you vandalise your own room, when *are* you responsible? Sometimes, when I look back to the way I was brought up, everything seems too easy for our children. It's handed to them on a plate.'

Alison stared at her husband as if seeing his true nature for the first time. 'Let me just get this right,' she said. 'You are now actually holding up your parents as models of child-rearing.' She gave a curt little laugh. 'The cane in the study? The locked door to your bedroom? All those battles over what you were going to do with your life?'

'I just think it's gone too far the other way. Our parents' generation was obsessed with punishment. We're afraid of it.'

From the hall outside, the telephone rang.

'Oh shit, someone's died,' said Alison, glancing at her watch. It was past midnight. 'On this of all nights.'

Matthew left the room, closing the door behind him. As he spoke on the telephone, Alison stared bleakly ahead of her. She thought of Mr and Mrs Turville – angry, disappointed pensioners living in Southwold – then of Stephen and Kate. She saw Matthew and herself standing between them, and wondered at the ease with which her husband now saw their generation as having achieved a higher level of civilized, sensitive and intelligent behaviour than the generation that had come before or that which was following behind. The old and the young – neither was somehow quite as evolved or sophisticated or sensible or grown-up as those now standing, proud but weary, on the pinnacle of middle age.

'Margaret Cowper,' said Matthew, returning to the room.

'At half-past twelve? Is she completely mad?'

'Apparently old Pearson's been found lying in the road – that was why the village was closed off. Fell out of his window.'

'Oh dear, poor old boy.' Alison sighed. 'Your suit's in the usual place.'

'Oh, he's not dead. They've taken him off to hospital in Norwich.'

There was silence in the room for a moment.

'If he's not dead, why exactly did Margaret ring?' Alison asked eventually. 'She doesn't seem like the gossipy type.'

'It's strange. She sounded odd – elated. Almost as if it was such great news it would make my night. Said something about his protest being no more.'

'*What*?'

'Bloody Pearson, she called him.'

'Gives me the creeps, that woman.'

'She works hard.'

'And she happens to be rather pretty.'

'Not bad. Colin Dunn's in love with her,' said Matthew sleepily. 'I wonder what made Pearson fall out of his window.'

'Pissed?'

'Yes. Suppose so.'

Miles heard the telephone receiver being replaced in the hall outside his office and glanced at his watch. 12.33 a.m. His new lodger had no discernible private life, never received calls. It was odd that she could find someone to call at this time of night.

He re-read the entry he had just completed.

DEATH, DOGS AND THE WEREWOLF MYTH: AN ANECDOTE

In 1723, the Duc d'Orléans died. While his heart was being removed (see HEART, BONES, ENTRAILS: TRIPLE POST-MORTEM DISLOCATION DOWN THE AGES), his Great Dane bounded into the bedroom and consumed 'a good quarter' of his master's heart.

Wolves, of course, have always been associated with death. When they roamed the forests of Europe, they were so frequently corpse-related sightings, graveyards, of course, being a ready source of food, that a mythology developed around them. It lives on today in tales of the werewolf. (See THE REVENANT AND IDENTITY: TOWARDS AN

Above his head, Miles heard the creak of a floorboard. Margaret had returned to her bedroom.

He hated gossip. The need to watch, to speculate, to pry into the darker corners of others' secrets was an aspect of village life that he had always regarded as intellectually and morally unacceptable. Rumour polluted fact, obscured reality with a haze of supposition and deferred longing. It was an item of faith, as far as Miles was concerned, that every individual had a right to live his/her life without his/her behaviour becoming the object of some tawdry spectator sport.

He hated gossip but he wanted to know more about Margaret Cowper.

Every morning she went to work with what he could only interpret as a sparkle of optimism and expectation in her eyes. Every night she returned, weary but strangely elated. She ate little but smoked adventurously, on one occasion even puffing at a cheap cigar she had bought at the village shop. Often he would catch her staring out of the window as mournfully as a prisoner dreaming of freedom. After dark, and no matter how cold the weather, she would sometimes go for long walks. On other occasions, she would go to bed early, firmly shutting the door behind her and – Miles noticed when he happened to pass her room – switching off the light. Jasper, his old cat, was less at ease with the stranger than his master was. Normally a sedentary and comfort-loving creature, Jasper had taken to living outside the house, returning only for meals which he ate quickly and warily.

Recently Miles had found himself entering the kitchen when Margaret was there in the hope of talking to her for a few moments. A sympathetic, quiet, if slightly humourless listener, she contributed little of herself to these conversations, but the fact that she imposed no value system, expressed no particular opinions, encouraged Miles to be uncharacteristically open about his own life. He would make casual reference to 'my friend in Norwich', discreetly pointing up the fact that, committed intellectual as he was, there was a romantic dimension to his personality. He had even allowed himself to hint at mild dissatisfactions, sources of impatience, with this friend in Norwich. So far, his hopes that Margaret would be encouraged to unburden herself (revealing, he secretly hoped, a heart in need of repair from a caring, worldly, sensitive older man) had not been fulfilled.

He stood up and walked slowly out of the study and upstairs. On the landing, outside Margaret's door, he hesitated. Then, with a sudden, furtive movement, he dropped to one knee and pressed one eye to the keyhole.

Margaret was fully dressed but shoeless. She was pacing up and down, puffing mechanically at a cigarette. Now and then, she would pause at the window and stare into the darkness outside. As Matthew watched, she stubbed out the cigarette and opened the window slightly. Decisively, like someone who is about to take a swim on a cold day, she peeled off her T-shirt, jeans and shoes. Soon she stood naked, lit by the single lamp by her bed. She gave a little shiver, then lay on the bed, stretched out straight on her back, palms upwards, her eyes staring at the ceiling. Breathing heavily now, she switched off the bedside light.

Frustrated by the darkness, yet horrified by what he had been doing, Miles stood up. He walked slowly downstairs, his mind teeming with visions of the slight figure, the glow of white with a smudge of darkness at its centre from which he had been unable to avert his eyes. He sat at his desk and gazed, unseeing, at the screen of his word-processor. He wrote nothing that night.

8

PONDERINGS

Our Thought for the Week comes from the Rev George Pardew, Vicar of Burthorpe

Someone once wrote that 'April is the cruellest month'. There will be those around our villages for whom the long, cold, dark month of February is the cruellest in the calendar. Nature seems to be a-slumbering, with no end of this long winter in sight. The robin redbreast on the bird-table. The hoary frost across the fields. The clear, still nights. How we long for that harbinger of spring, the snowdrop!

This February has been particularly oppressive for the folk of my own parish, Burthorpe. Two young teenagers have been taken from us in the prime of their life. Our beloved shopkeeper Harold Pearson has been grievously injured. Controversy concerning the so-called Chapel Meadow development has divided our community. Surely, as the Bard had it, the 'times are out of joint' – something is rotten in the state of Burthorpe!

This is not the moment to discuss the question of the new Garden of Remembrance. Suffice it to say that, in the kingdom of the Lord, there's 'a time and a place for everything'. At the end of the day, we need to consider very carefully whether 'change for its own sake' is always a good thing.

Perhaps then, and only then, this month of February may not turn out to be quite so cruel after all.

May your God be with you.

SCANDAL, DRAMA AND untimely death were so alien to the people of Burthorpe that the first instinct of villagers was to ignore the strange events that had been taking place. Darren Bugg, one of the dead teenagers, came from Garboldisham, so his fate impinged on them only marginally. Carol Power was generally thought to have been no better than she should be, the sort of girl who was anyway heading for trouble. If it was somewhat surprising that she had met her end beneath the branches of a falling elm tree on the outskirts of the village rather than in a crackhouse in South London, then Burthorpians were not about to quibble with detail. Frankly, she was asking for it, the way she carried on.

One might have expected that the accident to H.T. Pearson would have had a more marked effect upon the village – after all, there were few people who, short of a bottle of milk or needing to post a parcel, had not at some point made reluctant use of his Convenience Store but, oddly, Pearson was little missed. Groceries could be bought from Burthorpe Garage, now run by an Asian family; Post Office customers took to visiting the Fair Green branch in Diss. Although to a passer-by, the Convenience Store now seemed dusty, abandoned and inoperative, it had in fact changed little from the days when its proprietor was working there. These days, the shop merely had a permanent half-day-closing look to it.

Yet, while life continued in its normal, undisturbed way, there were few people in the village who were not subtly affected by these events. It was as if some vandal had placed two wholly unsuitable tableaux in an exhibition of local work, held at the church hall: there, among the agreeable still lifes and pastel landscapes, was Carol Power, her face forever affixed to Darren Bugg's private parts. Nearby was Harold Pearson, spread-eagled on the road, wearing, for reasons that still remained unclear, some form of skirt and displaying a noticeable absence of conventional underwear.

There was no escape from these visions. They adhered to the edge of the brain, undiscussed even in the public bar of the Greyhound, yet always there, reminders of something strange and out of control within the community.

The effect of injury and death, paradoxically, was to breathe more life into parts of the community. Errol Pryce decided that, if the travellers who were preventing development beyond the railway track were uninterested in his offers of money to move on, he would use more direct incentives. Simon Pygott signed the papers transferring Chapel Meadow into the partnership of Burthorpe Funerary Enterprises, and put Charlie down for Gordonstoun, having read in *The Times* that the Green Party had been invited to speak at Eton. The plumber Thurston Farr, finding that his ageing testosterone reserve had been strangely bestirred by recent events, paid three visits to the Squealer in one week and, while in a trance of post-coital muzziness, fell into a septic tank, from which he had to be rescued by one of Charlie Watson's farmworkers. Rose Hope felt a quickening of literary ambition within her.

One night in February, Rose parked the car on Railway Drive near Scrope Rise, from where one of Burthorpe's teenagers could be heard rehearsing a solemn one-note solo on his guitar. She stepped out of the car and walked slowly up the hill towards the main road and the Greyhound Inn.

Rose was unconcerned as to whether paranormal events had genuinely been occurring in the village or whether there was simply enough material to construct a plausible journalistic account to that effect – the line between reality and a good story had never been a powerful factor in her professional life. Her mind, increasingly preoccupied with thoughts of escape from this rural backwater, had fastened upon the idea of a story of true-life horror as the next great step forward in her career.

She entered the public bar at the Greyhound. One or two of the men seated around the gloomy room glanced up at her, their eyes betraying a wary curiosity. She ordered a spritzer from Carol Lownes who was standing behind the bar. Then, sitting on a barstool, she turned to take in the room, assessing where the liveliest source of information might be. She leant back, placing both elbows on the bar, crossed her long, spidery legs. It was a dull scene, this bar-room, but in her account of it, which in her mind was already a perfectly formed work of art, it would sing.

Rose recognised several people who sat, absorbed in their conversation, in the public bar. For a few moments she considered joining the contingent from Dick's Ducks, before she noticed Thurston Farr talking to the sinister builder Errol Pryce and his wife June. Thurston had attended to the occasional burst pipe at her house, Errol was an irregular and late-paying advertiser in the *DP*. Rose had not spoken to June Pryce, a sullen mountain of a woman, but then what she had seen of Mrs Pryce's social skills – monosyllabic answers, baleful glances at her garrulous husband – had never encouraged conversation.

'Thurston. Long time, no see.' Rose stood at the table, noting that the plumber's ginger toupee had an odd, electrified look to it, as if it had taken a recent chemical bath.

'Miss Hope.' Thurston nodded peremptorily.

'Could I join you?' Rose asked. 'I was supposed to be meeting someone but they seem to have stood me up.'

Thurston glanced in the direction of a nearby stool. Rose pulled it up and offered to buy the three of them a drink. Unsmiling, they accepted.

'So. Interesting times,' she said cheerily as she placed two pints of bitter and a large Scotch on the table. 'How goes the great Chapel Meadow debate these days?'

'It'll happen,' said Errol Pryce.

'Too many people got too much to lose if it doesn't,' said Thurston Farr.

'I don't know, I have a feeling poor old Pearson's accident might swing local feeling against it,' said Rose. 'And, with local elections coming up, the Planning Committee will be playing it safe. They've already got problems with the travellers on the station site.'

Like a slowly melting glacier, the conversation moved forward. Both men agreed that there was a new uneasiness in Burthorpe. Errol complained that the new crematorium would pollute the atmosphere. A friend of his lived in a village in which a mysterious grey substance had appeared, frosting the hawthorn hedges. 'Effluent from the old stiff ovens,' he said. 'Remains of people were settling on folks' heads and cattle. The smell of death was everywhere.'

Thurston Farr, whose profession had over the years inured him to all but the most unpleasant odours, nodded. 'This place will become a ghost town,' he said. 'People don't like death too near them. That's why cemeteries and graveyards were originally built away from houses. Who wants to live next door to corpses?'

'Property values.' June Pryce spoke up, looking angrily at her husband as if he had just insulted her. 'That's all we bloody need, isn't it?'

A distant look had entered Errol's eyes. 'Those gyppos have got to go,' he said. 'There's no place for people like that round here. It was when they pitched camp by the tracks that things started going wrong in Burthorpe.'

'What have the travellers to do with Matthew Turville's Garden of Remembrance?' Rose asked.

'The tree that nearly came down on me, remember that?'

They nodded.

'Whose motor bike had I been following? That little diddicoy bastard Dance. Then the teenagers – little Carol from Farthing Lane and Darren Bugg. Who goes down that path late at night? The same people who poach pheasant on the Garston estate, I'd say. Then there's poor old Harold Pearson – the most harmless man you'd ever care to meet. He only had one rule. No gyppos in his shop. Look what happened to him.'

'Evil eye,' said Mrs Pryce.

'They're behind it all,' said her husband.

Thurston Farr was making an odd humming noise to denote his uncertainty. 'Tinkers,' he said. 'There's nothing new in them visiting Burthorpe.'

'Tinkers?' Errol laughed, flashing his sinister white teeth. 'Wankers, more like. You're talking through your flybuttons, my man.'

'Eh?' The plumber looked down nervously. 'What d'you mean by that?'

'Enough said. I wouldn't want to, er, squeal on you.' Errol smiled nastily.

'Surely those people don't do much harm,' said Rose.

'They live by different rules.' Errol Pryce glanced at June's empty glass but sipped slowly at his own drink in the hope that the next round would be Farr's. 'No school. No rates. Scrounging this and that. And the police and social workers just leave them alone. Bloody scared of them, they are.'

'You're not actually claiming that Naughty Boy Dance killed those teenagers, or pushed Pearson from the window, are you?' asked Rose, mildly perturbed that her paranormal project might prove to be misconceived.

'I've seen some funny things down there is all I'm saying. They're incomers and, once you let incomers into a village and let them play by their own rules, to hell with the community, then things start going wrong. One way or another it happens.'

'There's certainly a strange atmosphere in the village,' said Thurston Farr.

Errol nodded. 'He's noticed,' he said to Rose. 'We've all noticed. You need to know the village to feel it.'

'They've got funny powers, odd habits, those people,' said June Pryce. 'It's all voodoo-hoodoo. I've heard all sorts of things about what goes on down there.' She pushed her glass forward, as if such a long speech deserved some kind of reward. 'Comings and goings, if you know what I mean.' .

Thurston Farr stood up hurriedly. 'My round,' he said rather too loudly. 'Same again?'

'So what's the solution?' Rose asked Errol after Thurston had made his way to the bar. 'If the police and the social services are doing nothing – '

'And the press is worse than useless.'

Rose smiled diplomatically. 'It's not our job to hound people from the area.'

'It's never anyone's job, is it?' said Errol. 'But, I tell you, if someone doesn't do something about that bastard Dance, it'll be done for them.'

'Done? How d'you mean?'

'Community action,' said Errol. 'Difficult for folk like you to understand how it is round here. We're proud of our village. We don't take kindly to some gaggle of black-toothed morons wandering in and upsetting the order of things. We don't stand by and watch.'

'Village people,' murmured Mrs Pryce. 'We're just simple village people.'

Thurston Farr returned with the drinks.

I ate at table now. A few weeks after he had first taken me to his room, he entered the dining-hall one morning while I was

*polishing knives and cliftes for dinner. We shall need an extra
setting tonight, he said. You will sit at the end of the table and eat
with us. I turned and gazed at him in the way a woman may gaze
when she has shared with a man what he called the Lord's greatest
gift. I reminded him that John Clarke, the Rector of Wretham,
would be among the invited that night, that Master Clarke was
friendly with the Bishop of Norwich. He smiled. Let polehatchet
Clarke flap his silly lugs, he said. A fig for my hallowed
reputation. Then, standing more closely, he whispered into my hair
that the world should know that I was his Meg, his make, and he
touched me so that I stopped polishing. Redeless to tell him that
his was not the only good name to be untwined were I to sit at the
head of his table.*

*He had a talent for spreading ease and good spirits wherever he
went. The guests gaured openly as I sat, eyes fixed on the plate in
front of me, in that noisy, good-humoured crowd of men, but
otherwise my presence was not acknowledged. Only when I stood
up to retire, leaving the men to their sack and conversation, was I
aware of being apposed as a woman, the rector's remedy, his
mutton. As I left the room, I was mindful of their lewd
imaginings, loosened by the drink they had supped.*

*It was not every night that he required my presence in his bed.
Perhaps one night in three would he feel the need for my company.
Sometimes when, as he said, the Muse was upon him, he would
write his words late into the night, waking me with a heavy hand
on my shoulder. Meg, come, he would say with the husk of need
in his voice, and sleepily I would follow him to his room.
Handmaiden to the Muse, he called me once.*

*And so it continued until Joseph announced his arrival into our
lives.*

As if it all wasn't complicated enough, Simon Pygott was now
confronted by one of those damnably delicate questions that only
he, as the master of Garston Hall, could resolve.

He slept badly these days. Now that Jess found it difficult to walk
up the stairs and stayed by the library fire all night, he missed the dog's

weight on his bed, the occasional old man's groan he would make during the night. Simon often found himself staring into the darkness, thinking around the most unlikely subjects – women, Chapel Meadow, his father, selling the rest of the cattle to move into arable, the boys. Sometimes he would switch on the radio and half-listen to a story or an interview with some actor fellow he had never heard of. Once he had gone so far as to ring Rose Hope to suggest she might let what he called bygones be bygones and pop over to the Hall for a bit of indoor sports right now. She had been really rather curt, using various terms which, old-fashioned as he was, he found faintly shocking coming from a woman, even at three in the morning.

So, one day late in February, he had awoken soon after six and had lain in bed trying to understand an item about wheat quotas on the farming programme. Then he had a bath, shaved, and made his way downstairs to the library.

Because Jess's tumour had now broken through the skin of his stomach, forming a crater of glistening white and pink, there was a distinct whiff of rotting flesh in the library. The old dog had left his basket during the night and was stretched on the carpet by the fire. When Simon spoke his name, he thumped his tail once, a nominal gesture of politeness, but failed to lift his head, only occasionally blinking his dull, dark eyes. Simon went to the kitchen to fetch a saucer of milk.

There he happened upon a scene of surprising domesticity. On each side of the kitchen table, enjoying a cooked breakfast and a pot of tea, were Jaime and a worried-looking young man with dark curly hair and a white open-necked shirt. Although Simon had no objection to Jaime allowing his friends to stay, there was something odd about this particular friend – perhaps the way he sat facing Jaime, perhaps the casual way his tie and the jacket of his suit hung over the back of his chair. There was an intimacy in the air which made Simon feel faintly uneasy.

'Ah, Jaime.' He stood at the door. 'I was after a spot of milk for the old dog.'

'Yes, Mr Pygott.' Jaime stood, walked to the fridge. As he poured the milk Simon smiled coolly at the guest. 'How d'you do,' he said.

'Hullo there.' At least the man had the grace to look embarrassed. 'I'm Derek.'

'Oh good.' Simon turned to Jaime. 'You should have told me you had a friend staying. He could have used one of the rooms at the top of the house.'

'It's all right, Mr Pygott.' Jaime handed the saucer of milk to Simon. 'Derek stayed with me in my flat.'

'Ah. Bit cramped, I would have thought. In fact, surely there's only one – Ah.' Simon looked from one man to the other, realisation slowly dawning.

'It's no problem,' said Jaime. 'You want me to take the saucer to Jess?'

'No, thank you.' Simon tried to invest his voice with heavy disapproval. 'I can manage.'

Bloody *hell*. Simon walked slowly across the hall, his eyes fixed on the saucer of milk he was carrying. He had always assumed the butler was a bit of a left-footer, a bit of what he called a shirtlifter – he was Spanish, after all – but really, tucking into breakfast with his boyfriend at the Hall itself was too much. Last month, he had vaguely mentioned to Susan that he had some pretty firm suspicions about Jaime but she had been remarkably unperturbed, turning those devastating eyes on him and saying, in words of ice, 'Welcome to the modern world, Simon.'

The modern world. So that's what one's own staff getting up to all sorts of business in the servants' quarters was called, was it? The modern world. Recently, Simon had seen rather too much of the modern world for his liking. For centuries, ordinary people, with all the tiresome problems that ordinary people tended to have, had been invited into the Hall once or twice a year – at Christmas or when beating the bounds at Rogationtide. Today they were at the gates, in the grounds, sneaking up the backstairs. It seemed to Simon that this modern world was like some ghastly infection which, if resisted at one point, would reappear in an entirely different form somewhere else. Councillors complained about his plans for Beggar's Hill Wood. Chapel Meadow was soon to be a final resting place for corpses from every walk of life. And now his butler seemed to be setting up home together with another man in the servants' quarters. It never used to be like this when chaps on the estate became involved in unsuitable liaisons. What were stables for? Or haystacks? Or hedgerows?

He walked slowly to the library and laid the saucer of milk by his dog's recumbent figure.

'There's bumming in the staff quarters,' he told Jess. 'Bad do, I'd say.'

The dog raised his head, and, twisting it, lapped messily at the milk before turning attention to the tumour on his stomach, which he licked with the earnest affection of a bitch cleaning her puppies.

From upstairs, Simon could hear the sound of the boys coming to life. Although it was half-term, they had become so used to rising early in the morning that, after a lie-in on their first day, they were usually downstairs by eight o'clock.

What if it had been they who had happened upon the romantic kitchen scene? Nothing wrong with a couple of chaps taking breakfast together, of course, but Simon worried about the way the old innocence was under siege, even threatening the boys one had taken the trouble to send to schools whose main purpose was to keep the modern world at bay for as long as possible. Not that, in the case of Charlie, his ruinously expensive prep school had managed even that small task. He had left home a slightly wet and tearful seven year old. Now he was a rip-roaring vegetarian conservationist who objected to everything the Pygott family had always held dear. These days, Charlie chatted to Jaime almost as if he were a friend rather than a butler.

No, he would have to say something. He was already worried about Charlie – frankly the idea that he might turn out to be, not only a nutcrunching lefty, but a bit of a Derek too, was simply unbearable. Simon gently pushed Jess's head away from the cancer, but the dog resisted with a low growl.

'Derekism,' he said despairingly to the dog. 'Exists at boarding-school, of course it does. Old Dicky Montagu was a complete and utter tart when we were at Eton, and look at him now – chairman of his own firm of stockbrokers, wife and children in tow, what I call the whole caboodle.'

Jess gazed at him without particular interest.

'But there's a world of difference between young chaps of like backgrounds horsing around together in a dormitory and Jaime and Derek at each other under one's own roof. Bloody *bloody* hell.'

It was going to be yet another problem to keep him awake at night. Maybe before Charlie went to public school this autumn, there'd have to be what he called a serious conversation between them.

'Charlie,' he murmured to himself. 'Now, er, Charlie. Something I've been meaning to tell you. Um, now, you may find some mornings when you wake up, or even during the day sometimes, you have certain thoughts or maybe one of the other boys has shown you a picture – you know what I'm talking about, don't you – girls, birds, with their things all, well, hanging out. Now what I'm saying is that, now and then, Charlie, what I call your old man might suddenly . . . stand to attention. And . . .' Simon closed his eyes, the day's first wave of tiredness sweeping over him. 'And when your old man stands to attention, things can get a bit scrambled, complicated. Because – '

'Dad? Are you all right?' Charlie stood at the door to the library.

'Oh, morning, Charlie.' Simon sat up in his chair. 'Just chatting to Jess. Had breakfast?'

'Yes. Jaime's friend Derek cooked us an omelette.'

'Derek, yes. That's excellent. Where's Jeremy?'

'He's gone out to murder some fish.'

'Good show. What are you going to do?'

'I thought I'd read my book. Keep Jess company.'

'Old dog.' Simon smiled in the direction of the Labrador. 'What a kind thought. Still, nice morning out there. Seems a shame to sit inside, not taking exercise.'

'I won't be long. I'll just read for a while.' Charlie sat down in one of the armchairs and opened his book.

'Don't you think there's a time and a place for reading?' Simon picked up an old copy of *Vogue* which Susan had left in the library during her last visit, and leafed idly through its pages. 'Before bed, by the seaside on hols, when you've done your prep. Awful pity to waste a lovely morning. Get a bit of fresh air, shake your liver up. That's what I'd do.' Seeing his son was absorbed in his book, Simon put down the magazine. 'What you reading, old boy?'

'It's called *Ring of Bright Water*,' said Charlie. 'It's all about otters.'

'Used to be otters in the Waveney. Hunted down as vermin in the old days.'

'That's probably why there are none left.' For a moment, there was silence in the library. 'When will Jess have to be put down?' Charlie asked in a more conciliatory tone.

'I doubt if he'll be here if you come back home for Easter holidays.'

'Poor Jess.'

Perhaps, Simon thought, it wasn't the moment for the speech about Derekism and old men standing to attention. 'Ready for Common Entrance?' he asked.

Charlie stared at the pages of his book. 'Yes,' he said quietly.

'You'll have the greatest fun at Gordonstoun.'

'Yes.'

'Jeremy's dead jealous.'

'Dad, I don't want to talk about it.'

'The great thing about a place like Gordonstoun is that it gives you a sense of independence – lets you discover your own mind about things.'

'I am independent.'

'Independent in the wrong way, old boy,' said Simon briskly. 'Stand on your own two feet, live in the real world.'

'Dad, I spend most of my life in a boarding-school,' said Charlie. 'It doesn't exactly seem like the real world to me.'

'Can I give you a bit of what I call fatherly advice?' Simon spoke more sharply than he had intended. 'There's no need always to walk out of step with the rest of the world, you know. Only makes trouble for yourself. Rather a boring habit at your age, to tell the truth. Can't think where you picked it up.'

It was his mother, of course. Simon saw Susan all too clearly in Charlie. The only difference was that while Susan's rebellion took the form of spectacular shopping sprees and going out to dinner with unsuitable young men, Charlie's led him towards any bleeding-heart cause that happened to be in fashion at the time. 'It really would be ghastly if you turned into the sort of boy who reached eighteen and was frightened of leaving home.' Simon spoke more gently. 'Anyway. None of my business. Just a worrying old dad, I expect. I think I'll put some ointment on this old dog.'

'I read the other day that one of the reasons why there's so much cancer is insecticides put on crops,' said Charlie quietly.

'Oh . . . *bunkum*, Charlie.' Simon slapped the arms of his chair. 'If you went out and actually looked around the farm rather than filling your head with all sorts of books and ideas, I'd have rather more respect for your opinions.'

Charlie lowered his gaze. 'It's not bunkum,' he said.

'There was a very good article in the *Field* the other day about country sports. I really think it would be worth your – '

'I don't believe in the *Field*.'

'Just *listen*!' Simon's voice echoed around the library, causing Jess to look up in mild curiosity. 'Sorry, old dog.'

Charlie stood up. 'I'll read upstairs,' he said quietly, then walked out of the library, head down, with quick, tortured steps.

'Just listen to your father,' Simon muttered to himself.

Lot of walking out these days, he reflected. Lot of closing of doors, slamming down of telephones. Chap tries to have a conversation with wife, girlfriend, son, pal, accountant, and, within a matter of minutes, it's all gone wrong. Raised voices, terrible, hurtful things begin said. Then off they went. Slam. Bewildering, that.

Another thing he couldn't help but notice. No one seemed to take him seriously. In the old days – surely he couldn't be imagining this – people used to have a certain respect for one's views, one's position in the world. They listened, they nodded, 'Too right, Simon,' they'd say. Laugh at his jokes. These days, it was as if the world was still sharing a joke but it was one from which he was excluded. His wife. The chaps selling him farm machinery. Freddie Pierpoint. Rose. Even Jaime. There was that smirk in the voice, that hint of cheekiness with which his fags at Eton used to address him. 'Are you being nervy, boy?' he used to ask them. 'No, Pygott.'

Couldn't say that these days. Are you being *nervy*? Wouldn't do.

It wasn't possible, was it, that he was the joke, always had been, always would be? Simon tried to distract his mind from this disturbing thought by reading the copy of *Vogue* but, such was his gloom, even the dreamy-eyed models in their wispy, expensive clothes seemed to look up from the page and mock the master of Garston Hall.

'You seem unhappy this evening.'

Margaret sat at the kitchen table, her hands around a mug of tea as if her whole body were drawing heat from it.

Casually, Miles opened the lid of the kitchen Aga and confirmed that it was full. Glancing down at his lodger, he experienced one of those lurches of the stomach, those breath-stopping, mouth-drying moments that surprised him even when he was prepared for them. 'Unhappy?' he said, trapped by the grey eyes, the half-parted lips, the downward curve of the narrow neck and, just visible beneath her loose T-shirt, the soft snowdrift swell of a breast. 'No. I was thinking about my plans for tonight.'

'You work too hard.' Margaret exhaled softly to cool her tea and, for the first time, Miles noticed that an odd whiff of something not entirely pleasant was carried on her breath.

'I'm not working. At least, not in the normal sense. I'm going to Norwich. Romantic duty.'

'I see.'

Did she? He was not sure that even he did. He had been seeing Dr Katherine Porter for the past five years, during the last two of which it had dwindled to an event that took place, more or less without fail, once a week. They had never officially been a couple, an unspoken agreement having somehow been established between them that, professionally, it was preferable to be seen as single and independent.

In the end, theirs was an arrangement of sexual comfort. For Katherine, he supposed, his visits provided a brief weekly thaw to her arctic ecosystem. As for Miles, the thought of no intimacy, no touch, no opportunity to step from the cerebral to the physical, had, until now, been more painful than any mild sense of futility that nagged at him after the event. He had read somewhere that men of middle years lacking sexual outlets ran a higher than average risk of prostate cancer in later life, information which had given his visits to Dr Porter a practical, muesliesque focus.

Their evenings would follow a predictable pattern – chat, some dinner, low lights and alcohol. Soon after nine, they would move to Dr Porter's perfectly ordered bedroom where, on her perfectly ordered sheets, they would make love, either in silence or with the light, ironical banter of the emotionally disengaged. At some point, Dr Porter would seem to make up her mind that this had gone on long enough and, arranging Miles upon her strong,-broad body like a hostess straightening a vase on her shelf, would achieve her weekly climax.

Unbidden, memories of his last visit to Norwich returned to Miles. Even during their early days together, Dr Porter had betrayed a certain post-coital restlessness, as if the generally accepted period of transition from the sexual to the non-sexual, the few minutes of touch and easy conversation, was just too slow for her; after little more than a minute, she would reach for the research paper which invariably lay on the bedside table and start to read, one hand trailing on his body for a few moments before that too was gone. But last week, when Katherine had been noticeably preoccupied by a forthcoming field trip to Ellesmere Island, had been far worse. Miles's moment of post-climactic mellowness had been shattered by an earthquake beneath him, a sudden, convulsive, upward twitch, followed by a deft pelvic swerve, which had effortlessly dislodged him, like a rookie cowboy catapulted out of the saddle at a rodeo. Face down in the sheets, Miles had lifted his head to see Dr Katherine Porter sitting up in bed, scribbling urgently on a pad.

'Yes, that's it.' He spoke out loud the words she had muttered to herself as she wrote.

'Maybe you should go out tonight.' Margaret was gazing at him as if she could understand his thoughts as clearly as any words.

'No, we don't do much of that. We . . . stay in.' Miles smiled sadly. 'To tell the truth, I wish I weren't going.' He hesitated, longing to add that he would prefer to spend the evening here with her, but the words froze in his throat. 'I have so much work to do,' he said.

'Me too,' said Margaret.

'Work? At night?'

'Yes. Do you know Sarah Dunn, the estate agent?'

'I've met her. I had no idea you were working together.'

'We have a project.'

As evening descends on Burthorpe, normal human sounds – the conversation of two women visiting a grave at St Botolph's, the laughter of children playing football on the green – give way to something more electronic and other-worldly. The air is thick with the whispers of a hundred television sets, the squawks and bleeps of computer games at the Greyhound, the hiss of rubber on wet tarmac as cars pass through the village at speed, the occasional stuttering chord from Gary Preston's guitar, the distant, nagging call of an unanswered telephone. It's as if Burthorpians have taken to their beds, surrendering the village to mechanical versions of themselves.

Few people knew the shadowy comings and goings of the village better than Errol Pryce. Because the activities of humans impinged directly upon property values and the availability of building material, he liked to wander about the streets and lanes, noting which lights were illuminated, who was visiting whom, where illness, or marriage, or death presaged an addition to the Burthorpe house market. Tonight, though, he was no longer merely watching.

Dutch Voight was ideally suited for the project Errol had in mind. A small, irritated man with (his only vanity) dyed black hair, Voight looked at the world sideways under heavy frowning eyebrows. A stranger might assume from Dutch's manner that he was a dangerous, sly cut-purse of a man; those who knew him saw him for what he was – a clumsy innocent whose glowering mien was no more than a social defence against a world that he had come, quite rightly, to distrust. Only occasionally did he misbehave, usually in late summer when, taking a holiday from Dick's Ducks, he would work on the harvest and get drunk at the end of the day. During that crazed fortnight, he would invariably become involved in a fight at the King's Head in Diss, and pay a visit to the Squealer for his annual sexual adventure, an experience so horrifying and traumatic that the dull glow of his libido would be doused until the following August when the process would be repeated. In crueller, more honest times, Dutch would be described as the village idiot.

'Lately?' He stood twenty yards from the Burthorpe Service Station, a hunched, evasive figure.

'Evening, Dutch,' said Errol.

'Lately?'

'Yes.' Errol had never enquired as to what Dutch's greeting signified, but he imagined the question had some grim sexual connotation. Certainly it required an answer for, until Dutch had ascertained whether or not you had lately done whatever he had in mind, he was liable to repeat the question, like the needle on a cracked record.

'Yes, lately,' said Errol. 'You bet.' He pointed down the road in the direction of Botesdale. 'I've parked the wagon on Railway Drive.'

The two men made their way towards the black van, pulled back the slide doors and sat for a moment in the darkness.

'We'll drive around for a bit, check the lie of the land,' said Errol. 'I reckon we'll make our move at about ten-thirty.'

'Railway Drive,' said Dutch.

Errol started the van. For twenty minutes, they patrolled the village. Occasionally, Errol had noticed, DC Penman of Eye Police would make a tour of Wortham, Roydon, Palgrave and Burthorpe. While the policeman was almost as easily outwitted as Dutch Voight, there was no point in taking unnecessary risks.

'Church. School. Mellis four miles.' Dutch commented quietly on the passing scene, as if committing it to memory. 'The Greyhound Inn. Camelot Carvery. Tuesday is happy night for happy knights. Pond.'

They turned down the hill past Scrope Rise. Errol pulled into the side of the road, switched off the engine and lights.

'Railway,' said Dutch conversationally. 'Pony.'

In the dim light emanating from a semi-circle of caravans, the travellers' encampment seemed harmless enough. A hairy piebald nag, head lowered in sleep, stood on a patch of grass near the tracks. From a bonfire on the wasteground that had once been Burthorpe Station, a thin plume of smoke rose lazily to disappear into the black sky. Reminders of daytime children's games – a plastic football, a hoop, two brightly painted skittles – lay in front of the caravans. Now and then, a large mongrel barked, shifting restlessly under the one horse-drawn cart in the group.

'Like ponies.' Dutch sniffed and wiped his nose with the back of his hand.

'Don't worry about the pony, old partner.' Errol glanced nervously at Dutch. The last thing he needed at this moment was an outbreak of scruples or rural solidarity from his colleague. 'We're not worried about him, are we?'

Dutch was gazing expressionlessly at the encampment.

'No, it's the bloody scroungers we're after, isn't it, Dutch?' Errol pointed to the ice-cream van. 'That little bastard in there. Doesn't go to school. Just wanders around the village, stealing as he goes. He's like a little rat, isn't he? Something bad happens, you turn round, and you just know it's that fucking Naughty Boy Dance, but where is he? Slipped back down his fucking rathole.'

'Fucker,' said Dutch, glowering with rage.

'The police want him, don't they? The social, too. But their problem is they play by the rules. Our little friend Naughty Boy wouldn't know a rule unless he was hit around the back of the head with it. Got to play by his rules, we have, Dutch. Give him a good blistering. It's the only language that little bastard understands.'

'Hit him round the head, good blisterin'.' Dutch spoke mechanically, either reminding himself of the job in hand or – it was difficult to tell – framing a question.

'Just a bit of direct action,' said Errol Pryce. 'A reminder that he's outstayed his welcome in Burthorpe. Calls himself a traveller. Well, it's time he fucking travelled. The others will follow him sure enough. It'll set an example, won't it?'

'That will. That fucking will and all.'

The door to the blue caravan opened. Walter Rusk, one of Charlie Watson's older farmworkers, emerged, hitching up his baggy trousers as he went. 'The Squealer,' said Errol. 'Never stops, that woman.'

Dutch looked away, down the railway track, as if his mind had suddenly filled with unwelcome memories.

'He'll come out at ten-thirty,' said Errol. 'Takes his mountain bike and heads for the fen. That's where we'll get him.'

'Naughty Boy.' Dutch laughed, an unearthly sound like the scraping of a knife along rusted metal. 'Fuckers.'

By ten-thirty, they were waiting behind a tree as Dance took the path from Burthorpe on towards Mileham Fen. The boy drove fast, apparently able to see his way in the dark. They heard him approach, the quiet rattle of metal, the chatter of the tape machine that filled his empty head with electronic music wherever he went.

Stepping forward, Errol jabbed the hazel walking-stick he had brought with him through the spokes of the front-wheel. Dance crashed to the ground where Dutch leapt on him, his knee pressing down on the boy's neck, his right hand grabbing Dance's hair, jerking the head backwards. Errol stood over the two of them and, annoyed that Dance had remained silent through the assault, thumped the back of his legs twice with the walking-stick.

There was no fight in Naughty Boy Dance. Errol tied his hands and elbows tight behind his back. When they pulled the skinny figure to its feet, Errol was irritated to find earplugs from a small tape machine were still in his ears. He tugged at the thin wire, then removed the machine from the pocket of Dance's jeans. He hurled it as far away into the darkness as he could. They bundled the boy into the back of the van, where Dutch sat on him, a Stanley knife held against his throat as he lay face down on the metal floor. Briefly, Errol considered backing the van over Dance's bicycle, but by now he was anxious to be done with the job. He carried it fifty yards and threw it into a stream.

He drove at a normal, casual speed past St Botolph's churchyard and into a turning off Bridge Lane, near the spot where Darren Bugg and Carol Power had met their end. He parked in a glade, switched off the lights, then climbed into the back.

'Time to talk, my man,' he said. 'Let the lad breathe, Dutch.'

'Little fucker.' Dutch Voight sat back against the side of the van, the hand that held the knife resting easily on his knee.

'Sit up,' said Errol, rather more roughly.

Naughty Boy Dance stirred, rolled on to his side. Then, with some difficulty, he pushed himself up against the van's spare tyre where he sat, arms uncomfortably behind his back, facing the two men. Dried mud from the floor of the van was embedded in his right cheek. The dark, unfocused eyes betrayed neither defiance nor fear, but a kind of holy resignation, as if this kind of event was always occurring to him.

For a moment, Errol Pryce found himself lost for words. He looked at this demon, this thief, this little bastard who flitted about Burthorpe like some fucking killer mosquito sucking out the lifeblood of the village, and saw no more than a scrawny, underfed apology of a little person. There was no avoiding it – for all his reputation, for all his quiet defiance, Naughty Boy Dance was still a child. Even Dutch was expressing a furtive embarrassment now, picking at a fingernail with his knife.

The boy looked at them both with unnerving directness, as if he understood what was in their hearts better than they did themselves.

130

'Time to talk,' said Errol quickly. 'You've got no friends in this village, boy. Nobody likes you. Nobody. In fact' – he paused reflectively for a moment – 'it's fair to say that we all hate you. You wouldn't disagree with that, would you?'

Dance said nothing.

'See, we just don't like people coming in from outside, setting up their Red Indian camp in our village, and going round robbing and stealing from ordinary, God-fearing folk. There's not one person in this village who, if they saw us now, would lift a finger to help you. Because tonight we're doing what everyone, every decent person in Burthorpe, has been wanting to do for a long time. We're teaching you a lesson. Not a school lesson, mind, not a police lesson – because you're not interested in them, are you, boy? – but a life lesson. A lesson in life. Tell me if you think I'm being unfair, Dance.'

The boy glanced at Pryce, briefly closed his eyes, then stared ahead.

'Dutch wanted to gag you. "What happens if he shouts?" he asked. Didn't worry me. You can holler your bollocks off for all it matters. No one cares. No one's going to help you. Even your own folk would be too pissed or frightened to lift a finger for you, fucking diddicoys. Then there's your mother – she has her hands full most nights, don't she?'

Dance muttered something.

'Sorry, boy. Didn't catch that.'

'Ain't got no mother,' said Naughty Boy Dance.

'No. Nor father, I expect. Don't go in much for family life, your lot, do they?'

Dutch Voight was showing signs of restlessness, as if the conversation was making him uneasy.

'Now this lesson Dutch here and I want to give you.' Errol smiled. 'It's very simple really. We want you to leave the village, Dance. Bugger off out of it. You don't really belong in Burthorpe – in fact, you probably don't belong anywhere – but we've put up with you for long enough. You may only be a little squirt but, if you move, the rest of them will follow soon enough. And if you don't, well, life will get unpleasant.'

In the darkness of the van, Dance seemed to nod. 'Can I go?' he asked.

'A lesson, I said. And that's not just words, boy. We're not the fucking social. It's time you had a bit more than a lecture and a pat on the head, eh, Dutch?'

Voight shook his head unhappily. 'That is,' he muttered.

'I want to get back,' Dance said quietly. 'I'm needed.'

'You'll get back, boy.' Errol leant forward until his beard almost touched Dance's face. 'You'll get back tomorrow.'

For the first time, the child showed signs of panicky resistance. Dutch held the Stanley knife to his throat once more as Errol reversed the van away out of the lane, then drove past the pond and the houses of Burthorpe to brick bungalows and sheds of Dick's Ducks. The two men unloaded Dance from the back of the van and, each of them holding an arm, marched him towards five low wooden duckhouses ranged in a row, like antique amphibian craft. They stood him before one of the pens. Errol, pulling a length of binder twine from his trousers, secured his legs together.

'D'you like animals?' he asked as he tugged the string tightly.

'Let me go home. I'm looking after someone.'

Errol stood up slowly. There had been a crack in Dance's voice, a sniffle, almost a sob. The eyes, Errol noticed, had filled with tears. 'Don't go blubbing on me now, will you, boy,' said Errol almost tenderly. 'Not when you're just about to get your lesson.' He nodded to Dutch, who pulled back a bolt and raised a door-sized latch in the low roof.

A clamour of crazed cheepings cut the night. Under the ghostly glow of ultraviolet lamps thousands of duck chicks swarmed and fell over one another, packed so tightly that it was impossible to see the floor.

'No,' said Dance. 'Please, sir.'

Errol grabbed the front of his T-shirt with both hands, manoeuvred him towards the opening over the seething mass of bird life, then lifted him. 'In you go,' he said cheerfully, pushing Naughty Boy Dance backwards. The child fell, crashing helplessly on to the soft, seething orange cushion.

They closed the latch, bolted it. There were no sounds of the ducklings now, only a series of thuds and tear-filled shouts as Dance flailed about within the chickhouse.

'Hope he doesn't squash too many of them birds,' said Errol, walking towards the van.

Voight glanced back unhappily.

'Don't you worry, my man,' Errol called out. 'I'll let him out at daybreak. You won't get into no trouble.'

Slowly, Voight followed him back to the van.

Dutch was restless that night. Long after Errol Pryce had left him at the cottage, he wandered through the village, thinking about what had happened and how it was that he always seemed to find himself involved in matters that made him unhappy, worried him when he was alone again, made him uncertain that he had done the right thing.

Soon after two in the morning, he found himself gazing over the railway track at the travellers' camp. Somewhere a baby was crying. It seemed to Dutch that the sound was coming from the ice-cream van of Naughty Boy Dance.

That morning, before it was light, Sarah Dunn drove through the village, in an attempt to clear her mind for the day ahead after her night spent with Superman. Her body still aching pleasantly from her exertions, she saw a slight figure making its way with uncertain steps down Railway Lane. It was Naughty Boy Dance, no doubt on his way home from some act of petty larceny. Sarah slowed the car, noticing that the back of his white T-shirt was covered in spots of dark red and what seemed to be some kind of yellowy fluff. As she passed, it occurred to her that his face was wet and blotched with colour, as if he had been crying. She accelerated away. She had problems of her own without worrying about Naughty Boy Dance.

Superman, in the context of Sarah's bed, and her body, was no dream. The term was not a nickname for Matthew Turville. It was the real man of steel who one moment during the previous evening had been engaged in light onscreen banter with Lois Lane on Sarah's screen, the next – after Sarah had allowed herself the briefest downward glance to the bulge in his blue suit, the merest nanosecond of erotic interest – he was there, standing before her, in her own sitting-room, very much in the flesh.

At first, Sarah had attempted self-censorship; had switched channels at the merest glimpse of a prospective bed-partner, but now she found herself succumbing willingly to her new, celebrity-filled secret life.

Superman, who had stayed the night, taking full advantage of Colin's presence in London, had not at all been as she had expected. Truth and justice played little part in his boudoir activities although – Sarah ran her tongue across her lips at the memory – he had been rather fond of the American way. He was, she reflected, as direct and dirty-minded as Tonto, or Robin Hood, or the Junior Minister for the Treasury who had – she blushed at the memory – appeared on *Panorama*.

These visits had been occurring for three weeks now. She merely had to experience the mildest of sexual thoughts towards some character appearing on a screen, and later that night, if she were alone in bed, he (or in the case, memorably, of the severe newscaster of *Channel Four News*, she) would join her. At first, Sarah had blamed stress or the effects of a course of anti-depressants she had received from Dr Gillette, but her visitors actually left evidence: a turmoil of sheets, her torn undergarments. Most alarming of all was the way that she felt. These encounters, she was forced to conclude, were no more dreamt than last month's vivid gynaecological problem had been. At first, she had been afraid. Then she found to her horror that she was becoming addicted to them. She moved into the spare bedroom, locking it behind her to avoid the danger of Colin surprising her in a moment of ecstasy with one of her many famous lovers.

She slept little. Her mind wandered while she was at work. Her body – this was the most alarming part of it all – had become a humming, tingling, yearning, keening instrument of desire, her skin feverish and sensitive. Sometimes, rocking back and forth in a sort of trance, she would search from channel to channel for a suitable partner. Such was her state of mind and body that her standards were slipping. Yesterday she had been visited by the smiling presenter of a daytime quiz show – his face against her skin had been papery from his TV make-up. Last week she had committed an act of startling intimacy on Scottie from *Star Trek*. There was no telling where it would end.

One of the first casualties of this surprising development in her private life had been her relationship with Matthew. When the visits had first occurred, she had attempted to deflect the erotic invasion by seeing her lover more often, breaking all the unspoken rules of an affair. She would call him at home, or blunder, almost weeping with lust, into his office where the dark-haired new secretary smiled knowingly at her, as if somehow she understood the sweet, churning agony of a woman on fire with need. Once Sarah had tried, halting and ashamed, to explain to Matthew how other men had entered her life, famous men, men of mythic proportions. His response had been a disconcerting mix of concern and relief. He took to discussing their children or the importance of friendship. Urgent appointments curtailed their meetings. Soon Sarah was finding that, beside the dangerous intensity of her nocturnal visits, making love to Matthew was becoming bedroom drudgery. His significance to her began to fade as if he, not her visitors, belonged to a lost fictional world beyond touch or feeling.

Matthew looked through the crack in the curtains and gave a silent, interior moan. She was there.

Nothing was simple any more. From the very moment that he had stopped seeing Sarah Dunn, he had found himself more besieged than ever. There were calls late at night – a single ring, then, when he picked up, the dialling tone, or an odd electronic hiss, like a call from a distant country on a faulty line. Sometimes, drawing the curtains at night or preparing for work in the early morning, he saw, or rather sensed, the presence of a figure in the shadows between the garden and the pond. Feeling besieged and guilty, he spent more and more time at his office where Margaret was there to screen his calls.

It had to be Sarah, he supposed. She denied any interest in him these days but clearly her grip on reality was loosening as she underwent some sort of mental or sexual crisis about which Matthew wished to know absolutely nothing.

Sighing again, he put his face closer to the windowpane. There was someone out there, he was sure of it.

'What sort of day is it?' Alison asked as she sat up in bed behind him.

'Cold. Miserable.' Matthew walked away from the curtains, down the corridor and into the bathroom.

He shaved, staring into the eyes of a man who had betrayed all the innocence and goodness around him, who had covered family memories, photographs, birthday parties, with the foul irremovable slime of his deception.

'What you thinking?' Kate stood at the door, watching him.

'Thinking of all the things I've got to do today,' he said, adding another small twig to the great bonfire of lies he had built beneath his family life.

'Boring,' said Kate.

Just one spark. Just one match. It was coming.

9

MERE TRAGEDY

A family of five ducklings and their proud mother were killed by a hit-and-run driver on Victoria Road on Monday afternoon. Mr Jim Foster, who has visited the Mere for many years and studies its birdlife, told the *DP* that the casualty rate had increased significantly with the amount of traffic going through Diss. 'This is just the tip of the iceberg,' he commented. 'Every spring we lose many birds to drivers passing through the town. People drive too fast. They just don't seem to care.' It is thought that a sixth duckling may have escaped but is unlikely to have survived.

DP *Comment – page 5*
Does Diss need a by-pass? Your letters – page 6
Spot the Duck Competition – page 13

I T OCCURRED TO Miles that his life might be entering a new and exciting phase, that the sun could be rising on an academic and possibly even an amorous Indian summer. Moving about his cottage, working on his book, cooking for Margaret (whose own new, bright sense of purpose Miles ascribed to a quickening of interest in himself), he felt more positive, more engaged than he had for many months. These days he left Burthorpe for the Anglia Institute with a sense of mild regret. At the end of the teaching day, he no longer hung around at the Union Bar, engaging in tetchy badinage with his fellow academics, but hurried home, his thoughts full of Margaret and the *Resource Handbook*.

For the first time for many years, he found himself looking back with a new honesty on the life whose stuttering progress, full of false starts and wrong directions, had nonetheless brought him to this point of opportunity and potential.

Until recently, he had been convinced that the disappointing second-class degree in sociology that, years ago, he had achieved at Sussex University could be explained by his involvement in casual sex, recreational drugs, radical politics, and other distractions of the time. Now he recognised that it had simply been post-adolescent torpor. Few, if any, of the contemporaries with whom he had kept in touch could recall doing sex or drugs or revolution with him and, while it was possible that they were out of their heads at the time, it seemed more likely that he was out of their heads, that he had been an anonymous, self-effacing youth with nothing exceptional about him.

During the seventies, Miles had dabbled in journalism, a career for which his temperament (seen by him as painstaking, by others as nit-picking) had rendered him peculiarly unsuitable. He had married a formidable and rather beautiful woman called Georgia in 1973 but, for reasons he still found baffling, she had accepted a job at Nanterre University shortly afterwards and had declined his offer to follow her. Today she ran a community for women painters in La Roche. As far as Miles could remember, they had become formally divorced at some point in about 1981.

For a long time during the eighties, he had felt he should have children – he possessed, after all, the kind of dewy sincerity expected of male parents at the time – but none of the women with whom he had had relationships had expressed the slightest desire to bear him offspring. Miles had once written an article on the new feminist independence, the political move away from motherhood, but, re-reading it later, he had worried that its autobiographical tone might be misinterpreted, and the piece now gathered dust, with many other half-completed projects, on the bottom shelf of his bookcase.

He had left journalism. He had tried to write for television. He had contributed the occasional article to the *Times Higher Educational Supplement*. A literary parody had won a £25 book token in the *New*

Statesman. Eventually, he had moved into academic life, teaching first in London, then, as he developed an interest in the sociology of death with particular reference to the Eastern counties, taking up his present post at the Anglia Institute in Ipswich, where he found a sort of spiritual home, surrounded by other middle-aged semi-intellectuals like himself.

During the ten years since he had moved into a small, untidy former labourer's cottage off Bridge Lane, Miles had done little to shake off the status of incomer. He rarely visited the Greyhound, or contributed to bring-and-buy sales. From matters of local import (discussions of the by-pass, a scandal involving the local MP, the triumphant progress of Diss Town FC in the FA Vase of 1994), he remained aloof. While others congregated in Diss for market day on Friday, he had avoided it. His rigid atheism had precluded visits to St Botolph's Church, except for the occasional funeral which he attended for professional reasons. Even the way he rolled his own cigarettes (spindly, elegant little constructs the width of toothpicks) was misinterpreted in the village: it was a habit, people seemed to think, indicating niggardliness, or eccentricity, or ideas below his station, none of which qualities was entirely acceptable in Burthorpe.

He was, Miles had concluded, a fringe character; it was a phrase he had once heard used at a faculty meeting where it had been intended as a term of withering abuse – Dr X was no one, a mere fringe character – but that was the way he now saw himself. On the fringe of village life, of academia, of love.

Miles thought about himself quite often. Until recently, these moments of introspection had been tinged with a certain melancholy as he contemplated his solitude and professional disappointments, his carefully noted physical decline. Of course, this mildly tragic sense of apartness and alienation was not entirely unpleasant. Miles had come to see himself as a contemporary version of the local Chekhovian scholar: a gawky yet wise intellectual, surrounded by country folk who were understandably ill at ease with his learning and academic sophistication.

Yet, back on that Tuesday evening in April, as he sat behind the paper-strewn desk in his small study, having partaken of a healthy vegetarian meal, and looked over his work, he felt genuinely happy. The sensation was partly explained by Dr Katherine Porter's imminent departure for the Arctic, which would provide Miles with a holiday from the grinding tyranny of those weekly visits, and partly by the accelerating progress of his ground-breaking handbook. Then, there was Margaret. More and more often, there were thoughts of Margaret.

He stood up and stretched, catching sight of himself in the dark reflection of the window in front of him. He even looked different – the uneven stubble on his chin which normally gave him a battered, hangdog look tonight endowed him with bohemian stylishness, the untamed *je-m'en-foutisme* of a free thinker.

He smiled, stretched, then sat down again at his desk. Work: that was the key to his new-found sense of self.

Glancing over the pages before him, he noted with pleasure that his *Resource Handbook* had taken an unpredictable and personal direction. Liberated by the funding arrangement facilitated by Colin Dunn, he was writing the kind of book which, he was sure, would be recognised as not only a work of academic authority, but also a playful and subversive commentary on intellectual life. Like those novels that weren't really novels, or travel books that were internal journeys, *Regional Death Studies: A Resource Handbook* would be both inside and yet outside a disciplinary tradition, conveying information to the student while skittishly providing a more personal perspective for the sophisticated general reader.

His introduction, which he had now written several times, established this tone rather well, he thought.

INTRODUCTION
Regional Death Studies: A Resource Handbook will be the first work of reference for students working within a discipline of growing importance, Local Thanatology, otherwise known as Regional Death Studies. Within the structures of an academic sourcebook, I intend to provide a 'double template' of objective and subjective analysis, reflecting (a) 'historic truth', and (b) 'narrative truth'.

Why do Regional Death Studies require at this point of time a compendium of source material? Indeed, what is the significance today of this particular school of study?

I believe we are upon the very cusp of change in attitudes to mortality. Over the past forty years, lessons learnt in European and North American societies have been 'unlearnt'. The subject, the reality, of death is now a matter from which we avert our eyes.

The discipline of Regional Death Studies attempts to understand society's aversion to the matter of mortality by regarding it in a defined local area. Many thanatologists, myself included, believe that paradigms for a redefined death-related thematic are to be found within rural communities where, in spite of the pressures of modern life, a socio-cultural rhythm retains its force.

SOME NOTES ON NARRATOLOGY

Because in this project I have attempted to 'marry' historical and narrative enquiries, thereby arriving at conclusions embracing both the empirical and the subjective (a 'felt' objectivity, if you like), a conventional syntagmatic narrative is, I have concluded, inappropriate. Instead I have 'cross-fertilised' my academic researches into death-related study fields with subjective perceptions of the community where I live. It is hoped that at the interstices of these two enquiries (what one might light-heartedly describe as a 'mix-and-match-narrative'), we shall arrive at truths that transcend traditional notions of the 'pure versus applied' variety.

THE VILLAGE AS SETTING FOR PRIMARY RESOURCE MATERIAL, INCLUDING CHARACTOLOGY

The region providing casebook material for the handbook is a small community containing 760 inhabitants, public transport facilities and several village-related accoutrements, including a pond, a green, a village shop (temporarily closed at the time of writing) and a church, with graveyard, situated some half a mile from the community's epicentre.

Suitability of the village for this project lies within its societal dichotomies: rural yet not isolated, socially homogeneous yet varied, traditional yet, as shall be shown, contemporary. It also has particular interest for the thanatologist in that it has its own undertaker.

I have been particularly interested in exploring dynamics

existing between the historical and contemporaneous within the village. The church and several houses date back to the fifteenth century. Yet, within a matter of 400 metres of the village green, a new housing estate was erected in 1983. There is even a troupe of travelling folk who have brought their mobile homes to the edge of the village – descendants of the medieval pilgrim or Elizabethan 'sturdy beggars', depending upon one's point of view! While, to the outsider, the community may seem to be steeped in traditional values, it is confronted by contemporary problems: development, crime, transport, vagrancy.

For these reasons, what might be described as a contingent dynamic tension between past and present, the village represents a highly fruitful source of material for this study.

'TO SEE A WORLD IN A GRAIN OF SAND': A BRIEF DEFENCE OF 'PARISH-PUMP METHODOLOGY'
The question of macro versus micro is as old as academia itself. Which study tells us more of medieval man: Huizinga's magisterial *The Waning of the Middle Ages*[1] or Ladourie's superb work of historical detail *Montaillou*[2]? What research is of more relevance to an environmentalist: that into the life of a cell or of an ecosystem?

Thanatology can boast many great works of general study, of which Philippe Ariès' *The Hour of Our Death*[3] is the greatest example. It is at the other, more modest, yet equally valid, end of the thematic scale that I shall be working in *Regional Death Studies: A Resource Handbook*.

[1] J.V. Huizinga, *The Waning of the Middle Ages* (Edward Arnold, 1924)
[2] Emmanuel le Roy Ladourie, *Montaillou* (Scolar Press, 1978)
[3] Philippe Ariès, *The Hour of Our Death* (Allen Lane, 1981).

'Oh yes.'

Miles Larwood smiled and sat back in his chair. It was a good tone that he had established. Authoritative yet accessible, it suggested the kind of man who would be as welcome at High Table at a Cambridge College as he would be at an agreeable dinner party held by the more sophisticated kind of country folk. While his project had been at concept stage, Miles had considered writing himself into the book as a village character, a trope which would subtly point up the fact that high learning was essentially just another craft, like building or thatching or farming, while giving the text the agreeable patina of postmodern self-reference. In the end, though, he had decided that this narratological *jeu d'esprit* might be mistaken for a lack of scholastic seriousness and had kept the autobiographical element to a minimum.

Tonight he would be completing an entry he had entitled 'Liminality and the living: the medieval model'. He intended to tease out the intriguing connection between the liminal period observed by mourners during the Middle Ages when it had been believed that the actual moment of death was merely part of a continual, or liminal, process, and modern burial practices in America. That would stir things up, Miles thought.

He was looking through his reference cards for a suitable quote from Gittings' *Death, Burial and the Individual in Early Modern England* when something in the darkness outside the window attracted his attention.

About thirty yards from the house, a dab of white caught the light from the window as it cut its way through the branches of an apple tree. At first Miles took it for a barn owl, but then, as it drew nearer to the house, he saw that it was a sort of cloud – white, about the size of a man's head, roughly circular but changing its constitution as it floated through the air. It slowed, descended, then passed a matter of feet in front of the window where he stood, before disappearing to his left.

Strange. Miles looked back to the apple tree and noted that there was no perceptible wind that night. Although his wood-burning stove was lit, it produced a thin bluish plume of smoke nothing like this.

In a sudden moment of self-concern, Miles feared that the decades of study and reading had begun to affect his sight. A cataract? A detached retina? He blinked earnestly into the darkness, then rolled his eyeballs upwards.

Distracted, he left his study and opened the front door. Covering one eye with his hand, he scanned the darkness looking in the direction of Burthorpe. He gasped: there *was* a light shape, only now it was wider and brighter, flame-like. When he opened both eyes, he found that the glow, appearing over the rooftops of the village, throwing the tower of St Botolph's into eerie silhouette, was still there.

It was not within his retina, but was real. A fire seemed to be blazing on the edge of the village.

'Shit.' Miles reached for his duffel coat inside the hall, then, pulling the door closed behind him, he began walking quickly up Bridge Lane.

There were already sounds of alarm from the dark around him. Two boys were running past the village pond, talking excitedly as they went. Behind him, Miles could hear the sound of a police siren and, as if in response, the brief, old-fashioned ring of the fire-engine as it made its way through Diss. As he walked, Miles could see that whatever was on fire was beyond Scrope Rise near the railway tracks. The air was thick with the smell of burning, but these were acrid fumes with an industrial smell rather than the burning timber of a house blaze.

Miles turned the corner before Scrope Rise and stopped, looking down on the astonishing scene before him. Beyond the estate, a great sheet of flame danced angrily in the night, illuminating the sad semi-circle of vans and cars that represented the travellers' settlement. At first Miles assumed that somehow one of their fires had illuminated a vehicle but now he saw that the conflagration had occurred on this side of the railway tracks, some thirty yards short of the vans.

There were two groups of onlookers. In the darkness beyond the fire stood the occupants of the vans, with their children and their dogs, staring in gloomy silence at the fire. Then, on this side, stood a more animated group of spectators, excited village folk whose voices and gestures were lost in the roar of the blaze.

Anxious not to be numbered among the village ghouls, Miles Larwood stood watching at the top of the hill. The first fire-engine had arrived now and, as the inferno abated, the dark skeletal shape of a small lorry or a van appeared through the flames like a ghost ship emerging from fog. A policeman with a torch was making his way along the front of the spectators, moving them along. Casting final reluctant glances in the direction of the spectacle, many of them now turned back towards the main road. On the far hill, two more policemen were walking towards the group of travellers, at the front of whom, Miles now saw, stood Naughty Boy Dance, a small child on

144

his hip. Belatedly, an ambulance turned off the main road behind Miles and raced past, its blue light flashing. As it approached the fire, the policeman who had been clearing the crowd spoke to the driver. No one from the ambulance seemed in a particular hurry to disembark.

The first of the spectators had reached him now – men, women and children silhouetted by the lights behind them. One of them, whom Miles now recognised as Rose Hope, stood before him.

'Somehow I don't think the ambulance will be needed,' she said, glancing back down the hill to the scene of smouldering devastation.

'Hmm.' Miles was momentarily embarrassed to be found staring at the accident. 'Maybe there was no one in it.'

'Someone thought it might be Errol Pryce's van,' said Rose. 'He wasn't in his usual place at the pub.'

'What was he doing there? And what the hell did he have in the van that went up like that?'

'Building materials, maybe? Petrol?' Rose started slowly up the hill in the direction of the main road and Miles followed her. For a minute or so, they walked in silence.

Miles had never felt close to Rose Hope. Because they were of a similar age and had worked in similar fields, she had always seemed to assume an intimacy which made him feel ill at ease, even slightly insulted. After all, while he had seen the error of his ways, trading in the empty cynicism of journalism for the more respectable virtues of academic life, she had become a local newshound. They really had nothing in common.

'Funnily enough, I was thinking of ringing you earlier this evening to discuss a project,' Rose said suddenly.

'Maybe now's not quite the moment.'

'Not journalism.' She smiled wryly. 'Something rather more substantial.'

'Ah.'

'Let me buy you a drink at the Greyhound. All that fire has made me thirsty.'

'I was working.'

'Won't take a minute, Miles. Tell you what, I'll walk with you back to your place – you can give me a drink, then I'll head home.'

Miles hesitated. 'I suppose it would be difficult to concentrate now anyway,' he said.

'Of course it would. Come on – we both need a drink.'

Men and children, it's a mystery. Search in his writings for a child and nowhere, among the seething clamour of carls and courtiers, among the beasts and the birds of myth or field, among the coistrowns and convent ladies, will you find a human who had yet to attain the age of discretion. I've heard it said that life, true and unvarnished, thronged the narrow lanes of his verse, but it was never so. The life of which he wrote had passed through a fine net, there to catch the truly rough, the unmannerly and bowsy. His life had no place for children. It had also, I was to discover, no place for me.

Yet, for weeks after Joseph was born, there was no keeping the man from my room. He would glose and gurgle over the boy as if this were the new and best of playthings. Here was experience. Here was life. Weary from lack of sleep, I would watch him as he lowered his head into the crib like some strange yet gentle animal feeding at a trough. Would the boy learn to read and to write, I asked. Would he be tutored in Latin and grammar and rhetoric? Joseph, he would murmur as he gazed into the sweet child's face, My Joseph will be a humanist, a scholar at court. My Joseph.

Fatherhood became him during those first few months. The restlessness, the rage for living, had abated. Often we would pass evenings together, the three of us, his need for the loud and witty company of men forgotten. When Joseph slept, he would take me to his bed, laughing as I protested that my body was bruised from child-bearing. Fathering, he told me, was his fancy. Like so much in his life, the fancy passed.

It was when Joseph was some several months old that an event occurred which was to mark the end of my happy days at the Rectory. On the eve of one sabbath, he surprised me by visiting us in my room, a pleasure rarely enjoyed since this was the evening on which he would prepare his sermon for the following day.

I was suckling Joseph and modestly I covered with a bedcloth

my glistening, heavy pap and his little head, now dark with fine,
shiny hair. Gently he pulled back the sheet. He sat himself in a
chair before us and watched with such serious intentness that I
might have been the Madonna herself, and Joseph Our Lord. A
proud mother, a loving wife, I smiled at him with tenderness.

Meg, he said, you shall be at matins tomorrow. Bring the boy in
a clean white swaddling cloth. Before I could protest, or at least
ask what good such a display would bring, he had left my room.

The reports of that Sunday are true. I entered St Mary's as the
service began and, ignoring some querulous and impertinent
glances from the more proper of our parishioners, I sat alone with
Joseph, on the back pew.

He rose to give his sermon, a magnificent, dazzling sight. It
seemed to me that his congregation cowered in fear as, in the
quietest of tones, he reported that there were those in this holy
place who were worse than knaves.

Why? His voice rose, shaking with the rage of the just. Why? It
echoed and thundered around the domed roof of St Mary's. I shall
show you, he said. You have complained of me to the Bishop that
I do keep a fair wench in my house. Yes. I do tell you, if you had
any fair wives, it were somewhat to help me at need. I am a man
as you be. You have foul wives, and I have a fair wench, of the
which I have begotten a fair boy, as I do think, and as you all
shall see.

His eyes, which had been searching the congregation as if to
burn out sin from their very souls, now raised towards me. For a
moment, he stared at me, my baby held sleeping to my bosom.
Thou wife, he said, ignoring the whispers of scandal that passed
about the pews and the aisles like wind-blown leaves. Thou wife,
that hast my child. Be not afraid. Fet me hither my child to me.

I stood. I walked down the aisle like the bride I had never been.
He descended from the pulpit and lifted my sleeping angel from his
white swaddling cloth, took him naked into the pulpit. The church
was cold and, as I stood at the foot of those steps, my back to the
congregation, Joseph began to cry.

How say you neighbours all? His voice was thunder. The baby
was held aloft as if my lord were Abraham himself, our son his

sacrifice. Is not this child the best of all yours? It hath nose, eyes, hands and feet as well as any. It is not like a pig, nor a calf, nor like no foul nor monstrous beast.

And so he continued, his gryl tones roaring above the pitiful cries of our child. I dared once to glance over my shoulder. The congregation was rapt, amazed, astonished by my husband's sermon. They saw me no longer.

If I had brought forth this child without arms or legs, he cried, I never would have blamed you to have complained to the Bishop of me. But to complain without a cause! I say, as I have said before in my ante-theme, vos estis, you be, and have been, and will and shall be lither knaves, to complain of me without a cause reasonable.

He brought me Joseph, handed him to me as if he were no longer his flesh and blood but some part of the church, a blessing, a thing. He nodded to me, not looking in my eyes. I wrapped Joseph in his cloth. I comforted him. Then I made the long journey through the congregation, my face a glede of shame, I left the church and walked slowly home to the Rectory. By the time I had reached my room, my Joseph was asleep once more. He was always a good baby.

Yes. Men and children, it's a mystery. From that day it was as if he had repaid some kind of tribute. He spoke to me distantly, in a manner once more convenable to a servant. Joseph he hardly seemed to see. The townspeople had taken to treating me with wary disdain. I was the Rector's musket. They avoided my eyes, moved away as I approached them, walking down Mere Street or up Market Hill.

Days later, he took us in his cart, past Fair Green, over the river, up the hill and down a narrow lane, at the end of which was a small, shadowy cottage. He explained that this was to be my home, that Joseph's crying disturbed his work. He would visit every day and sometimes at night. It was our home, a place where we would raise our family.

Your work? I stood at the door of this new home looking into the shadows, breathing in the dampness, the smell of earth and rotting timber. What of Joseph? What of me? Where shall your fair boy learn his Latin?

The look descended on his face which I had seen when guests

*had tarried too long at the Rectory. I have my work, he said. You
must understand that I cannot and will not be disturbed.*

*You are ashamed of us. For all your brave pulpit words, you
fear the Bishop of Norwich, you dought the melling tongues of the
people in the town.*

*He placed his great hand upon my back and pushed me into this
new and unwelcome habitance. My work. He said it again like
some form of incantation. He took some wood that lay near the
door and placed it in the fireplace. Then, wearied by this labour,
he stood before me. Meg, I have much to write, he said.*

*Words. I held Joseph before him. Is not the flesh of your flesh
worth more than all the words in the world?*

This time he took him not.

*In the beginning was the Word, he said. The Word was God
and the Word was with God.*

And it is God's Word you write? Truly?

*He looked at me now. Unread I may have been but I knew my
man. I may have lacked ornacy, yet I understood his work, his
words, better than many scholars.*

*It is my word, he said, stepping into the seat of his cart. He left,
the sides of the cart brushing against the hedges of the lane.*

*He would visit me, I would bear him further children, but I had
lost him.*

*Soon after this day, he took to visiting Lady Wyndham at the
convent by Carrow Abbey.*

Intellectual activity and movement of the more direct, worldly kind
make uneasy companions, Miles Larwood had discovered. His occasional social arrangements – even his relatively mechanistic and pre-
ordained encounters with Dr Katherine Porter – tended to distract the
mind from writing for several hours before and after the event. It was
perhaps for this reason that he found himself in no particular hurry to
be rid of Rose Hope's company when she sat late that night, drinking
whisky by the wood-burning stove and expounding her bizarre but
intriguing theories. His exploration of liminality and the living could
wait until the morning.

On reaching the cottage, Rose had made a couple of calls from his telephone, and, with swift professionalism, had established that the burning van had indeed belonged to Pryce, that Errol had left home earlier that evening and had not been seen since. The police were with Mrs Pryce now.

As she spoke, Rose sipped occasionally at the whisky in her hand, outlining what she had described as her 'project'. She seemed to have found a pattern in recent incidents of violence in Burthorpe: deaths, injury, insanity. She revealed that the smock H.T. Pearson had been wearing when he had fallen out of his window had not been the uniform of a morris dancer, as had been reported in the press, but an outsize gymslip. Similarly there had been more to the departure of Sarah Dunn to a private clinic than the rumoured nervous exhaustion, specifically her attempted rape of a young milkman from Palgrave while suffering under the illusion that the youth was the film star Kevin Costner with whom she had spent the previous night.

'I don't recall reading any of these stories in the pages of your newspaper,' Miles said at one point.

'We select. Lurid exposés are not our style.'

'Shame, that. I like a spot of salacity.'

'Yes.' Rose ran the tips of her fingers down the glass. 'So do I.'

Flustered, Miles reached the bottle from a nearby table and poured her more whisky. Then, realising that his motives might be misconstrued, he muttered, 'You don't have to drink it all if you don't want.'

'Miles, do you believe in the supernatural?'

'No. To be frank, I have serious intellectual problems with that general area.'

Maybe it was the whisky, or the hour; whatever the reason, Miles found that his mind was wandering, that he was considering, in a purely hypothetical, abstract way, what it would be like to go to bed with a woman like Rose. As he half-listened to the journalist's eccentric theory – paranormal forces had been stirred by the decision to move the Garden of Remembrance, she seemed to believe – he considered her narrow figure, her long and faintly witch-like fingers, the vulturous stoop to the shoulders, the predatory ·features of her face. He had always favoured softer, more pneumatic partners but, as she sat there, one long leg crossed over the other, he wondered vaguely how the ribs of Rose Hope would feel, the knees, the collar-bones, the little hips jutting sharply into him.

'What d'you think?'

Rose, he now realised, was sitting in silence and seemed to expect some reply from him.

'I don't quite see how all this affects me,' he said.

'I believe that you and I are at the centre of a major story for our times.' Rose sat forward in her chair. 'Together we could investigate it – write a book.'

'I'm already writing a book.'

'Are you?' A sharpness had entered Rose's voice.

'Yes. It's a sort of intellectual exploration of definitions and theories surrounding thanatological belief systems.'

Rose smiled, and seemed to relax. 'Miles, I'm talking mainstream here. This could be a bestseller.'

'But I'm not that sort of writer. I'm an academic.'

'You provide the authority. I provide the pace.' Rose held up a hand, warding off Miles's attempted interruption. 'Can't you see it? It's all so . . . zeitgeisty. Village life. A community trapped in the past. The calloused, gimlet-eyed sons and daughters of the soil and their weird, dislocated sexualities. And, underneath it all, a subterranean mythic power emerging – a life-force which has somehow been addled and corrupted over the centuries.'

Miles laughed. 'This is Burthorpe we're talking about, is it?'

'It's the Burthorpe of our bestseller, Miles – a Burthorpe of the mind, a universal Burthorpe. And it's got something else that's hot at the moment. Children. Think of all those horror films of the eighties – *The Shining*, *The Exorcist*, *Flowers in the Attic*. They all exploited a fear of children, of the weird, unworldly connection between inno-cence and evil – that frightening, feral purity of kids. These days you see it in the newspapers – child abuse, children who murder, out of control. We're afraid of our own children.'

'I've always rather liked kids,' said Miles, uneasily trying to lighten the atmosphere.

'Yuk.' Rose took a swig of whisky, momentarily distracted. 'When I see my friends who've done it, I thank God I never weakened. It all goes soft – brainpower, muscle tone, that redeeming sense of irony. It's as if every generation is leeched of its brightness and strength by these ghastly little sprogs.' Rose sipped at her whisky. 'You must see that, surely. You've avoided the trap.'

'It's not exactly how it happened.' Miles gazed unhappily at the stove. 'What have these theories got to do with your project anyway?'

'There's a rumour that the travellers have been involved in some kind of satanic cult. Hence the fire tonight. Then there were those two dead teenagers. Birth, death – a kiddie element would just make this story.'

'Rose, I'm not your man. Maybe there is something sensational to be discovered here, although it sounds of dubious intellectual provenance to me, but I'm a thanatologist, not a ghost-hunter.'

Rose gave a professional smile. 'Are we alone here?' she asked suddenly.

'Yes. Margaret goes to bed early.'

'Margaret? I thought you had some hulking male student living here.'

'Not any more.'

'Just you and her, eh?'

'Yes.'

'Cosy. I thought that was what you academics had students for.'

Miles blushed, but failed to deny the slur. 'It's not like that,' he said, smiling.

Rose stood up, her back to the stove, and ran her hands slowly down the warm seat of her tight jeans. 'Doesn't that put rather a crimp on your private life?' she asked.

Miles found that he was blushing. 'Not really,' he said, holding her stare, taking in the wide lips and slightly battered teeth. Perhaps in the end she was rather too worldly for his taste, he thought. He had always been drawn to women of a light and occasional erotic pulse, whose interest in sex took second place to other projects. On the other hand, Rose clearly found some rather powerful attractiveness within him, and that had not happened to him for quite a while now.

'It's very late for you to drive home,' he said with a craggy, raffish smile.

Rather to his surprise, Rose leapt to her feet. 'Christ, look at the time and it's press day tomorrow.' She walked quickly towards the door. 'Think about it,' she added. 'But don't wait too long.'

Miles laughed. 'Going to strike again, is it, this ghost?' he asked. The front door slammed in reply.

Alison Turville was awake again. She listened, as she did every night at this time, to the different sounds in the darkness – the sibilant breath of Matthew beside her, the occasional creak of timber in the wind, the muttering of Kate in her sleep across the hall, the occasional secret knocking, as if some very small person were trying somewhere to gain entry to the house, and, outside, the wind in the trees, the distant rumble of a car engine, the breathy call of an owl, a vixen barking on the far side of the village. No night was the same. The house experienced different dreams, sometimes restless, sometimes calm, was witnessed by different eyes from the dark.

But, inevitably, Alison felt outside it all – outside the night, outside the building, even outside the family, as her wakefulness removed her from the field of human strife, on to another plain. This brought no rest, only a powerless terror.

She had fought against insomnia, sometimes going to bed early in an attempt to catch a couple of hours' sleep before the long night's vigil began, or past midnight, hoping that sheer exhaustion would roll her downwards into slumber. In the end, the choice was simply between taking her few minutes' sleep as Matthew came to bed or in those awful defeated moments when night became morning and the fucking birds began their sodding dawn chorus. The sleeping pills prescribed by Dr Gillette made her feel torpid and suicidal the next day. Whisky gave her nightmares. Until the last few months, she would occasionally recourse to marital sex but, the more she emptied her mind of feelings of anger towards Matthew in order to concentrate on the sensations of her body, the more rage she felt, the further any kind of release drifted from her. 'All right?' Matthew would ask after a while. 'Yes,' she would say. Moments later, he would be asleep and another night in her private lonely world stretched before her.

It was a world in which everything became terrifyingly clear, when all the half-recognised truths of the daylight hours fell into place, yet where there was no relief or solution. On the night of the fire (of which neither she nor Matthew were aware until the next morning), she had a particularly bad time, thoughts of familial decline and failure crowding in on her. The children compared badly to their friends, she had decided. Her efforts to prepare them for the best of private schools – the lessons in English, Maths, recorder, ballet, violin, football, cubs, the afternoons spent driving around the country roads on the way to the next improving appointment – were all pointless. In the dark, the relentless treadmill of middle-class parenthood turned over and over in her head.

They were going to fail! Her children would be ordinary! Instead of being a great step forward, they would revert a generation, become as dull and unambitious as her parents or, even worse, Matthew's parents had been. Once she had imagined for them a future of weekend parties, and nicely spoken friends, and universities, and blundering, happy romances, a life of lawns and tennis tournaments and interesting, caring jobs. Now, as Stephen and Kate grew older, this dream seemed absurd. They lacked ambition, curiosity, drive. There was a listless acceptance of what was arranged for them which made her want to scream. Alison looked at the Dunns' children or the Pygotts', and saw a confidence, a certainty of purpose, in them which Stephen had never had – he was too damned *diffident*, anxious to please. He was doomed to be one of those people whose brightest and best moment had occurred when they were at primary school, whose subsequent life had been an inexorable slide into dreariness and mediocrity. Suddenly, she could see him, a pale and disappointed man in his twenties, hating the very parents on whom he was still dependent, a wastrel who was as weak, weaker, than his father. She would not allow it! In the darkness, she clenched her fists at the thought. With every ounce of energy in her body, she would lift him, *force* him to some form of success. And Kate, oh my *God*. Alison had always known that Kate was different from other children but, until now, she had clung to the belief that this quirkiness, this individuality, was a positive thing. Character – that *must* be good, surely. Maybe it wasn't! What if *less* character was what was needed? Did other children say the things that Kate did, have the kind of obsessions that she had, look at their parents in that odd, knowing way? Was there another six year old in the country who would take a pair of scissors to a window blind? Other people's children had been granted at least some advantage – those who were stupid looked pretty, or charming, or had interesting hobbies. Sometimes Alison studied photographs of the family and wondered (she hated herself for this, but couldn't help it) just *how* she and Matthew could have produced a little girl so plain, so awkward, so lacking in mental or physical grace, so fucking *charmless*. Oh shit, maybe Kate was mad. Alison's heart thumped with certainty at the thought. That was it, she had a mad daughter, one who was doomed to delinquency. Unless she did something (Matthew was useless), Kate was going to become alienated from the world of civilized values. She had to be saved, brought back into the fold before it was too late, the downward spiral had begun, and she was out behaving more and more strangely, sniffing glue and swearing in front of strangers and breaking windows and sleeping in haystacks with rough boys from Diss. What was the answer? Perhaps a new musical intrument would give her confidence, or the Brownies, or riding lessons in Norwich, maybe a new school. But *which* new school?

A clock at St Botolph's struck three. Alison knew where her thoughts were leading. Maybe – no, not maybe, definitely – all these problems, the failures and disappointments of her children, were not just bad luck, an unfortunate curdling in the gene pool she had created with Matthew, but were *all her fault*. What if, in spite of her best efforts, Stephen and Kate had somehow caught the malaise that existed within the marriage? As a wife, she had tried to continue as if nothing were happening, to retain the rhythm of family life while all her certainties collapsed around her, but now it seemed to be beating faster and faster every day, like a nightmare merry-go-round. What if it was her unhappiness, and Matthew's, to which the children were responding and the failure was not theirs but their parents'?

The house, the garden. She forced herself to think of those. There was so much to do, planting and painting and planning for the house, for the family.

The telephone beyond Matthew gave the briefest of rings and was then silent. He stirred and gave a long, weary sigh.

'Are you awake?' Matthew asked, his voice thick with sleep.

'I am now.'

'All right?'

'This is getting out of control.'

'The calls?'

'Everything.'

'It'll be better in the morning.'

He turned over. She concentrated her mind on the garden.

Miles sat in front of his word-processor, his staring, ill-shaven face illuminated by the screen. Attempting to banish restless thoughts of Rose, he had poured himself another whisky and was reading what his own *Resource Handbook* had to say on the subject of ghosts.

Had she really known him so little that she seriously expected him to risk his academic reputation for the sake of a lurid, quick-buck journalistic scam? Did she not realise that, almost of all specialists in the field of death studies, he was the least likely to lend any kind of intellectual support to populist notions of the so-called 'supernatural'?

In fact, a firm, fact-based scepticism towards what he termed the 'heeby-jeeby' school of thanatology was one of the recurrent themes, the guiding principles, behind his work.

THE REVENANT AND IDENTITY: TOWARDS AN UNDER-
STANDING OF THE MYTH OF THE SUPERNATURAL
It is beyond the scope of this study to reveal the full extent of mankind's adherence to beliefs in the non-physical return of those who are dead (see REVENANCE, THEORY OF), not to mention the tortured ratiocination in support of such theories. Briefly, however, we can discuss the more outlandish beliefs.
VAMPIRES, OR NACHZEHRERS: according to Barber[1], the true vampire (before being re-invented in the fiction of Bram Stoker) was believed to be 'a plump Slavic fellow with long fingernails, his mouth and left eye open, his face ruddy and swollen. His attire, naturally enough, would be a shroud'.
During the Middle Ages, a complex mythology surrounded

[1] Paul Barber, *Vampires, Burial and Death* (Yale University Press, 1988).

the vampire concept[2], particularly in the Eastern part of Europe. Variously, it was believed that, since vampires lived off cattle (as the vampire bat indeed does), it was dangerous to eat beef; that an animal jumping over a corpse (or the appearance of a black hen) could cause vampirism; that female vampires were frequently those who died in childbirth; that jade objects placed in orifices of the body, or poppy seeds (to aid sleep) were effective apotropaics; that stakes placed above the grave would destroy a vampire as he/she rose from the ground; that mourners should drink brandy mixed with the corpse's blood soaked in part of his/her shroud to ward off vampires; that for a stake to kill a vampire, it should be made of hawthorn. And so on.

The origin of these fears was both psychological and physiological. The powerful, obsessive fear of death by contagion, specifically from the Black Death or bubonic plague, was focused, by an act of transference, on corpses. Buried some distance from dwellings, it was found that they had occasionally moved from the grave, or that their arms had burst from the earth in an apparent attempt to escape the grave. When disinterred, fresh blood was sometimes found in their mouths. They were sometimes warm. There was a significant new growth of skin, particularly on the feet. Above all, they were vastly bloated, sometimes twice their normal size; when destroyed with a stake driven through the thorax, the body shrivelled – a sign surely that the vampire spirit had departed from it.

With the benefit of modern science, we can see the causes of these apparently 'paranormal' phenomena. The corpses were disturbed by such mammals as wolves (see DEATH, DOGS AND THE WEREWOLF MYTH: AN ANECDOTE). The grasping hand was simply a function of the expanding corpse in a shallow grave. The oral blood was not that of the vampire's victims but its own: pneumonic plague caused blood to be expelled from the lungs after death. The warmth, of

---

[2] It is perhaps worth noting here that the origin of cremation lies in the folkloric fear, originating in Eastern Europe, of the body rising again after death. Perhaps this explains why, to this day, cremation is more popular in Europe than in North America!

course, was caused by biological decomposition, and the growth of skin by a process known to pathologists as 'skin slippage'. As for the bloated corpse, which shrank so alarmingly when stabbed, the explanation was simply that gases had been produced by micro-organisms already within the body when it was alive. After a certain period *post mortem*, the abdominal cavity becomes hugely swollen – according to Evans, 'like an over-inflated balloon'. Hence the dramatic effect of the hawthorn stake.

Other mythic fantasies, as old as humanity itself, are similarly possible to explain with the help of science. Even the glowing presence of 'ghosts' in a graveyard may well have been caused by *protobacterium fisheri*, luminous bacteria emanating from a decomposing body, which can cause what is known as 'corpse light'.

I do not intend to devote much space in the *Resource Handbook* to figmental aspects of death. To the thanatologist, the only abiding mystery of these matters is that even today relatively 'sophisticated' individuals persist in their belief in wild and woolly versions of the myth of the 'revenant'.

'Was he there?'

Miles turned slowly in his seat. In the doorway, standing dark against the light in the hall, and somehow looking more imposing than usual, stood Margaret Cowper. Although it was almost half-past three in the morning, she was dressed in jeans and a loose white shirt which seemed to imbue her with the strangest kind of glow. She wore no shoes. Her hair was unkempt, as if she had just sleepwalked through a storm.

'Was he there?' she repeated.

'Was who where?'

'The fire? You saw it?'

'Yes.'

'It was a real blaze.' There was a lightness in Margaret's voice. 'Was Errol Pryce in the van?'

'They think so.'

'Oh dear.' Margaret walked into the room and sat in the chair which, only an hour or so previously, Rose had occupied. 'Your guest has gone.'

'Yes.'

'You wanted her to stay.'

Miles shrugged. It was true that he felt foolish, rejected. For some reason he had never been one of those men who could take such things easily, as if rejected advances were no more than pot shots at goal which had soared amusingly over the crossbar. 'I made something of a fool of myself,' he said quietly.

'You're lonely.'

'I just seem to come out with the wrong words. Or maybe they're the right words but said in the wrong way. People tend not to listen to the words themselves – they judge them for the way they sound, how they dress, the general feel of them.'

'Words are dangerous.'

Miles drank deeply of his whisky. 'I once went out with a girl I was really fond of,' he said. 'You know how I lost her? We were having a minor quarrel and I happened to mention that I had been unable to follow her somewhat tortured process of ratiocination. Fair enough, no?'

Margaret smiled and said nothing.

'Oh no,' Miles went on miserably. 'Not fair at all. Apparently this was, if I recall her phrase correctly, "the limp-dicked jerking-off of a pretentious pseudo-intellectual".'

'Yes.'

'I said – ' Miles swayed forward, his eyes fixed on the floor. 'I said – humorously – that this analysis was somewhat oxymoronic – that is, I was *either* limp-dicked *or* jerking-off.'

Miles glanced at Margaret but was not rewarded with a response. 'Both at the same time tends to be tricky. Categorical mistake.'

'She understood?'

'She left.'

Margaret leant forward and placed her hand on his. It felt as cool as a winter breeze.

She turned her grey eyes to the screen. 'More words,' she said.

'Yes. I like working at night.'

'And it's an escape.'

Miles smiled wearily. 'It's certainly simpler than the real world.'

Margaret stood up in a brisk, irritated movement. 'You have to choose,' she said.

She turned and walked out of the room, leaving behind her a faint and distant smell of diesel smoke.

10

WIN TICKETS FOR
THE 'MISS FROM DISS' STAR!

The year's most unlikely pop star, Winston the Singing Farmer, is to appear at the Park Hotel for two nights at the end of April. The East Dereham artiste, whose song 'Miss from Diss' has been played on national Radio One, will be supported by top local band The Planks at what looks to be a sell-out occasion.

Winston – whose real name is Winston Harrold – is Norfolk born and bred and hails from a long line of farming folk. His musical career started in the cowshed, at the age of ten, playing the mouth organ along with the cowmen, much to his father's disgust and the cows' delight!

Over the past two years he has become a firm favourite at pubs, clubs, and appeared at last year's Suffolk County Show in Ipswich. And, yes, Winston is still a farmer when he's not on tour!

The *DP* is offering five pairs of free tickets to see Winston the Singing Farmer at the Park Hotel on April 23rd. All you have to do is answer these three questions and send your replies, with this cutting and a SAE marked 'Winston the Singing Farmer Offer' to the *DP* offices by this coming Friday.

1) What musical instrument does Winston play?
2) Who had the original hit with the song 'Miss from Diss'?
3) Complete the next line from 'Miss from Diss':

I miss my little miss from Diss,

I miss her sister, too,

When one sister's missin', boy,

. . . . !

161

H.T. PEARSON WAS coming home, and a great reception awaited him in the village. Balloons hung from the branches of the line of plane trees stretching from the main road to the Convenience Store. Along the façade of Burthorpe Primary School, bunting fluttered in the breeze. A banner had been hung between two of the first-floor windows of the shop itself. 'WELCOME HOME, HARRY!', it read.

H.T. Pearson had never, in fact, been a Harry. For the years preceding his accident and subsequent celebrity, he had either been 'young Pearson' or 'Pearson' or, eventually, 'Mr Pearson'. His mother, in the days when she still remembered who he was, would refer to him as 'Harold'. Yet, thanks to a concerted campaign in the *Diss Press*, the lugubrious H.T. Pearson had been successfully re-invented as jovial Harry Pearson, the morris-dancing, twinkle-eyed traditionalist with ever a kind word for the kiddies.

It had been a journalistic achievement which Rose Hope would later rank alongside the tug-of-love toddler from Stradbroke or even the have-a-go Granny from Bressingham who had rugby-tackled a mugger while on holiday in Great Yarmouth. For some time, Rose had been looking for a story to lift the spirits of her readers during the gloomy season and, while the hospitalisation of Burthorpe's shopkeeper, under circumstances tactfully described by the *DP* as 'mysterious', may have seemed unpromising, she had identified its potential.

Weekly bulletins from the Norfolk and Norwich Hospital began to appear in the *DP*. Harry was still poorly after his accident. Doctors had been impressed by Harry's fighting spirit and good humour. Harry had received his first visitors, the Linighan family from Scrope Rise. Harry was now sitting up in bed and was pictured here surrounded by flowers and gifts from local wellwishers. Harry wanted to thank the readers of the *DP* for their many 'Get Well' messages. Despite his tragic accident, Harry planned to re-open his Convenience Store as soon as his health permitted. A group of local children, organised by Charles Pygott, twelve-year-old son of local landowner Simon Pygott of Garston Hall, had arranged to tidy and restock Harry's shop and (a nice touch) to install ramps where there had once been steps. And now Harry Pearson was on his way home.

So effective was the rehabilitation of Harry's reputation that the small handful of people who knew the truth behind his fall from the top-floor window had themselves all but forgotten its seedier details. Having removed certain videotapes from the Pearson flat, DC Penman of Eye Police had discussed the matter with his duty sergeant; although two of the videos, *Naughty Nymphets Through the Looking Glass* and its prequel *Naughty Nymphets in Funderland*, were strictly speaking illegal imports, the two men had decided that, at a time of rising crime, this particular can of worms was best left unopened. The sergeant had suggested that Penman would do well to lose the videos but, not being one to throw a good product away, the detective constable had taken them home. They had done little for him, to tell the truth, although, to this day, Mrs Penman has been known to invite a couple of girlfriends around of an afternoon, draw the blinds and enjoy the adventures of Anna, Ulrika and the plumber with the unfortunate skin.

At first, Rose Hope had been amused by her campaign, taking a perverse and cynical delight in the way the suspender-belted old pervert had, thanks to the power of the press, been reborn as a tragic local hero but, after a while, she had almost come to believe in the new version herself. The sad little shop with its 'CLOSED' sign, the reports from hospital, the touching contributions to the letters page: even before the devastating news was released ('TRAGIC HARRY WILL NEVER WALK AGAIN' ran the *DP*'s headline), his story had acquired an irresistible momentum. To report the great return, Rose had decided to use her best reporter, Jenny Floyd, a former weddings and funeral specialist who, when on form, could wring tears from a flower show.

That Saturday morning, as groups of local people gathered on the green outside the village shop in time for Harry's arrival by ambulance at eleven o'clock, Rose Hope walked among them, chatting to Jenny, briefing her photographer. She noticed, rather to her surprise, that Simon Pygott's Range Rover was parked some fifty yards down the road near the village pond, and wandered in its direction. Pygott was in the driver's seat, tapping his large hand on the steering-wheel. Looking up, he acknowledged her presence without any particular warmth. He leant across to switch off the tape that he had been playing and rolled down the window.

'Stranger.' Rose leant on the window, taking pleasure from the way

Pygott darted an anxious look in the direction of a nearby group of village people. Although she had more important concerns than her now-deceased affair with Simon, she was faintly irritated that he seemed embarrassed to be talking to her. 'How have you been keeping?' she asked.

'Ah. Busy.' Simon assumed the faintly impolite smile of someone trapped by a bore at a drinks party. 'Spring. Farm. School holidays. The usual sort of kit.'

'How's Jess?'

'Better.' He fiddled awkwardly with the cassette beside him. Rose noticed that it was 'The Greatest Hits of Bobby Vee'.

'I never knew you were a friend of Harry Pearson's.'

Simon nodded in the direction of the Convenience Store. 'Been whipped in by Charlie,' he said. 'He seemed to think it would be a good idea if I made it up with the old bugger.'

'Quite the little organiser, your son.'

'Yup. Full of the milk of human whatsit. Can't think where he got it from.'

There was a cheer from the main road. At a stately pace, an ambulance was making its way down the hill to the H.T. Pearson Convenience Store where it drew to a halt. Self-importantly, the driver stepped out and, with the help of a colleague, opened the back doors. As the ambulancemen set up a ramp, Harry Pearson appeared from the darkness of the vehicle. He was in a wheelchair, and waved jauntily to the crowd.

''arry,' said Simon suddenly and with uncharacteristic savagery in his voice. 'Suddenly we're all mad about 'arry.'

Sighing, Rose turned towards the shop. 'Duty calls,' she murmured.

Simon stepped out of the Range Rover as, in front of the shop, a small, hand-picked choir from the Primary School formed a semi-circle behind Burthorpe Brass, an ensemble which had been set up by Thurston Farr, the plumber. It had been agreed, at the small *ad hoc* village committee established for the occasion, that a spot of music would be nice for Harry's return and, since children were so important to him, the Primary School choir seemed the obvious choice. There had been a certain amount of discussion as to what song should be sung. 'Congratulations' had been favoured by some but had in the end been deemed inappropriate for the occasion, while the children's own favourite, 'Lord of the Dance', was thought a trifle heartless given Harry's new circumstances. In the end, they had settled upon the old Peters and Lee favourite, 'Welcome Home'. Now, the children's voices rising in comical yet oddly moving counterpoint to the elephantine farting of Burthorpe Brass, the choir was welcoming Harry home.

As the shopkeeper was steadied down the ramp by the ambulance-men, Rose took her place beside Jenny Floyd in front of the stores. A small presentation was to be made, marked by a speech from the editor and, of course, a photograph which would duly appear on the front page of next week's *DP*.

Harry was staring at the choir, a crooked smile of ecstatic delight suffusing his flushed and heavy features. 'Well,' he could be heard to say. 'Well I never.'

'The hero returns,' muttered Rose. 'I've never seen a man look so happy in my life.'

'Hasn't got much choice,' said Jenny Floyd quietly. 'The fall did it. His face is always like that.'

'Good God.' Rose gave a mayoral wave as the wheelchair made its way forward. It was true, she now saw, that there was something fixed about the rictal grin of delight on Harry's face, giving him the look of a man forever caught up in some intense, unseen pleasure. 'At least we don't have to ask him to smile for the cameras.'

Apart from his crazed facial expression, Harry Pearson looked well. Heavier than Rose remembered him, he was accorded a new dignity and authority by his throne-like wheelchair. Undeniably, handicap became him.

As the choir's rendition of 'Welcome Home' stuttered to a close, a group of morris dancers from Blo Norton moved into position. With the merest hint of awkwardness, they danced backwards and for-wards, bells ringing on their knees, waving their sticks, occasionally giving a self-conscious 'Ha!' 'Aho!' Harry Pearson tapped a hand on the arm of his wheelchair in time to the dance.

Not a moment too soon, the display came to an end. Rose Hope stepped forward and, holding her hands up for silence, addressed the small crowd.

'Well, the children have said it all with that beautiful song,' she said, smiling down at Harry. 'Ever since we at the *Diss Press* first reported your accident, Harry, we've been inundated with enquiries from the good people of Burthorpe – in fact, from folk all over the wide district currently covered by the *Diss Press*. And everyone has wanted to know the answer to the same question. When will Harry be back? When will the H.T. Pearson Convenience Store be open again?'

'Very nice,' muttered Harry.

'Well, today Harry is back. The Convenience Store is open. And we at the *Diss Press* wanted just to mark the occasion with this little ceremony and presentation.'

'Presentation?' Harry's smile took in every member of the crowd.

'And to help you on your way, Harry, *Diss Press* readers have made various contributions. Firstly, shopkeepers in the area have contributed stock so that the Convenience Store will, as ever, be groaning with goodies when you open for business today. Then' – Rose held out the first of two envelopes in her hand – 'the management at the Diss Pool thought you'd be needing a bit of exercise and came up with the idea of a weekly season ticket for swimming. Apparently you'll be very welcome at Kiddy Hour, when the schoolkids can help you in and out of the pool.'

Harry seemed briefly lost for words.

'And finally.' Rose looked at the second envelope in her hand. 'Here is, shall we say, a small contribution from your admirers at the *Diss Press*.'

As she handed over the cheque for £100, a series of photographs was taken. Charlie Pygott opened the door and Harry wheeled himself into the shop whose shelves contained more merchandise than they had seen since the days when Harry's father had been manager. Tears in his eyes, the shopkeeper wheeled himself behind the counter, which had been lowered to accommodate the height of the wheelchair.

There was a moment's awkwardness. A few of the villagers entered the shop and, in a self-conscious fashion, considered the items on the shelves, clearly uncertain as to whether some sort of purchase should be made to mark the occasion. Outside, the ambulance had left, and, as the choir and brass band dispersed, a faint air of anti-climax could be discerned among those waiting for something else to happen.

Now that Rose had entered the shop, murmurs of mild disapproval could be heard on the green. Who was this woman, after all? Where had she come from? Not from Burthorpe, that was certain. Surely, on this kind of special occasion, a local person rather than an incomer should make the presentation speech. One or two villagers even suggested that Pearson himself might have said a few words, at which point it was asked whether he *could* say a few words, whether he was in fact quite all right. There had been no suggestion in press reports that the shopkeeper was doolally but then there wouldn't be, would there? It wasn't exactly in the *DP*'s interest for the returning hero to turn out to be a nutter, was it?

Simon Pygott drifted uneasily through the crowd, unable to gossip (not part of one's education, sadly), and, despite his height and the faintly absurd tweed suit he had elected to wear, largely ignored. In past generations, the presence of the master of Garston Hall at such an occasion would have been a matter of note. Today few people recognised him and those who did felt no inclination to converse.

Emerging from the shop, Charlie Pygott made his way through the crowd and took his father lightly by the elbow.

'Dad, Harry wants to see you,' he said.

Smiling awkwardly, Simon allowed himself to be guided towards the shop door. He had not visited the Convenience Store for years and really had little idea what one did at the place. When his father had looked in, old Pearson used to dance attendance upon him, fetching goods from around the shop with a simpering, tearful smile, accepting money only with the greatest reluctance. Was that the way it happened? In which case, what was the form if the shopkeeper happened to be a cripple? Seemed wrong, somehow, chap on wheels fetching for someone with perfectly good legs.

'Mr Pearson,' he boomed, standing hugely in the doorway, then making his way past the biscuit shelves. 'Good to have you back among us.'

'Mr Pygott.' Pearson grimaced amiably. 'Your boy Charlie – '

'He's a good lad, eh?' Simon darted a blokeish smile in the direction of his son. 'Right. Well done. Good kit.' He turned to go.

'Dad.' Charlie nodded significantly.

'Ah yes, nearly forgot. You must come up to the Hall some time, Pearson. Things to discuss. Now's not the moment of course but, yes – make a plan, will you, Charlie?'

'The Hall?' H.T. Pearson managed to express surprise. 'Yes, of course. Pleasure.'

'Excellent, Charlie will sort it out, good day to you.' He turned and left the shop, nodding grandly to the other shoppers. He thought he had handled it all rather well under the circumstances.

They made their way towards the Range Rover through the few people who were still outside the shop. Simon acknowledged the villagers, glancing down occasionally at his son as if to share with him the innocent pleasures of local influence.

In the car, he pushed a cassette into place. The sound of fifties pop, bland and anodyne, filled the air.

'Bouncy, bouncy,' Simon sang.

'Dad,' Charlie protested mildly.

'"Rubber Ball" by Bobby Vee,' Simon explained, as he put the Range Rover in gear and moved off. 'One of my favourites. D'you listen to Radio Lux at school?'

'Never heard of it.'

'Oh come *on*. Fab 208. You can't be at prep school without listening to Fabulous Radio Luxemburg on the transistor radio under the pillow after lights-out.'

Charlie smiled.

'Every night I'd listen.' Simon tapped the steering-wheel in time to Bobby Vee. 'Tony Prince, the Royal Ruler. Itsy Bitsy Teeny-Weeny Yellow Polka-Dot Bikini. Everlys. Connie Francis. Horace Bachelor, the football pools man. Keynsham, spelt K.E.Y.N.S.H.A.M.' He laughed at the memory. 'Whatever had happened during the day at school, there was always good old Radio Lux to look forward to. Reminded me of the outside world away from prefects and games and lessons.'

'Who was Tony Prince?'

'I went to Luxemburg once. Travelling around Europe just after Eton, thought I'd have a deco at old Lux itself. Had this idea that it would be all juke-boxes and yellow polka-dot bikinis and jolly girls like Brenda Lee. All . . . well, bouncy.'

168

'What was it like?'

'Continental. Not fab at all,' said Simon gloomily. 'What sort of music d'you listen to, old boy?'

'Nothing much. Quite like silence actually, to tell the truth.'

Simon winced as he turned the Range Rover into the drive. Yes, *that* was what cheesed him off about his older son. You'd be making an effort, doing your best to give him the benefit of the traditional father–son chat (a bloody sight more difficult than people made out, in his opinion), thinking you were doing rather well, building bridges, establishing common ground, all that sort of kit, when, wallop, he'd spoil it all. It deflated one, made one feel silly, childish. Convinced one that *actually to tell the truth*, there wasn't any common ground between them.

'Everything has to be questioned these days, doesn't it?' he said suddenly. 'Nothing's just straightforward, good old fun.'

Aware that he had disappointed his father in some way he couldn't understand, Charlie looked out of the window. 'I only said I liked silence,' he said.

'I'm not saying there isn't a time for looking life in the eye, asking a few of the big questions, but' – Simon sighed – 'well, I didn't do it at twelve, that's all I can say. Too busy enjoying myself, getting on with things.'

'Sorry, Dad.'

'No no, don't be sorry. That's the way you are. Just have to make the most of it.'

'You're annoyed about Harry, aren't you? You didn't really want to see him.'

'Don't be daft, Charlie. Seeing Pearson's the sort of thing one has to do. No, it's that you sometimes seem so *disapproving* of everything. Even poor old Bobby Vee.'

Suddenly Simon realised that he had gone too far, that he was in danger of sounding foolish. Yet he *was* disappointed. It seemed to him that, ever since Charlie could talk, he had been asking damnfool questions to which there were no answers. Where would it all end? If, at the age of twelve, the boy couldn't accept school or meat or songs on the radio without pulling that pained, actually-to-tell-the-truth face, then how on earth was he going to cope with the rather tougher business of running the Garston estate?

Somewhere, at the back of Simon's mind, was a picture of the way it should be when a chap who owned a bit of land handed it all over to his son and heir. Chap would be in late middle age, walking the estate with the boy. He'd be fresh out of agricultural college, early twenties, bags of girlfriends staying the weekend and all that, a bit wild but no fool.

'Sting supports Greenpeace,' said Charlie, as they drew up on the gravel outside the Hall. 'D'you like Sting?'

'Never heard of it.' Simon stepped out of the Range Rover and marched briskly towards the house, leaving his son to follow a few paces behind him. It would be better when Charlie went to Gordonstoun, Simon thought. Sort his ideas out. He pushed open the door to the library.

Jess was lying by the fire. His cancerous ulcer seemed to glow against the dullness of his coat, as if what life and energy that was left to him was now concentrated in the bright pink flower of the wound. The stomach had shrunk, the muscles in his shoulders and haunches seemed to be wasting away. These days the dog was visited by the cruellest indignities of premature old age. His farts were lethal and many. Various stains caked the blanket on which he lay. Incapable of supporting his weight on one leg when taken out to the lawn, he squatted and splashed over himself, staring ahead with a martyred air. His eyes, sunk into the dark skull, now rarely looked at Simon and, when they did, it was without affection.

'He's very smelly, Dad.' Charlie stood at the door, staring at Jess.

'Yes. Jaime refuses to do the room when he's in here.'

'Well, it is rather disgusting.'

'Ees like a toilet, Meesa Peegot. I put smell dispenser on shelves and zat's eet, no more.' Simon crouched beside his dog. 'Bloody little dago queen.'

'Are you going to let Jess die?'

'Is that the environmental way?' Simon fondled Jess's ear with quiet rage. 'Keep it nice and natural? Let nature take its course?'

Charlie stood behind his father. 'If the vet came here, Jess wouldn't have to suffer. You could wait until the evening when he was drowsy.'

Simon considered the idea for a moment. 'My father used to shoot the dogs himself,' he said distantly. 'Up to Garston Wood. Took the

Holland and Holland he used for stalking in Scotland. Behind the ear. Bang. One thing he'd never ask his staff to do.'

'That was nice of him.'

'What? Oh, he wasn't worried about the staff. He thought it was unfair on the dog. They sense these things, you know.' Simon stood up and stared through the french window. 'I can still hear the bangs.'

'But we're not like that now, Dad.'

'No?' Briefly, Simon saw himself, caught in some strange way between his father and his son. It was contagious, this questioning of everything. 'Not sure about that, to tell the truth.'

'We could get another dog. From the same family.'

Simon looked down. 'Leave me for a bit, will you, old boy?'

'I could do Jess's ointment.'

'Please, Charlie.'

Simon sat down heavily on an armchair. Looking up after a few moments, he saw he was alone in the library with Jess. 'Bouncy, bouncy,' he said.

Like a river, a man's nature rolls on, its course unchanging whatever obstacles are placed before it. Sometimes it appears to move in a new direction but it will return to its old bed, its old course. Only now do I understand that.

His way was so frequently interrupted that fools were later to write that here was a man who harkened to change in his life, in history. The truth is that no man has changed less than he did. Merchant, courtier, teacher, maker, orator, scholar, countryman, rector, father, soldier: the river rolled on, undiverted.

I had refused him nothing, given him warmth, love, a child so perfect that it had been raised above the pulpit like a cherubim. To me, in those early months, he appeared no longer the clamorous courtier in love with empty talk, surrounded by bowsy educated fools with nothing to say and the Latin in which to say it, but a man who could sit by a fire and tell tales to a child.

This was my sentence. The world of the hearth, the greys and browns, mammocks of family life, were of no more than passing interest to him. The land of true feeling was, for him, painted in

171

the bright pall, the scarlets and byse and greens of court, where nothing is said direct, where the truth is seen only in the pretty glass of manners and poetry. From this land I was excluded as surely as if I were a goose or a pig or a donkey. My spirit, the spirit of my child, belonged to another, duller land, one that could never be graced by verbal description or celebration in song.

He would return from Carrow in what I believed, in my fondness, to be a creative turmoil but now know to have been a sweet agony of romantic love which could only be assuaged by my caresses. He would descend upon the cottage like a storm, rumbling with rage at the very sound of my voice, leading me to my bed not with love but with a sort of loathing which would have made me shrink from him if I had dared. He went at me with the rage of a madman digging a trench in a field. Then, half-sleeping, he would talk through the night, the sweetest of girls, a paradise of delights, my lips shall praise thee, snatches of Latin. Only later did I see that it was not me who was being praised by his lips, that I was no more than the poor faint shadow of someone else, someone so pure, so elevated by birth and breeding that the swinish expression of this noble affection, the base farmyard grunt and groan of it, could never be for her. That was my part. She was the shrine of all the pleasures, the virgo dulcissima, the divine inspiration for his love. I was the receptacle for it, the slop-bucket.

Shame is less than truth, he was to write when she, poor lady, expressed affront at his verses. It was, like most of what he wrote, a nice deceit. Shame was, and is, greater than any truth. Shame was to lie beneath a man who was loving another through you, his eyes closed tight, groaning as if his very heart was being torn from him.

The sparrow marked the end of his domestic days, of the diversion called parenthood. At the convent, he was taken back to the true road of youth, beauty, love, purity and, above all, gentility besides which the realities of marriage and children were a dark and muddy lane leading nowhere.

Pla ce bo! Who is there, who? Di le xi! Dame Margery. Fa, re, mi, mi. Wherefore and why, why? I have heard these lines, and

172

those that follow, many times over the years, though not read by their creator, of course. They have been praised for their newness, for the tenderness (hah!) of their evocation of a way of life lost in time. By carefully ignoring the facts that lay before them (in one account the dead and poetic sparrow was treated at twice the length of the 'musket', who had lived uncelebrated), scholars have averted their eyes from the fraud, from the delicate fakery that lay behind the lines.

Oh, the care with which he flatters his readers – it minds me of his early days at the Rectory when, with those nice words of his, he was stalking me as stealthily as Gib the cat was said to have stalked the sparrow.

Latin and English, the mythical and the homely, desirous and yet pure, a sheen of classical ornacy decorating and disguising his scaly old man's lust. This was truth! they cried. Here is a poet conjoining the sublime and the mundane, the spiritual and the fleshly, the noble and the domestic, the mind and the heart in one epic work! A poet who is yet a man, and proud of it.

A master of the observed life? It was I who told him the birds, gave him the list of names that has impressed scholars and naturalists down the years. He could never tell a raven from a robin redbreast because he never saw them. In those early days when we went walking by the river, I realised that he observed less than any person I had ever known. At the time, I mistook this blindness for courtly conning. Later I saw that his eyes were simply turned inwards, gazing at the fascinating and ever-changing landscape of his poet's soul.

Time passed. Soon we never walked together. It was rare now that he visited us, and, when he did, he wore the lere of distaste of a parson whose sad duty it is to visit the poor of the parish. His eyes were averted from young Joseph and our baby Mary. He forsook my bed. I imagined, without pain, that he must have found elsewhere the soft comfort that was so important to him, that he was worshipping at some other shrine of all the pleasures.

My cottage grew darker, vines and ivy enclosing the windows in a damp embrace as if the earth itself was reclaiming us. I found it

173

difficult to busy myself with family matters. Not being a poet, I was spurned as one failing in her God-given duties. He left me more money. I spent it on beer or mull or sometimes lost it in the mud and leaves outside the cottage. He ceased to visit us at all.

Mary died of fever. She had seemed fretful, uninterested in food and one morning I found her cold and blue in her cot. Joseph was taken from me. Starving as he was, he still cried piteously. My talk of the Rector was dismissed as the ravings of a poor soul who had lost her wits although each of them knew who had fathered my children.

Once I visited the Rectory but by then he had gone. He had returned to his life after the brief diversion that was his family.

Something was happening to Alison. Maybe it was the birth of spring, or simply unhappiness – whatever the reason, her mind would drift away from the busy, distracting routine of domestic life. Sometimes she would stare out of the kitchen window, gaze over the gentle swell of Charlie Watson's field of spring barley to the coppiced wood on the edge of the Garston estate. Birds would be singing, the hares so rarely seen during the rest of the year might be doing their demented courtship dance in the field. Everywhere, among the animals, on the undulating landscape, she sensed a juicy vernal yearning. Then, uneasy with these thoughts, she would shake her head, swear softly and try to think of work to do in the house or the garden to distract her mind.

She had once read in a book the story of a married couple who had not spoken to one another, except in the company of others, for seven years – so perfectly did they play the parts expected of them that no one had the slightest idea that they cohabited in a state of simmering, silent loathing. It was, she had thought at the time, one of fiction's more absurd conceits. Today she understood. She realised that, unwittingly, she had for some time been waiting for someone to pass by with the key to her cage.

Then, one day in early May, she found him.

She had been on her way back from Kate's recorder lesson, which had gone badly. They had stopped at the world's least romantic spot, the H.T. Pearson Convenience Store. Harry Pearson was busy in earnest negotiation with a man in a dark suit.

There was something about the man's voice. She looked, noting the gentle slope to his shoulders as he spoke to Harry, his hair, his back. As Kate chose her sweets, Alison willed him to notice her. He turned and looked, swallowing and – this touched her – completely losing the drift of what he had been saying.

They were in one another's company for slightly over a minute. Their conversation was unexceptional.

'I'm sorry, are you waiting to be served?'

'No, I'm fine. No hurry.'

'(There is hurry, Mummy. I want to go home.)'

'(Don't be rude, Kate.) Sorry about that.'

'No problem. (Harry, why don't I leave you this card and I'll call back next week. Say, Wednesday, four-thirty?) Sorry to have kept you waiting.'

'No no. My . . . pleasure.'

'(Why's it a pleasure, Mummy? Why did you say that?)'

'(Don't be silly.) Kids!'

'(Bye, Harry, thanks, next week then. Bye, Kate.)'

'(Say goodbye, Kate.)'

'(Bye.)'

'Goodbye.'

'Goodbye.'

After he had left, Harry Pearson grumbled about the man. Ever since the first rumours that the Post Office would be privatised, this spiv's firm had been pestering him to sell out. He had told them he wasn't on the market, not after all that had happened to him, all the marvellous support he had received. As Harry talked, Alison, with the daring of the truly smitten, picked up the stranger's calling card from the counter and put it in her pocket.

Did it matter that he was clearly younger than she was, that his job ranked him, among contemporary undesirables, alongside, say, a property developer specialising in turning hospitals into hotels, that his car and clothes suggested a certain lack of sophistication? It did not. Alison kept his calling card beneath the lining paper in her knicker drawer. She referred to it occasionally. She turned his name over in her mind. Paul Gilchrist. Paul. Paul and Alison. Alison and Paul. She liked it.

Rose Hope had become convinced that she was approaching one of those moments in her life when a change of speed, a switch in direction, was required. It had happened in the early seventies when she had abandoned the alternative press, with its attendant pleasures of dope and multiple partnership (Rose Grope, one of her many passing lovers had called her), for a job on a women's magazine. There had been another natural break when the editor of a Sunday newspaper, with whom she shared her body on a regular, orderly basis, gave her a job on the diary page in 1981. With the end of both the decade and the affair (a bitter moment of betrayal, involving a younger, firmer, more pliable version of Rose Hope), she had resolved to search for a less glittering reality in the heart of East Anglia.

Now, she realised, there were few profound truths to be found here. A coffee morning was a coffee morning, a rural affair was – apart from its more agreeable setting – not markedly different from its urban counterpart. She longed for the thrust of city life, the edgy pleasure of duplicitous competition.

As she had done so often in the past, Rose turned to a past lover to facilitate her next career move.

Like the birdwatchers who pass through Burthorpe on their way to Minsmere or Redgrave Fen, Rose had, over the past years, been an acquisitive and systematic collector. Ranging widely both in the professional and social spheres, she had found herself in circumstances of one-on-one intimacy with a considerable variety of men from all walks of life. What had once been no more than the natural charge provided by power and success had, with experience, developed into a more considered and predatory system of professional advancement. It really was rather useful to know that, whenever she needed expert advice, she could turn to someone with whom she had once shared a few moments of desire. Although her preference was for married men – their response to requests for assistance had an element of slightly panicky urgency which was helpful – there was nothing sinister or planned about Rose's system. She never slept with men she found entirely repellent, and she rarely repeated the experience. Once twitched, the man entered Rose's address book as an old friend, a useful contact, but no more than that.

When she had first met Philip Gross in the mid-seventies, he had been a brilliant young pathologist whose startling intelligence, shoulder-length hair and actress wife had made him one of the rare academics who had genuine colour-magazine appeal. Today the wife had gone, as had the hair, but enough intelligence had remained to secure the Chair of Pathology at Nottingham University. Hearing from Rose, and after a few reminders of what direction the interview at Brown's Hotel had taken all those years ago, Gross was eager to accommodate her. Yes, of course, he would be delighted to examine the blood specimen she had found. But why? Blood is blood is blood.

Rose had reminded him that, as a journalist, she had to be careful not to reveal too much, a fact that he should know better than most, and Gross abandoned his line of questioning.

The letter now lay on the desk in front of Matthew Turville. It was late in the afternoon and the undertaker's secretary Margaret had, with a touching reluctance to leave her boss working without her assistance, left the office.

'Have you heard of Professor Gross?' Rose asked.

'No.' Matthew had with only the greatest reluctance agreed to see her. His voice, she now noted, betrayed an edge of irritation which even years of experience in aftercare and grief counselling failed to suppress.

'*The Chemistry of Death*. It's quite a well-known work. I would have thought it would be part of your bedside reading.'

Matthew remained impassive, unamused. 'What's all this about, Rose?' he asked.

She picked up the letter and started to read. '"Dear Rose, Pleasure to hear from you once more after all these years. Your request was no imposition and, even if it was, I can think of absolutely no one by whom I would prefer to be imposed upon – "' Rose looked up. 'We're old friends,' she explained.

'Go on.'

'"Your blood: I was not, as 'twere, sanguine as to the chance of "reading" too much into the stained fabric that you sent me and I regret that my forebodings have proved amply justified. There are no signs of any DNA indicators, nor is it possible to ascertain to which blood group it belongs. There are certainly the basic chemical properties of blood – but it appears to be of such antiquity as to preclude any serious or detailed analysis. And here's where I confess to being somewhat stumped. Normally, the colour of blood this old would have faded or disappeared altogether. In other words, it should, at best, be a dark, anonymous stain. The fact that it retains a distinct reddish pigmentation is quite simply a mystery. I can only assume that freak conditions (was it discovered below ground? In a cellar?) have conspired to keep this particular sample at such low temperatures that it has retained its original characteristics. Does this make any sense to you? I long to know more about what you're up to. Talking of which – " The rest is personal stuff.'

Matthew rubbed his eyes wearily. 'You're not still on about that stain?'

'Listen, Matthew, I'm as sceptical as you are, but look at the facts. A burial ground is about to be moved across the village. Suddenly, trees are falling on people for no reason, vans are bursting into flames, a shopkeeper's jumping out of his top window, there are other mysterious deaths like your Mrs Kirby – and, on each occasion, a red mark is found near the scene. According to an expert, the substance consists of blood so old that the fact that it retains its colour defies logical scientific explanation. Christ, how much more evidence do you need?'

'Are you saying you want me to reverse the decision to move to Chapel Meadow? Another great campaigning triumph for the *DP*.'

'Not at all. I just want your help. This could be an extraordinary phenomenon which I plan to follow up. I'm getting help on the historical background from Miles Larwood – '

Matthew raised his eyebrows sceptically.

'– and, more importantly, I've managed to get a production company interested. There might be a few TV cameras in the village over the next few weeks.'

'Looking for ghosts.'

'This is serious, Matthew.'

'The answer is no.' He spoke quietly. 'Before you bother to ask, I won't do an interview. I won't give them information. This is a stupid publicity stunt of which I want no part. Clear?'

'In which case, we'll have to do the story without you. You'd be sensible to co-operate.'

'Ah.' Matthew smiled coldly. 'The traditional journalist's threat.'

'Just a statement of fact.'

'I don't want a TV camera within a hundred yards of this funeral home.'

'Not even if it's a matter of public interest?'

'And if you want that in writing, I'll speak to my lawyers.'

Rose shrugged. 'I thought you might welcome the exposure.'

Matthew was looking at her coldly. Under the bright office lighting, he looked pasty and unhealthy, with dark shadows under his eyes, his hair uncharacteristically lank and untended. He suddenly appeared to Rose like a man in some sort of decline. 'It's not the dead that cause problems around here,' he said pointedly. 'It's the living.'

'You seem a bit haunted yourself, come to think of it,' she said.

He held her gaze for a moment, then looked away, like someone who has allowed too much of his inner life to be revealed. 'It's a busy time,' he said.

'Nothing odd to report, then? No spooks hanging around the Turville household? No messages from beyond concerning Chapel Meadow.'

Matthew stood up and glanced at his watch. 'Not that I've noticed,' he said.

CREMATION, ENVIRONMENTAL IMPLICATIONS OF
The practice of consuming a corpse to ash, originally introduced as a 'pre-emptive strike' against returning spirits (see THE REVENANT AND IDENTITY: TOWARDS AN UNDERSTANDING OF THE MYTH OF THE SUPERNATURAL and REVENANCE, THEORY OF) has now reached such a level of popularity in countries such as Britain that questions are increasingly being asked about the environmental viability of cremation-related burial practices.

According to no less an authority than C. J. Polson[1], 'An adult

[1] C. J. Polson, *The Scientific Aspects of Forensic Medicine* (Oliver & Boyd, 1969).

body of about 160 lbs (73 kg), cremated in a purpose-built furnace fired by gas, and with recirculation of hot gases, is destroyed to ash in three-fourths to one hour of steady burning at a temperature around 1,600°F (870°C).' Advances in cremation technology have reduced the consumption of fossil fuel: in earlier types of furnace, air was admitted cold and uncontrolled, each corpse requiring from 10 to 15 hundredweight of coke.

Contemporary usage:

Gas – 1444 cu. ft – 1964 cu. ft.

Electric furnace – 180 kw at operating temperature.

Oil – approximately 24 gallons.

Environmentally, it is a positive factor when a sophisticated 'in the round' furnace is used, since combustion only takes place where oxygen reaches the client[2].

THE LOSS OF AFFECTIVITY, OR THE WAY WE DIE NOW

No age has turned its face more fearfully from death than our own. Over the past half-century, modern man/woman has developed strategies to obscure the reality and significance of our mortality; death-wise, he/she is 'in denial'.

A growing sense of death as something unseemly and shocking established itself within the popular psyche during the thirties and forties; the advance of medical science over the past fifty years has done the rest. 'Our senses can no longer tolerate the sights and smells that in the early nineteenth century were part of daily life,' wrote Ariès[1]. In 1949, 50 per cent of all deaths took place in hospital. By 1994, the figure had reached 80 per cent. Society isolates the dying from the living to the detriment not only of those who see out their days in solitude, but also to the society that survives them. If, as St Bernard reflected, 'Mors janna vitae'[2], we are excluded from life itself.

Even in hospitals, death has come to be regarded as something squalid and shameful. An American undertaker[3] has revealed how nurses will sometimes leave a patient who has

[2] W. E. D. Evans, *The Chemistry of Death* (Thomas, 1963).
[1] P. Ariès, *op. cit.*
[2] 'Death is the gate of life.'
[3] Vanderlyne R. Pyne, *Caretaker of the Dead: The American Funeral Director* (Irvington, 1975).

died to be discovered by the next shift, or even, in order to minimise the need to handle a dead body, do some of the preparations *while the patient is still alive.*

The eminent American doctor Sherwin B. Nuland expressed the personal thematic of this crisis in death-role identity in the following terms: 'An intensive care unit is merely a secluded treasureroom of high-tech hope within the citadel in which we segregate the sick so that we may better care for them. Those tucked-away sanctums symbolise the purest form of society's denial of the naturalness, even the necessity, of death. For many of the dying, intensive care, with its isolation among strangers, extinguishes their hope of not being abandoned in the last hours. In fact, they *are* abandoned, to the good intentions of highly skilled professional personnel who barely know them. Nowadays the style is to hide death from view.'[4]

[4] S. B. Nuland, *How We Die* (Chatto & Windus, 1994).

'It's all going terrifically well. I never thought this could happen to me but the project actually wakes me up in the early morning, *demanding* to be written. My eyes snap open, I feel a kind of tightness in the stomach, rather as you feel when something very good is about to happen to you. As soon as I'm in front of the word-processor, it just, well, flows out of me and on to that screen. Page after page after. It's almost as if the project is writing itself – as if I'm merely the intermediary of some, I don't know, some – '

'Ghost?'

'No, I wouldn't go that far. Some force greater than myself, shall we say?'

'Goodness.'

'Yes.' Miles Larwood smiled at the small, dark figure seated across the kitchen table from him. So still, so attentive, her pale, serious features framed by dark curls, she listened and understood how a writer can be writing all day, 'running on empty' – literally *drained* – and yet by the end of the day still need to talk through his ideas, unwind with a sympathetic companion. 'You seem to understand the creative process,' he said.

'I once knew a writer.'

'A lot of people don't understand how it works.' Miles held the bottle of whisky up to Margaret but, even before she had shaken her head, he was pouring himself another glass.

'To them, it's just words,' she said.

'Exactly.' Miles took a hurried, preoccupied sip of his whisky. 'To tell the truth, that's the problem with my friend in Norwich. She sees this handbook of mine as just another job. I might be trying to explain some small satisfaction from the writing life and, as soon as I start talking, I can sense her tuning out. It's as if she's not listening, but searching in her mind for one of *her* little triumphs, a more glittering equivalent from the world of Environmental Studies to anything I could achieve, with which to cap my story.'

'Yes.'

'For her, conversation's like chess – there's always a bloody counter-move.'

'I see.'

Miles brooded for a moment. 'Friend, I say "friend" in the broadest, loosest sense. Between you and me, it was just one of those relationships that sort of happen and no one can quite think of a way to make them unhappen.'

Margaret said nothing.

'It's different with you,' Miles said, choosing to sound drunker than in fact he felt. 'I enjoy talking to you so much. We really communicate, don't we?'

'Yes.'

'It's important to listen to people, *that's* what Katherine doesn't understand. When someone else is talking, it's not just in order to give you time to think of something else to say about yourself.'

'No.'

'You give, you take – it's like life.'

'Are you including those stories from village life you were considering?' Margaret asked.

Miles smiled. She had proved the point. This woman didn't only listen: she heard. She was genuinely interested in his work. 'I'm coming to that in Part Two,' he said. 'At the moment, the general stuff is just spilling out on to the page. I want to get that raw material down, the basic clay. *Then* I'll start sculpting in earnest.'

'Would it be helpful to have a reader?'

He hesitated, frowning. It occurred to him that there may have been more of him in the pages he was to write than he immediately wished to reveal. 'Perhaps I've somewhat overplayed the popular, anecdotal element,' he said, choosing his words carefully. 'Most of it's rather technical and academic.'

'I can read, you know,' she said sharply.

'I'm aware of that but – '

'You don't think I can read your book. You think I'm foolish.'

'Good Lord; no. I – I merely meant that, to the average lay non-thanatologist, some of the terms of reference may verge on the abstruse.'

'I see.'

'What I'm trying to say is that, if it wouldn't bore you too much, I'd be delighted if you would read for me.'

'No,' she said, standing up. 'I'm going to bed.'

'Margaret – '

But she had gone. He heard the small angry feet stomping up the stairs. Cursing his ineptitude, Miles poured himself another drink. Hell's teeth, maybe he had sounded a trifle high-handed.

The misunderstanding could not have happened at a worse moment. He had found that he was thinking more and more frequently of Margaret, of her serious, quiet grace, her lack of small talk, even (although he liked to think he was not taken in by appearances) the way she looked. Increasingly, he had found himself considering a scenario in which Margaret took Dr Katherine Porter's place in his affections. He imagined a quiet, easy relationship, in which the perfect balance between intimacy and independence had been established.

It occurred to him that the open, adult way of dealing with this evening's gaffe was to 'set the record straight' regarding his view of Margaret's reading capabilities; perhaps a few words called through the door as he passed on his way to his bedroom would, if deployed in an appropriately light-hearted tone, preclude any overnight brooding on her part.

He switched off the light in the kitchen and began to climb the stairs. At first he thought that the faint crackling noise he could hear ahead of him was simply an effect of the alcohol that he had consumed. Then, noticing that the sound, like the rapid flicker of a faulty electrical connection or of the fuse on a firework, seemed to be coming from his lodger's bedroom, he stealthily made his way to the top of the stairs and on to the corridor. He called her name. The noise grew louder. He knocked gently. Receiving no answer, he crouched before the keyhole.

Inside the room, Miles could see the bed, illuminated by moonlight shining through the window. It appeared to be empty, although there was something on the bed, moving either underneath or even, in some strange invisible way, on top of the blankets. The moving valley in the centre of the bed was growing smaller all the time.

He knocked again. Margaret was not in her room and, if she had left the house for one of the late-night walks which she occasionally enjoyed, Miles was sure that he would have heard the front door close. He turned the handle and entered the bedroom.

By now, the uneven electrical buzzing had faded. Yet it seemed to Miles that there was an unusual ambience in the room – a chill not entirely explained by the open window. He shivered. Above the bed, he noticed what seemed to be a tell-tale sign of Margaret's recent presence: a barely perceptible haze of bluish cigarette smoke which hovered above the pillow, then spiralled slowly upwards and through the narrow gap of the window.

He looked out into the night but saw nothing apart from the smoke, still adhering to itself in the strange way that smoke occasionally has, drifting across the pale full moon.

Hanging in the air of the room was the faint but unmistakable smell of burning.

The old dog moaned, then growled half-heartedly as Simon Pygott crouched beside him in the dark. Ignoring the odorous force-field of rotting flesh that assaulted his nostrils, Simon placed one arm under Jess's haunches, the other in front of his shoulders, and lifted him into the dark interior of the Range Rover.

Their departure had taken some organising, but then Simon had recently come to the conclusion that it was in organisation that the answer to all his problems lay. He was going to organise one thing, then organise another thing, one step at a time, until he had organised his way into a bright, new, orderly day. He would be like one of those painters who does a tree one day, a cloud the next, then a couple of sheep, until he looks up to find the whole bally landscape is just there, all organised and in apple-pie order.

First Jess. Then the boys. Then Chapel Meadow. Then the farm. Then Susan. One step at a time, that was the way.

For a moment, he stood on the gravel beside the vehicle, in which Jess had carefully stretched out on the back seat. Simon looked up at the dark shape of the Hall, the reflection of moonlight on the moat. He had originally planned to take Jess to the wood at a time when Charlie was still awake in bed – a shot echoing suddenly in the dark outside would remind him in a relatively painless way of the traditional Pygott way of doing things – but, in the end, the organisation had been too tricky. What if the boy had looked out of his window, had guessed in a flash what had been organised? There would be grim scenes in front of the house – whining dog, blubbing child, Jaime prancing about, wringing his hands like something out of a ghastly continental comic opera.

Simon stepped into the driver's seat. Nearby, leaning against the passenger door, were a spade and a twelve-bore shotgun, which he had taken the precaution of placing in the Range Rover and covering with a blanket before he had brought Jess out. The old dog was still likely to get over-excited when he saw a shotgun, and the idea of telling him that tonight there would be no retrieving for him, nor ever again, come to that, was pretty bloody unbearable. Organisation, planning, what he called forward thinking.

But now, as the engine turned over, Simon's thoughts went not forwards, but backwards. In his mind, he saw Jess, a young Jess, bounding ahead of him, occasionally looking back, head questioningly on one side, as they went out for a spot of rough shooting at dusk. A man and his dog waiting for wood pigeons to come into roost. That was peace, that was happiness. Why hadn't he realised it at the time? What strange, inexplicable impulse had caused him to let even that simple pleasure slip through his fingers? One day, he had been about to fetch his gun when he had suddenly realised that he no longer wanted to kill birds any more. He hadn't mentioned it to anyone, of course, but just quietly let Colin Dunn take over the syndicate, pleading pressure of work. He had tried to explain to Jess, but even now the old dog would still prick up his ears when distant shots echoed across the valley from Watson's land.

Sitting in the darkness, Simon felt the cold of the night on his cheeks which seemed to be wet. He wiped his nose with the back of his hand. Oh bloody hell, he was actually blubbing now. He reminded himself that he was a father, a landowner, but somehow that made the tears fall faster.

Everything that had once been so simple was now so damned complicated. The certainties around which his life had been built seemed to be rotting away as inexorably as the flesh on Jess's flank. His mind slithering into nostalgia, Simon saw bright, sunlit images in the dark lane before him. His father returning on a Friday evening, loud voices, the dogs barking and bundling gladly against his legs as he entered the Hall, Susan and the boys taking tea on the lawn, a summer landscape quilted with the gold of perfect, heavy crops, the green of meadows containing their fine, healthy dairy herd. Then what? One moment things seemed to be getting a bit tricky, the next it had all disappeared like a dream, Dad off to Italy, Susan to London where these days Jeremy was spending more and more time, leaving him and Jess and Charlie at Garston as everything decayed all around them.

The Hall had somehow seemed fuller in those days. Every part of it had been overflowing with good things. Biscuits and meringues in the kitchen, the porch cluttered with croquet mallets and fishing rods and tennis rackets. Flowers, fruit bowls full of figs and peaches, on the tables in the hall and dining-room. Dogs and people and staff and noise and life.

Yet, even before the pictures and the books had been sold off, gaps had mysteriously seemed to appear at Garston. No horses in the stables, just one dog, the kitchen full of empty shelves, carpets threadbare. After Susan had lost interest, he had occasionally invested in what he called homely items that he happened to see in shop windows in Diss – green spotted leopards, some Victorian prints, amusing framed cartoons by Giles for the loo – but they always looked out of place at Garston. Outside, the fields were now full of other people's cattle, animals which appeared somehow smaller and meaner and wilder and more ordinary than the gentle Jersey cows he remembered from his youth. Even the flowerbeds around seemed second-rate and suburban when he thought of the rampant colour that used to surround the house like an opulent necklace.

It was odd that, apart from the occasional consignments to Sotheby's or the auction in Diss, Simon couldn't remember any of these things actually going. Had his father supervised the slow draining of the Hall's lifeblood? This evening, Simon had looked into the gun cabinet and had been astonished to find that the Holland and Holland, Dad's favourite stalking rifle, had disappeared. Flogged off? Or had Jaime's neat, dark, little fingers magicked it away? Simon sighed and glanced down at the twelve-bore. It would do the job, if a little messily.

The vehicle rocked as it took the pitted lane that led down the valley past Chapel Meadow and, from the back seat, Jess groaned.

'Outies, old dog.' Anxious that Jess should have no idea of the aim of their journey, Simon tried for a cheery tone, but there was a crack in his voice. 'Going for a midnight run.'

The dark shape of Garston Wood loomed up in front of them, the headlights of the Range Rover illuminating the track leading into the trees, from which, with no particular urgency, rabbits hopped into the undergrowth.

'Bloody animals, eh, Jess?' Simon remembered as a child sitting on the front of his father's Land Rover, a 4/10 in his hands, shooting rabbits caught, mesmerised, in the headlights. He had felt close to Dad on those occasions, useful. Father and son, going out at night, working together; it gave him a sense of belonging. For a while, when Charlie and Jeremy had been babies, he had imagined the day when they too would sit on the front of a Land Rover, one on each wing, blasting away, doing their bit for the farm, but now he knew it would never happen. Even Jeremy would whinge about giving the bunnies a chance to run away. As for Charlie, he would be traumatised for life.

While organising this afternoon, Simon had driven down to the wood and had trudged around considering where Jess might be buried. A glade surrounded by old beech trees had seemed suitable at first but it was too close to a public footpath frequented by so-called 'ramblers'. The idea of his dog being trodden underfoot by the good folk of Burthorpe Simon had found distressing.

Then there was the stream that cut through the wood on its way to Chapel Meadow. Remembering the way Jess used to love plunging into water when he was young, Simon had explored the bays and sandpits by its banks before deciding that a shift of wet earth during winter would risk uncovering his dog's poor old bones.

It had been quite late, as the light began to fade, that he had found himself making his way between the row of tall lime trees that had been planted by Sir Charles Pygott in the late eighteenth century to mark the Sunday walk he would take with his family on his way to St Botolph's Church. Near the edge of the wood, no more than fifty yards from the beet field that marked the start of Charlie Watson's land, there was a clump of tall poplars whose upper branches had been colonised by rooks, forming a kind of roof. There was something about the place, its darkness, the clamour of the birds over his head, that made the right connection. He had stood, hands sunk deep in his Barbour jacket, and had known this damp and lush enclosure had been created to be Jess's final resting place.

Now, slowly, he drove the Range Rover down the avenue, headlights catching the bright, small, silver-and-red reflections of night eyes in the shrubbery. Despite the thought of the task ahead of him, he felt the peace of a man who had made a decision and was now acting upon it. Over the last thirty yards, a narrow footpath leading from the avenue through the undergrowth to the clearing would need to be walked. As Simon stopped the vehicle, switched off the engine and headlights, Jess briefly raised his head, then gently let it fall back on the seat.

Simon stepped out. He opened the passenger door, took the spade and the torch, and, having reassured Jess that he would return soon, made his way down the footpath.

Standing in the centre of the clearing, Simon prodded the earth twice with his spade, the click of metal against small stones making a brief, muffled sound in the still of the wood. He was about to start digging when something attracted his attention. High above his head, the branch of a poplar tree trembled distinctly, almost as if some animal was moving through it, shaking it, making the tree's shimmering leaves catch the silver of the moon. Then silence returned. Moments later, another branch, lower and on the other side of the clearing, began to tremor as if in response, before that too died away. A young beech beside the path was the next to move, then another poplar. For several minutes, the breeze traversed from one side of the clearing to the other, setting up a conspiracy of whispers, bewitching Simon with its seductive, sibilant rhythm. Then, remembering why he was there, he lifted the spade high and let it fall, cutting deep into the dark, peaty earth.

The grave took fifteen minutes to dig and was about three feet in depth. When he had finished, Simon stood straight and stabbed the spade into the mound of black earth that was heaped on one side of it. Whatever had caused the trees to move had gone now and, apart from the sound of his own heaving breathing, the wood was perfectly silent. He wondered if his father had taken this amount of trouble when disposing of his dogs. Somehow he found it difficult to imagine Dad digging a ditch.

Reluctantly, Simon applied his mind to the grim practicalities of the task that lay ahead. It was essential that Jess had no idea of what was happening – a problem since, even now that he was mortally sick, the dog's instincts were razor-sharp. Last week, for instance, when Simon had been obliged to take Jeremy down to London to join Susan, he had specifically said, '*Not* going to London, old dog. Just a little drive,' but Jess – Simon could tell from the resentful, almost contemptuous expression on his face – had seen through the lie.

He would smell the oil on the gun. The deep hole would arouse his suspicions. It was tempting to do the deed near the car, just after Jess had jumped out, was getting his bearings – sneak up behind him, sorry, old dog, bang – but then he would have to drag the corpse, its head blown away by twelve-bore shot, down the path to the grave. Simon shuddered at the thought. He would feel like a murderer.

'Here's what we'll do.' He spoke quietly to himself. 'Get him out. Bring the rug. Walk him down the track. Lay the rug near the hole. Tell him that you've forgotten something. Put him on the rug. Go back for the gun and – oh bloody *hell*.' Simon's mind recoiled from the scene he was imagining.

Swaying in the dark, he thought of his father. He thought of Charlie, the Pygott tradition.

He walked to the Range Rover and briskly opened the back door.

'Outies, Jess,' he called.

The dog looked up incredulously.

'Yes, I know it's a bit dark, old dog but – hey – maybe we can catch some rabbits.'

Jess pricked up one ear, half-interested.

'That's right, *rabbits*, Jess.'

Some enfeebled vestige of the sporting instinct propelled the dog to his feet and, with a grunt, he clambered out of the car.

'*Where's* a rabbit, Jess?' Simon blinked awkwardly.

The dog looked around him, bending his body in a painful imitation of pleasure.

'Yes, down that path. *Let's* go.'

Jess led the way. Taking the rug from the back seat, Simon followed.

When, moments later, the dog stopped his brisk waddle through the undergrowth, Simon almost fell over him.

'You bloody old fool,' he muttered.

Jess seemed to be frozen to the spot. He had broadened his shoulders as if in response to some threat, his hackles rising, a low but unconvincing growl rumbling in the base of his throat. The behaviour was so uncharacteristic that, for an awful moment, Simon became convinced that the dog had seen his grave, had understood in an instant the fate that awaited him. Then he saw what had stopped Jess in his tracks.

A luminous grey shape was passing through the shrubbery some ten yards ahead and to the right of where they stood. It was moving so quickly and soundlessly that only when it glided into the clearing and paused by the mound of earth did Simon notice that it had a human form.

Jess was pushing back in terror against Simon's legs but seemed unable to look away from the apparition. It stood, gazing, head bowed, into the freshly dug grave, a small figure, probably female, although its brightness precluded any detailed memory of what she was wearing or of her features, even when she turned to face them. Then, as if a gust of wind had gathered her in the still of the night, she was spirited away through the trees until all Simon could see of her was a faint shadow of light fading in the direction of the village.

'Did you see that?' Simon whispered.

After a few moments, he glanced down. For the first time, he noticed that Jess was no longer pushing against his legs. The dog was lying on his belly on the path, legs buckled beneath him, his chin resting flat on the ground like the head on a tigerskin rug.

'Old dog?' Simon placed a hand on the dark shoulder.

Jess rolled lifelessly on to his side as if some unheard voice had bidden him one more time to die for the queen. A speck of dirt adhered to the dark eyeball. His dark top lip twitched in an expression which might have been his last growl, or his last smile. The mouth was slightly open, its tongue extruding, a silver, glistening trail of saliva dribbling on to the grass.

Simon knelt down and felt for a pulse in the neck. There was none.

'Rose, I must see you.'

'Are you quite mad, Simon? It's after midnight. I have to be at the printers' tomorrow.'

'Something really quite extraordinary happened.'

'Tell me about it tomorrow evening.'

'Rose, don't laugh at me, but I've seen an angel.'

'An angel.'

'I took Jess to Garston Wood because I had decided that I had to, that the time had come – well, I just did.'

'And saw an angel.'

'Yes. An angel. In the wood. In the Temple of Jess.'

'For fuck's sake, Simon. Have you been drinking?'

'She was just floating through the woods. Through the trees, Rose. Then she stopped and sort of looked at us. When she went, she took Jess with her.'

'*What?*'

'Not literally. I mean, Jess is dead.'

'Oh, I'm sorry, Simon. I know how much he meant to you. Look, what you should do is pour yourself a brandy, take yourself off to bed, then in the morning – how d'you mean she took Jess with her?'

'Not literally, but when she floated off, I looked down and Jess was dead.'

'Floated off?'

'I mean, she passed *through* the trees, as if she were made of air – as if, well, she was an angel, it's the only way I can describe it. She was the most astonishing thing I've ever seen . . . Rose, are you still there?'

'I'm on my way over.'

11

THE COURTS
ANGER AT 'YOBS.' CHARTER' VERDICT
There were angry scenes outside Diss Magistrates' Court on
Tuesday after a fifteen-year-old boy was given a twelve-
month suspended sentence after being found guilty of
theft, possession of drugs and evasion of TV licence duty.

Gavin Dance had stolen a quantity of pig tranquilliser from
a local farmyard with the intention, police claimed in court,
of selling it as an illegal substance to London dealers.

But, according to social workers from Mid-Suffolk Council, Dance – known locally as Naughty Boy – had been
looking after the two-year-old child of a neighbour and
had financially supported the group of 'travellers' who live
in vans beside the old railway station in Burthorpe.

Local MP Christopher Hamilton-Martin said he was
'deeply disturbed' by the case. 'Surely to goodness, it's time
to recognise that evil is evil, whatever age the criminal
happens to be,' said Mr Hamilton-Martin who described
the verdict as 'a yobs' charter'.

Eye police have expressed disappointment at the sentence.
'This sort of thing does make our job that much more
difficult, to be honest,' said a spokesman. Dance refused
to speak to our reporter.

DP *comment: page 5*
*Naughty or just plain evil? Your chance to vote on the Dance
case.*

'**M**ORE TEARS?'

Paul Gilchrist lies diagonally across the bed, running his left hand over the blonde head that rests on his chest. The movement is gentle and repetitive, like someone calming a fretful child.

Paul and Alison. They are together in a hotel in Bury St Edmunds.

'I thought I was hurting you at first,' he murmurs. 'Now I'd be disappointed if you didn't cry when we made love.'

'I can't help myself,' she says. 'Suddenly it all crowds in on me. Good and bad. The past, the future. You, the children. What I have and what I want. It's a sort of ecstatic drowning, as if I'm sucked under, losing control.' She smiles, embarrassed. 'It's never happened before.'

'Never?'

'Never.'

'It must have been good once with your husband.'

'You know, it wasn't.' It's as if Alison has never realised this fact until now. 'I told myself that we were good together, but we never were. I always thought that it would get better, or that, if it didn't, I would begin to mind less. Because everything else was fine. I believed that for years.' She sighs. 'Maybe it's the same with all unhappy marriages. Behind all the angry talk, all the silences, is just a simple, sad little sexual tragedy.'

'It does matter.'

Alison sits up in bed. She reaches for Paul's cigarettes which lie on the bedside table, offers one to him, takes one herself. They both light up. She, her lungs unused to the smoke, coughs briefly, then rests her head on his shoulder. 'It's the great lie that the old pass on to the young,' she says. 'Never mind the sex, they say. It's friendship that matters – conversation, affection, shared interests.'

'Maybe you'll do the same one day.'

'No. When my daughter wants to get married, I won't ask her if his intentions are honourable, or if he's a nice boy with decent job prospects.'

'Yes, yes, dear – but is he a good fuck?'

They both laugh.

'And your son?' Paul asks.

Alison thinks for a moment. Stephen has always been afflicted by his father's weakness for conformity, his need to fit in. The nerves are already being dulled, covered by a hard skin of expected, correct behaviour. He has learnt the rules, knows how to play the game without being hurt too badly. 'I'll probably tell him the same thing,' she says.

Mention of the children has brought a chill to the room. She will soon have to return to Yew Tree Cottage, once more the good mother. Back at the house, she will still feel Paul's touch on her skin. As she walks from the kitchen she will remember the things they have done in this hotel room. Climbing the stairs to bed, the hint of soreness between her legs will make her smile.

'I don't know what to do. My husband's walking around like a man in a trance. The telephone seems to have taken on a life of its own. Everything seems disordered, somehow. And here I am with you.' Her hand smooths his chest, crosses his flat stomach. She holds her lover's penis in her hand, gazes at it, as if in that dark absurd thing is contained the answer to all the questions in her mind. 'I'm fiddling while Rome burns,' she says distantly.

Paul puts his arm around her and pulls her close to him. 'I love you,' he says. 'We're going to work this out together.'

It's what she dreads, yet wants, to hear.

Among those who knew him, the general consensus of opinion was that Simon Pygott had lost whatever precarious fingertip hold he had once had upon reality and was now in free-fall through the icy blue wastes of harmless insanity. Rose Hope had declined his request to send a *DP* photographer to the scrubby woodland he now called the Temple of Jess and, irritated beyond words by the miasma of general goodwill in which he now enveloped himself, rarely spoke to him. Carstairs, his farm manager, had abandoned his daily meetings at the Hall, discomfited by Simon's new, breezy informality and occasional enquiries as to whether they shouldn't be thinking about harvesting souls. Susan, having coolly expressed her sympathy for the demise of Jess, had become increasingly concerned at Simon's state of mind and had agreed to drive up from London on the boys' last weekend before returning to school.

Through it all, Simon responded to the anger, bafflement or concern of those around him with the same beaming insouciance with which he greeted the Vicar of Burthorpe, the Reverend George Pardew, when he made an unscheduled visit to the Hall the Friday after Jess's death.

'An *angel*, George.' Simon stood at the french window, having ushered Pardew into the library. He now stood gazing out as if, at any moment, the heavenly host might form up on the lawn. 'That's got to be a sign from above, hasn't it?'

Pardew sat, legs crossed, in an armchair, looking apologetic and uncomfortable. More and more often these days, he found himself actually dissuading people from belief – too much belief, or the wrong kind of belief. The old-fashioned Church in which he had always believed was simply part of the social fabric, a timeless Sunday morning institution. He was alarmed that, in the case of certain individuals, its gentle, calming influence was being replaced by something wild and dangerous. He found it disturbing that even Simon Pygott appeared to have been touched by this farouche spiritual extremism. Now *that* was a sign from above, if anything was.

'The extraordinary thing is how uncomfortable the whole business seems to make people feel,' Simon was saying. 'One mention of the angel of the Lord and it's almost as if a chap had said something unforgivable or made a rude noise in public. In fact, hats off to young Charlie – he's the only person who's really listened to me. Said he hadn't actually made up his mind about the angel but he was glad if the whole thing had made me happy.'

'Christian spirit,' said the Vicar vaguely.

'What no one has been able to explain is how it was that, if this is all my imagination, my old dog died a painless death and without a mark on his body.'

'Was it painless?'

'Of course it was, George – that dog died happy. His old face had a sort of post-dins tranquillity to it, you know? For months, I had been dreading the moment when he had to pop off but, thanks to the angel, it all went marvellously. Frankly, I haven't felt so alive for years.'

'Oh, excellent.'

'And now – ' Simon strode towards the Vicar and sat on a chair opposite him with an ominous sense of purpose. 'Now I want to do some good. Which is where you come in.'

'Yes?'

'George, I've suddenly seen that, over the years and for the best of motives, my family have been rather better at what I call taking things than giving things. Not being disloyal to the old family name here but, if you look around the pictures of my precious forebears' – he waved an arm in the direction of Sir Marcus Pygott – 'they all have that closed look, you know – a sort of what-I-have-I-hold defensiveness.'

'I hadn't noticed that.'

'Now, after my recent experience, I've decided to change all that. I'm going to put something back. With your help, I'm going to give, for a change.'

'Give.' Pardew placed the palms of his hands together like a man pondering a new and not entirely welcome concept. 'You know, I've always liked that bit in the Bible about the need for moderation in all things. There's an awful lot to be said for that.'

'How d'you mean exactly?'

'Well, when I see you in your place in the front pew of a Sunday morning, I feel reassured that all's well in the village. The lesson you read at matins on Christmas morning is always something of a high point in the Burthorpe church calendar.'

'Is it?' Simon looked pleased.

'So I was wondering whether one way to respond to your new enthusiasm – to give in a very real sense – would be for you to read a few more lessons at St Botolph's. I'd be most happy to arrange that.'

'You and me, George.' Simon moved closer, his eyes sparkling. 'The land and the cloth. We could be *dynamite*. We could change everything around here.'

'Yes.' Pardew stared at the ceiling for a moment, then lowered his gaze to smile evenly at Simon. 'I'm all for change – in its place,' he said.

'Century after century, same old bally set-up at Garston. Out for yourself. Never mind the other chap. I really believe it's time for what I call a new broom.'

'Oh yes, sure.' Pardew frowned as he considered his next move. 'But d'you remember that marvellous old hymn we sometimes sing – "The rich man in his castle, The poor man at his gate, God made them high or lowly, And ordered their estate"?'

'Rings a bell, yes.'

'It says an awful lot, you know. The reason why the name Pygott is revered around here is because – ' The Vicar stalled temporarily. 'Well, the reason why it's revered is because you're there – in your castle, or at least in your Hall. And I'm down there in St Botolph's Parish Church. It is, as it were, how God has ordered his estate in Burthorpe. Now if one day I were to be found ruling the roost at Garston while you suddenly popped up in the pulpit at St Botolph's, well' – Pardew raised both hands, then let them fall in eloquent despair – 'where would we all be? More importantly, where would ordinary folk be?'

'You don't think God likes a new broom?'

'He likes evolution. Not revolution.'

'I've been having thoughts about the Hall,' said Simon, changing the subject briskly. 'I've decided to hold a family meeting this Sunday tea-time – Susan's idea, actually, but I go along with it. Clear the air, make plans, next step forward, that sort of thing. Want to come?'

Pardew looked startled. 'If it's a family meeting, I'm not sure – '

'We're all God's family, aren't we?' said Simon, with a hint of impatience.

'Yes, true. I suppose we are – in a way.'

'When I said that to Susan about God being part of the family, she just couldn't see it – banged on about how it wasn't God who paid the bills or bought the Christmas presents or decided which school to send the boys to, so a fat lot of good He was as part of the family.'

'A little simplistic, maybe.'

'She's not a great one for giving, old Susan. Between you and me, George, she's never quite got the hang of it.'

'The Lord moves in mysterious ways His wonders to perform.' The Vicar smiled as he intoned a formula that he had always found useful on difficult occasions such as these.

'Anyway, you're very welcome on Sunday.'

Pardew glanced at his watch. 'Busy day, the sabbath,' he said, standing up and patting the pockets of his tweed jacket. 'But I'll do my best. Now I promised my wife I'd call in at Pearson's for some bread,' he said.

'Oh, right.' Simon walked slowly towards the door.

'We should talk about those extra lessons.'

'Extra lessons?' Simon stopped, hands in pockets. 'You don't need prep to learn the word of God, do you?'

The Vicar smiled. 'Lessons for you to read at matins, Simon. God made them high or lowly, eh?'

'And everybody sharing. That's the way it's going to be from now on.' Simon shook the Vicar's hand with unusual warmth. 'Remember, God loves you and so do I.'

'Oh, good.' Pardew took the car keys from his pocket and weighed them in his hand as he attempted to come up with a suitable response. Unable to find one, he murmured, 'Excellent,' and walked towards his car.

That evening Simon took down the several photographs of Jess that were on shelves and tables around the house. He looked at them, then placed all but one in the bottom drawer of his desk in the study. He took a small silver-framed photograph – taken on the lawn before Jess's very first shoot – and placed it on the bedside table in his dressing-room. He sat down on the bed, deep in thought. An end, and yet a beginning. A death that brought with it life. He stood up and slowly walked downstairs.

THANATOS AND EROS: DEATH AS AN ANTI-EROTIC MECHANISM

During the fourteenth and fifteenth centuries, there developed a belief system in which man was seen to be in a permanent condition of corruption: life was a relentless preparation for death. Because disease was essentially an eruption of the rottenness within, divines such as Odilon of Cluny used the fear of death to discourage fornication: 'Consider that which is hidden in the nostrils, in the throat, in the bowels: filth everywhere. We, who would be loath to touch vomit or dung, even with our fingertip – how can we desire to clasp in our arms the bag of excrement itself?'

This thanatoptic preoccupation, a fascination for the very putrescence of humanity, has been re-examined by late twentieth-century writers in whose work death, technology and desire are frequently portrayed as fractal units of essentially the same thematic configuration (see BORROUGHS, BATAILLE, BALLARD AND THE 'DEATH OF AFFECT').

MORTALITY, IMPIETY AND DEBAUCHERY

It was the German Lutheran doctor Christian Friedrich Garmann (1640–1708) who first noted that male cadavers he studied on the battlefield appeared to be experiencing erections. During the subsequent decades, the erotic potential of death itself became something of an obsession among intellectuals. When the body of an alleged vampire in Hungary (see THE REVENANT AND IDENTITY: TOWARDS AN UNDERSTANDING OF THE MYTH OF THE SUPERNATURAL) was said to have 'wild signs (which I pass out of respect)', the reference will have been understood to refer to his engorged member.

From here it was but a short step to the positive eroticisation of death. During the late seventeenth century, there are reports of bored young aristocrats experimenting with semi-suffocation as a means of enhancing sexual pleasure. Corpses became an object of prurient curiosity, bodysnatchers doing a busy trade and anatomy lessons taking on the social popularity of a masked ball! Gothic novels of the time were marked by ghoulish necrophiliac obsessions; indeed, there is evidence that unhealthy desires existed outside the pages of fiction. A memorandum to the Procurator General of Paris, dated 1781, reported 'most infamous violations' taking place in the city's graveyards. 'On the pretext of study, certain persons, not content with the bodies that are given to hospitals, also steal dead bodies from cemeteries and commit on them everything that impiety and debauchery might inspire'.[1]

The connection between romantic necrophilia and the Victorian yearning for the 'good death' and ecstatic reunion with a loved one beyond life is explored elsewhere (see THANATOPHILIA AND THE POST-ROMANTIC IMAGINATION).

[1] Quoted by P. Ariès, *op. cit.*

Miles sat wide-eyed and motionless in front of the screen, as if somehow he was now the text, the subject, and the machine was examining him. He was utterly absorbed. The thing was taking shape, coming alive beneath his galloping fingers. He had worked late into the night, sipping occasionally at the glass of whisky beside the keyboard, blind and deaf to the real world outside that of his project.

FOLKLORIC BELIEFS AND THE EROTIC POWER OF DEATH

Gittings has pointed out that the connection between sex and death was enacted most explicitly in early modern England at public executions. The man about to be hanged would be dressed as a bridegroom. By custom, a man could be saved from the gallows if a woman from the crowd agreed to marry him. In 1701, an Italian called Gemmelli witnessed an execution after which the young man who had been hanged was 'carried with a white sheet, the said sheet was held up by maidens in white, with innumerable women, maidens and children following'.[1] Just like a wedding, in other words!

The phenomenon is explicable by society's need to balance opposite extremes of behaviour and experience. Just as there is humour at a wake, so those present at a hanging need to remind themselves of the life-giving erotic impulse.

PUBLIC HOLIDAYS: A THANATOLOGICAL PERSPECTIVE

An overt erotic subtext was first explicitly recognised in the late sixteenth century when scholars argued that sex and death were the two societal weak spots through which our innate savagery could still penetrate and disorder society. Nature was kept in check by custom and taboo; in this context, the role of the public holiday was to provide a discreet safety valve for the release of instinctual feelings of desire and/or violence.

Almost as if to formalise the connection between desire and

[1] Quoted in C. Gittings, *Death, Burial and the Individual in Early Modern England* (Croom Helm, 1984).

death, the day after a public execution was granted a holiday and was often an occasion of near-orgiastic merry-making.

CROSSROADS, SYMBOLIC FORCE OF

For centuries, any form of suicide was regarded both as an affront to God, the King and mankind (see SUICIDE, SOCIAL ATTITUDES TOWARDS), and perhaps as a symbolic configuration of our own deepest fears. The clearest manifestation of these fears lay in the commonly held superstition that suicides are 'prime candidates' among the dead for the unhappy gift of life on earth beyond the grave. Since the thirteenth century, it was believed that those who had died by their own hand should be buried at a crossroads or on parish borders in the hope that their spirits would inhabit the 'no man's land' between parishes (see REVENANCE, THEORY OF).

The case of one Thomas Maule of Pleasley, Derbyshire is typical. 'Tho Maule found hung on a tree by the wayside after a drunken fit April 3. Coroner's inquest in church porch April 5. Same night at midnight buried at the crossroads with a stake in him, many people from Mansfield present.'

These burials have meant that, over the years, crossroads at a parish border have seen a number of midnight burials for suicides – a chilling thought perhaps for those who live near such a spot, as does the author of this *Resource Handbook*!

Miles leant back in his chair and rubbed his eyes wearily. The unhappy gift of life on earth beyond the grave. Revenance. Desire and death. He had dreamt of this moment, when the work would take over, when the years of research and thought would find expression, tumbling almost independently of him on to the page, yet he was unnerved by what was appearing before him. Thanatos. Eros. It was not the way he had seen the *Resource Handbook* developing. Somehow it seemed to have moved beyond his control, from the cerebrum into the real, from behind the bright screen of words into his life. He felt almost afraid of where he was being led.

It was too late for work. His mind was rambling, becoming illogical. On the desk in front of him, the snowman alarm clock which, in a rare moment of humour, Dr Katherine Porter had given him, revealed that it was past two o'clock. Miles yawned, switched off his computer and rose to his feet.

He had thought that his life was acquiring a sort of order, an acceptable balance between professional forward movement and emotional stasis. Now he saw that, sooner or later, he would be obliged to take action. The restless enquiries of Rose Hope, the unexpected mental implosion of Simon Pygott, strange events, lurking suspicions, the course of his own work: they were all leading unavoidably to the moment when it was no longer enough for him to observe, the sardonic but good-humoured outsider. It was not something he welcomed, this involvement. At thirty, he might have acted, even thirty-five; now he felt afraid, fragile.

Outside Margaret Cowper's door, he hesitated. The thing beyond comprehension, which all logic told him should make him fearful, in fact held fewer terrors for him than the simple but radical disruption of his everyday life. It was odd, and yet Miles was not anxious to find an explanation for it.

Without bothering to look through the keyhole or to knock, he entered the room. She would not be back for another thirty minutes or so. He switched on the bedside lamp and looked around the small room. She was a neat person, and the only sign of her occupancy was a pile of her clothes folded carefully on the chair in front of her dressing-table. Miles nodded, almost with approval. He liked neatness.

Glancing towards the window which, he saw, was slightly open through half-drawn curtains, he lifted the covers to her bed. There were no clues to be found on her sheets. He carefully rearranged the bedclothes, then walked to the window. The night was still, a vernal dampness hanging in the air, the quietness only broken by the occasional hum and hiss of a passing vehicle making its way through the village on the main road. He looked more closely at the pale-yellow curtains. There, six inches below the curtain rail, he found what he had been looking for – the faintest traced lines, sketched so lightly on the fabric that, were they not red in colour, they might have been human hairs. He ran his fingertips down the border of the curtain, then walked quickly across the room, picked up the pile of clothing and laid it on the floor. Glancing around the room, he moved the chair to a corner beyond the wardrobe from where he would be able to see both the window and the bed. He switched off the lamp and sat down to wait.

He had been in the room no more than fifteen minutes when he noticed signs of movement at the top of the curtains, almost as if, from the night outside, fingers had extended to twitch at the material. Then, as Miles watched, hardly daring to breathe, the grey presence poured languidly into the bedroom through the gap in the curtains. The temperature in the room seemed to drop so that the air that touched Miles's face and hands felt like a tangible presence. The shape gathered silently above the bed, glowing palely, before descending on to the bedcovers. It took a few moments to settle there, like a cat trying to make itself comfortable. Then the faint crackle which Miles recognised filled the room. The amorphous incorporeal mass took substance, assuming the dimensions of a small human being. Within no more than ten seconds, the bright, naked figure of Margaret Cowper illuminated the bed where she lay on her back, eyes open, palms downward. The hiss of noise faded now as, with her eyes closed, Margaret sucked air deep into her lungs, exhaled one weary sigh, then, after a moment, began to breathe slowly and regularly, with a certain, sad relief, like someone who has emerged from a long dive underwater. Her hands touched her breasts then rested on her stomach as it rose and fell.

Miles became aware that, in rapid counterpoint to Margaret's sighs, his own heartbeat was pounding in his ears. Through the darkness, he gazed on her spare, trim body, the small breasts, the narrow waist, the legs slightly apart in a position of weary self-abandon. Despite the coolness in the room, he felt a glow of heat within him. Some distant outpost of logical thought was signalling alarm, telling him that his desire was misplaced and dangerous but he felt no fear, only a sort of longing to step forward, lie down and welcome the figure on the bed back to the world of human warmth.

Margaret turned her head and, with no particular surprise, stared at him. She smiled. Then, unhurriedly, she sat up and, with her right hand, pulled the bedclothes over her.

'You've returned,' said Miles.

* * *

I have returned, but there is no reason for alarm.

Although we are everywhere, we rarely intrude in your affairs. Only now and then do we break out of our spacious prison to enter the world of time and space. For you who are corporeal and breathing, this is fortunate.

Integration can sometimes be a problem for us. We are like a disastrous guest at a party. There are broken plates, tears, various forms of unpleasantness before we leave. We try to behave, but the standards by which you live, the concerns which keep you awake, are so insignificant to us that we simply forget ourselves. Darren Bugg, Carol Power, Errol Pryce, Enid Kirby – are they missed, really? Yes, of course they are. But put those minor human experiences, a few lives less, a few tears more, in the context of centuries and they are nothing.

My loss, the loss of Meg, was scarcely noticed in the village. I had served my purpose. Musket, muse, mother. It was done. Now I was merely filling a space which could be more usefully occupied by another servant girl who would follow the same path, more or less.

My fall might have been measured in months or in years. At the time, they passed in a damp, gloomy haze of hunger and solitude, punctuated by visits from the village men, visits which became less and less frequent as my body withered and rotted, a corpse before its time.

Joseph had been taken miles away. To Stradbroke, I was told. My master had left for court. It was said that he had travelled with the King to France and witnessed the siege of some French town but of this I had my doubts. He was a man of words not work and used his craft for gentler, more perfumed pursuits than war. Either way, I cared little for what became of him. In this, I was at one with Jane Scrope, who departed Carrow to marry a Suffolk gentleman. From there she would daintily complain of the harm that the sparrow had inflicted upon her.

I recall my leaving only hazily. It was winter and had rained for weeks. The water meadow below my cottage was in flood. Every day the brown and restless tide moved nearer. Something happened, some act of anonymous violence was inflicted upon me.

One early morning I awoke, face down near the door, my body aching in a way not fully explained by hunger.

We know our moment has come, each of us. Even Darren and Errol, Enid and Carol will have known, if only for that second which can last a lifetime. I was dead before I walked barefoot from the cottage at the first grey, cold light of that day. Perhaps I had been dead for years. I collected the stones of flint that were lying in the muddy lane leading towards the village and placed them with care in my garments as if to stop being blown away by any passing gust of wind. I turned, walked back, past the cottage, into the field. I was so cold that I saw but did not feel the dark water swirling around my feet. Between my toes, the mud oozed, holding me back with every step.

Between the field and Garston Wood, there was a ditch, not deep but deep enough. I walked forwards, my eyes fixed on the darkness. The water moved swiftly where there would usually be a stream. I looked down at its dimpling, glittering surface, then fell, face forward, as if I would embrace it. In that moment before I welcomed the water into me with one last, heaving breath, I saw his face, lit by the flame of a taper, his small dark eyes staring at me down the length of the table at the Rectory, drawing me downwards into love.

Why do we return? Why do we come back to meddle in your lives? Perhaps because there is something unresolved, some unanswered question which will not let us rest until we find, even if it takes centuries, the time that will furnish the answer, the person who, in an act of love and revenge, will release us and give us peace.

MEDIEVAL LOVE AND DEATH: SKELTON'S REMEDY
No discourse upon regional death studies would be complete without mention of a poem by a local author that is both a playful variation on the Office of the Dead and cunning deployment of mortal fears in the cause of love, John Skelton's 'Philip Sparrow'.

Since his rehabilitation during the early 1920s, notably by

Robert Graves[1], a certain mythology has developed around Skelton. Although it is not within the terms of reference of this *Resource Handbook* to discuss his value as poet, or as repository of late medieval intellectuality or moral values, we can briefly consider how he impacts upon thanatological themes and customs.

Skelton lived, it is believed, from 1460 to 1529, and his life was nothing if not experientially discursive. He was tutor to Henry VII's younger son Henry, Duke of York, attended court from 1488. Awarded a laureateship, a less prestigious post in those days but nonetheless one about which he frequently boasted[2], his early translations and poetry suggested that he tended to the humanist rather than new renaissance models of scholarship, quoting Petrarch, Erasmus and Boccaccio and arguing from the dialectical position of medieval logic. 'In education Skelton was all for the modes of signifying – grammar with a solid logical foundation,' Edwards[3] has written. Throughout his life, he was convinced that 'logic was the keystone of the intellect and deeply suspicious of the new enthusiasms he saw everywhere around him'. Nonetheless, both his use of the English vernacular and many aspects of his lifetime place him in the Renaissance tradition of Rabelais, Ariosto and Folengo.

Despite being created subdeacon in 1498, Skelton was not averse to 'enthusiasms' of a less cerebral nature. His early poem 'Mannerly Margery' reveals a sensualist's appreciation of such Westminster 'rough trade' as Long Meg, a gigantic Lancashire woman known at court for her house of ill-repute.

Shortly after the death of Prince Arthur, Skelton was removed from his post – possibly because of the concerns expressed by the King and his wife Lady Margaret that the Duke of York's tutor, something of a 'loose cannon' at court,

---

[1] Graves's poem 'John Skelton' first appeared in the 1917 collection, *Fairies and Fusiliers*. His verse was said to have influenced the early work of W.H. Auden and Edith Sitwell.
[2] 'Written by me, Skelton, laurelled Bard of Britons' was the way he signed 'Philip Sparrow'. In 'Why Come Ye Not To Court?', his self-confidence is even more pronounced with the lines 'This the bard wrote/ Whom thousands quote.'
[3] H.L.R. Edwards, *Skelton: The Life and Times of an Early Tudor Poet* (Cape, 1949).

might teach the future King 'less seemly things'. He was appointed Rector of Diss.

It is generally thought that Skelton remained in Diss from 1504 to 1511 or 1512 when he was invited back to court; he was appointed Court Poet to his Majesty King Henry VIII. During the so-called 'Diss period', his reputation as a versifier grew, with works such as 'Ware the Hawk', 'The Tunning of Elinour Running' and, of course, 'Philip Sparrow', announcing a new, vigorously English form of poetry whose most obvious characteristics were short, uneven lines, linked together by alliteration, parallelism and repetitive rhyme: the so-called 'Skeltonic'[4].

According to Ferrar's study of Skelton's life in Diss[5], there was no sense in which the poet was simply passing time there until he was rehabilitated into court life. He had twelve acres of glebe at the Rectory (later to become Mere Manor), on which he grew crops and raised livestock. He also cultivated an impressive number of enemies, as was his custom. He used his position to bully and cajole his fellow priests and parishioners: the poem 'Ware the Hawk', for example, was a powerful attack upon a cleric, possibly the Reverend John Smith of East Wretham, who allowed his falcons to pursue a pigeon within the confines of St Mary's Church, Diss. Never above using his position as poet-priest to pursue a personal agenda, Skelton took to writing vitriolic epitaphs[6] to condemn (once they were safely dead) members of his congregation of whom he disapproved. On at least one occasion, he found himself in conflict with his immediate superior, Richard, the Bishop of Norwich.

A particularly contentious issue was the question of 'Skelton's musket', a common-law wife by whom he bore children (two, my researches suggest) yet who was apparently of so little significance that her name is nowhere recorded. According to Braynewode's 1549 *A Hundred Merry Tales*[7] (admittedly an

---

[4] In his study *John Skelton, Laureate* (New York, 1939), William Nelson convincingly points out that this much-discussed form is, in fact, little more than crudely rhymed prose. A modern equivalent might be the 'rap' lyrics of the pop world.

[5] James R. Ferrar, *John Skelton – the Diss Period* (unpublished dissertation for Loughborough University, 1983).

[6] 'Epitaph for Adam Udersall' and 'A Devout Trental for Old John Clarke'.

[7] Collected by Bale, edited from his notebook by Lane Poole and published as Ioannes Baleus, *Index Britanniae Scriptorum* (Oxford University Press, 1902).

unreliable source), the Rector kept a woman whom he had married (secretly, 'for fear of anti-Christ') in the guise of a concubine. Even the relatively liberal Edwards commented that 'regrettable as it may seem to the modern reader, Skelton must have regarded the lady less as his wife than as his 'remedy' – to use the Abbot of Walden's convenient term – an Ovidian cure for the pangs of love'.

Apart from a bizarre incident at St Mary's, when the Rector 'confessed' to having a family and even displayed his baby son to the congregation, there is one further reference to the unnamed woman. During the nineteenth century, a poem said to have been written to her shortly before the birth of their first baby was 'discovered' and published[8], but was later discredited. 'Only the inveterate itch for "revelations" could ever have led to the ascription,' Edwards points out. 'In any case it is more than doubtful whether Skelton ever wrote poems to the lady of Diss Rectory. She formed part of his domestic life; and one suspects that Skelton, in common with most writers of his century, kept that side of him strictly detached from his poetic activities.'

What have the life and times of this dissolute, noisy and faintly fraudulent man of letters (a sort of medieval version of Frank Harris, one might say) to do with Regional Death Studies? Just as, for literary figures like Elizabeth Barrett Browning[9], Robert Graves, and E.M. Forster, Skelton has been held up as a new spirit in English poetry, so, for the thanatologist, he represents a significant moment of change.

A perusal of Skelton's extant works suggests that his concerns – mortality, sexuality, the court, religion – were entirely those of his period. Yet, as he grows older, from the Diss period onwards, he develops a tone of detached ironic playfulness that has more distinctly contemporary echoes. In 'Epitaph for Adam Udersall' and 'A Devout Trental for Old John Clarke', he actually uses religious form to mock two of his parishioners in death:

[8] *Atheneum Magazine*, 1873.
[9] 'He is as wild a beast as a poet laureate can be in his wonderful dominion over language; he tears it, as with teeth and paws, ravenously, savagely. It is the very sansculottism of eloquence.' E. Barrett Browning, *Book of the Poets*.

Jam jacet hic stark dead
Never a tooth in his head

Here, the words of a rector on the passing over of one of his
flock, is an entirely new 'take' on mortality!

Bibite multum
Ecce sepultum
Sub pede stultum
Asinum, et multum!
The devil kiss his *culum!*[10]

The tendency towards parodic irreverence in matters of love
and death reaches its most frank and open form in the poem
regarded by some as Skelton's masterpiece, 'Philip Sparrow',
which was written during the Diss period, probably in 1508.

Apparently inspired by a minor domestic incident – the
killing by a cat of a pet sparrow named Phip which belonged
to Jane Scrope, daughter of Lady Wyndham, who was resident
at Carrow Convent near Norwich – the poem begins, char-
mingly and touchingly, in the form of the Office of the Dead,
with Jane herself imagining a service for Philip Sparrow in
which the entire animal kingdom join in her lament.

A porta inferi[11]
Good Lord, have mercy
Upon my sparrow's soul,
Written upon my bead-roll

An account of the sparrow's life before his untimely end
provides the first glimpse of the direction in which the poem
is headed.

And on me it would leap
When I was asleep
And his feathers shake,
Wherewith he would make

---

[10] Both quotations are from 'A Devout Trental'.
[11] 'From the gate of hell'. A versicle from the Absolution for the Dead.

Me often for to wake,
And for to take him in
Upon my naked skin.
God wot, we thought no sin:
What though he crept so low?
It was no hurt I trow.

At which point, Skelton startlingly abandons his chosen narrative voice of Jane Scrope and, in the second part of the poem, entitled 'The Commendations', steps forward, reveals the true dynamic of the text[12]: a hymn of romantic and erotic praise directed at Jane Scrope herself! The apparently innocent voice intones Latin phrases in praise of this *'gloriosa femina'*:

Retribue servo tuo, vivica me![13]
Labia mea laudabunt te[14]

Yet the medieval reader will have noticed that something distinctly unusual is happening here: the two lines are from separate Psalms and are, under normal circumstances, declaimed in praise of God. The implication of the phrase 'my lips shall praise thee' acquires a distinctly secular resonance when addressed to a young woman who 'causeth mine heart to leap'. Soon Skelton is going even further:

Legem pone mihi, domina, viam justificationum tuarum![15]

Here Skelton not only quotes from the Psalm but replaces *'dominus'* (the Lord) by *domina*, his lady – a startling act of blasphemy repeated throughout the rest of the poem.

Thus, with much throat-clearing and clammy scholarship, the poet lists, with increasing frankness and evidence of poetic desire, the virtues of his *'domina'*.

---

[12] Claims made in a recent issue of *Middle English Review* (Issue 254, November 1993) that Skelton was in effect foreshadowing postmodern narrative structures have failed to convince critical theorists.
[13] 'Deal bountifully with thy servant that I may live.'
[14] 'My lips shall praise thee.'
[15] 'Teach me, O lady, to justify Thy ways.'

Her lusty ruby ruddès
Resemble the rose buddès;
Her lippes soft and merry
Enbloomèd like the cherry:
It were an heavenly bliss
Her sugared mouth to kiss.

And so it continues, moving uneasily from coyness to frank
arousal:

I tell you what conceit
I had then in a trice,
The matter were too nice
And yet there were no vice,
Nor yet no villainy,
But only fantasy.

The 'fantasy' reaches a level many might find somewhat
inappropriate for a clergyman to direct at a young girl in a
convent:

Her kirtle[16] so goodly lacéd
Under that is bracéd
Such pleasures that I may
Neither write nor say!
Yet though I write with ink,
No man can let me think,
Thought is frank and free;
To think a merry thought
It cost me little or nought.

With that dubious line of argument, Skelton scurries back
behind the mask of scholarship, wishing that 'mine homely
style/ Were polishéd with the file/ Of Cicero's eloquence/ To
praise her excellence!' And so, with that merest hint of
embarrassment, Skelton closes what Coleridge has described
as 'an exquisite and original poem'.

From the thanatalogical point of view, the belief systems

---

[16] 'Girdle'.

embodied in 'Philip Sparrow' are significant, envisioning in explicit form the first early questioning of medieval man's fear of death and passionate love of life. The forms and traditions of the funeral service (including religious texts) are cynically deployed to express base human desire, as are classical scholarship, contemporary science and the traditions of courtly love poetry[17]. This new sense of balance anticipated what Ariès[18] called 'a world in which moderation must reign'. The Good Death of the sixteenth century was to have neither the intensity nor the excitement of the Middle Ages' *ars moriendi*.

[17] There are incidentally arresting features to 'Philip Sparrow' which may interest the student, including a moral subtext of some significance. Skelton the scholar exploited his scholarship for personal ends; Skelton the man of God betrayed and undermined his own religion. But what of Skelton the man? While his biographers have attempted to defend him against the charges of callousness, hinting at poems written to his wife, depicting emotional deathbed confessions, the fact is that 'Philip Sparrow' was a public proclamation of adulterous ambition of a rector towards a convent girl almost thirty years his junior. Records remain of Jane Scrope's entirely justified objections to the lurid tenor of 'Philip Sparrow' – Skelton was later obliged publicly to defend the poem ('Alas that goodly maid/ Why should she be afraid?') – the reactions of his own 'unofficial' family have not, of course, been recorded. My own researches have revealed that the luckless 'musket' or 'doxy' who had given the Rector of Diss a family by the time 'Philip Sparrow' was written herself met an end of some misery – that, far from benefiting from any will by the Orator Royal, she had, by the time of his death, lost her reputation, her children and finally her life in the cause of the self-styled 'laurelled Bard of Britons'. She was, of course, no more than a 'remedy' and therefore, perhaps worthy of little more than a footnote in biographies of the man who had destroyed her.
[18] P. Ariès, *op. cit.*

With bold, confident strides, Simon Pygott crossed the hall on his way to the dining-room. All traces of the old boredom, the languid apathy of the privileged depressive, had vanished. He walked like an athlete entering a stadium, aware that this was his moment. He felt new, different, empowered by faith.

In the dining-room, an uneasy gathering awaited him. Standing in front of the portrait of Sir Thomas Pygott (1805–1869) was Susan, in a grey cashmere cardigan, her left hand, holding a long cigarette, poised in front of her. The two boys had, at their mother's insistence, put on tweed jackets, cavalry twills and dark-red ties and looked like gentlemen farmers in miniature. Beside them was George Pardew, florid in comparison to the other three, his Sunday uniform – ecclesiastical shirt and dog-collar beneath a worsted jacket – providing an appropriate balance between the man of God and the man of the world.

'So. Here we are.' Simon looked at the scones and biscuits that had been laid by Jaime on the table. 'Excellent scoff.'

'Can we start?' Jeremy asked.

'We're just waiting for Nigel to come up from the farm. Then we can tuck in.'

'No.' Susan inhaled deeply on her cigarette, and spoke through a cloud of smoke. 'He mentioned that he had been invited to lunch in Bury. I told him we could get by without him.'

'But all this affects him.'

'Grow up, Simon.' Susan stubbed out the half-smoked cigarette in an ashtray. 'Even if we do make any decisions here, we can tell him afterwards.'

The sound of a car crossing the gravel outside reached them.

'Perhaps that's him now.' Simon smiled. 'Good old Nigel. Late as usual.'

'Probably Freddie Pierpoint.'

'Freddie? I had no idea he was coming. Our money man,' Simon explained to the Vicar. 'Poor sod.'

'You know, I really think I'd better attend to parish business.' George Pardew glanced at his watch. 'Lovely to see you all – '

'Stay, George,' said Simon. He pulled back a chair from the table and gestured in its direction. 'You must be able to stay for tea.'

Nervously, the Vicar lowered himself into the chair. Charlie and Jeremy also sat at the table. Ambling past her husband, Susan muttered absently, 'Don't bully the Vicar, darling. He's meant to be on your side.' She sat, a distant, chilly smile communicating an exquisite boredom of the soul.

'Sorry I'm late, Susan.' The small, dapper figure of Freddie Pierpoint stood at the door.

'Freddie, old man.' Simon spread his arms dramatically. 'What a surprise. Take a seat.'

Pierpoint scuttled across the room and sat at the table, like a schoolboy trying not be noticed by the prefects. As Jaime entered with a silver tray, Simon, at the head of the table, introduced the accountant to the man of the cloth. 'If you ever want any advice on the old portfolio, George, this chap's your man,' he said.

Pierpoint leant forward. 'Has Susan explained the situation?' he asked Simon.

'The number of times he's saved our bacon, money-wise,' Simon continued. 'Lots of my pals told me I should be a Lloyds name. Freddie took me aside. "*Cave*," he said. "Something a bit whiffy in the wind. Best not *pro tem*." Just like he was back at school and Matron was patrolling the corridor. *Cave*.'

'Simon, it was me who asked Freddie to come along.' Susan spoke quietly. 'He's acting on my behalf.'

'Of course he is,' said Simon. 'We're all in this together. Jaime – ' He turned to the Spaniard who had been standing near by and who now stepped forward to place a teapot on the table. 'You can join us, too.'

'Sir?'

'This involves you, too. Take Nigel's place down there.'

'I don't think so, Jaime,' said Susan, glancing up as if declining a second helping.

'Sit, Jaime,' said Simon.

In an agony of embarrassment, Jaime danced around a bit behind the chair before, with an apologetic smile in Susan's direction, he slowly sat down.

'What's that Spanish word they use in cowboy films, Jaime?' Susan asked across the table.

'Madam?'

'Loco, that's it.'

'Loco?'

'Plum loco. Mr Pygott's gone plum loco. Sad.'

'Well.' Simon sat at the head of the table and placed two large hands behind his head in a gesture of extreme relaxation. 'Here we all are. Pour us all a cup, darling. It'll be getting cold.'

'Jesus wept,' said Susan.

Socially, the tea was an uneasy occasion. Charlie and Jeremy ate mechanically, so paralysed with awkwardness that they hardly dared raise their eyes from the plates in front of them. George Pardew spoke loudly and inconsequentially. Freddie Pierpoint conversed in quiet tones to Susan who occasionally darted looks of glacial disdain in the direction of her husband.

'I can't make up my mind which I dislike more – sad Simon or happy Simon,' she said, allowing her voice to carry through a gap in the conversation. 'On balance, I think I prefer him in his normal stunned walrus mode. You know?'

Freddie glanced up at Simon who smiled as if receiving the most gracious of compliments. 'Certainly seems to be happy now,' he muttered.

Simon tapped the rim of his cup with a silver teaspoon and an uneasy silence descended on the room. 'I just wanted to say one thing before I set the ball rolling on this discussion.' He looked around the table significantly. 'Something that I hope you'll bear in mind when I reveal my plans for Garston.'

'Get on with it,' said Susan.

'– and that is, well – ' Simon's smile took in the whole table. 'I love you all very much.'

'Oh dear,' said Freddie.

'Dad, please,' muttered Charlie.

Susan drew herself upright in her chair. 'I think I'm going to be sick,' she said.

'Yes, that's right, don't be embarrassed.' Simon ignored them all. 'Frankly, there's not enough love about the place at the moment. I want to open all our hearts to it.' He paused briefly before continuing. 'I love you, George. I love you, Freddie. God, I love you, Charlie and Jeremy. And of course I –' He looked into the ice-blue eyes of his wife, gazing back at him with the mild contempt with which she might have regarded a beggar on her doorstep. He swallowed and looked away quickly. 'I – I love you all.'

'Good. Well, let's get on with it, shall we, old boy.' Freddie tapped his watch with amiable impatience.

'Yes. To business. Now, as you are all aware, we have recently been privileged – what I call blessed – by a somewhat unusual visitor. I know your feelings on our visitor because I've spoken to you individually about it.'

'And how,' said Susan.

'Setting aside what I'd call the spiritual dimension, this event has cleared up a few things in my head – answered questions which, to tell the truth, I hadn't even realised were questions until now. The first, but not the most important, matter is about money. As Freddie will confirm, I've never been terribly good with the old readies.'

Freddie made a polite but unconvincing gesture of protest.

'It just seems to slip through my fingers like water. We were knee-deep in the stuff when my father was around. Then he had his problems and there was a bit less. Sold land, books, a few things around the house, but investment in the farm seems to go up every year while the old turnover goes down. Today, let's be frank, it's pretty thin on the ground, the loot. Eh?' Simon smiled cheerfully. 'And getting thinner by the minute, I'd say. So what I'd like to do is devote myself to a cause which I just know I can make a decent fist of – '

'Oh do tell,' said Susan.

'– and that is the cause of our Lord. For the first time in my life, I want to do something to help people.'

'Excellent idea, Simon,' George Pardew interrupted. 'But, you know, it's well known that God helps them who helps themselves. And, I'd say, in all frankness, that you're helping yourself and the good people of Burthorpe by being what you are. I mean, can there be a more worthwhile – spiritually worthwhile – job than that of a farmer? Think of it – all that food and crops and flocks of, you know, cattle and things.' He tapered off feebly.

'Others do it better than I ever will. That's why I'm handing over all decision-making to Nigel.'

'Sounds very sensible,' said Susan. 'He virtually runs the place anyway. All you do is interfere and spend money on those ridiculous machines.'

'Won't you get a bit bored without the farm, Dad?' Charlie asked.

'Glad you asked that, Charlie. Because, as it so happens, I'm going to be busier than ever before – I'll be spreading the word.'

'Oh, Simon.' Freddie shook his head wearily.

'The day after the visitation, I happened to have been glancing through *The Times* when the Lord guided my eyes to a little paragraph about some Christians who were being hounded off their premises in Leighton Buzzard.'

'I remember,' said Pardew. 'American charismatics, weren't they? Sounded very dubious to me.'

'Yes, but d'you remember the name of their church?' Simon paused dramatically. 'The Seventh Holy Temple of Jesus.'

'Don't quite follow you, old boy,' said Freddie Pierpoint.

'The date when the angel visited me was the 7th of April. And where did she appear? At the Temple of Jess! Maybe a coincidence, maybe not – makes not a jot of difference to me. The fact is, the Lord was delivering his message to me loud and clear.'

'Quite, quite bonkers,' Susan murmured.

'So of course I looked them up in the book, rang the chappie, who was charm itself, toodled down to see him and he put everything in my life into the most tremendous sort of what I call context. Clever chap, quite young. Described himself as "one of God's Area Marketing Managers". Come to think of it, he did sound a bit American – sort of half and half, like the disc jockeys you hear on the wireless sometimes. Reminded me a bit of Tony Prince on Radio Lux.'

'How exactly did he put your life into context?' asked George Pardew.

'Turns out that he and his people know all about angels. That's how the Seventh Temple of Jesus was started – a holy angel appeared before this fellow in Illinois. Told him to go forth and spread the word, get disciples. Apparently angels appear quite often if you're the the right sort of person, what Marvin – that's the marketing fellow – calls "tuned in".'

Pardew shuddered.

'Now I know it all sounds a bit what I call iffy,' Simon continued. 'But the fact is, these people are doing exactly what I'm interested in. They're collecting money from the rich and giving it to poor people all over the world. I want to help them.'

'How exactly will you do that?' asked Freddie Pierpoint.

'Going to become one of their trainee Templars. Many called, few chosen, that sort of thing. Have to do some sort of course.'

'What's a Templar, Dad?' asked Charlie.

'That's what I'm going to find out on their spiritual traineeship course.'

'Before you spend the rest of your days, wandering door to door pressing cheaply produced, sub-literate pamphlets into the hands of bemused surbanites, I suppose.' A sardonic, unamused smile played on Susan's pale features. 'Really, Simon, you are the biggest bloody fool that's ever walked this earth.'

Simon nodded amiably, as if this reaction was entirely to be expected, even welcomed. 'I'll be collecting money, too. It's going to be terrific fun.'

'Simon peddling God and collecting spare change in a bucket,' said Susan. 'I've heard it all now.'

'Better than that, darling. The very best and most important bit of news concerns this house. I've discussed it with Marvin. We've talked it through – carefully and prayerfully, as he puts it. My very first act of charity is going to be to put Garston Hall at their disposal. It will be the new spiritual HQ of the Seventh Holy Temple of Jesus.'

There was silence in the dining-room.

'*Madre de Dios*,' said Jaime.

'Bloody hell,' said Freddie.

'What's going to happen to my fishing?' asked Jeremy.

'The Seventh Templars are fishers of men,' said Simon breezily. 'I'm sure they won't mind if you catch the odd roach in the moat.'

'I think we've heard quite enough of these ravings.' Bright dabs of red showed through the powder on Susan's cheekbones. 'Children, go and get your tuckboxes ready for tomorrow. Jaime, help them raid the kitchen, will you?'

As, with evident relief, the boys left the room, followed by Jaime, Susan turned to her husband. 'You *bastard*,' she said quietly. 'You pathetic, weak, inadequate little creep.'

Simon smiled, but looked shaken. 'You wouldn't understand,' he said quietly.

'Marvin.' She gave a contemptuous little laugh. 'He's what you've been looking for all these years, isn't he? A headmaster. A school pre. A daddy figure to tell you what to do.'

George Pardew stood up. 'Now, I really must be on my way,' he said.

Ignoring him, Simon set his jaw and stared ahead. 'Marvin isn't – '

'Fuck Marvin.'

'Well, let me put it in the words of Jesus – '

'Fuck Jesus.'

The Vicar smiled tolerantly as if, although that wasn't quite the way he would have put it himself, he understood Susan's position.

'Fuck Jesus and Marvin and Seventh fucking Temple of whatever the fuck it is.' Susan leant across, her hands gripping the edge of the table. 'Fuck you, Simon Pygott. I wish I'd never met you.'

'Yes, well, duty calls.' Pardew extended a hand which Susan mechanically shook, while still staring at Simon. 'I'm sure this will . . . with the help of goodwill on all sides.'

'Thank you for calling by, George.' Susan glanced up. 'Don't mention any of this outside, will you?'

'Oh please. Confidentiality of the cloth, you know.' The Vicar nodded nervously in Simon's direction. 'I'll see myself out.'

After he had left, Susan glanced towards Freddie Pierpoint, who was looking as if he would like to escape, too. 'Don't go, Freddie,' she said quietly. 'We have some sorting out to do.'

'Perhaps when we're all feeling a little calmer.'

'No.' Susan reached for her cigarettes, lit up, leant back in her chair and exhaled a cloud of smoke. 'You know, when I was in my teens, we lived in Kenya.' She spoke to Freddie as if Simon was no longer there. 'We used to see wildlife every day – elephants, hippo, lion, giraffe. But the animals I used to enjoy watching more than any other were the baboons. I'd study their games, the way the mothers carried their young, how the adolescent baboons would be kept in order by their parents, the fights, the chattering rows. What fascinated me was the fact that, behind what seemed to be confusion, there was an order. Each baboon knew its place in the group. The baby looked up to its parent. The young stayed clear of the adults. And all of them – *all* of them – respected and feared the head of the group, the leader, the alpha male. He could go anywhere he wanted. The path cleared in front of him. If he wanted one of the females, he'd have her, just like that.'

'Would life were that simple,' said Freddie uneasily.

'When I came back to England, I did the season, the usual deb dances. And one weekend, there was a dance near Bury, and I stayed at Garston Hall. I met Simon.' She looked at him now, as if remembering that moment. 'His father seemed a funny, sad little figure – he must have known that he was going to have to do a bunk sooner or later. Simon was in charge. All that weekend, I watched him – the way the other men deferred to him, how the girls tried to catch his eye, the bigness, the authority he had – so effortless, somehow. And I remember thinking, at about three in the morning as Simon lumbered around the dance-floor with me, laughing and making too much noise, this is him, this is the one I want. This is my alpha male.'

'You were so pretty.' It was a whisper from Simon. 'I'll never forget that night.'

'What happened?' Susan seemed genuinely curious. 'I mean, look at him, Freddie. A husk, a great big empty nothing. No character, no . . . substance. He's hardly an alpha male now, is he? Not even a beta male. Or a ceta.'

'Gamma,' said Freddie.

Simon looked up. 'I'd rather hoped you'd see that we had to change,' he said evenly. 'What we're going to do is move into Hall Farm. There's too much room for us here anyway. Rattling around.'

'I'm not living in a bloody farmhouse,' said Susan. 'Sorry, I'm not. That's final.'

'Have you actually signed anything?' Freddie asked, relieved that the conversation had moved from the emotional to the practical.

'Marvin's popping over tomorrow. He's preparing a few papers, bit of documentation.'

'I'll bet he is,' said Susan.

'Now, the Hall is in your name.' Freddie spoke like a man thinking out loud. 'And so, of course, you can reach any form of tenancy arrangement with whomsoever you choose.'

'I suppose so,' said Simon.

'The only impediment to such a move being – well, obviously, as a friend of the family, I'd hate to see this – if you and Susan decided that you had reached the end of the line, matrimony-wise.'

Simon frowned. 'Bit rocky recently, a few harsh words,' he said. 'Not the first time, though. Been here before. We'll muddle through.'

'You are joking, Simon Pygott,' said Susan. 'I'm going to get you registered as a loony. I'll get the men in white coats around here, just you watch.'

'I wasn't aware that wanting to help people was grounds for insanity,' said Simon. 'Some might argue that it's the sanest thing a person could do.'

'Of course, you're right, old boy.' Freddie spoke up. 'We live in a Christian society and all that. On the other hand, in the event of divorce, a court would simply divide your assets.'

'Haven't got many of those, apart from property and land. Bit of farm machinery, a few paintings, bloody great overdraft at the bank.'

'The property being the flat in London and Garston Hall.'

'Yes.'

'In other words, Susan would have the right to half of this place.'

'I say, Freddie.' Simon laughed nervously. 'Don't you think you're being a little bit biased here?'

'I thought you realised – '

'Freddie's acting for me,' said Susan crisply. 'I explained the situation. Told him he had to choose. He chose me.'

For the first time, Simon looked genuinely shocked. 'But we were at school together,' he said. 'He knew me ages before he knew you. Freddie?'

Pierpoint spread his hands. 'Difficult decision, old boy. In the end, I felt Susan and I were on the same wavelength. I don't know, this angel business – makes it difficult for a chap to talk finance.'

'I see. So, between you, it's been worked out that you'll have a claim on Garston Hall. I suppose I'll just have to mention that to Marvin. Could be a bit of a wrinkle in the old plan.'

'Maybe. Maybe not.' Freddie reached into the inside pocket of his jacket and took out a sealed envelope. 'Susan and I have discussed a scenario that might be acceptable to you in the unhappy event of marital breakdown.' He handed over the envelope, which Simon opened. It was a short letter, but he seemed to have difficulty understanding its contents.

'It's just a draft for you to think about,' said Freddie. 'But, in the unhappy event and all that, there's not much room for manoeuvre.'

'The London flat, custody of the boys and – that's a ridiculous amount of money.'

'Not if you sell the land and the plant,' said Susan.

'And you would be left with the Hall,' said Freddie. 'Then you'd be free to donate it to your friends at the Seventh Temple.'

'You can give it to the devil, for all I care,' said Susan. 'I've always hated the place.' She stood up. 'Freddie, you've been too kind. We mustn't detain you.'

As Susan escorted Freddie Pierpoint to his car, Simon sat at the table, staring at his hands, listening to their voices as they walked slowly towards the bridge over the moat.

'Are you all right, Dad?'

Charlie stood at the door.

'Yes.' Simon sighed. 'Well, no. Didn't go quite as well as I had hoped, to tell the truth. Mum called me a baboon.'

'She was never going to understand. You must have seen that, Dad.'

'It all seems clear to me. Thought it would be to everyone else.'

Charlie sat down at the other end of the table. 'It's clear to me,' he said. 'You did what you thought was best.'

'I did.'

'You just weren't very tactful about it. That's always been a bit of a problem with our family, hasn't it?'

'I suppose so.' Simon looked up at his son and smiled. 'It's just the Pygott way,' he said.

Knock, knock. Knock-knock. Knock.

Alison listened to the sound of nature stirring behind the plaster wall of her bedroom. Seated at her dressing-table, she held up her finger like someone testing the direction of the wind.

'What?' asked Kate, who lay on the floor, a half-completed jigsaw puzzle before her.

'Listen.'

Knock-knock. Knock.

Kate gave a gasp of astonishment. 'Someone's knocking to come in,' she said. 'What is it?'

'Guess.'

'Um.' The little girl screwed up her eyes. 'Squirrel,' she said. 'Squirrel on the roof with a nut.'

'Nope.'

'A mouse?'

'Not a mouse.'

'Don't say it's a rat.'

'No, thank you very much.'

'I give up.'

'Well. I *think* that it's a little beetle. Tapping away in one of the wooden beams.'

'Oh *yes*, a beetle.' She stood up and put her ear to the wall. It was one of Kate's many eccentricities that she actually loved the insects from which her friends would recoil. At first Alison had worried about her daughter's ladybird farms, the way she put moths and flies into the webs of spiders in the garage, but she had come to the conclusion that Kate's pleasure lay more in seeing the spider well fed than in any incipient sado-masochistic tendencies.

'He's calling,' said Alison. 'Calling for his wife.'

'Or girlfriend. They might not be married yet.'

'No, I think that sounds like a married knock.'

Kate tapped the wall with her small knuckle.

She seemed to be warming with the weather, Alison reflected, watching her daughter. The fights with Stephen were less frequent and better humoured these days. She was sleeping at night. Even her hair was more ordered and was losing its enraged frizziness.

'It's spring,' said Alison quietly.

In past years, April would mark the opening of nature's siege of Yew Tree Cottage, when the rampant army of greenness threatened to engulf the house and garden. It was a battle for supremacy which Matthew and Alison enjoyed, knowing that, by the end of June, the invasion would have been quelled, an amiable truce called until next year.

Now she felt differently. Let the grass grow, the moles dig, the starlings build nests in the rafters, the bindweed entangle the roses, the ivy continue its stealthy suffocation of the hazel hedge. Let the deathwatch beetle tap its semaphore of lust and destruction within the precious oak beams.

Normally, Matthew would be mowing and cutting back foliage and treating timbers ready for the invasion but he too seemed distracted and had let the house and the garden fend for themselves, as if the lifelessness at the heart of their marriage was no match for the teeming fecundity outside.

Yet the rhythm of life somehow drove them on. Returning from an afternoon in the Bury St Edmunds hotel, Alison would slip back with very little effort into the evening's routine. Sometimes, at a moment when the discord and misery between the Turvilles had flared into acrimony, the telephone would ring, a friend or a parent calling. Either of them would talk coolly and competently, as if the rage and the tears were no more than a performance out of which they could step at will, when family or social duty demanded.

She saw now how easy it was to join the adultery game. Once she had imagined that it would be difficult, a strain – all that emotion, all those lies, the different roles that one was required to play – but now she realised that the sophistication of modern sexual life, the ubiquity of deceit, prepared virtually anyone for a life of quiet, well-ordered infidelity. Easy – logical, indeed. What better way was there to keep the terrors of loneliness and middle age at bay, to stay alive while retaining both the reputation and the comfortable way of life of a grown-up, responsible person?

Alison wondered whether it had always been like this. She thought of her parents, trapped together in their tidy little house in Norwich. So normal had been parental disagreement during their childhood that Alison and her sister Mary had become habituated to meals spent in silence, or to hearing, from downstairs after they had gone to bed, the poison hiss of marital discord. Did Dad cheat? Did Mum have a salesman? She hoped so, but suspected they didn't. After she and Mary had left home, their parents had seemed to come to terms with one another. Occasionally, her father would put an arm around her mother's shoulders, awkwardly, in a way that spoke of years of sexual misery. At Christmas, the two of them stood together, surrounded by the two families of their daughters, looking like old enemies who have been persuaded to pose for the cameras after signing a truce. Perhaps this was what awaited her and, after her, Kate and Stephen, an unbreakable chain of inherited bleakness.

'Don't be absurd.'

She heard her mother's voice, concerned and incredulous, when she had made the fateful telephone call to Norwich yesterday morning.

'What on earth are you trying to tell me, Alison?'

'It's over. The marriage is finished.'

'He's met someone. I knew it.'

'I've met someone.'

'Oh for heaven's sake, Alison. Grow up.'

'That's just what I've done.'

'This is nonsense, darling. Now I'm going to pretend we haven't had this conversation. You have your little fling – these things happen in a marriage, you just have to be careful and well-organised – but don't you dare betray those darling children and your husband all for a bit of sex. You're an adult, for God's sake – you have responsibilities.'

'It's not a fling.'

'These things pass. They happen to everyone. Surely you can see the difference between a little affair and what's really important in your life.'

'Happiness is important.'

'Happiness!' Her mother had laughed bitterly. 'What is it with your generation? You seem to think you have a God-given right to this happiness thing – as if it's some pill handed out on the National Health. Children, family, the house, the whole set-up you've spent years building – that's where you'll find happiness.'

'A set-up is just a set-up. Change isn't that terrible. I'll explain to the children. They'll come with me. I think Kate has sensed it already.'

'And does Matthew have a say in any of this?'

'I haven't told him. We're beyond the discussion stage, Mum. It's just words that go round and round in the same circles.'

'You're mad. Why don't you get away and think about it? Stay here, if you like.'

'Mum, this is decided.'

'And when would all this happen?'

'Soon. I'll know the moment.'

'Just consider what you're doing, darling. Promise me that.'

'I promise.'

Kate was pulling at her mother's hand. 'What were you thinking of?' she asked. 'You went into a dream.'

Alison placed an arm around the small shoulders and kissed the crown of Kate's head. 'I was thinking we should visit Grandma and Grandpa,' she said. 'We haven't seen them for ages.'

From downstairs could be heard the sound of Matthew and Stephen returning from the football match they had been watching.

Kate leapt up. 'I'm going to tell Daddy about the beetle,' she said, running from the room.

Alison heard the murmur of voices in the kitchen, interrupted by Kate's excited news. It took a few moments for the full significance of what she was saying to filter through to Matthew. His questioning became terse and annoyed. 'Beetle? Knocking? Oh *shit* – ' Alison imagined his face as it darkened from fatherly tolerance to the rage of a man who had just been told that his beloved house was being eaten alive. She started laughing. The beetle knocked, as if belatedly replying to Kate's invitation. She heard the her husband's heavy, head-of-the-household steps on the stairs.

'What's all this about a beetle?' he asked, standing at the bedroom door.

Alison lay back on the bed, her eyes wet with tears, her stomach aching from laughter. It was several seconds before she could confirm the bad news.

From the shadow of the yew tree, a small figure in a dark sleeveless shirt watched the scene taking place beyond the closed bedroom window. She saw the wife, head back, laughing soundlessly, the blonde hair and pale face catching the glare of the room's central light. The husband's solid, broad-shouldered presence stood still before her dancing, moving lightness. The daughter was there now, looking from one parent to the other.

Family life, bright and unbreakable.

The figure's right hand, which had been smoothing the skin of her left forearm, buckled suddenly in a sort of paroxysm, then slowly descended, its nails digging deep, leaving bright-red furrows in the white flesh. Blood trickled downwards and dripped softly on to the grass.

12

PETWATCH

Losing a pet always involves heartache and pain. Every week the *DP* helps readers find pets that have gone missing in the region. If you have recently lost or found a pet, why not call Daphne Rose at the *DP*'s Petwatch desk?

Pounce, black cat, 18 months old and very greedy! Owners think someone might have been 'adopted' by Pounce. If so, please push him out! Victoria Road area. Reward. (01379) 461991.

Tiffany, Wortham's most beautiful cat has gone missing! £25 reward no questions asked. Answers to the name of Tiff. (01379) 465544.

Connie, 12-year-old black-and-white cat. Owners have just moved from Scrope Rise, Burthorpe to Attleborough and think Connie may have homed. (01953) 54732.

Pepsi, a 4-year-old brown-and-white terrier. Lost in Stuston on June 6 while in an 'interesting-to-other-dogs' condition. Have you seen her? (01379) 46725.

Remember, regular updates on DP's Petwatch *column can be heard on the* Roy Waller's *Tea for Two and a Half Show on the 'Talk of the County', Radio Norfolk.*

TO THOSE EXCLUDED by accident or design from Simon Pygott's social circle, the gathering that midsummer night at Garston Hall had seemed of no particular significance. Just as certain herds of wildebeest are taken by the urge to migrate, plunging crazily into raging torrents or the mouths of lions, so the upper middle classes will occasionally gather to throw food, spill champagne over one another, and engage in para-sexual activities beneath rhododendron bushes in the early hours of the morning.

Yet later, people like Miles Larwood, who had actually turned down the chance to attend that last gasp of the Garston Hall set, were obliged to mention the fact, as if even a declined invitation provided a worthwhile connection to the bizarre events of that evening.

'I'd be out of place.' Miles Larwood sat at the kitchen table, a glass of whisky in front of him, trying not to stare at Margaret Cowper who stood near by in her party clothes. Over recent weeks, Margaret had seemed to bloom with the fine weather, becoming relaxed, almost playful, in Miles's presence. There were times when he forgot that she was over 500 years old, allowed himself the illusion that the two of them were living together as partners, sharing jokes, intimacies, a future. 'I know how these things are,' he continued gloomily. 'I'd sit in a corner, getting drunk and making sarcastic comments. They'd think I was a supercilious prat. At the beginning of the evening, we'd make polite noises at one another. They would drift away to get drunk and have fun. I'd get drunk and resentful.'

Margaret leant against the rail of the kitchen Aga, sipping wine. She was wearing a long-sleeved black evening dress of crushed velvet which somehow imbued her with both purity and wantonness. Ever since he had seen her materialising from vapour into physical form, Miles had been tortured by thoughts of her. He had tried, with a dismal lack of success, to convince himself that her body was figmental, not flesh but a dream of flesh which disguised the corruption beneath. He wanted to be near her; even the trace of her breath, a distant memory of unspeakable graveyard odours which sometimes hung in the air after she had left a room, had begun to seem sweet to him. Day by day, Margaret seemed to him less of a ghost, more of an intoxicating reality.

Now, deploying one of those easy silences of hers, she shifted her weight, crossing one slim ankle in front of the other. She touched the dark hair, stacked in careful disorder on her head, then rested a slender hand on her throat. Where she was leaning, the rail of the Aga caused a small, heartbreaking swell of muscle tissue to the side of her hip, straining against the black velvet.

'It won't just be Simon Pygott's friends,' she said. 'Rose Hope will be there, Pearson – '

'Matthew.'

Margaret looked into the wineglass she was holding. 'I believe Mr and Mrs Turville have been invited,' she said quietly.

'Rose Hope's TV crew will be there, too.'

'Her project.'

'Yes. So tonight you behave.' They laughed, comfortable with their shared secret. 'I'll be thinking of you as I work,' Miles said. 'Up there among the smart set. *Le tout Burthorpe.*'

'Too what?'

'Fashionable Burthorpe people.' As he stood up, Miles was unable to take his eyes off Margaret. She was frowning, annoyed that her centuries of observation and self-improvement had failed to cover the use of French phrases in English usage. 'Did you always look like this?' he asked.

Self-consciously, Margaret touched the drop earrings on her small, elfin ears. 'Not exactly,' she said.

'I meant the rest.'

'I made small changes.' Margaret ran a hand across her stomach, then closed it gently on her thigh, as if to remind herself of a body that was not entirely hers. 'I watched the men and women of Burthorpe, listened to their talk. Maidenhood, I discovered, was no longer treasured by girls. It was like a wearisome younger brother who followed them about, spoiling their games. To men, it was a strange, exotic gift, exciting yet a challenge, something to be taken.'

'I suppose it's true. Purity has become depraved over the years.'

'I would return a woman, yet not a mother.' She looked away unhappily. 'In the end I denied my little ones, just as he once did.'

'He must have been mad.' Miles stood up, stepped forward and kissed her briefly on the lips, his left hand resting for a moment on a velvet hip.

Margaret's grey eyes held his. 'He was a man,' she said.

'Bastard.' Miles turned and picked up his keys from the kitchen table. 'I'll drive you there.'

It was less than a mile and a half from the cottage to Garston Hall and most of the way they drove in silence. Miles was suddenly relieved that he wouldn't be there tonight to witness her triumph; beside her, he felt faded and battered and middle-aged.

Although it was only nine o'clock, the BMWs and Rovers were already parked from the moat up the drive to beyond the barns.

'If they ask, you'd better say I'm your taxi-driver,' Miles said, half-joking. 'How are you getting home?'

'I'll walk, probably.'

'In that dress?'

'I can hitch it up.' As usual, Margaret avoided the opportunity for flirtation. 'Maybe someone will give me a lift.'

'Maybe. You could always take the direct route over the trees.'

Margaret laughed. 'And what would I do with my clothes?'

As they drew up outside the Hall, she laid a cool hand on his. 'Thank you,' she said.

'Have fun.'

She looked towards the house, unsmiling. 'I'll try,' she said.

Colin Dunn stood on the lawn, discussing the decline in property values with Henry Gibson, the second richest man in Burthorpe and a partner in the estate agency where Sarah Dunn worked. Beside Colin, Sarah stood closely, her hand linked through her husband's arm. Only occasionally did she look away from him while Henry Gibson spoke.

The Holmead Clinic had worked impressively, returning Sarah the perfect model of an addiction-free partner, full of a new honesty concerning relationships to her husband and to the world. Alarmed at first by this new candour and naturally concerned that the years spent building up a civilized marriage of balanced infidelity might have been wasted, Colin had recently discerned within himself an odd sense of relief. He was glad that his wife liked him again, that she had returned to the marriage bed with a distinct and renewed enthusiasm. With genuine relief, he had told Nina (whose response had fallen some way short of sisterly generosity) that he had fallen back in love with her sister.

'Golly, look at Turville's secretary,' he said, seeing Margaret emerge, dark and elegant, from Miles Larwood's car. 'Talk about dressed to kill.'

'Sexual compulsion is something we've both experienced in the past but have put behind us,' Sarah explained to Henry Gibson. 'But, you know, with the right degree of self-approval, you can connect with your interior powerhouse without needing the jump-leads of infidelity. Colin and I are enjoying the best sex we've ever had, aren't we, darling?'

Dunn shrugged modestly.

'Oh, well done,' said Henry Gibson.

'Own your power. Easy does it. One day at a time.' Sarah squeezed her husband's arm. 'Hello, Margaret,' she called out. 'You look lovely tonight.'

'Margaret.' Colin kissed her lightly on the cheek. 'Let me get you a glass of fizz.'

'That would be kind.'

'I'll give you a hand with the glasses,' said Henry, glancing anxiously in Sarah's direction.

'He's such a thoughtful man, my husband.' Sarah smiled as she watched the men depart.

'Yes, he is.'

'He used to be rather keen on getting you into bed but we've embarked on a new programme of mutual commitment so you won't have much luck there, I'm afraid.'

'Sorry?'

'We're expanding the comfort zone of our marriage as part of a twelve-step recovery programme.'

'Oh.' Margaret nodded politely. 'That's good.'

For a moment, the two women looked across the lawn. From a marquee in front of the library could be heard the sound of electric guitars being tuned up.

'Simon's booked the Coffin Dodgers,' said Sarah vaguely. 'Pals of Simon's. Rhythm and blues. Rather fun.'

'I don't recognise these people. Do they come from Burthorpe?'

'All over. Simon knows everyone. I tell you when these religious types move into Garston, there's going to be a hell of a gap in a few people's social calendars. Simon may not be much cop at farming but he certainly knows how to organise a good party.'

For the first time, Margaret noticed Matthew and Alison Turville. They were standing silently, amongst a group of six, each wearing the stunned, wary look of an unhappily married couple on public parade.

'Matthew Turville is a good lover but he has failed to come to terms with his inner child,' Sarah said conversationally, seeing the direction in which Margaret was looking. 'He's what the clinic called one of the walking wounded on the interior battlefield.'

'Matthew's my boss. I don't think of him like that.' Margaret reached into her small velvet bag and fumbled with a packet of cigarettes.

'I think you do. He's an attractive man,' said Sarah. 'And I'd thank you not to smoke.'

'Sorry?'

'Cigarettes. Passive smoking undermines my recovery programme.'

'You used to smoke.' Margaret closed her bag.

'I've come through the self-harming process. Thank you, Margaret. You have just taken the first step towards recovery. You feel better?'

'No.'

Colin Dunn was making his way towards them, bearing three glasses. 'Henry's gone to see Simon about something,' he said, handing Margaret, then Sarah, a glass of champagne.

'This is how I imagine heaven will be.' Sarah sipped at her drink. 'Everyone equal. The men looking handsome, the women pretty. Glorious summer's evening. Anticipation in the air.'

'Yes, it is rather heavenly,' Colin muttered.

Margaret noticed that Matthew was staring at her. Although a hint of the defensive attended him these days, there remained a dark-eyed seriousness which set him apart from the other guests.

'I need to smoke,' said Margaret, moving away from Mr and Mrs Dunn.

It had been a mistake to come to the dance, Alison Turville thought, sensing a faint quickening of interest from her husband's direction as Margaret Cowper, looking unrecognisably sultry and seductive, walked towards them. She smiled a cool welcome, then turned away pointedly, pretending to participate in a conversation to her right as Matthew began to talk to his secretary.

It was from this that she needed to escape before it was too late.

233

Appearing together at social functions for fear of arousing suspicions that all was not well with the marriage. Smiling through the pain (or, worse, the absence of pain, the absence of anything) in order to maintain appearances, to keep the show on the road. Turning her head as Matthew skipped off for another round of the faithless fandango. Perhaps joining the dance herself. It had not been some obscure standard of family unity that until now had bound her to Matthew, she now saw, but fear – fear of an existence without the rhythms and routines of Yew Tree Cottage.

Alison became aware that Margaret was displaying the signs of interest in Matthew which over the years she had learnt to identify but which he, like most men, rarely noticed. The secretary was leaning towards him, as if to catch not just his words but the breath upon which they were carried. There was colour in her cheeks, a lock of dark hair had fallen forward. Poor girl. When Matthew realised what was going on – and, by the look of her, the secretary would be dragging him off to the woods at any moment – he was likely to be a severe disappointment. Female need brought out the wimp in her husband, made him feel trapped and panicky. Alison smiled to herself. It had been her own lack of enthusiasm, the fact that she had never really desired him, that had brought them together. Common interests, a perfect social fit, good company, a controlled and passion-free sex life: it had been a truly English marriage.

Her husband had always been ambitious – even his affairs had betrayed an innocently guileful element of social planning – and for this reason alone, his poor, pretty little secretary with her haunted eyes was doomed to disappointment. An employee at the Home? His own secretary? She hadn't a chance.

'Lovely as ever, Mrs Turville.' The booming voice of Simon Pygott, accompanied by a large arm thrown around her shoulders, disturbed Alison's thoughts.

'Thank you, Simon. What a wonderful party.'

'Not bad, eh? What I call the last hurrah. Moving into Hall Farm next week.'

'With Susan and the boys?'

Simon looked away, narrowing his eyes, as if seeing someone he knew approaching from the direction of Chapel Meadow. 'Bit messy, that. All down in London. Not looking good on what I call the marriage front, to tell the truth.'

'Oh Simon, I'm sorry.'

'Can't move for lawyers. Freddie Pierpoint has brewed up the most bloody awful shit-storm about this place.'

Matthew turned, with some relief, from his secretary. 'I hope someone's representing your interests,' he said.

'The Temple's people are being helpful. I've got a lawyer involved. Now –' Simon held up both hands, as if to forestall any further discussion. 'I have a much more important question for you chaps.' He paused dramatically. 'Do you want to change your life?'

Like most parties, the dance at Garston Hall unfolded like a socialised version of the effects of alcohol upon the brain – anticipation, animation, garrulousness, confusion, depression, stupor. By eleven o'clock, most of the guests had drifted into the library where they messily consumed the culinary efforts of Toff Scoff, a catering firm specialising in deb dances and charity balls. At twelve o'clock, the results of a raffle in aid of a new wheelchair for H.T. Pearson were announced, with the shopkeeper himself wheeling across the dance-floor to present the prizes, accompanied by loud and only slightly ironic cheers. By one o'clock, the babysitter brigade, aware that the party was becoming rather too wild for their tastes, had hurried back home with barely disguised relief. By two, Nina Hebden had removed her upper garments (a sure sign of a good party) and was dancing topless as D'Arcy Disco played 'The Birdy Song'. At around three o'clock, a trainee auctioneer from Larsson's caused something of a stir by falling into the moat. By four, Emma Pardew, the Vicar's seventeen-year-old daughter, had been relieved of her virginity by Nigel Carstairs, who specialised in this service.

Yet, even before Simon's party reached its premature and entirely unexpected conclusion, the more observant of guests might have noticed that an atmosphere of dangerous excess was prevailing, as if Garston Hall was bidding farewell to centuries of bad behaviour with one last demonically hedonistic celebration. The Coffin Dodgers had never been more deafening. More Toff Scoff was thrown than consumed. The code of sexual etiquette observed in politer circles was repeatedly and openly breached. The warm summer night throbbed with such sounds of music and merrymaking that, the *DP* said in its front-page report, the party could be heard as far afield as Mellis in one direction and Dickleburgh in the other.

As Miles Larwood had predicted, Margaret was in constant demand, her air of mildly distracted vulnerability attracting men, young and old, married and unmarried. She was pushed and pulled around the dance-floor, her body being held in an increasingly shameless way as the night progressed. Before midnight, she had discovered, the men with whom she agreed to dance at least managed some pretence of social chat but, as soon as H.T. Pearson had been wheeled off into the night, the search for a partner became more pressing and urgent. Smiling, with more colour in her cheeks than there had been for centuries, Margaret declined one sexual overture after another. 'Shall we go somewhere?' they would ask, squeezing or caressing her absent-mindedly. 'I don't think so,' she would reply. Once rejected, her dance partners wasted little time before heading off for their next quarry.

It was past three in the morning, as the last of the amateurs and part-timers were departing, and Margaret was resting between part-ners at a table occupied by Matthew and Alison Turville and Sarah and Colin Dunn. 'Rose is busy tonight,' Sarah said vaguely, looking across to the other side of the marquee where Rose Hope was talking earnestly to a man with a pigtail who was carrying a camera.

'She has a project, I believe.' Colin's head swayed above a half-empty glass of champagne. 'Got the telly people interested in a ghost in Burthorpe.'

'Burthorpe?' Alison laughed. 'Why on earth would a ghost choose Burthorpe?'

'She's probably still recovering from the break-up with Simon,' said Sarah. 'It's called emotional displacement activity.'

'Somehow Rose has managed to convince herself that, since this party is connected to the sale of Chapel Meadow, we're all in for some whizzo paranormal show,' said Colin. 'Got the cameraman running around filming all sorts of weird things happening in the bushes.'

'I've just told her I won't do an interview at the Home.' Matthew spoke quietly to Margaret. 'She'll probably corner you later.'

'What should I say?'

236

'Tell her to leave us alone. Life's difficult enough without spooks.'

'I'll say I have no comment.'

'Great.' Matthew held Margaret's look for a few seconds, then turned to the Dunns. 'This woman is the perfect secretary,' he said.

'How sexist you are, Matthew.' Agnès Babineau had appeared out of a throng of dancers behind the table. Her dark hand rested on Matthew's shoulder. 'As punishment, you have to dance with me. If Alison is *d'accord*, of course.'

Alison glanced up. 'I'm *d'accord*.'

As the Coffin Dodgers moved into a rock 'n' roll medley, Matthew and Agnès jived, their bodies moving backwards and forwards, touching occasionally.

'She dances well, Agnès,' said Sarah.

'Yes.'

The two women watched, their thoughts taking a similar direction.

'I hear she's providing pews for Matthew's new chapel.'

'Yes.'

'Her shop's doing really well. She's quite a power in Diss these days.'

'Why don't you just say it, Sarah?' Alison spoke quietly, her eyes still following the dancers. 'She'll be fucking Matthew before the month's out.'

'Alison, I wasn't suggesting –'

Alison stood up. 'Tell my husband I've left,' she said, smiling coolly in the direction of Margaret and Colin Dunn. 'I'm going.' She nodded, as if reaching some important, wider decision. 'Yes. I'm going.'

Before Colin could make the awkward semi-squat gesture with which he normally marked the departure of a woman, Alison was out of the marquee walking briskly into the darkness beyond.

'Oh dear,' said Sarah.

'Slight lack of tact there, darling.' Colin smiled at his wife, the unhappiness of others reminding him of his own good fortune. 'Poor Alison.'

It was just past four o'clock and an early morning chill was dampening the fag-end of Simon's party. In the marquee, D'Arcy's Disco had moved into easy-listening mode. A few guests slouched about the dance-floor, draped over one another. In one corner, Nina Hebden sat, sobbing and shivering, clad only in a pair of knickers, some food in her hair. Occasionally an optimistic, partnerless male guest would approach her in a spirit of fake condolence, only to be roundly abused and to retreat, a sheepish grin across his face.

Matthew and Margaret were among the dancers. The undertaker was undeniably flattered by the attentions of his secretary whose light touch, swaying body and melting glances communicated unmistakable erotic promise. He was probably not displeased at finding himself the object of interest both of Margaret and of Agnès Babineau, who was now sitting with Colin and Sarah Dunn, pointedly ignoring what was happening on the dance-floor. A decision would be required, and really rather soon.

As Alison had understood, and Agnès suspected, there was no competition.

A glutinous ballad drew to a close and Matthew escorted Margaret back to the table. Agnès was tapping her glass with the merest hint of impatience. She said something in French to Matthew, then, smiling coldly at Margaret, ambled off, hips swinging, out of the marquee.

Margaret, whose entire attention was focused on Matthew, failed to appreciate the change of atmosphere at the table, the awakened curiosity of Mr and Mrs Dunn. She had no knowledge of French. All she saw was Matthew, sitting back in his chair. Then, fatally, he nodded slowly and gave her a long, languorous stare. It might have been embarrassment, or perhaps a vaguely polite idea that, before he went, he should at least leave her with a smouldering sense of what might have been. Whatever the motive, it made Margaret's mouth go dry. He stood up.

'Well,' he said. 'I'll see you good people later.'

He left, Margaret watching him until he disappeared into the dark night outside the marquee.

'Gee, thanks, Matthew,' muttered Sarah. 'Leave us to clear up the pieces, why don't you?'

Awkwardly, Colin asked Margaret if she would like to dance. She declined, an odd smile of triumph and anticipation still on her lips.

'I must go,' she said.

'Home? Already?' Sarah spoke with evident relief.

Margaret laughed. 'Not home,' she said, still gazing after Matthew.

'I really would go home,' said Colin. 'Bit late, you know.'

'Don't follow him, Margaret,' said Sarah. 'It will end in tears, believe me.'

She moved away slowly. 'I don't think so,' she said in a distant, dream-like voice.

'Ah,' said Colin after she had gone.

'Oh shit,' said Sarah.

Margaret made her way across the lawn and over the bridge. She hesitated, peering into the darkness before her, then lit a cigarette. She took off her shoes and began walking towards the clump of trees from which the first birds of the morning had begun to sing. The dew was cold between her toes. She smiled as she picked her way carefully, hesitating occasionally to look around her.

When she reached the trees, she stood, her fingers smoothing the velvet sleeves of her dress. It had been a long wait, and now that wait was almost over. Ahead of her, through the trees, she caught sight of a small flame, like that of a cigarette lighter or candle, moving away from her. Small branches cracked beneath her feet as she made her way forward, hitched her black dress up to her waist as she climbed the small stile into Chapel Meadow.

Her eyes were accustomed to the dark now. Some fifty yards away stood the family chapel into which the flame disappeared. The chapel: yes, it was right. She let the cigarette fall from her right hand, making a soft hiss in the wet grass. Breathing lightly, her eyes sparkling, her lips slightly parted, Margaret dropped first one shoe, then the other. Holding her dress daintily above her knees, she walked slowly towards the chapel.

In the porch, she stood for a few seconds, savouring the moment. Then, softly, she raised the catch on the heavy oak door. She slipped into the small building where the air was cooler and a gentle sighing could be heard.

The candle was on the altar. She saw Matthew kneeling before the great stone upon which, down the centuries, the coffins of lately deceased Pygotts had been lain while the Office of the Dead was declaimed over them. He seemed to be at prayer. It took moments for

Margaret to realise that the stone had life, that Matthew was working delicately, as she had seen so many times before, on a body. Only it was not like the bodies that she had seen him transform in the Preparation Room. It was no corpse. Matthew was working on a body writhing with life, his head, lowered in worship, between the thighs of Agnès Babineau.

Margaret stepped back, her dark small figure merging with the shadows in the chapel. Breathing heavily, she leant against the wall. Her hands, flat against the plaster, curled slowly as Matthew stood up, took off his dinner jacket, undressed languidly, then eased himself on to the stone where, laughing and gasping, their bodies flickering in the candlelight, the couple made love beneath the altar.

So they would not have heard the long, low sigh of lament, nor been aware of the whispered words, 'Ware the hawk', nor seen the small hand take the heavy metal key from the door and the figure leave the chapel with just one glance behind her. The sound of a key turning in the lock would have been lost in their gasps of lust.

They were, of course, aware of the single gust of heat, the flame that burst like the Devil's breath across the chapel, igniting the pews, the panelling, the curtains, cracking the stained-glass windows. But beyond that, and a few minutes of inexpressible terror, they knew remarkably little.

A single light shone at the cottage when she returned, opening the front door softly. Miles Larwood was at his desk, staring so intently at the screen of his word-processor that Margaret had to clear her throat before he realised that she was standing behind him in his study.

'Couldn't sleep,' he said. He looked more closely at Margaret. 'Are you all right?'

She sat down on an armchair, staring ahead of her. He saw now that there was blood on her feet and her hands were scratched. The beginnings of a bruise were appearing on her right cheekbone.

'Looks like it was quite a party. Did you walk home?'

She turned to him, her grey eyes wide and unblinking. 'He is dead,' she said. 'Matthew.'

Miles sat back in his chair and closed his eyes wearily. 'Why?' he asked eventually.

'I loved him. I needed him to release me.'

'Five hundred years. And you chose Matthew Turville.'

'I was never good at choosing men.'

'So it seems.'

Margaret stood, wide-eyed, arms hanging loosely by her side, a picture of weariness. 'It's cold out here. We have needs, too.' When she spoke, it was in a low monotone. 'We watch you and long for the love and the death which you enjoy. A passing moment of expressed desire between the ugliest daw and the lewdest callet can make us ache with longing. Those of us who have remained on this earth rather than passing through it enjoy a sort of freedom within our confinement. Some use the gauds and tricks invisibility allows us. Others, sad beings, derive pleasure from instilling terror in the hearts of innocent village folk. I have made mistakes. In my time, I have meddled in all manner of unlust, but, finally, I knew I had to return, to be rescued from eternity by love. It would not have to be transcendent, or even pure, but it had to be love.'

'Funny sort of love.'

'Love. Rage. What's the difference?' She sighed. 'I chose the undertaker. I watched him as he corrected the dead, made handsome the haggard and the reasty who lay on his table. I believed that he could correct me, too. He had the eyes, the tender hands. He reminded me of a man who changed people, too.'

'Poor Matthew. He had little chance either way.'

'He smiled at me at the dance. It was our moment, I was sure of it. He nodded, as if he understood everything.'

'People nod. People smile. It means nothing. Matthew understood very little.'

'I see that now.'

'How will you escape?'

Margaret looked up. 'You tell me.'

He turned to his screen. 'Let me read you the entry I've been trying to rewrite all evening.'

'Entry?'

'From my book.'

'Words.'

'Listen. "Revenance, theory of".' Miles looked up at Margaret and smiled. '"Contiguous to, and paradoxically subversive of, the notion of death as the facilitator or signifier of recontextualised desire, is a dynamic positing that an interest in death may be a displaced or even deferred model of erotic syntagma. So, with an eye on philological and linguistic critiques, one is led to conclude that there is more than a dichotomised fractal connection between the term "revenant" in its French and English interpretations. Is it possible, one might ask oneself, that this state of fear for invisible otherness (our spiritual alteriority, if you like) could, under certain circumstances, express itself in an actualising moment of focus as a state that one might term "desire"? For this hypothesised condition, I have coined the word "revenance".'

'You write beautifully,' said Margaret. 'But I'm not sure I quite understand.'

'I suppose I'm talking about a kind of return for warmth, for the affective process one could broadly describe as love.'

'Revenance?'

'It's a word that I've invented – a development from the concept of the revenant, one who returns from a previous life. Then there's the secondary meaning, "revenant" in the French sense of pleasing, prepossessing, or attractive. So revenance, at least in my theory of it, embraces both the other-worldly and the . . . well, the erotic.'

'Love, sex and death.'

'Yes. Though not necessarily in that order, of course.'

Margaret moved forward and placed a cold arm around his shoulders. He closed his eyes and allowed his head to rest against her breast.

'They'll be here soon,' she said.

'And you have nowhere to go.'

'Yes. I have.'

She stepped back and extended a hand. He took the hand and stood up. Without another word, they made their way out of the study, through the hallway and upstairs to his bedroom.

*   *   *

242

A blanket of summer mist hung over Charlie Watson's freshly cut hayfield as Margaret and Miles walked slowly east, two hours later, in the direction of Scole. Through the greyness around them, the disembodied sounds of the village reached them – voices, the whirr of a milk float, cars on the main road – as if overnight it had been Burthorpe that had somehow become a community of ghosts.

They skirted Garston Wood until they reached the point where Watson's land ended. There Margaret spoke briefly to Miles Larwood before kissing him softly on the lips. He stood as she turned away from him to continue on her way.

After five yards, Margaret seemed to check as if suddenly she had to push against some great force. An unearthly, echoless crackling sound cut through the morning stillness. Ten yards away from Miles, the contours of her body were becoming less clear, lost in a shimmering transparency. Two more strides and she was almost indecipherable from the mist that surrounded her. Then, slowly, even the sound of her faded until Miles no longer knew whether what he heard distantly was what was left of Margaret or merely the memory of her within him.

He walked forward to where she had disappeared. Looking down, he noticed something, a line of darkness on the dewy ground in front of him. He stooped and touched the grass with a single caress. He held his hand before him and, noticing a trace of red, closed his eyes and kissed it. Then he looked into the mist of which Margaret had become a part, turned and made his way back home.

FOR SEVERAL WEEKS, Burthorpe achieved the relevance to national and local news for which it had waited centuries. Journalists arrived – edgy, loud-voiced people carrying wallets full of large-denomination notes. They interviewed the wrong people, ran up large bills at the Greyhound, and quickly grew disheartened. There was speculation in the tabloid press as to the identity of Margaret Cowper, the raven-haired lovely who only had eyes for her boss and who had disappeared the day after the fire, but her landlord disobligingly was able to account for her movements at the time of the fire and confirmed that she had caught a train to London the following morning. The Eye police put out a search for her, and paid close attention to the activities of Dr Miles Larwood, but the trail was cold. Soon the interest of both the law and the press shifted to other, less mysterious matters.

At the height of journalistic interest in Burthorpe, Matthew Turville was buried. It was a fine ceremony, worthy both of the deceased and the firm of undertakers, Browns of Long Stratton, who had been brought in to organise the last journey of their former business rival. Pale and dry-eyed, the widow walked slowly down Farthing Lane, beside her son, holding the hand of her daughter. Behind her, the ranks of Burthorpe mourners were swollen by journalists, photographers and, an unnoticed presence, Paul Gilchrist.

A few weeks later, Alison and the children moved from Burthorpe, for reasons less to do with rumours about her husband's death (a tragedy it might have been, but no decent explanation had been found for his presence in the chapel with a Frenchwoman at four in the morning) than with an openly expressed desire for a new life. Yew Tree Cottage was put on the market and, despite being riddled with beetle, was bought by a couple from London.

Stephen misses his father but is already turning his mind to thoughts of a career, possibly in retailing. Kate is exasperating, difficult and happy. To her mother's astonishment, the first report from her new school contained such words as 'contributes', 'gregarious' and even, for two separate subjects, 'bright'. Alison continues to be courted by Paul; they will be married at the end of the year.

Burthorpe has also been the subject of a flurry of interest from Hollywood. In a largely successful bid to revive her career (she now works for the *Sunday Express*), Rose Hope produced a film treatment which, having been discussed in air-conditioned offices on the West Coast of America, brought hired Daimlers to Bridge Lane. Tanned, bouffant-haired men in designer jeans and cowboy boots stepped into the H.T. Pearson Convenience Store, from where they emerged moments later, bemused and disappointed. It wouldn't play. The components were there but somehow the story lacked the aspirational theme necessary for conversion to the silver screen. The fear, first expressed by the *Diss Press*'s new editor Chris Beattie, that Burthorpe might become a mecca for *cinéastes* – a North Suffolk version of Marienbad or Paris, Texas – quickly receded.

In the meantime, other visitors have arrived in the village, pilgrims for whom Burthorpe is not a step along the way but a destination in itself. For it is here that the new headquarters of the Seventh Holy Temple of Jesus has been established.

Pasty-faced young men and women can now be seen drifting about the village, their gentle eyes vague and unfocused. It was rumoured at first that hallucinogenic drugs were regularly consumed at the Hall. Then it was said the Templars were bringing too much traffic to the village, or they were lowering the tone, or that their picnics were causing bald patches on the village green, or that they were engaged in acts of group depravity at Garston Hall. H.T. Pearson would fulminate against the incomers in those early days but there was something half-hearted about his protests, as if he had come to recognise that these people would at least provide regular custom for his Convenience Store.

It was also believed that Nirvana, the tiny shop that had opened next door to the petrol station and sold crystals and divining rods and other kinds of new-age merchandise, was a covert supplier of forbidden substances to the Templars. There were regular police raids and the shop's manager, Gavin Dance – formerly known as Naughty Boy – was obliged to make frequent visits to Diss Police Station.

To this day, the local officers remain convinced that the mumbo-jumbo sold by Dance is no more than a cunning diversion from a trade supplying pig tranquilliser to the denizens of Garston Hall, but they have reached a sort of accommodation with Dance, as if the sheer bare-faced cunning of the scruffy little bastard merits some kind of grudging professional respect. The fact that Dance might genuinely be innocent and be building a new life for himself has yet to occur to them.

'Do you want to change your life?'

With these words, the former squire of Garston Hall will sometimes appear on the doorstep of villagers throughout the area. Simon Pygott's own change, which has seen the end of his marriage, the dispersal of his land, a troubled hiatus with one of his sons, and the loan of Garston Hall to the Seventh Holy Temple of Jesus, has aged him, but the wide blankness of his face now radiates with religious conviction.

The press soon became aware of Simon's conversion. Reporters investigated the Temple and found, to their editors' displeasure, that large sums of money were indeed sent to the Third World where good work was dismayingly evident, that the organisation was not a cover for the CIA, nor were young innocents being manipulated for financial or sexual gratification. Simon was interviewed on television. His broad features and uncomplicated, charitable world-view suited the medium. He has become a minor celebrity and is occasionally to be seen or heard on earnest programmes devoted to matters of faith.

These days, he is often accompanied door to door by a small female presence named Sister Karen. She is wan, young, and appears content to be in a world where all significant decisions about her life are made by men. Now that the Temple has recognised his worth, Simon and Sister Karen stay in his old bedroom at the Hall and dine on the top table with Marvin. They hope soon to join the Seventh Circle of Parenthood, an event that Sister Karen anticipates with the same gentle equanimity as she regards everything else in her life.

Jeremy Pygott does not, of course, fish for roach in the moat. While Marvin would probably have no particular objection, Jeremy was upset on the one occasion when he returned to his old home and now spends most of his time in London with Susan, who is often seen in the company of a nice, but ineffective viscount.

On the other hand, Charlie frequently visits his father. He has made it quite clear that he has no intention of becoming a Templar, even going so far as to decline the dry fruit cake whose consumption, the Temple believes, can save the soul even of non-Templars, but his quiet affection and respect for his father have convinced even Marvin, who is not the most flexible of God's servants, that the boy's visits are acceptable.

Charlie, incidentally, was never to benefit from the vigorous regime of a Gordonstoun education. Cleverly pointing to the small earthquake in his family circumstances, he declined to pack a trunk and take the train north. He now goes to a day school in Fulham and has his accent mocked by his mother. Can't think where this ghastly little oick of a son came from, you know? I blame the father, frankly.

And yet, behind all this movement and development, Burthorpe itself has not changed from the village to which Margaret Cowper returned. Cars and lorries still thunder through, their drivers glancing with unseeing eyes at the village buildings and shops and lives. Such is the weight of traffic today that the *Diss Press* has lent its support to the campaign for a Burthorpe by-pass – a development which, should it take place, will confirm in tarmac the process of marginalisation that has existed and accelerated down the years.

H.T. Pearson is against the by-pass, as he is against most things.

Even Harold's weekly trips to the Diss Pool have proved a source of rumbling, unexpressed dissatisfaction. What should be paradise – young, friendly hands easing his poor broken body into the paddling pool – has become a subtle form of torture. Not only can he feel nothing in his lower body, he can no longer imagine what it was once like to experience desire. In the early days, his need had lived on, bubbling away unhealthily at the back of his cortex, but, like the muscles in his legs, it wasted away. Briefly, Harold considered cancelling his trips to the baths but recently he has discovered that talking to the young swimmers, hearing their jokes, discussing their problems, is something he rather enjoys. As for the children, they actually like this funny bald man who sits in the pool, his bony legs floating in front of him like half-inflated water wings.

Miles Larwood stares into the darkness outside his study window. His *Resource Handbook* has become a strange hybrid, a swirling confusion of the academic and personal, the studied and the confessional. It is now a towering manuscript to which he regularly adds a few pages, writing more as an act of devotion than with any serious thoughts of publication. He never draws the curtain these days but remains vigilant, watching out for the wisp of grey, the tell-tale scent of smoke that marks her return. Does Margaret really visit him late at night, bringing those cold, perverse pleasures to which he has become so addicted? Or is it that his imagination has taken over his life, creeping like some irresistible fungus from the pages of his book? No matter: Dr Katherine Porter has not heard from him since her return from the Arctic Circle. He has changed.

Sometimes, tired from writing, he reaches for a book, battered and coffee-stained, that he keeps beside his desk. He reads:

> *Pla ce bo!*
> Who is there, who?
> *Di le xi!*
> Dame Margery.

Then he sits back, and waits.

AUTHOR'S NOTE

SEVERAL BOOKS HAVE been helpful in the writing of *Revenance*, and I would particularly like to acknowledge a debt to Philippe Ariès' *The Hour of Our Death* (Allen Lane, 1981), Katharine Doughty's *The Betts of Wortham in Suffolk 1480–1905* (John Lane, 1912) and H.L.R. Edwards' *Skelton: The Life and Times of an Early Tudor Poet* (Jonathan Cape, 1949). The contributions of the poet and undertaker Thomas Lynch to the *London Review of Books* have also been useful.

All quotations from Skelton's poetry were taken from Philip Henderson's excellent edition, *John Skelton's Complete Poems 1460–1529* (revised edition, 1959), whose glossary I also pilfered, and I am grateful to the publishers J.M. Dent and Sons for their permission to quote. Lines from Allan Smethurst's 'Miss from Diss' were reproduced by kind permission of Dick James Music Ltd.

Above all, I would like to thank friends – Dyan Sheldon, Roger Deakin, Sue Roe, Melissa Horn, Nigel Harding, my agent Gill Coleridge and, at Bloomsbury, Liz Calder and Mary Tomlinson – for their invaluable editorial advice and encouragement.